NET OF JEWELS

BY ELLEN GILCHRIST

In the Land of Dreamy Dreams

The Annunciation

Victory Over Japan

Drunk With Love

Falling Through Space

The Anna Papers

Light Can Be Both Wave and Particle

I Cannot Get You Close Enough

Net of Jewels

Praise for Ellen Gilchrist

NET OF JEWELS

A Novel by

ELLEN GILCHRIST

LITTLE, BROWN AND COMPANY

Boston   New York   Toronto   London

First Paperback Edition

The characters and events in this book are fictitious. Any similarity to real persons, living or dead, is coincidental and not intended by the author.

A portion of this novel was previously published, in a slightly altered version, as "1957, A Romance" from *In the Land of Dreamy Dreams.* Copyright © 1981 by Ellen Gilchrist.

Acknowledgments of permission to reprint previously copyrighted material appear on page 360.

Library of Congress Cataloging-in-Publication Data

Gilchrist, Ellen, 1935-
    Net of jewels : a novel / by Ellen Gilchrist. — 1st ed.
        p.   cm.
    ISBN 0-316-31423-4 (hc)
    ISBN 0-316-31432-3 (pb)
    I. Title.
    PS3557.I34258N48   1992
    813'.54—dc20   91-32958

10 9 8 7 6 5 4 3

MV-NY

Published simultaneously in Canada by Little, Brown & Company (Canada) Limited

Printed in the United States of America

For Hoyt Hughes Purvis

"Like a war between magicians it can last a long time, and even then the outcome may not be what it appears to be."

Tom Robbins

NET OF JEWELS

Preface

My name is Rhoda Manning and I am a writer. I'm not a great writer like my cousin Anna Hand, but I'm not bad either. I make a living at it and that's more than I can say for most writers. I want to get this straight at the outset, before we set up camp for three hundred and fifty-nine pages.

I meant this as a book of short stories and I started writing it that way. Then the stories started to bleed into each other and I decided to go on and let them bleed. I should have known when I decided to call a book *Net of Jewels* I was going to be in trouble. Well, I'm the one who did it, so let's start with me.

I was cathected by a narcissist. That's how shrinks put it and it means, my daddy is a vain and beautiful man who thinks of his children as extensions of his personality. Our entire lives were supposed to be lights to shine upon his stage. We were supposed to make him look good. We were supposed to be better than his brother's children, smarter, faster, more accomplished. Then his mother would like us more than she liked them. And so on and so forth. You have to know that to understand this story, which is about my setting forth to break the bonds he tied me with. It took a very long time and almost destroyed a lot of innocent people along the way. In the end I got free, so it sort of has a happy ending.

That's what this country is about, isn't it? Getting free. Freeing people from their pasts. Creating our own crazy dazzling lives.

This story is also about Charles William Waters, who was along for part of that journey and sparked or inspired me into telling about it. Charles William spent his whole life making things beautiful and building houses for people to live in that made them view the world in different ways. He liked cathedral ceilings and lots of glass and creeks running into living rooms and people playing Ravel on the record player and girls wearing handmade cotton underwear trimmed with lace. He lived and died for beauty and was scarce adjusted to the tomb when one who died for truth was lain in an adjoining room. That will be me.

About Charles William's tomb. When he found out his heart was failing him, he went straight down to the Dunleith Funeral Parlor, the black funeral home that he designed and built after the old brick one burned down, and picked himself out a coffin. It has The Last Supper in raised figures on the inside of the coffin lid and he is resting in it now. "I'd had my eye on it, Dee," he told me when he called me with the news. "I told Spavineau, Spav, you know I've been wanting it. How much do you want down to hold it for me? So, of course, she burst into tears. Don't cry on the lining, please, I told her. Unless you want to come down on the price."

Part One

DUNLEITH

Chapter

1

"We're moving to Dunleith, Alabama." It was my momma on the phone. I was a freshman at Vanderbilt and I had just completed my next-to-last swimming meet of the spring semester. I was sitting in my room letting my roommate cut my hair when my mother calls me up to tell me this dreadful news. "Why?" I screamed. "What is he doing now? What are you going to do?"

"He wants to move to Dunleith. He wants to go back to the South. I want it too." There was something strange in her voice. My mother was never forceful, but this was forceful. "Wait a minute. He wants to talk to you."

"I'm getting my hair cut. Lilly's cutting my hair." She had followed me out into the hall and was standing beside the phone booth with the scissors still in her hand. At that time there were not many telephones in the world and people had to go out into the hall to answer them.

"Sister." It was my father. "Sister, don't go starting one of your fits now. Your mother and I want to move back to the South. We went down to Dunleith last weekend and bought a house. I'm going to bring you a car so you can drive down there when school's out. When do you get through up there?"

"Don't you want to know about the meet? I came in first in

three events. Don't you read the papers? You didn't even call to see if I had won."

"Of course you won, Sweet Sister. Now settle down. Dunleith's only twenty miles from Aberdeen and we can be near your grandmother. Your mother bought a fine big house and you can help her fix it up."

"I don't want a house. I've lived in five towns since I was five years old. I don't know where I live. You drive me crazy, Daddy. You should have told me. You should have asked me if I cared."

"Well, Sister, I'm not going to ask any little half-baked girls if they like what I do with my life. Here's your mother, talk to her." He handed the phone to my mother and she tried to calm me down. "Your father will bring a car and leave it for you. Bring some friends home if you like. You're going to love the house, darling. It's really a wonderful old place. We'll have fun restoring it."

"I have friends in Franklin, Mother. Val thinks I'm going to write for him all summer. I can't believe you'd do this to me. It's the end of April. You should have told me. How could you do this without telling me?"

"He did it, darling. You know how he is."

So they had done it to me again. Uprooted me without notice. Destroyed my life. Ended everything I had worked to create. Always before I had been dragged along without complaining, but this time something snapped. I went back into my room and let Lilly finish cutting my hair. She had created a new hairstyle for me. It was very short, as short as a boy's, a little cap of reddish gold curls that would not be in my way when I was swimming. Where would I swim in Dunleith, Alabama? Where would I go? Who would I talk to?

When Lilly finished my haircut I went back into the hall and called my parents back. "Did anyone tell Val I won't be back to write my column? Did anyone think of that?"

"You can call him and charge it to our phone. I'm sorry you'll be inconvenienced, darling, but this is going to be the best for everyone."

"Sister." It was my father again. "Our old friends the Halli-days own the paper in Dunleith. As soon as you get there we'll go down and tell them you want a job."

"I don't want a job, Daddy. I want my own newspaper. I want my own desk next to Mr. Valentine's. How could you do this to me? Why didn't you tell me you were doing this?" But he had hung up. He always hung up if you tried to yell at him. Criticism rolled off him like water off a duck's back, he told my brothers or me or anyone who didn't like anything he decided to do. But then, he was the oldest son of a woman who thought she could walk on water. So maybe it wasn't his fault either.

"Are you okay?" Lilly asked. She was a tall blonde Atlantan who had stuck by me through sorority rush and all the other assorted horrors of our freshman year in college. She had pledged the best sorority on campus but she hardly bothered to notice it. She just kept on cutting my hair and going to breakfast in the dining hall with Cutter Mayberry, a tiny nondescript banker's daughter from a small town in Tennessee who later turned out to have an exotic secret life downtown with a sailor. Lilly and I always ate breakfast with her because her room was next door and no one else in the residence house liked her. "What are they doing to you now? Come back here, Rhoda. Come sit down and tell me what they said."

"It's done. We're moving away from Franklin this week. I won't even get to be there. I won't even get to tell my friends goodbye or pack the things in my room. They always do this to me, Lilly. They've been doing it forever. Both of them were born in places where they always lived. They think it's fun to move around. But I think I'm going crazy. God, I think I really am." I went back into the room I shared with Lilly and fell down on a bed. Lilly sat beside me and rubbed my soft still-wet hair. "Let's go over to the pool and swim," she said. "I love to watch you swim. And then we'll go to the Waffle House and eat waffles. You want to do that? There's a bloodmobile at the Kappa Sigma house. We can eat up everything in sight and then go and give a pint of blood and we'll come out even. Remember the last time we did that and Doc McElroy fainted in the hall? Please don't be sad, Rhoda. We can't do anything about the things they do. They're our parents. They get to run our lives."

"They won't run mine. I won't go. I'll stay in Franklin and live with Val. He'll let me. I won a state contest with my column when I was a junior in high school. I won it two years in a row. A contest for grown people. They're waiting for me to come back and write for them. I was going to work there all day in the summer. I was going to make three hundred dollars a month. I can't believe they'd do this to me, Lilly. No one could do this to someone else."

"Our parents can." She began to stroke my back and neck. "They can do anything they want to do. Let's go swimming, Rhoda. I love to watch you swim. Please don't stay here. If we stay here, we'll only end up crying."

"Okay. Find a bathing suit. I'm getting up. Let's go."

We went over to the indoor pool and put on our bathing suits and began to swim. There were only two or three different kinds of bathing suits back then. I had a pretty blue Jantzen for swimming in meets or outdoors in the summer where people could see me and a two piece baby blue Catalina for when I was feeling especially thin. But the suit I liked to practice in was made of dark gray wool. It was very old and my mother had worn it the first time she swam in the Atlantic Ocean. When I was small I had used it to make Catwoman outfits. I had swum a million laps in it but it was still as thick and good as new. No one now would swim in such a heavy wool suit, but I had been wearing it for different things since I was ten years old and it was my lucky suit. I was wearing it the day I broke 1:06 in the hundred-yard butterfly and the day I swam the five-hundred-meter freestyle in 6:52.

"Where'd you get that suit?" Lilly asked. "It's so fuzzy looking. It looks so professional. Is that what real swimmers wear?"

"No, it's what I wear, for luck. It's my lucky suit. I don't race in it. I practice in it. It's real heavy so when I take it off I think I'm a lot lighter. It's like taking off a starched dress. Did your mother used to make you wear starched dresses?"

"Yes. I hated them. I used to cry if I thought about it."

"I wouldn't wear them. I tore them off. I tore one right down the middle one day when my uncle was visiting from medical school. It's a good thing he was there. My dad might have beat me to death."

"Did they beat you?"

"They hit me with a belt if I was bad. They beat the boys. Daddy beat them anytime he wanted to. He still beats Dudley. Dudley lets him do it. Dudley does anything my daddy wants him to."

"My daddy just talks to me." Lilly leaned against the ladder going down into the hot chlorinated water of the pool. The water rose up in clouds and curled her light blonde hair, which was cut off as short as mine, but not as well, since she did it herself and couldn't do a good job in the back. "He's a baby doctor. He doesn't believe in beating children or even spanking them."

"My daddy's daddy used to beat him too. In Aberdeen, where he comes from, they think you have to beat children to make them mind. Well, that's where we're moving back to. Back to Alabama where he knows the governor. My daddy's family owns the whole county where they live. So now he's rich and he can go back there. So now they're going to pack all the stuff in my room without me even being there." Tears were beginning to run down my face into the dark blue chlorinated water. "Lilly, do you have that stopwatch I gave you?"

"I've got it."

"Well, start watching it. Tell me when it gets to the top." I took a position in the second lane and lay my arms back behind me and began to count into my stroke. One, two, three, four, five, six, seven, eight.

"Now," she said, and I dove into the water and began to swim. Like the wind, I told myself, like wind in a canyon, tear the rocks off the wall, turn the stone to pebbles, goddammit, Sister, swim.

Six minutes and forty-two point three seconds later I pulled myself up on the side and Lilly told me the time. "Oh, you're kidding. No one can swim that fast. You didn't time it right."

"I pushed it when you touched the end. It was so beautiful to watch, Rhoda. You look like you don't even move. I can hardly see you move. The water moves all around you."

"Let me see the watch. You timed it wrong. Of course, there wasn't anyone else in the pool. When you're making the only waves it helps. Goddammit, if I did that. If I really did."

"Try it again."

"Okay. Let me catch my breath and get a drink of water and I will. God, if I did that. If I did it once. See, if you can ever do it once, you can do it again." I went out into the hall and drank from a water fountain. I thought about the swimming pool I had helped build in Franklin, Kentucky. I had written column after column in the paper about how much it would help the town and how much fun we'd have and had vowed to teach swimming to little kids if they built it. A promise I had kept. Well, that was all behind me now. I would never see Franklin again. Never see the newspaper office or the swimming pool or our white frame house or the roof where I slept beneath the stars on summer nights or my room that I had decorated to look like a newspaper office or Sue Beck Bailey or Betty Clinton or Stanley Walther, status genius, age fourteen, or my brother's baby goats or Mr. Mobly, the mayor of Main Street, or the Sweet Shop or the park where Joe Davis had taken me swimming on the third of May or the train station where they shipped me off to a girls' school in my senior year in high school and where I had wept uncontrollably when the train delivered me home for Christmas. I stopped with my hand on the water fountain and tried to suck up my guts. Suck up your guts, Sister, my daddy always said to me. Act like a man.

"Rhoda, what are you doing? I thought you were going to swim the five hundred again."

"I can't right now, Lilly. Let's just swim laps, okay? I'm really feeling bad. I'm tired. I'm really tired. I don't know why. Let's swim some laps and then we can go eat a waffle. I'm tired and starving."

"Try it one more time. You broke your record. Please try it. I want you to." She stood in the door to the pool area with her soft wet hair and her long skinny legs and her amazing kindness and praise and I went back in and swam the five hundred again. But this time the time was fifty-four, so I supposed the other had been an accident or a mistake after all.

Back in Franklin, Kentucky, the movers were hauling my bed and desk and books and clothes out of my room. The next morning they would be on their way to Alabama with my parents and my little brothers in two cars behind them. My mother had the baby, Johnny, who was four, and my father had my brother Alford, who was seven. They drove down to Aberdeen first to see my grandmother and have tea and biscuits on her blue-and-white china and talk about me.

"She needs to settle down," my grandmother would say. "She's such a scatterbrain."

"You never did like her," my mother would put in. "You only like the boys."

"Sister'll be all right," Daddy decreed. "She'll marry a nice boy someday and have some babies. She's still wet behind the ears."

"She won some race," Momma put in. "People talk all the time about the columns she used to write."

"Well, don't encourage that. Look what happened to Sissy Arnold. They let her work for that Hodding Carter down in Greenville and now she's in New York married to that drunken man who wrote all that bad stuff about Clarkesville and all that nasty stuff about Aunt Frances's house. After he was her guest. He said she had the family portraits held together with masking tape. He said her silver was black as coal."

"She's eighty-three years old," Momma agreed. "Imagine having all that nasty stuff written about you in *Newsweek* magazine. When he was her guest."

"He and Sissy were down there last summer handing out birth control things to the Negroes. She let them stay. Frances let them stay after he wrote all that nasty stuff about her."

"She must be senile," Mother said. "I don't think she can think very well."

"She is not senile. She has some trouble hearing. I don't know where you got your information, Ariane, but my sister Frances is

not senile. People in our family do not lose their minds. There has
not been a single case."

"Where are the little boys, do you think?" Momma would
quickly ask. "I believe we should go on to Dunleith, Dudley. I think
the movers will need us to be there when they arrive."

Chapter

2

I swam a 6:45 in the Southeastern Conference Championships in Knoxville and a 1:09 in the 100-yard breast-stroke and took home two blue ribbons. My butterfly had been off all spring and I placed third in that. Also, I completely quit going to Chi Omega meetings. I had only joined to save face anyway and I was reading Shakespeare in the Joint University Library at night hoping my English teacher would notice me on his way in or out of the stacks where he was locked up every night working on his Ph.D. He was a lanky Jewish intellectual who reminded me of Bob Rosen, my long-lost love in Harrisburg, Illinois. I had noticed him staring at my Chi O pin one day in class so I took it off and never wore it again. I think now he was looking at my breasts but who was I to know that back then? I didn't even know it was against the rules for teachers to have love affairs with students. Not that I knew what a love affair was either. Once a boy had put his hand inside my underpants every night for twelve nights, but aside from that it was lost love in Illinois and things I wrote and stuff I read. I wish I had the notebooks I used to keep in those years. I wish I could read the lies I used to tell the pages in my careful legible teenage script.

My father showed up one day in early May and left a Cadillac at a friend's house for me to drive to my new home when school was over.

"Your momma's got the house in good shape," he said. "You've got a big new room with a ceiling fan and all your things are right there where you had them. I've lined up all your cousins. They're waiting for you. And there's a dandy girl right across the street. Little Irise Lane. Her father's the assistant editor of the paper so you can go right back to being a newspaper writer if your heart's so set on that. I told him you were coming and he and little Irise are waiting for you. She's a KD at the University of Alabama. I wish to hell you were down there at Auburn or Tuscaloosa instead of this goddamn liberal place. I tried to talk to those people at the administration building but they're a bunch of nuts. I swear, Sister, a college education is the worst thing a man can have. I'm about to live mine down at last." He paused, pulled out his billfold, and laid it on the table. We were eating dinner at a campus restaurant that specialized in beef fillets on biscuits. I was proud to be there with a man as handsome as my father, in his gorgeous handmade clothes from Harold's in Lexington. This town had belonged to him once. He had played left field for the Nashville Volunteers in the old Southern League and the sportswriters in town knew and remembered him. He had been famous and I was only a slightly overweight, wet-behind-the-ears little girl who had not been invited to join Kappa Alpha Theta. "You shouldn't have sent me here," I said. "You talked me into this. You should have sent me somewhere where Chi O was the best. I didn't even have any Kappa recs. If it hadn't been for that girl who knew Uncle Jimmy in Mobile, I wouldn't have even been invited to the second party. It was the worst thing that ever happened to me in my life, Daddy, and it was your fault. You got me to come here and then Dudley got in all that trouble last year and was disgraced and you didn't even tell me that. You should have told me that. I was here for three months before the Kappa Sigs told me why he left. It's too embarrassing. I hate it here. You can't be at Vanderbilt if you aren't a Kappa. I hate it all and now you're going to make me move down there." I pushed my plate away from me. I began to eat my chocolate ice-cream pie. I ate it as fast as I could. He sighed. He pushed his chair back from the table. He laid his fork and knife down on his plate and began to fold his napkin across his knee.

"Now you're going to start hating your brother, Sister? That's the ticket now? You're going to believe what these sapsuckers tell you about your brother? I'll tell you one goddamn thing. He's got more spunk and guts than this whole goddamn place and all its teachers put together. He's down there in Knoxville playing with the varsity team at night and taking care of his family and running one of the mines for me on the weekends."

"He lost his scholarship."

"We don't need any goddamn scholarships, Sister. He wouldn't tell on his fraternity brothers. Just like I've tried to teach you all your life. You don't tell on your friends, Sister. But you're a tattletale anyway. Always have been. I guess you'd have just gone on and told their names."

"He let people copy off of him in tests. He cheated, Daddy."

"Sister, finish up that cake and let's get out of here. I've got to drive three hundred miles tonight and I'm tired. You make a fellow very tired, Sweet Sister." He stood up and put a tip on the table and picked up the check. He took three one-hundred-dollar bills out of his billfold and laid them on the table and said, "That's for clearing up everything down here before you leave. You've got the map I gave you, haven't you? Your mother will be waiting for you. Dudley and Annie will be in their new house by the time you get there. It's right around the corner. Little Ariane's the cutest little girl you ever saw in your life. Well, come on, let's get out of here."

I stood up beside him. He was so beautiful, so perfect, so powerful and impossible and brave. Nothing I would ever do would make him love me.

"I won the five-hundred-yard freestyle and the hundred-yard breaststroke. Did Momma tell you?"

"Good for you, Sister. What happened in the butterfly? You let them take you to the cleaners there, didn't you?"

"I swam the five hundred in six forty-two point three in practice. I couldn't believe I did it."

"Did you read about that new Channel swimmer in England? She broke the men's record last week. Well, hurry up, Sweetie, I've got to get on the road."

* * *

The semester dragged on to its end. I got permission to bring the car Daddy had left for me onto the campus during exam week and park it in front of the residence house. It was a dark red Cadillac, embarrassingly long and heavy and funereal. I packed all my belongings in the trunk with my typewriter stowed beneath piles of sweaters and cutoff blue jeans. I stacked my books on the backseat and threw all my 45 rpm records on the shelf beneath the rear window. On the morning of my last exam I drove the car over to Ransom Hall, the domain of the history and English departments, and parked it in the back and went inside to take the exam. The exam was in World Lit, "The Ancient World Through the Renaissance." All my life I had loved to take exams and write essays. I grabbed a stack of blue books at the door and began to fill them with opinions. I discussed Job in the Old Testament, then moved on to Homer, then to Plato's *Symposium*, then to Dante, Rabelais, Cervantes, and Shakespeare. "Then you will do your duty," said Don Quixote, "for it is not necessary to be dubbed a knight to engage in battles such as these." That was the text I chose to open my essay on simile and metaphor, an extra-credit question. I wrote happily away. When I looked up two and a half hours had gone by. There were only three other people left in the room. "Anything *can stand for something else*," I wrote in conclusion. "Any key will turn the lock into the secrets of our brains. Everything is like everything else and everything is hooked up to everything else and everyone is included. 'Cast a cold eye on life, on death. Horseman, pass by!' "

I closed the blue book, picked up the stack of them I had filled, there must have been nine or ten, and began to gather up my things. My English teacher, whom I had worshipped so desperately from afar, came over to me. "You wrote all of these?" he asked.

"I had a lot to say."

He grinned at that and carried them before him up to his desk and put a rubber band around them and then walked with me outside. "I have a surprise for you," he said. "I didn't want to tell you until you'd finished writing. I was afraid it might distract you."

"I got an A?"

"Oh, I'm sure you got an A, Rhoda. No, it's something else. You won the freshman writing contest. I entered that essay you wrote on The Fugitives and you won first place. Not even edited. I'm proud of you."

"What did I win?"

"A set of books. They'll send them to you this summer." He stood with his hands folded in front of him. We were outside on the steps now. Wide marble steps that led down onto the beautiful lawns of a quadrangle with huge old oak trees.

"I don't know what to say. That's wonderful. That's so good. I mean, thanks for entering it. It's really wonderful. I won first place?"

"You did indeed. I thought it was a fine piece of writing. When are you leaving for home?"

"Right now. I have a car to drive. They left me a car because my family moved somewhere this spring. I won first place?"

"You did. When you get back next fall, come and see me. I want to set you up with some extra studies. I'm going to be in charge of the honors program for English students. Hopefully, I'll have finished my dissertation by then." He smiled and laughed to himself. "God knows I'm sick of working on it."

"I will. Well, thanks again. I mean, thanks so much."

"You did it. Well, goodbye then. I'll look forward to reading your exam." He laughed again and shook his head.

"I'll see you in the fall."

"I'll see you too." I walked on down the steps, putting each foot down into a pool of sunlight, so exhilarated and pleased, so thrilled and excited it seemed that my whole life had been lived to arrive at this one conversation on this one day. I walked down the steps and around the building and got into the car and started driving. I glanced in the rearview mirror once and noticed that my entire collection of 45 rpm recordings had melted in the sun into crazy little warped black sun hats but it didn't mean a thing to me. I had won the freshman writing contest. I was a writer. I could write things and win. Nothing mattered in the world but that. I left the campus and turned onto the highway leading out of town and began to drive to my new home.

Chapter

3

North Alabama, in the middle years of the twentieth century. Towns with names like Sheffield and Florence and Tuscumbia. Muscle Shoals and Elkmont and Tanner, Aberdeen and Dunleith and Wheeler. The Tennessee River flows through this country, flowing southward to meet its eastern half at Guntersville Lake. This is the Appalachian Valley, the Appalachian Highlands, and the Piedmont Plateau. This is where my father's people came when they left Scotland. They are cold laughing people, with beautiful faces and unshakable wills. They are powerful and hot-tempered. They never forget a slight, never forgive a wrongdoing. They seldom get sick. They get what they want because they believe they are supposed to have it. They believe in God as long as he is on their side. If he wavers, they fire the preacher. I had never been comfortable with them. Never liked to visit long in Aberdeen, their stronghold in the middle of their cotton fields. They had settled the land on Spanish land grants and cleared it with slave labor. They loved to read the old wills in which their ancestors left slaves to each other. It made them sad to think they couldn't keep slaves anymore but had to let the black people do anything they liked, might soon even have to let them vote.

I came due south from Nashville and drove into the sleepy little town of Dunleith in the afternoon of the last day in May. I found the main street, using a map my father had drawn for me, and followed it to Wheeler. I turned onto Wheeler and immediately began to be seduced. Huge elm trees lined the street on either side. Behind the elms were magnificent houses, each one bigger and more elaborately Victorian than the last. I began to want to live in one of these huge painted houses. I do not know what I thought such a house might do for me, but I wanted the biggest one of all. Three blocks from the corner there it was. A huge chocolate-colored palace with turrets and balconies and porches. I parked the car and got out and looked up at the door. My mother came running down from a screened-in porch. She was wearing the black Mexican wedding skirt she had bought the year before when my father was having his love affair and she had run away to New Orleans for her nervous breakdown. She came flying down the steps with her hair all in ringlets and began to hug me. "My goodness, honey," she said. "You've gained so much weight. I thought you were on the swimming team."

"I won the freshman writing contest, Momma. I didn't even enter it. I won first place."

"We'll take you to a doctor tomorrow and get you some of the new pills. We'll go in the morning. Well, come on in and see the house. Isn't it beautiful? Don't you like it?"

"Are Dudley and Annie here? Have they moved in yet?" I spotted my little brother Alford lurking on the porch with his B-B gun. The summer before he had shot a B-B in my hand when I tried to take the magazine out of his gun at an ice-cream party we were having. "I can't believe you still let him have that gun. I can't believe you do it."

"Don't start a fight with Alford. Come on in, Rhoda. Everyone's on the porch waiting to meet you. Some of your cousins. They've been here all afternoon waiting for you to come." I walked up on the porch and was introduced to my cousin Martha Ann, who lived across the street, and her husband, Frank, and Mrs. Hunter Waits, Senior, from Aberdeen, and Daddy's cousin James's wife, Lelia. I shook hands with everyone and answered their questions, then Momma and Lelia took me to see my room and tour the house. It had fifteen rooms and an attic and a basement. It had three screened-in porches and three parlors and a den. It had six or seven bedrooms depending on if you counted the maid's room. My bedroom was on the second floor. It was three times as large as any room I had ever had. Its windows looked out upon the high branches of a majestic elm. My cherry furniture was all arranged and a new bedspread was on the bed. A quilted spread in subtle shades of yellow. There was a ceiling fan above the bed and a braided yellow rug was on the floor. Mother stood beside the bed waiting for me to tell her how wonderful it was.

"Where's my eiderdown comforter, Momma?" I asked. "Please tell me where you put it. It better be here."

"It's in the chest at the foot of the bed. That's my old chest that held my trousseau. I'm giving it to you."

"That's nice. That's really nice. Look, are all those people down there going to stay all afternoon? I'd really like to get my stuff out of the car. My typewriter's in the trunk. I want to see if I can find a copy of that paper I wrote that won in case anyone wants to see it. I've forgotten what it says."

"Of course, darling. I'll bet you're tired too. I'll have the maids bring your things up and help you put it all away. You go take a bath and change clothes. You look like you're worn out." She was opening my dresser drawers. "See, honey, everything's here. Right where you left it."

"Well, not quite." I walked over to the window and looked out through the trees and across the street to where a small brown-haired girl was standing on the porch of a small blue house. "Who's that, Momma? Who's that girl?"

Momma came and stood by my side. She put her hand on my shoulder. "That's Irise Lane, honey. She's just your age. She's dying to meet you. Shall I call her over? Shall I invite her over?"

"No, wait until tomorrow. I'm really tired, Momma. I had to drive a long time to get here. Who's in our old house in Franklin? Did someone buy it?"

"Daddy sold it to Val's cousin Donald. Val said to tell you goodbye. He said you could keep on writing columns and send them to him in the mail if you wanted to." I was still watching the girl on the porch of the blue house. A heavy boy in a loose white shirt and a pair of shorts came walking up the sidewalk and took her arm and the pair of them went into the house.

"Who's that with her?"

"That's Charles William Waters. He's very artistic. He's studying architecture at Georgia Tech. He's Doctor Freer's nephew. We really need to go see Doctor Freer tomorrow and do something about this weight. I don't want you to be fat. You've never been fat."

"You shouldn't have sent me to that goddamn school without getting me some Kappa recs. It's been terrible. It's the worst thing that ever happened to me in my life." My voice was rising. Daddy's cousin James's wife, Lelia, backed out into the hall. "I had to join that goddamn new Chi O chapter you and Aunt Lucille cooked up for me. It's the worst thing that ever happened to me in my life. You didn't even tell me about Dudley being kicked out of school for cheating. You let me go up there with that hanging over my head and you didn't even tell me." I turned on her then, so full of rage and incomprehension and despair, so glad to find a target for my wrath.

"Oh, darling, please don't start anything. There are people in the house. Don't come down here and make everyone's life a hell. There's a wonderful country club in town. Tomorrow we'll go out and you can see the pool. So you can keep up with your swimming."

"Leave me alone, Mother, will you? And I'm not going to a doctor. I'm not fat. There's nothing wrong with me. I'm going to kill myself if you don't leave me alone." She moved toward the door and I pushed her through it and slammed it shut and walked over and lay down on the bed and cried myself to sleep.

Chapter

4

Of course in the end I agreed to go to the doctor. By ten o'clock the next morning my mother and I were down at old Doctor Freer's office and he had weighed and measured me and given me a diet and a prescription for some "pink pills" to take half an hour before breakfast, lunch, and dinner. I took one at the drugstore as soon as we had the prescription filled. By the time we got home and started fixing my diet lunch I was in a marvelous mood. Momma ran the cook out of the kitchen and fixed the lunch herself. She fixed me four ounces of steak and a very small lettuce and tomato salad and a piece of melba toast. She set the dining room table with a crocheted placemat and heavy Strasbourg silver and made me a glass of iced coffee and sat with me while I ate. I was chattering away, happy as a lamb on twelve milligrams of Dexedrine.

After lunch I went out onto one of the screened-in porches to sand a chair. I had the record player in the den blaring away, playing Tchaikovsky's Piano Concerto Number 1, a perfect complement for a brain speeding away on Dex. I was feeling thin already. This was a great diet. You didn't even get hungry. This was perfect.

"We heard you were coming. We've been waiting for days for you."

I looked up. Outside the screen door were the boy and girl I had seen the day before. They were standing side by side, a tall heavy-looking boy with his shirt unbuttoned to the navel and some odd-looking cross hanging down on a chain. He was barefooted. Beside him was the girl I had seen on the porch of the blue house. "I'm Charles William Waters," the boy said. "And this is Irise Lane. We know your name is Rhoda, but I'm always going to call you Dee. For Dirty old Rhoda, for what you did to Lizzie."

"Who is Lizzie? I never knew a Lizzie in my life. What did you hear about me?" I opened the door and they walked in, both smiling widely.

"Lizzie used to live here. She's furious because she had to leave. This used to be her house."

"To hell with some goddamn mythical Lizzie. I don't know why Daddy bought this goddamn monstrosity anyway. We're completely redoing it. It's going to take months to fix it so anyone can live here. Well, anyway, hello. I saw you yesterday. I'm Rhoda."

"Excuse me for not wearing shoes. I never wear them in the summer."

"He always goes barefooted," Irise said. "Because he is flat-footed."

"We're dying to see the house," Charles William added. "I came over about a week ago but they were still tearing out walls. Is that Tchaikovsky? I love classical music. The only other thing I listen to is jazz."

"I love jazz. The boy I love taught me all about it. He plays a saxophone. But I'll probably never see him again. He's in southern Illinois dying of cancer."

"Oh, Rhoda, that's the saddest thing I've ever heard." Irise moved near to me and I really looked at her. She was very small, smaller than she had seemed from my upstairs window, and she was very old-fashioned looking, like a girl out of an old picture of a perfect life. She had soft brown hair and wide eyes that could fix on you and hold. She was wearing a thin white cotton dress trimmed in lace. She put her hand upon my arm and moved nearer. I caught a whiff of roses, some divine soft smell.

"I don't know. He may be all right. I had to move away and

leave him anyway. Well, I don't care. What's that perfume? What a great perfume."

"It's Joy. Charles William got it for me. He brought it back from Cuba."

"A woman in a bar was wearing it," he said. He laughed out loud. "I said, what is that perfume? Joy, she answered. The most expensive perfume in the world. Then she got her husband and brought him over. They were these fabulous tacky Yankee people. He'd made a million dollars before he was forty and he was trying to retire but he didn't know how. Hunter McCormick and I had gone to Cuba for two weeks, this was last summer, we saw all these blue movies. You wouldn't believe what we saw, Dee. So then I got Hunter and we started helping these people have fun. They rented a fifty-foot sailboat for the weekend and took us out on it. They kept trying to give us money and all they talked about was money. Every time we'd admire something, they'd tell us how much it cost." He laughed again and hugged Irise to his side.

"Oh, my God," I said. "How tacky. Well, look, come on in and see what Momma's doing. She's got this whole place full of carpenters. They woke me up at seven o'clock this morning. I may have to go to Cuba."

"You'd love it, Dee. I know everywhere to stay. By the time we got through helping Patsy and Myron, that was their names, have fun we had seen the island."

"I wish I could go. I've never been anywhere. My life's passing me by."

"Let's see the house," Irise said. "I've been visiting here forever. I can't wait to see what your momma's doing."

"She's doing everything. She didn't want this monstrosity, but Daddy had to have it. He said she could do anything she wants to with it, so she's doing it."

"We love Ariane," Charles William said. "We met her at Saint James's. We think she's a doll, an absolute doll." He stopped to inspect a piece of wainscoting that was being nailed up beside a chimney. As if on cue, my mother came flying down the stairs with her hair tied up in a turban. She was trying to look like a person who could boss workmen around and had taken to tying up her hair and wearing canvas wedgies instead of her usual two-inch heels.

"Oh, Charles William," she exclaimed. "Irise. You darlings. How nice to have you here. You've met Rhoda. Isn't she precious?" She stopped by me and squeezed my shoulder. It was still early in the day and we hadn't had time to have an argument yet. Every day she woke up thinking she could understand me and "stop fighting with me." Every day I broke her heart.

"Make your guests some coffee, honey," she said. "Take them in the den. Charles William knows all about decorating. He helped your cousin Martha Ann do her whole house. See if you think the sofas are all right, Charles William. I can still send them back. Joe January said he'd take them back if I decided I didn't like them."

"I can find you a mantel for that chimney in the hall, Ariane," he said. "If you want one. They're tearing down a place in Fairfields that has some fabulous ones still in it."

"Oh, would you? Please get one. Whatever you think will fit."

"I'll do it tomorrow. I'll take Dee with me. Do you mind if I call her Dee, Ariane? Rhoda is too closed for her. She needs an open sound."

"He always gives people nicknames," Irise said. "He never even calls pets the names you give them."

Twenty minutes later we were in the den smoking Pall Malls and drinking coffee and listening to Ravel's "Pavanne for a Dead Princess."

"It's divine," Charles William said. "I could listen to it forever. I think I'll play it at my funeral."

"You won't be at your funeral," I answered. "You'll be dead."

" 'This I do being mad: gather baubles about me, sit in a circle of toys.' Edna Millay." He raised his coffee cup, exhaled a lungful of smoke.

"My favorite poet," I answered. " 'Come and see my shining palace built upon the sand.' No, listen to this. This is my absolute favorite. 'What lips my lips have kissed, and where, and why, I have forgotten, and what arms have lain under my head till morning.' "

" 'But the rain is full of ghosts tonight, that tap and sigh, upon the glass and listen for reply, and in my heart there stirs a quiet pain. For unremembered lads that not again will turn to me at midnight with a cry.' "

"Oh, my God, you really know it." I jumped up, ran up to my room, got all my books of poetry and we sat in the den for half the afternoon, reading poetry out loud, talking about death, drinking coffee, smoking Pall Malls, totally enraptured with each other. Irise fell asleep on the sofa, all curled up in her soft white dress and sandals. Charles William sat cross-legged on the floor, his fat legs sticking out of his camp shorts. I sat on a chair, my fat stomach sticking out of a midriff. We kept on listening to the Ravel while we read. Wanda Landowska's brilliant renditions of "Pavanne pour une infante défunte," "A la manière de Chabrier," "A la manière de Borodin," and "Sonatine" played over and over on the record player.

They stayed all afternoon. At six I took another one of my pills and Mother asked Charles William and Irise to stay for dinner. "Rhoda's on a diet," she said. "But we can fix you a real dinner."

"I'll go on the diet with her," Charles William said. "I'll eat whatever she's having."

"I can eat anything," Irise said. "Let me help you set the table."

At six-thirty I sliced the artery between my thumb and index finger with a steak knife in my excitement over not being hungry for the four-ounce steak Mother cooked me.

Irise and Charles William rode with us in the car to get my hand stitched up at the hospital. "We needed some excitement," Charles William said, when we were driving home with my hand bandaged. "And here you are, willing to amputate your hand, just for us."

"He loves excitement," Irise said. "He never stops doing things."

"Neither do I. Well, meeting you has made this town seem like someplace I can live. I'll see you in the morning, won't I? Will you come back over?"

"As soon as we get up," Charles William promised. "We'll go find Ariane a mantel and have you an ankh made."

"A what?"

"This." He removed the strange cross from his neck. "It's the Egyptian symbol of everlasting life. See, the circle represents the female sexual organs and the cross represents the male. Put them together and you have a key to unlock everlasting life. Isn't it marvelous? I found a man in Huntsville who can make them. Here, put it on. You can wear mine until your hand gets better." He lifted the chain and put it around my neck.

"My goodness," Mother said, and stopped the car before Irise's driveway.

"He loves old things and cultures," Irise said. "Egypt is his favorite now. He knows everything about Egypt."

"It's getting late," Mother said. "Rhoda better get to bed."

"I was interested in the Greeks," Charles William added, getting out of the car and giving me a kiss on the cheek. "But then I moved into the Egyptians. Good night, Ariane, thanks for bringing Dee here. We'll see her in the morning."

Mother backed the car across the street and pulled into our driveway. I was sitting in the seat with my bandaged hand in my lap and the other hand holding the ankh.

"I wouldn't wear that pagan thing if I were you," she began, but I got out of the car and walked away.

"Shut up, Mother," I called over my shoulder. "Please mind your own goddamn business."

Chapter
5

Then six weeks went by. I had lost my home and my
budding profession as a newspaper columnist but I had found a
friend and a new life so rich and spoiled and pampered and charming that I never shed another tear for the small town of Franklin,
Kentucky, and its sensible midwestern inhabitants. My mother and
father had turned their house into a party. My mother's cousins
came up from the Delta and my father's cousins came in from their
plantations near Aberdeen to eat and play bridge and sit on the
porch discussing whether we should have dropped the atom bomb
and if insurance was worth having and how soon it would be before
the niggers took us over. Every afternoon by five o'clock they would
gather on the screened-in porches while Mother ran in and out
carrying whiskey sours and scotch mists and gin and tonics.
Around the corner my brother Dudley and his wife were settling
down into the red brick house Daddy had bought for them. Across
the street his cousin Martha Ann held her own court and next door
to that was another Victorian mansion Daddy was fixing to buy for
his brother. Anywhere I moved, anything I touched belonged to
him. Anything I wanted I could have. All I had to do was stay on
my diet and be "nice to people" and get acquainted with north
Alabama. Charles William and Irise were my guides. They took me

all over Dunleith and the outlying countryside. They took me to meet the famous Mimi Huffington who painted portraits of anyone who caught her fancy and sometimes even painted them for money. She had a Greek column in her living room and a bedroom she had turned into an artist's studio. She was first cousin to the fabled Lizzie who hated me for living in her house. Finally I was even taken to meet Lizzie. "Come see what we did," I volunteered. "Come over anytime you like."

"I didn't want to move," she answered. "I can't even drive by the place." She squinted up her freckled face.

"If you change your mind, call me up," I answered. "I didn't want to move either. I didn't want your house."

Still, I had her house and I had her friends, Charles William and Irise. Charles William was my first true running buddy, my first imaginative peer. All my life I had wanted a friend who knew what I was talking about. I had angelized plenty of people, one in each town where I lived, endowed them with whatever it was I needed, then overwhelmed them and made them love me, but I had never before found anyone who didn't need any filling in. Charles William was with me all the way. Of course, when two people like us get together there is always a chance things will get out of hand. We had Irise for an occasional voice of reason, but she was too polite to really put a brake on us. If we started doing something she didn't like (such as wearing the ankhs to early communion), she just said she wanted to stay home. Which is why she wasn't with us the night we went to meet the Klan.

"Y'all go on," she said. "I'll see you when you get back."

It started out innocently enough. It was about six weeks after I moved to town and Charles William asked me if I wanted to go and see a cockfight.

"Sure," I said. "Whyyy not."

"It's in a field they use for Klan meetings. I've been wanting to go and watch. If something like that's going on, you ought to go and see it."

"That's great. I'd like to see it. I read about it but I don't know what they do." I didn't know what they did. I had not lived in the

Deep South since I was a child. Everything I knew about the Klan I had read in *Gone With the Wind*. I thought their job was to keep black men from raping me. I didn't even know about the hangings.

All Charles William and I really wanted to do was to go and watch some white trash in their bad behavior in the night. We wanted to drift down into the real dark heart of the night and see what we could see. We wanted to do any exciting thing we could think up to do and we had already been caving, been swimming in a borrow pit, gotten drunk a dozen times, played bridge with an old lady who drank cough syrup all day, driven up to Guntersville Lake and gone through the locks in a motorboat, let Charles William's cousin give us Stanford-Binet intelligence tests (we were waiting for the results to come back from California), had my ankh made by a silversmith in Huntsville, put in an order for a copy of *Lady Chatterley's Lover* to be smuggled in from France, and anything else we could think up to do, not to mention taking the pink pills Doctor Freer gave me. Not to even mention that. I took them three times a day, and after he found out how good they made you feel, sometimes Charles William took them too.

Now we were in Charles William's mother's Buick going to a cock-fight. It was eleven-thirty at night, a Tuesday, and I had sneaked out the side door after my parents went to sleep. "Don't talk much when we get there," Charles William was saying. "Just be quiet and act like you're interested in what they're doing. Junior and Winston know we're coming. They'll take care of us, but don't talk too much. They don't really like women coming to these things."

"Who are Junior and Winston? I forgot what you told me."

"They used to work for my dad. They'll do anything for me. Pass that bottle please."

"The Coke or the bourbon?"

"The bourbon. The only way to understand white trash is to do what they do. I learned that in the theater. I want you to meet the theater people here, Dee. I bet they'll want to put you in a play."

"I was in a play once. I was the ingenue. I had to wear these lime green lounging pajamas Momma made me. They had frogs for fasteners. I hated them. I don't look good in Chinese clothes."

"Oh, Dee, I can just see Ariane making lounging pajamas for you. I don't see you in green, though. I see you in mauve and violet and white. You're so golden. You need mauve to cool you down."

"Someday I'll get rich and let you build me a house. What would you build?"

"White brick with many windows and gardens everywhere. A bedroom with a raised dais and a bed with mauve sheets and walls the color of shells."

"God, it's dark out here. Where are we?"

"Warwick County. It's the worst place in Alabama. These people can't even read. The white people can't even read."

"Then why are we going out here? It's spooky. It gives me the creeps."

"I think you ought to see this. If you're going to live down here, you ought to see what you're up against. Junior's going to be waiting at the store. Nothing can happen to us."

"It's just so goddamn dark."

"Dark of the moon," he answered and took another drink out of the bottle and passed it to me. I took a sip and shuddered, then chased it down with Coke and took another sip. The two-lane asphalt road wound up into the hills of Warwick County. This land had never been under cultivation. All people out here did for a living was raise a few hogs or pigs or chickens or maybe cows. It was the stronghold of the Klan, where the main obsession morning, night, and noon was keeping the white race pure. This was partially achieved by incest. But the main work was keeping the Negroes in their place, keeping the night as dark as it could be. We turned off the asphalt onto a gravel road and drove a few miles and came to a stop before a country store. Cars and pickup trucks were parked all around the building. A jukebox was playing. The porch was filled with groups of men wearing overalls and dark pants. Some of them were wearing capes. Long white satin capes with hoods and designs in red. Light shone from the windows of the store onto the figures on the porch.

"No," I said. "We can't go in. Turn around, Charles William. Let's go back."

"You need to see this, Dee. You're safe. They won't hurt you. Junior's here." As he spoke a man released himself from the crowd and came down the wooden steps and walked up to the car. A dark face leaned into the window on the driver's side.

"Who you looking for?" he asked. "What'd you need?"

"I'm looking for Winston Strange. We're supposed to meet him here. We came to bet on the fights."

"You got a girl with you?"

"Winston said she could come." I moved back into the seat. I had dealt with white trash before. They worked for my father at his coal mines in Kentucky, but I had never been alone with them in a place where I wasn't the boss's daughter. You couldn't tell what white trash would do. Up in Kentucky they still had feuds and killed each other.

"I don't care if I come or not," I said. "It doesn't matter to me if I see a fight. I just came along for the ride."

"Park over there by that Chevy," the man said, indicating a white car under a tree. "I'll see if Winston's here."

"I don't think we should be out here," I said when he was gone. "They're wearing capes, Charles William. They've got those capes on. They look like vampire movies. Let's go."

"We went to all this trouble. Let's just look at what they're doing. We don't have to stay long. Junior and Winston won't let anybody hurt me. Jesus Christ, Dee. Don't look like that. Nothing's going to hurt you."

"Charlie-Boy." A second face was peering in the window. "I'm glad you made it. Who's that with you? Who you got in there?" The face came all the way into the window. I shrank further back into the seat. The dark-faced white trash of the Delta always made me feel this way, as though some disaster was already happening, as though at any moment I might be captured and become one of their pale frightened women.

"This is Rhoda. She wants to see a cockfight."

"No, I don't. I mean, I don't care if I do or not."

"Well, get on out. It's okay. Kleet didn't scare you, did he?

He's an Avenger. We had a meeting called but it's over now. Some niggers over in Huntsville acting up. Come on, get on out.'' He opened the door on Charles William's side.

"So what happened to little Irise?'' he went on. "She quit on you?''

"Her momma won't let her out at night. Rhoda snuck out, didn't you, Rhoda?''

"We don't need to get out of the car. We could just sit here.''

"Get out,'' Winston said. "Come in the store. Have a beer.''

"It's okay, Dee,'' Charles William said. "You're with me. Nothing can hurt you here.''

"What are we going to do?''

"See a fight. The cocks love to fight. They fly at each other. You can't keep them from fighting.'' He came around to my side of the car and helped me out and took my arm and we walked up on the porch. The groups of men parted as we passed. Winston stood in the doorway holding open the door. He had taken off his cape and laid it across a chair. It sat upon the chair, just as evil on the chair as it had seemed when he was wearing it. The hem was muddy and the hood hung down into the satin folds. On the front was a red satin cross inside a circle. I walked around the room, smiling as hard as I could at the men sitting at the tables. When in Rome, I counseled myself. The Romans were drinking beer and eating pickled eggs and pickled pig's feet from filthy-looking glass jars on the bar.

"You want an egg?'' Winston asked.

"I'd like some of those potato chips if I could have them. And a Coke. Could I have a Coke?''

"You want anything in it?''

"No. A Coke will do. Just a plain old Coke.'' The bartender reached down into an ice chest and brought up a Coca-Cola and popped the top and handed it to Winston, who handed it to me. "What about my potato chips,'' I said. "I'd like them too.'' The bartender reached behind himself and took down a package of potato chips and handed it to Winston and he handed it to me.

"Oh, Dee, look at this. Isn't this hilarious?'' Charles William had a punchboard in his hand. On the front was a photograph of an aircraft carrier. There was a small metal punch attached to the board. "You want a punch? You can win a hundred dollars or ten or five. You want to try? I'm paying for it." He handed the board to me. The men at the tables were all watching us. I moved closer to Winston. I concentrated on my potato chips. "Come on, Dee," Charles William insisted. "Have a punch. I'm paying for it." He held the board out toward me. I took it from him and punched out a number. I unrolled the tiny piece of paper and read out loud. "Not today. Better luck next time."

"Oh, God," Charles William said. "Isn't that great? Here, let me try." He took the board from me and zeroed in on number seven. "You win five," the paper said. "Pay this man and let him go. Where he lands nobody knows."

"I won." Charles William brandished the paper toward the bartender. "Who pays for this?"

"I'll take it." The bartender took the paper and deposited it underneath some cash in the cash register and handed Charles William a five-dollar bill.

"You lucky stiff," Winston said. "I haven't won anything in six months off them goddamn boards."

"Let's go find Junior," Charles William said. "I want to show him this."

We went around back to where men were gathered around a wire enclosure. There were fires going farther back from the store and a burning cross from which smoke seemed to endlessly ascend, a black burning cross against the sky. It was the most evil thing I had ever seen. Somewhere, I could not remember where, I had seen a photograph of such a thing or heard a story of it. There was a blackened corpse on it in my memory. A figure hanging from a rope. "I want to get out of here, Charles William," I said. "I can't stay here. I want to leave."

"Oh, come on, Rhoda. We'll just watch one fight. I want you to see this. We'll see one fight and then we'll leave."

"What's wrong?" Winston asked. "What's wrong with her?"

"Nothing. There's nothing wrong."

"I have to get home," I said. "The mayor of Dunleith is coming to see my dad. My father is a good friend of the mayor's."

"She's all right," Charles William said. "I'm taking care of her." He led me over to a circle about ten feet in circumference. Men were gathered around it in groups of two and three. On one side a man was squatting, holding a small bird that was trying to peck his hand. The bird's beak was taped with adhesive tape and its feet were tied. The man held the bird with one hand and stroked its head with the other. On the opposite side of the circle a second man had a bird upside down and someone was tying something onto its feet. They were little knives, very small two-edged razor-sharp knives. Even from a distance of several feet and between the backs of the onlookers I could see the tiny glints of steel in the lantern light. I looked away. All around it was dark.

Dark of the moon. July twenty-fifth. I wanted to turn and run, but I could not move. I was transfixed. I thought that at any moment a rooster would escape and come flying at me, cutting my face to ribbons with his deadly legs. I backed away. Charles William put his arm around me and pulled me to his side again. "Don't be scared, Dee. They won't hurt you. They want to kill each other."

"How will they stop them? Who will catch them with those things on their legs?"

"Nobody wants to catch them," Winston said. "It's a fight."

We were joined by a man who turned out to be Junior and the story of Charles William's luck with the punchboard had to be told and exclaimed over. Junior was still wearing his cape. He had it rolled back from his shoulders. The hood fell down his back like a crumpled camellia. Keep away from me, voodoo and witch, I began reciting. Steer my path from the jailhouse gate. "I think we ought to go now," I said, hanging tighter and tighter onto Charles William's arm. "I need to get on home."

"Not yet, Dee. They're about to start." The cock owner had finished arming the second bird. A man stepped into the ring and began to announce the rules. "No poking the birds from the sidelines. No loud yelling. Stand back. Stay back behind the circle. Everybody ready? Okay, on three. One, two, three." The cocks were released and began to circle. Suddenly, one spread its wings and flew at the other. They met in the middle. The crowd moved back. "I'm going," I said. "I'm not watching this."

"No, wait. You have to see it. It's their nature, Dee. This is nature. This is what really happens." He stood there in the firelight, perfectly at ease. Junior and Winston stood on either side of him, two scrubby little terriers. Charles William was only nineteen years old but somehow he had power over these grown men. Not just his father's money either or because he was the late boss's son. He had some other kind of power, some self-assurance or will that made him safe even in this primitive unsafe place. Because of that I held on to his sleeve and let him make me stay. "Okay," I said. "But just one fight. Then we're leaving." The cocks were circling again. Then they flew into each other and blood flew out in all directions. It splattered all over Charles William's white shirt and on my hand. Before I could scream the birds were at our feet and blood was all over me. "Oh, goddammit," I screamed. "Goddammit all to hell. Oh, no, not this." I turned and ran toward the store, wiping blood from my face with my hand. Charles William came after me. "Come back, Dee," he called. "Come let me help you."

"You better take me home this minute," I screamed. "Come and take me home. YOU TAKE ME HOME THIS MINUTE. I HAVE TO GO HOME THIS VERY SECOND, DO YOU HEAR?"

He caught up with me. "Okay, Dee, calm down. It's okay. I'm sorry about the blood. We shouldn't have been so close. Come here. It's okay. Everything's okay. You want anything from the store before we leave?"

"No. I want to go to the bathroom but not in there. We might get lice or something. Just get me in the car and get me out of here."

"Well, let's go in and get some paper towels and wipe off the blood so we won't ruin Momma's car. Do you mind waiting that long? Can I go in the store?"

"Sure. Go on. It's okay. No, wait a minute, I'll go with you. I don't want to be alone."

The crowd on the porch had thinned. There were only three men left and only the bartender was in the store. We got two plain

Cokes and another bag of potato chips and took some paper towels and wiped off the blood as well as we could.

"The bathroom's right there," Charles William said. "Go on in. You won't catch anything, Dee. Go on. Don't be miserable."

I went into the bathroom and urinated and tried not to read the nasty graffiti. Then I washed my hands with soap and water and looked up into the mirror. A terrified Rhoda looked out at me. An initiate of some pagan blood cult, kidnapped, plundered, pressed into service, recruited from my dreams into the rank and file of White Trashdom, Inc. I looked into the cheap wavy mirror lit by a yellow electric light bulb festooned with dead insects and knew that I was lost. I was in some great swamp or marsh, walking without direction. A wide marshland stretching out as far as I could see. In one direction only, toward the morning sun, it looked as though there might be slivers of land, islands I could step upon. If only I could reach them.

I looked at myself without expression. I was not a part of this bathroom or this store or this goddamn cockfight. I could leave anytime I wanted to. I breathed in the terrible odors of toilet cleaner and rusted sink and unwashed board floors, of a thousand drunken urinations and the skull and crossbones on the label of the bottle of lye sitting on the floor. I turned the rusted handle on the door, knowing past all biology that I was touching something which all the Roget and Gallet's sandalwood soap in my mother's linen closet would not erase.

"Let's get out of here," I said, coming out the door. "Come on, Charles William. Take me home."

"I'm coming." He was holding the punchboard. "You want one more punch? I'm paying."

"No, goddammit, I want to get out of here." I grabbed him by the arm and dragged him behind me out the door and walked over to the car and got into my side and scrunched down into the seat. "Start driving," I said. "Get me out of here."

We were ten miles down the road before either of us spoke. "You wanted to go," he said. "You wanted to go with me."

"You didn't tell me about the capes. I didn't know they were going to be wearing capes."

"I didn't know it either. For God's sake, Dee. Don't be mad at me."

"I'm going to throw up," I said, "so you better stop this car." He pulled over to the side of the road and I tore open the door and began to throw up into a ditch. The terrible sweet taste of Coke and bourbon filled my nose and throat. I threw up for what seemed an eternity, then I got back into the car and rolled up in a ball and fell asleep. Did they really kill people? Did they really march around in those capes and kidnap people and hang them from trees? What a terrible dark world it was. How could I live in a world with terrible dark things in it? What a mess I was in.

In the morning I resolved to change my ways. I cleaned up my room and helped my mother take care of the baby, Johnny, and even offered to polish silver. When Charles William called I told him I was busy. It was almost four o'clock that afternoon before I called him back and told him to come on over.

"That was really bad," I said. "That was a terrible thing to do."

"Why do you always feel guilty?" he answered. "You feel guilty about everything you do."

"I don't know. But I know one thing. I have to start swimming again. Starting tomorrow I'm going to the pool every morning and swim at least four miles."

"You're getting so thin. You're almost too thin, Dee. Maybe you should go off your diet."

"No. All I need to do is start back swimming. No more sneaking out after this, Charles William. From now on I'm going to be a lady." I poured tea for him from the silver service I had brought out onto the screened porch. Irise was coming across the street wearing a pink sundress. People were starting to come over to have a drink with my parents. It was all right. We were not in Warwick County. Warwick County had nothing to do with us. We were right here on the porch of my momma's house in Dunleith.

Chapter

6

It was so hot that summer it was easy to keep a promise to start swimming. I started going to the pool every morning. I would swim laps for a while, then smear myself with Coppertone suntan lotion and lie by the pool and order bacon, lettuce, and tomato sandwiches and sign the chits. I had never signed chits before and I thought it was very grand. I thought the Dunleith Country Club was very grand. I forgot all about the pool I had worked so hard to have built in Franklin, Kentucky. This was a private club without any weird people hanging around the dressing rooms. Yes, perhaps my father had been right and it was good we had moved home to Alabama. He had begun to corner me in the evenings and campaign for me to leave Vanderbilt and go to school in the state. "It would save me a lot of money, Sister," he would say. "You could have a car and more money for your clothes. Of course, Auburn's my first choice, but you can go down to Tuscaloosa with little Irise, if you like."

"I won the freshman writing contest," I would say. "I think I should go back."

"I wouldn't mess with those sapsuckers if I was you. Your momma says there's an ace chapter of Chi Omega at Tuscaloosa. Well, you think about it."

I was thinking about it. Meanwhile, I was swimming every

morning at the country club. I would dive into the cool water of the pool and begin my count, one, two, three, four, five, six, seven, eight. I would go out early while the pool was deserted and swim sometimes for an hour. I think now it was the only time of the day when I actually understood what I was doing. The rest of the time I floated in and out of consciousness, being acted upon by any influence at any moment, floundering in search of grace.

There was an exotic woman who came to the pool that summer. Her name was Patricia Morgan and she had had polio and wore steel braces on her legs. She was from Massachusetts and had come to Dunleith because her husband was a physicist at Chemistrand, the new industry that was going to save the town. She wore gorgeous white linen blouses and khaki-colored skirts and brown and white saddle oxfords. If a Chinese mandarin had decided to start dropping by the pool in the mornings it would not have been stranger or more seductive to me. She represented something I longed for, but barely knew existed, a world of rational thought, coolness, Puritan simplicity. I had known a girl in Kentucky whose older sister had gone off to Massachusetts to school, to a place called Wellesley. She had come home from her freshman year in college bringing notebooks full of notes concerning a book called *Ulysses* and had let us read the notes. I lay in the sun and thought it over. Devoe Tyson and the *Ulysses* notes, the possibility of a place like Wellesley, this strange, exotic woman in her saddle oxford shoes. The heat played with my brain, mixed with the smell of chlorine from the pool and the melting mayonnaise on my half-eaten sandwich.

The heat that summer was like a force. During the night it invaded you and fluffed you up. Dared you to move your legs out from underneath the sheets. All sheets were white back then and bleached and ironed and applied like poultices to beds. It was cooler underneath those sheets than on top of them. I do not know what physical theory explains this. Perhaps it was connected to the fans. My father was a passionate believer in fans. He had ceiling fans in every room, tall fans to blow the air through the doors, short fans to cool our feet and legs, oscillating fans which he would bring into a room and continually adjust to blow on whoever was around. "I don't want that fan on me," I was always saying, but he would ignore that and fix it so the oscillation was a constant breeze, six inches to the left, then six to the right, blowing my hair into my eyes and back again. I would get up and move to another part of the room. He would follow me and adjust a fan to blow on my legs and feet.

I did not know yet that I was made of light, of star carbon and molecules. But I gravitated always toward my source. I was always hurrying outside in the early morning to watch the light filter down through the trees. Birds would call, robins and raucous blue jays, and, always, the long low notes of the mourning doves. People died suddenly back then, without warning, quickly left us, heart attacks, pneumonia, snakebite, drownings. We were aware of our mortality and the suddenness of leaving. The finality, the possibility of loss was always with us, even in the hot heart of summer. North Alabama, 1955, as the century took shape and began to grope toward its meaning. *As the World Turns* was all the rage. We stared into the fat thick television screens and began to imagine the world spinning through space, began to sense our daily lives meant something, were full of drama, illusion, change. Up until then our main metaphor had been the cross. A man nailed up to die on wooden two-by-fours.

I was reading Durrell that summer. I had read a review of *Mountolive* in a British newspaper my English teacher showed me and gone immediately downtown to a bookstore to find out how to get a copy. There were quotations in the review, brilliant descriptions of interior states. I drew in my breath while reading them. I had never encountered such writing, except in poetry. A month later the bookstore owner called me.

"You're in luck," he told me. "I had a friend coming this way and he brought them to me. Come and pick them up." I cut my afternoon lab and went downtown to pick up the books. *Justine* and *Mountolive*. That had been in April. Now at last it was summer and I had time to read them. I started *Justine* one morning right after breakfast. It seemed very complicated and turgid in the beginning. Then I got to a sentence, almost an aside, in which Durrell mentions that Justine is looking for her lost child in the brothels of

Alexandria. Then I was reading like mad, caught up in the drama of the search.

At ten that morning I was still reading as I drove to the country club to go swimming. Keeping the book on my lap and reading at stoplights. There was so little traffic back then and we were innocent of cars. As soon as I got to the country club I settled myself on a chair to read. "These are the moments which possess the writer, not the lover, and which live on perpetually. One can return to them time and time again in memory, or use them as a fund upon which to build the part of one's life which is writing. One can debauch them with words but one cannot spoil them."

I was upside down on a lawn chair, the book underneath my head, turning the pages as fast as I dared, reading breathlessly. I looked up. The woman from Massachusetts was watching me. She had arrived at the pool without my noticing it and was settled down in a chair, her legs in their elaborate braces, the cane leaning on the chair, the bright saddle oxford shoes on the footrest. Her fabulous brown eyes were watching me. When I looked up, she smiled.

"I've read that book," she said. "Where did you get hold of that around here?"

"I got it in Nashville. Someone brought it from England to a bookstore I go to."

"What do you think of it?"

"It's fabulous. I want to go to Alexandria. Where is it anyway?"

"In Egypt. On the Mediterranean and the Nile." Her beautiful brown eyes smiled into mine.

"Oh, I should have known. I was reading so fast, trying to find out what happened to her daughter who was stolen." I pulled my legs down from the back of the chair, got up, went over to stand near her. "I love your shoes. You look wonderful in them."

"They're Spaldings. Spalding saddle oxfords. I can tell you where to order them if you want."

"Oh, God, could you?" I leaned near her. She was holding a cup of coffee. She was reading the *New York Times*. I had never been to New York City. The very sight of the name excited me. "I want to go to New York someday. My cousin lives up there. She works for *Time* magazine. She went to Sweet Briar." It was all I had to offer. I sat down on a chair beside her beautiful withered legs, her braces and cane, her *New York Times* draped across her knees.

"I'll write down the name of the place where you can order the shoes. You can use my name if you like. They make them and send them to me." She smiled at me again. I was still holding the book. My forefinger stuck between pages to hold my place.

"What is your name?" I asked.

"Patricia Morgan. What is yours?"

"Rhoda Manning. It's nice to get to meet you. I see you out here every day. I wanted to talk to you."

"And why is that?" She was smiling widely, leaned back in her chair, placid, at peace. Her soft light hair swung around her cheekbones, held in place by a bobby pin carelessly stuck in the side. Her skin was freckled and tanned, her clothes fit loosely on her body. She *was* a Chinese mandarin at the Dunleith Country Club. The world seemed to revolve around her chair.

"Because you're different. Are you Jewish? I had a lab instructor at Vanderbilt who was Jewish. He's the only Jewish person I ever met except for the Rothschilds in Clarksville. And the boy I used to love. Well, I still love him. He's a grown man really. His father was Jewish and his mother was a Catholic and they got a divorce when he was two."

"I'm an Episcopalian from Massachusetts."

"Oh, God, I'm sorry."

"Please don't be. I really am flattered. You're looking for your peers, Rhoda. Anyone with a good mind does that at your age. What happened to your boyfriend, this boy whose parents got a divorce?"

"He got cancer of the thyroid gland. He's in the hospital half the time. He has another girlfriend, anyway, a girl his age. I was just his little kid friend. I think he would have loved me if I hadn't had to move away from Harrisburg. If I could have stayed there until I was older. Well, I shouldn't talk about myself. I wanted to know what those papers are you bring out here. All that stuff in folders. Are you a lawyer or something?"

"I'm working on a plan to feed breakfast to children in the public schools. Many of them can't study because they're hungry. Their blood sugar is too low to concentrate. We're putting together a plan to put before the legislature. Here, you can look at these if you like." She pulled some papers out of a folder and handed them to me. "These are studies we did in Meridian, Mississippi, last year. To see how many children in grades one to six had eaten breakfast before they came to school."

"I hate to eat breakfast. They used to have to beg me to eat when I was little. My momma would cut the toast up into eight pieces and pretend to be feeding it to a bird to get me to eat it. Oh, God, I can't believe I'd tell you a crazy thing like that. I just mean, maybe those little kids don't want to eat it."

"They want it. Many of them didn't eat supper either. We're going to start a study here in the fall. If you're around you might want to help with it. We pay people to do the field work. Not much, but their expenses."

"I'll be going back to school. I go to Vanderbilt. Well, I told you that. You know what happened?" I slid the copy of *Justine* up onto my lap. I held it in my hands like an offering. "I won the freshman writing contest at Vanderbilt last year. My professor came out and told me right after my last exam. I can't stop thinking about it. They were supposed to send me some books but they haven't come yet. I think they lost my new address. But I shouldn't tell you that. It's bragging on myself." I looked up into her face and met her eyes and for a minute neither of us spoke.

"Who told you not to be proud of your accomplishments?" she said at last.

"Well, they mostly want me to stop being fat. It embarrasses them if I'm fat."

"You aren't fat. Who told you you were fat? Why are you listening to such a thing?" She leaned forward. I was sorry I had started the conversation. And somehow I knew not to tell her about the pills.

"Well, I'm not now. But I was when I first got home from college. I weighed a hundred and forty-three pounds. I was fat as a pig and my mother took me to a doctor and put me on a diet. I'm glad she did.''

"I don't mean to say your mother did anything wrong. Well, let's see what time it is.'' She looked at her watch. "It's eleven-thirty. I really should be starting home. It's nice to talk to you, Rhoda. It's very heartening to see a young woman reading a real book. It gives me hope for the future. Come and talk to me when-ever I'm out here.'' She began to gather up her things. She had a way of abruptly ending conversations that disconcerted me. I felt that I had said the wrong thing, made a wrong response. I think now that it was only her way of being cautious. She didn't know what was appropriate in Dunleith. How far she could go with a nineteen-year-old girl. The Chemistrand Corporation had had semi-nars for its northern employees and their wives to prepare them for moving to the South and warned them against stepping on the toes of the natives until the plants were firmly established.

She gathered up her bags, stood up on her braces, put the crutches under her arms, the bags on her shoulders, made a series of small adjustments.

"Let me help you. Can I help you carry things to the car?''

"No. I have a system. I get it all balanced, then I can manage. If I start letting people carry things for me there would be no end, would there? I'd get in the habit, then I'd have to wait on them to move. You could put that folder back in the brown bag. There, that's it. Thank you. Well, I'll see you soon then.'' She smiled down from her structure of braces and crutches and bags. The placid peaceful look had returned. She had a journey to make and she was about to make it.

"I'll be back tomorrow. Will you be here then?''

"If it doesn't rain. If nothin' happens.'' She laughed out loud. She had made a joke in a black dialect. If nothin' happens. It was what the maids said when they left the white houses in the eve-nings. It was a phrase that struck terror in the white women's hearts. It meant, maybe I'll be back tomorrow to clean your house and nurse your children and iron your clothes, and maybe I won't.

"I hope you do. I'll be waiting for you.''

"Well, here I go. I'll see you soon." She began to move very
slowly and deliberately across the flagstones and down the path
toward the parking lot. It was exciting to watch her. Each step
weighted and planned. *To find my peers.* What did that mean? *Who
is telling you such a thing and why are you listening to what you hear?* I
went back over to my pile of books and towels and suntan lotion
and found the bottle of diet pills and took one and then dove into
the pool and began to swim laps while I waited for it to take effect.

I think now what it must have been like for her to come to Dunleith
from Massachusetts. To be dumped down into a sleepy little Alabama town with instructions to be careful of what she said. A town
where the ladies spent the mornings getting dressed and the afternoons playing bridge. Whose intellectual food was the *Dunleith
Daily* and the *Birmingham News* and the main selections of the
Book-of-the-Month Club. Who thought New York City was where
you went to spend the day at Elizabeth Arden and the evenings
seeing Broadway musicals or carefully selected plays without any
dirty language. Where everybody went to church and sent money to
Africa to save the heathen but took it for granted that the black
people in Dunleith couldn't read. A few of them could read. My
father's cousin Martha Ann taught her servants to read so they
wouldn't make mistakes giving medicine to her children.

"Do you believe in God?" I asked her the next day.
  "No, but I go to church. I go to the Episcopal Church. I think
I met your mother, by the way, but I haven't talked to her. I was
introduced at a tea for the new rector."
  "They make me go. I've never believed in God a day in my
life. I don't believe in hell and I don't think you stay alive after
you're dead. Why do you go if you don't believe in it?"
  "Because it's a force for good. I was raised by devout people.
I don't know. I suppose I go out of habit. Especially since I was in
the iron lung. I want to keep on doing everything. I don't want to
get into the habit of staying home. Max, my husband, is a very
busy man. He works sometimes twenty hours a day so I can't
depend on him for amusement. I have to stay active. Of course,

it's solace too.'' She was quiet for a moment. "One of our children died. In a car accident. Our oldest son. Our other boy, Clay, is at Brown. He'll be coming home soon. He's never been to Dunleith. Maybe you would show him around the town and introduce him to people.''

"I'd love to. I have this friend, Charles William. I bet Clay would love him. He's studying architecture at Georgia Tech. He reads as much as I do. We have this literary society.'' I smiled and looked down, starting to get tickled. "It's just a joke. We use it for an excuse. Anytime we want to go somewhere we tell our mothers we're having a meeting of the Literary Society. Isn't that stupid?'' I was sitting next to her now. I had pulled a chair up beside her. I had taken Mrs. Morgan for my property. I was as close to her as I could get. I had been at the pool when it opened, waiting for her to arrive.

"Don't wait for Clay to get here. Bring your friend out to Fairfields anytime you like. Do you ever go out there? On the way to Huntsville?''

"Oh, sure. That's where Imogene Uzell lives, the society editor for the paper. She comes to our house in the afternoons for a drink. Everyone comes to my parents' in the afternoons to have a drink. They sit on the porch and drink. Would you like to come? Oh, you wouldn't like it, though, I bet. I bet it would bore you to death.''

She smiled at that. I could just imagine her sitting on the porch listening to my daddy and his cousins talk about politics and football and Big Jim Folsom and keeping the Negroes in their place and which church was the best, the Episcopal or the Presbyterian. "You wouldn't like to come there. I shouldn't have said that. They have all these boring people there. These old cousins of theirs from Aberdeen. Sometimes they stay until after supper. You can't get away from them and they ask you all these questions and talk about the past.''

"Nothing is boring if you know who you are, Rhoda. If you have autonomy. Try not to judge the world. Judge not, that ye be not judged. That's one thing the church got right. I like truisms and time-honored clichés. I've thought of making a collection of southern ones while I'm here. I could make a book of them, or at least a Christmas letter.'' She began to laugh at that. She seemed to think it was divinely funny. "So you think I might be bored by the parties on your mother's porch, do you?" she added, still laughing, squeezing the very last giggle out of her amusement.

"I think you'd be sorry you were there if my Aunt Hattie Manning got hold of you about General Joseph Wheeler and the Civil War. She digs her fingernails into your arm while she talks to you. I can just see your husband listening to that."

"Oh, Max likes the South. He'd probably be fascinated. He might even agree with her. He's very broad minded about history."

"I'll come out to Fairfields and see you. I've been out there to a tea at Imogene's. Do you know her?"

"She gave me some plants for an herb garden I'm starting. If you've been to her house you can find ours easily. We live at the end of her street, in the old brick farmhouse. Please come out. And bring your young architect. He might be able to give me some ideas. We're still working on the place."

"I want to meet your son when he comes. What's his name?"

"Clay. He's very nice. I'll write and tell him I've found him a friend. He's hesitant about coming here. It was difficult for him to think his home would be in a different place when he finished school. Of course, he can always go back to Woods Hole, where we're from. He has friends there and Max has a brother in the area."

"They did that to me. They moved last year when I was at Vanderbilt. They didn't even ask me about it. They just did it. All of a sudden we were here."

"I thought you had always been here."

"My father's family are from Aberdeen. They built Aberdeen. Aberdeen belongs to them. So now we're home."

"And are you happy with that? Are you adjusted to it?"

"I guess so. I went on this diet, I told you that, so at least I stopped being fat. And I have these new friends, Charles William and Irise. And I met you." She was watching me with an intense serious look. I don't believe I had ever talked to anyone who entered into what I was saying with such intensity. I started to tell her about the pills, how wonderful they made me feel. How sometimes they made me want to run around the yard. How once, the first week I took them, I had run around the house twenty times while my father stood on the porch and roared with laughter. "I better go back to my book," I said. "I think I'll go lie down by the shallow end and quit talking your arm off and read my book."

"Come out to Fairfields anytime. Come see the garden I'm making."

I went down to the shallow end and spread a towel in the sun and added suntan lotion to my arms and legs and got out my book. I called the dining room to bring me a glass of iced tea so I could take my pill. I lay down on my stomach and began to read.

> Pompal finds much of this banal and even dull; but who, know-ing Justine, could fail to be moved by it? Nor can it be said that the author's intentions are not full of interest. He maintains, for example, that real people can only exist in the imagination of an artist strong enough to contain them and give them form. Life, the raw material, is only lived *in potentia* until the artist deploys it in his work. Would that I could do this service of love for poor Justine. (I mean, of course, "Claudia"). I dream of a book powerful enough to contain the elements of her—but it is not the sort of book to which we are accustomed these days. For example, on the first page a synopsis of the plot in a few lines. Thus we might dispense with the narrative articulation. What follows would be drama freed from the burden of form. *I would set my own book free to dream.*

I read on, keeping one eye on the page and one eye on Patricia. I didn't want to be a part of the life around the pool. I even forgot the lifeguard in the presence of her strange Yankee power. After a while the waiter brought my iced tea and I drank it and took the pill and then I dove into the pool and began to swim laps while the Dexe-drine moved through my blood and into my brain. Everything became more intense, the feel of the water, the color of the water, the color of the sky. I pulled myself up at the deep end and saw Patricia gathering her things into her bag. I climbed out and held it for her while she adjusted her legs and took up her cane. "I'll see you again, Rhoda," she said. "Don't forget to come to see me."

"I won't," I answered. "I promise you that."

* * *

After she left I swam ten more laps, then gathered up my things and drove home in my bathing suit. Three cars were parked in the driveway. Everyone was always at our house. People came and went at all hours. My friends, my mother's friends, my father's friends, my grandmother, my great-aunts, my aunts and uncles and cousins. I cannot imagine how my parents had the energy to deal hour after hour, day after day, with such a crowd of people.

"Is that you, Rhoda?" It was my mother, hurrying into the kitchen to find me. I had parked the car beside the basketball hoop and come into the kitchen through the back door. "Where are you, honey? Is that you?" She came into the kitchen, her pale green and white flowered dress cinched at the waist with a belt. Her legs and feet encased in nylon hose and high-heeled shoes. It was almost a hundred degrees outside but she was completely dressed. "Oh, darling, put some clothes on. You really need to cover up. You can't drive around like that. Here, put this on." She picked up a towel that had been lying on the dryer and draped it around my waist.

"I have a shirt on, for God's sake. Leave me alone, Mother."

"Did you take a pill? We have your lunch ready. It will only take a minute to grill the steak. Fannin, put Miss Rhoda's steak in to cook, will you?" She turned to the woman beside the stove. I pulled the towel off my waist and threw it on the washing machine.

"I'm not hungry yet. I want to take a shower first. Tell her to wait. Don't do it yet, Fannin."

"You didn't get anything at the pool, did you?"

"No. I didn't eat anything at the pool. It's my diet, Mother. I'm on the diet. Not you."

"Well, I'm only trying to help."

"I'm not hungry yet."

"Doctor Freer said you had to be sure and eat thirty minutes after you take the pill. You have to eat on time. He said it was very important."

"Well, I don't care what he said. I'm not hungry right now. I'll eat when I come down." I turned and walked up the back stairs and left them there.

* * *

I took off my clothes and got into the bathtub. "Rhoda." She had followed me up the stairs. "Darling, I want you to go on and eat. Fannin has other work to do. She can't stand around the kitchen all morning waiting for you to eat lunch."

"Then tell her not to. I'll fix it when I come down. I know what to do." She was in the bathroom now. Picking up my clothes from the floor. She put the clothes in the hamper and straightened up the bathmat and sat down on a little painted chair to watch me bathe.

"Mother, stop looking at me."

"You look wonderful, Rhoda. Your body looks very beautiful." She reached out a hand, touched my shoulder, caressed my arm. "I can't believe you're getting so grown up. My little baby girl. Darling girl."

"I met this fabulous woman at the pool, Mother. She's from Massachusetts. She wears these darling shoes because she had polio. She's going to give me the catalogue so I can order some. Can I have some?"

"I guess so. What kind of shoes?"

"Saddle oxfords. Like we used to have for cheerleading. Only these are so beautiful. They are the most beautiful leather."

"Who is she?"

"Mrs. Morgan. Her husband works for Chemistrand. She goes to Saint James's."

"Oh, I know who she is. She's a friend of Imogene's. Well, that's nice that you met her."

"Can I have the shoes?"

"We'll see. I have to see how much they cost. I've been spending so much money on the house. Don't you think it looks nice? Don't you like the carpet downstairs and the drapes?"

"Oh, yeah, they're great. Well, look, get out of the way so I can get out, okay?" I stood up. She watched me as though I were the archangel Gabriel. She worshipped me despite my faults. She handed me a towel.

"I'm going down and get your lunch ready. Come down as soon as you get dressed."

"All right. I will."

* * *

I ate my diet lunch. Then I went back upstairs and shut the door to
my room and turned on the ceiling fan and read myself to sleep.
"Somewhere else, in a great study hung with tawny curtains, Justine was copying into her diary the terrible aphorisms of Herak-
leitos. The book lies beside me now. On one page she has written:
'It is hard to fight with one's heart's desire; whatever it wishes to
get, it purchases at the cost of the soul.' "

I sank down into my cherry four-poster bed. The heat of summer penetrated the thick board walls of the house. The force of heat,
the passion of heat. Even the Dexedrine could not fight it off forever. I sank my face down into a satin pillow. The sounds of the
house moved up and down the hall, footsteps, a maid ironing in a
bedroom, a radio playing in the kitchen. My baby brother Johnny
was being bathed in the bathroom I had so recently vacated. Charles
William and I had removed the old wallpaper from that bathroom—six layers of flowered papers. We had spent days at our
task, stripping off layer after layer of roses and yellow forsythia and
ivy on trellises. Then the paperers came in and covered the walls
with a pattern of Williamsburg blues. It was my favorite room in
the house, a testament to my native if untapped industry. We had
worked feverishly; it was the first week I took the Dexedrine and
Charles William had been caught up in the tide. Now the room was
finished and my baby brother was in there throwing water and toys
at the Williamsburg pattern.

It smelled like heaven that summer in the chocolate-colored
house on Wheeler Street. Smells stayed in their places. Even
Daddy's fans could not move those smells. The smell of furniture
polish on the dressers and chairs and tables. The smell of new
carpets made of the miracle fiber being spun from oil out at Chemistrand which was going to save Dunleith from extinction. The smell
of ironed clothes hanging in the closets, ironed starch, soap powder, and bleach. Wallpaper paste and hair spray with plenty of
fluorocarbons since we had not even named them yet and certainly
didn't know they did anything but turn our hairdos into helmets.

The kitchen smelled of toasted bread and fried chicken and
green beans cooked in melted fat. Of whiskey sours and scotch and

water and sweetened tea. Of biscuits baking and bacon frying and
coffee being endlessly percolated in the old aluminum percolator
that later Dudley and I would press into service as a martini shaker.
The smell of Daddy's and Dudley's mud-covered boots and dust-
covered work clothes. The pickup truck covered with the red clay of
roadbeds.

It was a rich life. Even I, the most selfish and least satisfied and
most sensitive and wary one, even I knew I was living in a blessed
time. I would wake from sleep in that chocolate-colored house and
stretch my legs down between the ironed sheets and caress my
nightgown with my fingers. I slept in old-fashioned white cotton
nightgowns made on a foot-pedal sewing machine in my grandmother's house in the Delta. Every few months a new nightgown
would arrive, packed in scented tissue paper in a box from Nell's
and Blum's in Greenville.

I would rise from bed and go stand by the window, which
looked out upon ancient trees full of birds and squirrels and spiders
and crickets and tree frogs. In the stand beside my bed were the
journals of my imaginary love affairs and the notebooks of my
imitation Emily Dickinson poems and the copy of *One Arm and Other
Stories,* by Tennessee Williams, which Charles William had given
me to read. I had gotten as far as ''Desire and the Black Masseur,''
then put the book away.

I would open the drawer and look inside, then quickly close it
and take off my gown and go over to my dresser and open my
underwear drawer and find my underpants and bra and put them
on. I would add a pair of pink corduroy shorts and a cotton off-the-
shoulder blouse and find my sandals and go downstairs, following
the smell of bacon and coffee. Perhaps the kitchen would already
have begun the work of dinner, filé gumbo or vegetable soup or the
famous Aberdeen stew, which took three days to prepare. It was
made of fresh tomatoes and new corn, okra and chicken and ground
black pepper. It had to cook for forty-eight hours to reach the
desired consistency. Only the descendants of Highland Scots could
have invented a way to make stew the exact consistency of oatmeal,
but they had triumphed, and it was my father's favorite meal. Tears
would come into his eyes at the thought of Aberdeen stew and

when my mother's kitchen was at work creating that wonder he looked at her with disarmed, tender eyes. It must have been in such a mood that my unexpected brother, Johnny, was conceived.

Not that conceived had any meaning to me except in reference to the Gettysburg Address. I was looking up the wrong words in the dictionary in my continuing attempts to find out something about sex. Why didn't I ask Charles William? I wonder now. Why didn't he volunteer some information? Maybe he thought I knew. I was so innocent, I didn't even know what to ask.

All I knew of sex was menstrual blood. I loved the sight of it upon my panties. Sometimes I would wash the blood off in the sink, scrubbing and scrubbing until the last trace of it was gone. Sometimes I just dropped the panties down the clothes chute. The panties floated down the wooden chute, landing atop my father's dusty work clothes on the basement floor. A hidden tribute to Electra, Sophocles, Freud. Ah, my poor innocent father. Indra's net, the net of jewels, in which each jewel contains the reflections of all the others. A universe of life is a drop of dew at any intersection. Every morning one of the maids would go downstairs and collect all the clothes and bring them up into the kitchen and sort them out and stuff them in the washing machine. Into the white tub they would go, there to mix their blood and dust and eggs with bleach and lye and water and emerge like vestal virgins to hang out on the clothesline. Later, they would be submitted to the ritual of the iron. A week later I would lift them from my dresser drawer and put them on and wear them off to spend my daddy's money or drive his car. He, meanwhile, would be off somewhere in his khaki pants, wheeling and dealing to buy a road grader or a coal mine, never knowing his pockets contained the last vestige of a packet of his genes. Ah, sweet mysterious, boundless feast at which we so often wander blind and bound and starving. If we could understand one thing entirely, we might understand it all.

There were four servants in the chocolate-colored house. Fannin, the cook, a maid named Adeline to clean the bedrooms, a maid named Edith to sweep the parlors and the porches, and a gardener to keep the yard and run errands. Later, when I came home with my babies, my father would add another servant for each grandson I delivered. I certainly never imagined taking care of them myself. They had come unbidden into the world and they were welcome to it but somebody else would have to keep them amused and fed. Babies bored me to death.

All of that was waiting for me, presaged by the blood on my underpants, but I did not know or sense it. It was the golden summer, the summer we came home to the South to live among our people.

In the days following my conversation with Mrs. Morgan I made every effort to be at the pool when she came. I would sit across from her reading. I finished *Justine* and moved on into *Mountolive*. I pictured Mrs. Morgan as Lelia Hosnani, the tragic heroine who gives up the beautiful Mountolive. Later when he returns to Alexandria as the British ambassador it is too late. Lelia's beauty has been ruined by smallpox and she will never leave her summerhouse. In one terrible scene she covers herself with veils, gets into her carriage, and goes to see him one last time. I was weeping all over the book as I read. "Where are you now?" Mrs. Morgan asked.

"Where she goes to see him covered with veils."

"Oh yes. Well, adultery nearly always turns out badly. But it makes good fiction, doesn't it? By the way, Rhoda, Clay is coming this weekend. We want to have dinner to celebrate. On Saturday night. Will you come out and join us? Nothing elaborate. Just the four of us."

"I'd love it. Sure I'll come. How old did you say he is?"

"He's twenty. He's a junior. I think you'll like each other. I talked to your mother the other day, by the way. Did she tell you?"

"No, I don't think so. She said she met you though. Oh, God, she's so boring. I hope you don't think I'm anything like her."

"I thought she was charming. It isn't good to hate your mother, Rhoda. It's like hating part of yourself. Our parents create us. We have to make our peace with that, you know."

"I just mean she drives me crazy. She's always watching me."

"She adores you. She was praising you to the skies. She told me about your newspaper column. She said people read your pieces on the radio."

"Oh, well, that was a long time ago. That's over now. I don't think about it anymore. I'm a lot more interested in making sure I don't gain back any weight. But I forgot, you don't think people should go on diets."

"I have too many opinions. Don't take them to heart."

"I'm sorry I said that about my mother. It doesn't mean I don't like her. I like her a lot."

"Well, I'm glad you'll come on Saturday. Come at six so I can show you the place. I want to show you the root cellar and the gardens. Are you sure you know the way?"

"Of course. I'll be there. I'll show him everything about Dunleith that Charles William has shown me."

"On Saturday then. At six." She sat back in her chair and I went over to the diving board and showed off doing half gainers and back dives for a while and then swam my laps. I was half thinking about giving up swimming entirely. I had always done it to keep my body thin, but now I didn't really need it anymore.

On Saturday afternoon I dressed up in a blue and white flowered dress and drove out to Fairfields, a small community ten miles from Dunleith with three streets of restored houses and a post office and a store. The place the Morgans had bought was an old farmhouse with brick chimneys and porches with brick floors. Patricia was waiting at the door when I drove up in the yard. Her son, Clay, was beside her. A tall, happy-looking young man with brown hair and soft brown eyes. Dr. Morgan, the mad scientist, was nowhere in sight. I walked up onto the porch.

"Your dress is very pretty," Patricia said.

"Mother told me all about you," Clay added. I looked him over. I liked him. There was no way anyone could help but like him. There was something childlike about him. He seemed so young compared to the young men I knew. The young men I knew drove cars fast and talked fast and moved in fast to put the make on me. This young man kept standing beside his mother. He kept waiting for me to do something.

"Clay's been in summer school at Brown," Mrs. Morgan said.

"He's going to be at Woods Hole when he goes back, to study marine life."

"It's pretty silly," he said. "It's just a lot of work."

"Nonsense," Patricia said. "Of course it's not."

"Is your husband here?" I asked. "I'd really like to meet him if I could."

"Oh, Max. Of course. I think he'll be out soon. I wanted to take you around first and show you what I've been doing." We began to walk through the house. Patricia leaned on Clay's arm. talking gaily as she showed us things she had been restoring, bricks that had been stripped, boards that had been uncovered and revealed, old artifacts she had found in the yard and was polishing. We went out to the root cellar and looked at that awhile. Every now and then I would meet Clay's eye and he would smile at me. He seemed perfectly content. He seemed to think nothing else was supposed to happen but walking around looking at old junk his mother thought was worth polishing and hanging on the walls. "Clouds are gathering," she said, pointing past the root cellar to the west. "It might rain later."

"I doubt it," Clay said. "They're stratocumulus. They're too high for rain."

We moved up onto the porch again and were inspecting some cowbells Patricia had soaking in acid when Dr. Morgan appeared on the porch. He was a small stoop-shouldered man with a smile that made me move to his side. "I heard you were in Chicago when they made the first atom bomb," I said. "I've never met a physicist. I've been hearing all about you."

"It was a nuclear reaction. Would you like to come into my study? Would you like to see the photographs?" He smiled the fabulous smile again and I forgot all about Clay and Patricia and followed him into a small office off the kitchen. It was very plain. Pads of yellow paper were on a steel desk. Books were on bookcases along the wall. There was a modern-looking light fixture hanging from the ceiling. The floor was covered with woven mats. He went around behind the desk and took a framed photograph from the wall and held it out to me. It was of three men standing in front of a cement bunker. "Enrico Fermi," he said. "And one of the young assistants and me. This is where we did it, but it began in the minds of men. Many minds down through the years contributed to this moment. Flashes of intuition and years of thought. I was lucky to be there. I was in a lucky place." He held one end of the photograph while I looked at it. I was too lucky, too fortunate. What was I doing in this room with this great man? This man was far away from anything I had ever known. This man was a quantum leap away from my reality. Why was he letting me stand here? Why was I being allowed to touch his picture? I looked up at him. He was smiling at me. He was very still. Did he know what he was giving me? Did he know how thick life was in that room at that moment, how distilled and thick and brilliant and translucent that moment would always be for me? Did he know what he was offering?

I held on to one end of the photograph. He held on to the other.

"Dinner is served," Patricia said. "Come along, Max. Bring her in to dinner."

There was asparagus casserole and roast beef and hot homemade bread. There was wine, and later salad. I picked at the food, and chattered away about my family and Vanderbilt and my exploits with Charles William. My voice rose and fell. I drank more wine. I was charming. I was undone. I was elated.

"Clay made the bread," Patricia said. "Isn't it delicious?"

"You made the bread?" I answered. "How did you know how?"

"She taught me." He laughed uproariously at that. Everything seemed to make him laugh. There was no aggression in the young man, no secrets, nothing I could recognize.

"We can go into town after dinner and find some people," I said. "We can go over to Charles William's house and you can meet him. You want to do that?"

"That would be wonderful," Patricia said. "Oh, Clay, you should do that. Rhoda can introduce you to people."

"We can go to the pool if it doesn't rain," I added. "We go out there a lot at night. Do you like to swim at night?"

"Of course he does." This from Dr. Morgan. "Who wouldn't go swimming at night with a pretty girl?"

Clay had gotten up and was taking the plates and salad plates to the kitchen. He was waiting on the table. A boy who made bread and waited on the table. I had never seen such a thing. I jumped up and began to help him.

"There's peach cobbler," Patricia began. "Rhoda, you can help Clay serve it. The ice cream's in the freezer on the porch."

"I'd love to help him." I met his eyes. We smiled together. Then we moved the rest of the plates and serving dishes and served the dessert and dessert wine and coffee and brandy. We were a family. Max and Patricia and Clay and I. We were a family in a dream. A family waiting on each other. I drank the sweet white wine and Dr. Morgan got up and filled my glass. Then I drank my brandy and he refilled that.

"Tell me how they do it," I asked. "Tell me how they make carpet out of oil."

"It's all sun," he began. "It all begins as hydrogen."

Later, when we had done the dishes and talked on the porch awhile, I called Charles William and told him we were coming over. Then Clay and I got into my mother's car and I began to drive down the two-lane asphalt road leading into Dunleith. There were no seat belts in cars back then. We had never even thought of having them. "Your parents are the nicest people I've ever met," I began. "Where did they go to school? Where do you go to learn things like that?"

"She went to Vassar." He was sitting beside me in the dark front seat. I was driving sixty miles an hour, then sixty-five, as fast as I could drive and make the curves. "And he went to the University of Chicago. My brother was going there before he died. But I go to Brown. Do you know where that is? Maybe you should turn on the windshield wipers, Rhoda. It's starting to rain."

"Okay. If I can find them. This is Mother's car. I haven't driven it very much." I reached for the switch to turn on the windshield wipers. Then the car began to skid and I threw my foot on the brake and the car began to spin. It spun around once and then again and again and again. I put my hand on Clay's knee. "Nothing can happen to me," I said. The car stopped and lights were coming toward us and then the car exploded and sailed out across the road and I heard the sound of gravel underneath the wheels. I felt my head hit against the side of the window.

When I woke rain was falling and men were leaning over me and somewhere, in a world I could barely see, Clay was being lifted from the seat and put upon a stretcher.

"He's dead," I heard someone saying.

"No, he's not," a second voice answered. "He's breathing. Goddammit, Joe. He's breathing."

Men were all around me. Someone gave me a shot. Then I was being moved and stars were falling all around me. A sea of stars was falling on my arms and legs and belly and shoulders and face. It was a baseball field full of stars. It was a baseball field or a pillow. It was dark in the room and my mother was sitting by the bed and a nurse was leaning over me.

"Is he dead?" I asked. "Is Clay dead?"

"Yes," my mother answered. "Go back to sleep, Rhoda. It wasn't your fault. Please go back to sleep."

"I don't know what happened. I don't know how it happened. I don't know what happened to the car."

"You spun the car around and a car hit its side. It wasn't your fault. Try to go back to sleep. You've had a concussion, Rhoda. You have to stay still."

"What happened to him?" I was beginning to cry. Tears were rolling down my cheeks and onto the pillow. I couldn't move my head to get the tears away. My head hurt so much I could barely move it. My mother had my hand in her small tight hand. She was squeezing my hand. It was too dark in the room. "Turn on the lights," I was screaming. "I don't know what happened. I can't see anything in here." Then the nurse left and when she returned other people were with her. Someone took my arm and gave me a shot and my mother kept holding on to my hand.

The funeral was in Saint James's Church at ten o'clock in the morning a few days later. I was dressed and wearing bandages on my head and my mother and father and brothers were all around me. My mother and Fannin and my sister-in-law had dressed me and done my hair. "You have to go," my mother kept saying. "You have to be there."

"It's not your fault, Sweet Sister," my father was saying. "There were brand-new tires on that car. It's that goddamn asphalt. I've been telling them to modernize that road. That old asphalt's a hazard when it rains."

"Oh, Daddy, I'm so sorry. I don't know why you're all being so nice to me. Someone should be mean to me. I think I was driving too fast."

"No. You weren't driving too fast. Ariane, hurry up and finish whatever you're up to with her hair. Come on, let's get going." He had moved out into the hall outside of Momma's bedroom. My sister-in-law, Annie, was sitting on the bed. Momma was combing my hair. "I want you to go on and sign up to go to the university, Sister. I want you down here near us, especially after this."

"Then call them up and tell them I'm coming." I looked at him. He was so good to me, so perfect, he never let anything happen to me. No matter what happened he would fix it. "Tell someone to call and get an application. I made A's at Vandy, Daddy. I can go to college anywhere I want to."

"I'll take care of it this afternoon. Come on now, Sister, let's get on down to the church and get this over with." I walked to the door and he took my arm and led me down the stairs and put me in the front seat of his Cadillac with Momma on the other side. My little brothers rode with Dudley and Annie.

When we got to the church, Charles William and Irise were waiting on the sidewalk and walked in with us. The coffin sat on a stand before the altar. The priest intoned the service with tears rolling down his cheeks. "I am the resurrection and the life saith the Lord: he that believeth in me, though he were dead, yet shall he live: and whosoever liveth and believeth in me shall never die.

"I know that my redeemer liveth: and that he shall stand at the latter day upon the earth: and though this body be destroyed, yet shall I see God: whom I shall see for myself, and mine eyes shall behold, and not as a stranger."

*   *   *

Doctor Morgan and Mrs. Morgan sat on the front row with people
from Chemistrand and their old friends and brothers and sisters
who had chartered a plane to come and be with them. Their other
child was buried in Massachusetts, but for some reason they had
decided to bury Clay here, in the cemetery behind the church.
Although there had not been any room in the cemetery for years, a
plot was found for them and a stone put into place. A tall plain
stone of Carrera marble. "Clay Alexander Morgan, 1934–1954. 'I
Have Let Fall Death.' Hadrian, A.D. 1."

After the service and the burial, my family and I went out to the
Morgans' house and stayed a long time on the screened porch
talking to people and standing shoulder to shoulder with our hands
folded. At some point my mother led me back to Patricia's bedroom
and the three of us talked for a while. "You mustn't blame yourself," she said. "I gave you the wine."

"It was the rain," I answered, as I had every time we had the
conversation. We had had the conversation in the hospital after
Clay died and in the church before the ceremony and now we were
having it again. "It was the rain, not the wine."

"It's not a judgment," Patricia said. "It's only that he's
gone." She was sitting on the bed and my mother was sitting beside
her and I was standing. One of the Morgans' friends from Massachusetts came into the room.

"There's nothing to do now," she said, "but go on. We have
to go on, Patricia. You have to go on for Max."

"Where is Max?" she asked. "He should come and talk to
Rhoda."

"He's out by the root cellar," she answered. "He was out there
with Drew and Arthur. He told them to leave. He said he wanted to
be alone."

"Go out and talk to him," Patricia said to me. "He wants to
talk to you, Rhoda. He's worried about you. He talked about you last
night. He doesn't blame you. No one blames you."

"They should blame me. It's my fault. It was my car. I was
driving the car. I was driving it too fast." It was the second time

that day I had said it. I looked straight at my mother as I said it. I couldn't believe I had said it again. It was wonderful to say it. I wanted to say it over and over again. Light poured in the windows as I said it. Light was everywhere. "I was driving sixty-five miles an hour. I was driving like a maniac. I shouldn't have been driving that fast. I did it to show off." My voice was rising. I felt the light penetrate me and blow me open. My mother jumped up from the bed and came to me. "No, Rhoda," she said. "Not now. Don't do this to Patricia. Come on, let's go outside and talk to Doctor Morgan." She tried to lead me from the room, but I didn't want to go. I wanted to scream my crime. I wanted to tell Patricia what I had done. All of a sudden I could see Clay, in this room, beside his mother, his gentle body folded over hers, his head beside her head, his hand on her arm.

"Come on, Rhoda," my mother said. "Please, honey, for God's sake, come with me." She got me to the door, then I broke away from her and began walking down the long hall that led to the backyard.

"Where are you going?" she asked. "I'm going to go and get your father."

I turned around. I became very cool and poised. "Please, Mother, I have to go and talk to him. Please don't follow me. I'm okay now. I swear I am." I stood very still and she waited, then began to back off.

"All right," she said. "Go on."

I walked past the kitchen full of people making drinks and eating food and talking. I walked all the way down the old board hallway and out onto the unused back porch and down the back steps toward the root cellar. Doctor Morgan was standing there, by the closed door to the cellar. Just standing there, staring at the mound of earth and the closed door. Beyond the mound the soft hills of summer rose up in brilliant greens. Clouds were moving in from the north. It would rain again by evening and wash all this away.

He heard me walking toward him and he turned and looked at me.

"I'm so sorry," I began. "So terribly sorry. I will never be the same now that I killed Clay. I killed him, Doctor Morgan. I killed your son."

"No." He reached and took my hand. "Come here, Rhoda. I want to show you something." He led me back toward a row of apple trees. Old thick trees with blossoms and leaves and fallen apples piled on the ground beneath them. There was a smell of apples there. Of apples and fallen death and decomposition. He led me to a tree and reached up and laid his hand on a branch. "Atoms into molecules," he began. "Molecules into bases, into amino acids, into proteins, into cells, into tissues, into simple animals, into complex animals, into you and me. I want you to remember that. I want you to remember that I told you that." His voice had not changed as he spoke, had not risen or fallen, had not accused or begged or charmed or forgiven. He kept on holding on to my hand as if he could impart something by osmosis.

"Oh, Doctor Morgan. I can't live after this. I won't ever forget it. What can I do? There is nothing I can do."

"You can learn to think, Rhoda. You can think harder than you do. You can do better than you're doing. You can learn."

"I don't know what that means. You hate me. You think I killed him."

"No. Look at this." He pulled the branch toward me. "Look at it. Find out what it means. I don't hate you and I don't want you to feel guilty. I know you wouldn't kill another human being. You would never kill anyone, would you? Would you?" He had let go of the branch and was holding my arms. "Would you kill someone? Even to save your life?"

"To save myself I would." I was fixed by his eyes. It would have been impossible to lie to him, even if I wanted to.

"Did you need to save your life on Saturday night?"

"No. I don't think so. I wanted him to like me, though. I was driving fast to show off for him. Maybe that was to save my life. Why did I drive so fast?" I kept looking at him. He was still, then he let go of my arms.

"Because we let you drink wine. Because we gave you wine. Because we wanted you to like us and take Clay off our hands and reconcile him to this place." He walked a few feet away from me and stuck his hands into his pockets and turned his fierce and brilliant eyes on me. This time they were different eyes. This time there was nothing to recognize.

"I'm going to raze this house," he said. "And build a modern house with concrete floors and modern materials. You can put the heating of a house into the floors now, Rhoda. Did you know that? You can build windows that catch the sun and then you don't need fires. You can get fire from the sky." He rounded his shoulders down around his chest and stuck his hands deeper into his pockets. "Shall we go in?" he asked. "Let's go in now and see who needs us." I moved beside him. I took his arm, which was fixed deep down into his pocket, and we began to move back toward the house. Cars were still driving up from everywhere. Muted voices and the clink of bottles and glasses from the kitchen flowed out into the yard. It made us a wave of sound to follow. A little path, or current, or drag, or magnetic field. We followed it like pilgrims. Nothing we did or said on that or any other day was going to stain the white radiance of eternity to which Clay had returned his colors.

Later, on our way home from the Morgans' house, Daddy started in on me again. We were alone in his car, Mother had gone ahead with Dudley and Annie and my younger brothers. "Mighty hard," Daddy said, as we passed the place where Momma's car had been dragged up from the ditch. "Mighty hard to know what to do with you, Sister. Your momma said you showed your ass in front of that dead boy's momma."

"I did not. What did she say? God, she says anything she wants to about me."

"She said you acted like a fool and went spouting off about driving fast. Those people could sue me for everything I own. Do you know that, Sister? Goddammit, you're the most selfish little girl I've ever seen. Your mother said you were spouting off about how fast you were driving with everyone listening. I don't know, Sister. I just don't know." He shook his head, then continued. "I brought you back here where you could be somebody. Your ancestors came here as pioneers and made this country for you. My people have

been respected down here for two hundred years and you and
Dudley are going to ruin all that for me, it looks like. You've been
running all over town with that Waters boy, he's a queer duck if I
ever saw one. Everybody in town talks about how crazy you talk
and act. I just don't know, Sweet Sister. Well, I'll get some applications to the university and maybe if you go down there you'll settle
down. Maybe you got all those crazy ideas up at Vanderbilt. I hated
having to raise you kids in the North but I had to do it until I could
make my stake. I've been working twenty hours a day all my life
to give you a chance to make something of yourself and this is how
you pay me back."

"It's your fault," I screamed. "You're the one who did it.
Every time I start doing good you make me move. You made me
leave Harrisburg and you made me leave Franklin. Now you want
me to leave Vanderbilt. I don't know what to do. I'm tired of trying.
I can't start over every time I turn around. I don't want to go to
Tuscaloosa. I want to go back to Vanderbilt and finish my life
there."

"I thought you hated it so much. You said you hated
the sorority. You told me I'd ruined your life by sending you there.
Now you're going to change your mind about that? Is that the
ticket now?"

"I don't care. Who cares? What difference does it make?" I
was crying now. "I hate you so much, Daddy. I killed someone. I
killed him right here on this road. Stop the car. I want to get out and
walk. Stop the car. I want to walk home." I pulled on the door
handle but he reached across me and grabbed it and pulled it shut
and locked it and kept on driving. I grabbed his arm and bent my
face down to bite him but he stopped the car and took my arms and
held them to my sides. "You stop all this crazy acting, Sister. You
killed that boy but now it's done. I don't want to hear any more
about how fast you were going. I don't want to hear any more out
of you about anything until we get home. You just suck up your guts
and get a hold of yourself."

I laid my head back against the seat. My arms went limp and
he let go of them. Usually I fought him longer and harder than
this but today it didn't seem to matter. He pulled back out onto

the road and began to drive. I closed my eyes. I tried to remember standing by the storm cellar and Doctor Morgan talking to me. Atoms into molecules, molecules into bases, bases into amino acids, into something else. Remember that, he had said. Remember I told you that.

"We'll get you down to Tuscaloosa where you can know some real people," Daddy was saying. "Where we can keep an eye on you and you can know some folks that are our kind of people."

Part Two

TUSCALOOSA

Chapter
7

So the con was on. He knew when to strike. Whether or not the accident had been my fault the guilt was mine and it was a vein anyone could mine for years. So of course Daddy was the first to get a pick and go to work on it. I felt guilty and I was vulnerable. For many nights I would wake up in the middle of the night with lights coming at me and the car turning and turning into the crash. Sometimes the impact would be on my side and I would be lying in the coffin. Sometimes alive in the grave. Sometimes the car would be coming toward me and I would turn the wheel to sacrifice Clay. Always in the dreams Doctor Morgan and Patricia and Mother and Daddy would line up to call me to judgment.

It's a wonder I went back to college at all. Also, Doctor Freer had taken away my diet pills and I suppose I was having what would later be called withdrawal. I spent a lot of hours plotting ways to get him to give them back to me, then I forgot it in the aftermath of the accident. It would be almost a year before I found another source for Dexedrine.

For now, I let Daddy con me and tell me not to worry and buy me a baby blue Chevrolet with leather seats and put six times too much money in a bank account for me and send me down to Tuscaloosa to join the Crimson Tide.

"You be careful down there," my mother said. "Be careful of

your reputation, Rhoda. Try to act like a lady. Let people love you."

"Let people respect you," my father said. "You don't need a bunch of love."

About my father and the con job he did to get me to quit Vanderbilt. Well, we owed him a lot that year, although we didn't know it. He had given up his true love for us. So we owed him our lives, didn't we? Not that he didn't already know about Abraham and Isaac. He knew children had to sometimes be sacrificed. He was big on young men going off to war and was almost ashamed when my uncle came home unscathed from the South Pacific. That was his code and his culture that had been beat into him in Aberdeen and he had beat it into my brothers. He never hit me again after I was thirteen. I always said I was menstruating and that terrified him. Besides I was fiercer than my brothers. I might have killed him if he hit me. There were furies I went into that no one dared mess with. Lack of pigment, red hair, those old ancestors sacrificing their strawmen, king for a day, oak knives. I was a throwback to that Celtic violence. I was also the shortest person in my family, several inches shorter than my mother. Enough of all that for now.

As I was saying, Daddy had given up his true love in Kentucky, although we didn't know it yet. A short, large-hipped, slightly tacky lady who had done his books the year he made a million dollars. By the time that first summer in Dunleith was over my brothers and I had figured all this out. So the reason for the new house and the new life and my discomfort was a woman. Doesn't it always come down to a woman? someone would later write. Not just a woman either, but my brother's mother-in-law. My sister-in-law Annie's mother.

Still, if we imprisoned him, forced him to move back to a place that was sixty percent black at a time when it was out of fashion to keep slaves, later it was we who set him free. When we got bad enough, when we started taking what we wanted in the world, he went on and took his too. More about that later. For now, I was packing up my new blue car and heading south to Tuscaloosa.

* * *

Irise was driving with me. I backed the car across the street and added her bags to mine. Charles William stood on the sidewalk waving and throwing kisses to us. "Don't forget you're coming to Homecoming," he called to me. "I've got you a date picked out. He's got the greatest body in the state of Georgia."

"How can we leave him?" I said, turning to Irise. "God, I wish he was going with us."

"We have to. It won't be for long. We might get married next year, Rhoda. If his grades are good enough they're going to let us."

"Well, which way do we go?" I had pulled out onto the main street.

"Just find Highway Sixty-five and start driving. I'll show you what to do. I've been on it a thousand times."

"I can't believe I'm doing this. I haven't even told Vanderbilt I'm not coming."

"Maybe you won't like it and you'll go back up there."

"No, I'll like it. I can't wait. They really have parties on week nights?"

"They really do."

"And the Chi O's are good?"

"They're the best, except for KD."

Chapter

8

We arrived in Tuscaloosa in the middle of the afternoon. It was a brilliant fall day. The streets near the campus seemed gentle and familiar. I would be welcome here. I had Irise by my side and a trunk full of pretty clothes and a car. They would love me and let me be a college cheerleader or a yearbook beauty or something worthy of me. "Let's go by the Chi O house," Irise said. "I'll go in with you if you want me to. They know you're coming. Your momma said she called."

"Would you go with me? Oh, would you do that?"

"Sure I will. I told Ariane I'd take care of you." She seemed larger suddenly, sprightlier, here on her turf, where she was a Kappa Delta. "Turn down that street right there. It's the house on the corner." She pointed down a street lined with oak trees. I drove down it and came to a stop before a white frame house with girls in the yard putting up signs for rush week. *Follow the Yellow Brick Road,* the signs said. *We're off to see the Wizard.* We went in and Irise introduced me to the Chi Omegas. "She makes A's," she told everyone. "She's a genius. She wrote for a newspaper. She's so wonderful. You're so lucky to have her here." They drew around me, really pretty girls, girls with beautiful clothes and faces. "Oh, we're so glad to have you. It's so good you're here. Will you help us with rush? We don't even have a skit yet."

"I'll write you a skit. What do you want it to be about?"

"She's going to write a skit." It echoed up and down the living rooms. "There's a transfer from Dunleith who can write."

Two of the girls went with me to drop Irise off at the KD house. Then we put my stuff in the dorm room I had been assigned. "Don't worry about that," the girls said. "We'll get you in the house soon. It takes a while but someone always leaves. As soon as someone leaves you can have their room."

"Just put those clothes in the closet and get my typewriter," I directed. "Let's go back to the house and get started." We drove back to the Chi Omega house and I set my typewriter up on a dining room table and wrote a skit while they watched. It had two acts and three songs set to the music of popular ballads. In the finale the star (to be played by me) came out on the stage wearing a red towel and sat down on the edge of the stage and sang:

> I'm tired of wearing my clothes.
> I'd rather go naked, God knows.
> I'd much rather wear Chi O pins in my hair
> And sit on the curb till I froze.

They adored it. We rehearsed it six times, ordered the costumes prepared, and went in to dinner in the dining hall. I was surrounded by admirers. I had campus beauties all around me. I was a hit. I was going to be popular. "She wrote for a newspaper. She won a writing prize at Vanderbilt. She can write book reports and everything. She makes wonderful grades. Can you believe she came here? We're so lucky to have her. Oh, maybe now we can get off academic probation after all."

The honeymoon between me and the Nu Beta chapter of Chi Omega lasted about three weeks. It lasted through rush week, during which time I was still such a celebrity that I was able to pick out two girls I really wanted and railroad them through. One of them was the niece of Scott Fitzgerald's wife, Zelda. It was a great disappointment to me to learn that she had never read his books. "Oh, they wouldn't let me," she said. "They have disgraced the family."

It lasted for the first week and a half of classes and the first three meetings in the crowded attic room where the votes were taken on burning issues such as whether or not to accept an invitation to enter the Sigma Chi Derby. "Rhoda can write us a skit," the president said. "Rhoda, will you do it for us?"

"If you'll find me a room in the house. I hate that dorm. I want to live here in the house."

"As soon as one's available. As soon as someone leaves. Someone usually flunks out after midterms. The minute there's a room you can have it. We want you here." All eyes were upon me. I was their whole new thing, their writer, a girl who was smart and also reasonably pretty.

"I'll write it. But not this week. I really have to start going to my classes."

It lasted through going to my classes. It lasted through the knowledge that I didn't have a single teacher who inspired or interested me. Through the dirty chemistry lab with its antiquated equipment and the distracted young woman teaching American literature who didn't even know poetry. It lasted until I got bored. All of a sudden the exhilaration dropped out of the adventure and I was walking around in the afternoons all over the campus of the University of Alabama trying to find someone to talk to. I thought about going to the newspaper office and asking for a job on the student newspaper but when I dropped by one afternoon it was closed. I took a copy of the paper home and read it and it bored me. Everything bored me. I was getting deeply tragically bored and there is nothing in the world as dangerous as a bored Celt.

It was on such a walk one Sunday afternoon that I met May Garth Sheffield at last. Charles William had told me about her. "Be sure and look up May Garth Sheffield from Birmingham," he told me. "She's the craziest girl I've ever known. She's crazier than you are, Dee. She's six feet tall. I went to Episcopal camp with her when I was little. Wait till you meet her. I'll tell her that you're coming. Don't forget to look her up. I've got a feeling you will need her before it's over. Remember I told you this."

Prophetic. I needed anything I could find but I had forgotten about the conversation because I had been so caught up in solving my sorority status problem and making sure I could be popular. Then one Sunday I was out wandering around by myself, quoting T. S. Eliot out loud and thinking about death and how I would end up a dried leaf in the wind and probably in hell, if there was one, for killing Clay. The universe will not forgive such a slight, I was thinking. It will shadow me wherever I go. Who knows, maybe I'm like that man in the Li'l Abner cartoon, wherever I go, clouds of death are overhead. Everyone I love, first Bob Rosen, then Clay. Well, I might have fallen in love with him. We might have been madly in love and I could have gone up to Brown with him and met some poets. When you are dead, think no more of me from your heavenly cloud. Oh, my beloved, oh, my darling lost husband. Well, I don't want to marry anyone as long as I live anyway. I don't want to wash dishes and run the vacuum cleaner and have babies. I wouldn't have a baby for all the tea in China. I couldn't stand to do that. I wouldn't let anyone do that to me no matter how much I liked them. Maybe I find people that are going to die so I won't ever have to swell up like Dudley's wife. I can't stand to think about it. It's so disgusting. Oh, world, I cannot hold thee close enough. If I should die, think only this of me: that there's some corner of a foreign field that is forever England. I shouldn't have come down here. The minute this semester's over I'm going back to Vanderbilt.

So my little nineteen-year-old mind would meander through its maze of hope and fear as I moved from one end of the campus to the other, walking hurriedly, usually in the early evening and always alone. With other people I was always cheerful and hopeful and optimistic and in a good mood. I had too much pride to allow anyone to know I was unhappy. Of course, I would throw Bob Rosen into a conversation to let them know I was human and had darknesses and secret sorrows. In the same way I would pretend to hate school to make stupid people feel at ease. I had never needed Nietzsche to tell me that the weak hate and fear the strong. I knew how to play that game. The wonderful thing about the past summer with Charles William was not the Dexedrine or the freedom but the fact that every morning I could walk down the street and find someone to talk to who wanted the best I had to give, the best my mind could offer. I had not found anyone in Tuscaloosa who

sparked that in me. It certainly never occurred to me that I could
find a boyfriend who was *smart*. My mother had programmed me
to breed with her kind of man. He had to be six feet tall and a good
dancer. Nothing else would do. I kept having a hard time finding
anyone who fit the bill. The tall boys couldn't dance and I wasn't
supposed to take the short ones seriously. None of them could think
as fast as I could or read or write as well. The brilliant, intellectually
curious boys were all off hiding somewhere, as miserable and unfinished as I was. *The higher the intelligence the slower the rate of
maturation,* I would learn later. For now, *I knew nothing* and I was
passing by the boys I could have talked to. Comtemptuous of their
needfulness, I wandered around being in love with mythical
Bob Rosen and an occasional professor and drunken fraternity
boys when they were drunk enough to be self-assured. I spit on the
grave of my twenties, one of the Algonquin wits had written. It
should have been engraved over the lintel of the Chi Omega
house.

It was on such a walk, full of such morbid thoughts, that I
finally encountered May Garth Sheffield.

As I came within sight of the Tri Delta house I saw an extremely tall girl standing on the steps that led down to an aban-
doned garden and wisteria arbor. She was standing alone, staring
at the sky, so still I thought at first she was a statue. ''Hi,'' I called
up. ''I'll bet you're May Garth, aren't you? I'm Rhoda Manning.
Charles William Waters told me to look you up. Did he tell you
about me?''

''Oh, yes.'' She came down the stairs and opened the iron gate
and moved out onto the sidewalk. She was at least six feet tall. Back
then that was the social equivalent of having terminal cancer. Back
then girls were supposed to look like children. Not everywhere, of
course, but certainly in the culture of the Deep South. Perhaps this
was because southern men were so mother-ridden they had to
believe they were kissing little girls to get excited. A woman as
large as their mothers might suck them back into the womb, control
them body and soul, make them keep on hating themselves forever.
Fortunately for the human race the system was imperfect. There
were very few mothers who could control their sons' minds after

the testosterone kicked in and very few women who could make their bodies smaller and keep them that way, so breeding kept getting done and babies kept getting born and the species rolled on to better days. Of course, even an imperfect system can be made to work by a genius, and May Garth was that. She was the most tenacious person, man or woman, I have ever known. She could focus and she could concentrate. If she had been born thirty years later she might have been a great basketball or tennis player or distance runner. Alas, she had been born in the wrong time in the wrong place. There she was, with that big brain and those long arms and legs and nothing to do all day but brood upon ways to squeeze herself onto the tiny little Procrustean bed of north Alabama society's feminine ideals. The long torso bent like a mast in the wind, curved down to meet gravity and fate. Stooped. The long legs walked apologetically. The arms barely moved.

She had status. She was a triple legacy to Tri Delt and in those days sororities took their legacies even if they were six feet tall. Also, there was the matter of her family's banks. The Sheffields of north Alabama owned thousands of acres of cotton land, six gins, and several banks, including the Bank of Birmingham.

"What are you doing?" she asked. "Are you going anywhere?"

"I'm just walking around. What are you doing?"

"Nothing. I'm just standing here."

"You want to go for a walk? I want to walk over to the architecture school. It's a very inspiring place. I need to be inspired."

"Okay. I'll go. I don't have anything to do until six. I have to do something at six but I'm free until then." When she spoke, she curved her back and stooped my way. When she listened, she did the same. Immediately I wanted to do nothing that would make her stoop. I began to walk. She walked beside me. If I so much as glanced her way, she stooped to meet my glance. "What are you doing at six o'clock?" I asked.

"I have to take my iodine. I take it every eight hours. Two drops of iodine in a glass of milk. It makes you lose weight. I'm doing it to lose weight."

"My God. That's great. I never heard of that." I had a vision

of poison iodine dripping into milk. Huge globules of iodine falling, falling through the white silky milk.

"It burns the fat. It makes you burn the fat."

"How long have you been doing it?"

"For two months. I lost nine pounds already."

"Oh, my God," I said. "That's really great."

We began to walk at a faster rate. We left the brick wall that
surrounded the Tri Delt house and began to walk in the direction of
the school of architecture. It was the newest building on the campus, very modern, an icon from a bright new world we had only
begun to hear of in Alabama. We walked past a row of maple trees
and up a flight of stairs to an atrium with tall glass windows on
three sides. May Garth seemed even taller here, surrounded by this
vast, high-ceilinged room. Perhaps this symbol of a new world cast
a spell on me, or, perhaps, up here I didn't have to worry about
being seen out walking with a six-foot freak. One way or the other,
here, in this tall marble-floored temple of a room, I began to see
May Garth in a different light, as a Valkyrie or Joan of Arc, a female
warrior who at any moment would go back to the Tri Delt house and
drink iodine in milk. I had been on every diet I had ever heard of,
but even I was not prepared to drink iodine in milk.

"I lost twenty pounds this summer," I said. "I got so fat they
had to take me to a doctor. He gave me some pills. Then he took
them away. I wanted to lose some more but they wouldn't let me.
I never eat now. I starve all the time."

"So do I. I can't eat a thing. I have a thyroid problem. I get
bigger and bigger." She hung her head. She stooped even more at
the thought. Then she straightened up and the warrior appeared
again. She squared her shoulders, determination reigned. She
stared out the windows toward the west.

"Could I watch you take the iodine?" I asked. "I'd like to see
you do it."

"Sure. Come back to the house with me. I have an attic room.
We play cards up there. You want to come sometime? Do you play
cards?"

"Sure. I play bridge mostly, but I can play anything. Do you play bridge?"

"We play poker and we get drunk. We get drunk every Wednesday night. Oh, well." She hung her head, half a stoop, almost a stoop. "I guess the Chi O's don't drink, do they? I heard they didn't drink."

"Are you kidding? They drink like fish. They just like to keep it hidden. They don't like for anyone to get in trouble."

"We get in trouble." She laughed, a great foreign-sounding laugh, a wicked full-throated laugh. She raised her head and stood up straight. She laughed as though she had remembered that she owned some banks. I began to think I had underestimated her. Maybe being six feet tall didn't matter if you owned banks. Maybe she didn't even care. Maybe she just stooped to be polite. I took her arm and led her to a window that looked out on the engineering building. "I knew a girl as tall as you at Vanderbilt who was studying to be an engineer," I said. "She got chosen to be Miss Vanderbilt. Bob Hope judged the contest. He told the newspaper she was the prettiest girl he'd ever seen."

"She studied engineering?"

"She made straight A's. We had a good time at Vanderbilt. I had a good time there."

"Why did you leave?"

"I had to. I couldn't stand it there. I wanted to come down here."

"I have to go now. I have to get back before six." She looked down at me. She was very close, barely stooping now. "I have to take it before dinner. It doesn't do any good after you eat."

When we got back to the Tri Delt house, May Garth invited me in but I wouldn't go past the brick steps. "I don't feel like meeting people," I said. "I'm not in the mood."

"I can bring it out here." She looked down, curved into a half moon of conspiracy. "If you really want to watch."

"Okay. Go get it. I'll wait here." She disappeared into the front door and returned in a few minutes carrying a glass of milk and a bottle of iodine. We moved to the side of the stairs behind a brick pillar and I held the glass while she opened the iodine and took out the glass stopper and dropped two drops into the milk. It spread on the surface, a little red poison lake, then disappeared. She took the glass and drank it off in three long gulps. "Well, that's that," she said. "You really ought to try it. It really works."

I was speechless, dazzled by the casualness of the act. "I guess I better get on home," I said. "I've got to work on a skit I'm writing. I'm writing our skit for the Sigma Chi Derby."

"Come back and see me. Come Wednesday night. Bring some money if you have it. We play for money. Do you have any money?"

"I've got plenty. My dad gives me anything I want."

"That's good. I like money. I like it to add to my collections. I'm collecting Coke bottle aprons and telephone conductor caps. I was collecting stuffed animals but I finally got enough." She was still holding the empty glass and the iodine bottle. I kept thinking someone would walk up and arrest us.

"I've got to go," I said. "I'll see you soon."

"Come over Wednesday. Come play poker with us."

When I got back to the Chi O house I told one of the girls I had met May Garth.

"Oh, don't get mixed up with her." The president of the sorority stepped forward. "Her father is, well, it's hard to say it, because it's not her fault, you know. Her father is a, well, a nigger lover. He made some statements after the Supreme Court did that thing."

"What thing? What are you talking about? I thought she owned banks."

"Well, her family does but her father's a renegade. No one receives them anymore in Birmingham. He's a judge that went bad. He's worse than Hugo Black. I'll tell you all about it later, Rhoda. Come see me after dinner. Her father is a traitor to the South."

"Where will you be after supper?"

"I'll be in my room. Come on up so we can talk alone." She raised her eyes, as if to say, don't let the younger girls hear all this. I was embarrassed by the speech, embarrassed by the whole thing, and went off to a table and ate six biscuits with butter and honey and drank several glasses of milk. That was just like me, I decided, to get involved with some nut just when I was getting popular.

After supper I went up to the president's room and she explained to me about *Brown versus Board of Education* and Autherine Lucy and how the Supreme Court had said the schools of the South had to let black children go to school with whites whether they wanted to or not. "That's terrible," I agreed. "They can't come down here and tell us what to do. A bunch of Yankees can't boss us around."

"May Garth's father is the worst traitor in the state. The Tri Delts don't know what to do about her. Don't be rude to her, of course. A Chi O has to be polite. Have you finished the skit yet, by the way? Everyone's so excited that you're writing it."

"It's almost finished. I have it all thought up. I just haven't finished writing it. I'll finish it tonight. I need something interesting to do."

"We need it soon. We ought to start rehearsing."

"Okay, I'll go home now and work on it."

"You aren't unhappy, are you, Rhoda? We'd love to get you some dates, you know. Donie said she suggested it and you turned her down. You don't have to get interested in them. Just go out with a few boys we could suggest."

"I've been in a funny mood. It's how I am. I'm moody. I'll think about it though. Right now I want to go home and finish up this skit." I stood up, full of the power of creation. Muse power. I had the muse by me. She might disappear now and then when I was pouting, but she always returned to save me. Like my imaginary playmates, Jimmy and Sally, the muse always surprised me by showing up.

"Stay for the singing. We're going to sing old camp songs at nine. Leta's leading it."

"No, I have to go. When I want to write something, I have to do it right then." I left her room and walked down the stairs and out the door. I walked to my dorm and went upstairs and closed the door to my room and lit a Pall Mall and started typing.

"THE MUSES COME TO TUSCALOOSA," I typed. I giggled,

looked up into the ceiling where my own muse was dancing in a cloud of cigarette smoke. I began to type in a heat of passion. By eleven o'clock I was finished. I snuffed out my last cigarette, tied the laces on my Spalding saddle oxfords, walked down the back door and let myself out through the service entrance. I paid little or no attention to dormitory rules when I was busy. There was always a way around everything. I walked out across the campus in the midnight air. Artist at work. Do not disturb. I walked all the way to the triangle. I thought about going to the Chi O house to spend the night. It would save sneaking back into the dorm. I looked at my watch. It was twelve-fifteen. I was just passing the Tri Delt house. There was a light on in May Garth's third-floor room. I decided to see if she was playing poker. I was too excited from writing to go to sleep. I wanted someone to talk to. "May Garth." I stood out in the yard, calling up to the light in a stage whisper. "May Garth, come to the window. I want to talk to you."

A tall girl in a robe came to the front door and told me to be quiet. "Don't wake up the housemother," she said. "Who is it, anyway?"

"It's Rhoda Manning. I'm a Chi O. I have to talk to May Garth. It's really important. It can't wait."

"Well, come on in. But be quiet. Our housemother's been drinking sherry and she finally went to sleep but if she wakes up she'll go crazy. She's been driving us insane lately."

"Yeah, I heard about it. I heard she was turning out to be a mess." I walked in the front door and the girl in the robe led me to the stairs.

"She's the third one we've had since last January. They're getting harder to find."

"Get one who's fat," I advised. "The fat ones are in a better mood. Well, look, I'm going on up. Are they playing tonight, do you know?"

"I think they were. I don't know if it's still going on." I walked as quietly as I could up the sets of stairs and knocked on May Garth's door. "It's Rhoda," I called out. "I have to talk to someone."

"Oh, good," she said. "Come on in." She opened the door to

a large attic room with a double bed and two dressers and about a hundred and fifty stuffed animals piled against the walls. Some of them had been arranged into pyramids that looked like they had an order. Others were just in piles. All along the edges of the room were animals of different sizes and kinds. In a large center space was a card table with poker chips and decks of playing cards. "God, I'm glad you came over. I couldn't sleep either. We were supposed to have a game tonight and no one came. Did Gena let you in?"

"Someone did. She said you're having trouble with your housemother."

"She gets drunk every night. She drinks sherry while she eats dinner. I think we ought to keep her anyway. After she passes out she isn't any trouble to anyone. Where have you been? What have you been doing?" She pulled me into the room and shut the door. Then she went over to a closet and opened it and began to take out beers from a shoe bag. "You want a beer? They're hot but they're pretty good. My brother brought them last week from Birmingham."

"Sure. Open it. Why not." I looked around for somewhere to sit. The only chair was full of stuffed bears.

"Sit on the bed," May Garth said, knocking the bears off the chair. "Get comfortable. I don't guess you want to play, do you?"

"Not right now. I'm really excited, May Garth. I just wrote the best skit you ever read. For the Sigma Chi Derby. God, it's so good I can't stand it." I took my beer and settled back against the pillows on the bed. From this angle the room seemed even more interesting. All along the ceiling were suspended small silver airplanes on long threads. They were held to the ceiling by Scotch tape. In one corner was a model of a World War II bomber. In another a model of a fighter. Beside the dresser was a poster. NO MAN IS FREE UNTIL ALL MEN ARE FREE, in huge red letters on a yellow field.

"Tell me about it," she said.

"Well, it's called 'The Muses Come to Tuscaloosa.' In it, nine Chi O's, dressed as Clio, Euterpe, Thalia, Melpomene, Erato, Polymnia, Urania, Terpsichore, and Calliope, come down to visit the Sigma Chis and civilize them. The Sigma Chis have this terrible housemother named Slut. In the conclusion of the skit she gets into a fight with Mnemosyne, the mother of the muses, played by me. Mnemosyne wins because she remembers everything that ever happened and reminds Slut of the trashy lives young men live if they don't have girls around to empty the ashtrays and put out flowers and bring music and poetry and beauty to the place. Slut repents, begins to cry, and swears to change her ways. She combs her hair and begins to take the whiskey bottles off the bar. Then the Sigma Chis come back in and start pinning fraternity pins on the muses. Isn't it great? Don't you think it's great?'' I sank back into the pillows, clutching a brown bear I had picked up from the floor. May Garth sat across from me in the chair.

"It's wonderful. How did you think it up? How did you know all that stuff?''

"My mother was a classics major at Ole Miss. She told me about the muses and the Greek gods ever since I was born. I used to get them all mixed up with the stuff they taught us at church. I guess that's why I'm an atheist.''

"You're an atheist?''

"Yes, I have always been.''

"I am too,'' she said. "I don't believe a word of that crap.''

"Let's drink your beer,'' I said. "I want to get drunk and celebrate.''

We drank several beers and then we drank some bourbon she had hidden in a Listerine bottle, then we lay around on the bed and talked about our lives and boys we used to love and what people did in bed. "My sister got married last year,'' May Garth said. "You wouldn't believe what she does with her husband. Listen, you can't ever tell this.''

"I won't.''

"They put their mouths on each other down there. They do it every night. I can't believe she'd do it, my sister.''

"I'm sorry. I don't know what to say. That's too terrible. That's the nastiest thing I've ever heard.''

"My own sister. I'll never speak to her again.''

"Why'd she tell you?''

"I don't know.'' May Garth was lying across the bottom of the double bed now, her legs hanging down onto the floor. "She made me listen."

"Have you got anything to eat? I really think I'd better eat something."

"There's a lot of stuff in the closet. See what you can find in there." I got up off the bed and opened the closet with the shoe bags full of beer. I found a box of Ritz crackers and a jar of peanut butter and brought it back to the bed and we ate Ritz crackers for a while. "Why do you have that poster?" I asked. I had finally gotten drunk enough to broach the subject.

"My dad and I made it for a contest. At Mountainbrook, where I went to school. It didn't win. A girl won with a poster about good posture. I don't know. I just like it."

"What do you think it means?"

"I don't really want to talk about it. You want any more of these crackers, Rhoda?"

"No, I want to go to sleep. Can I sleep here?"

"Sure you can." She got up and turned off the light and we settled down in the bed. I could feel the huge rush and power of her breath. There was a terrible sadness in May Garth's breathing. "My dad's a wonderful man," she said finally. "He's so good to me. He took me last summer to see the pyramids. Next year he's going to take me to Australia. We're going on a boat. I might just decide to stay there. Everyone in Australia is as tall as I am."

"Can I ask you something?"

"Sure. Go on."

"Why do the Tri Delts let you do all this? I don't get it."

"My aunt bought this house. She paid for the whole thing. If they want something fixed, she pays for that. You can buy anything you want from most people, Rhoda. It's disgusting. My dad taught me that. But not from me. They can't buy anything from me. You know what he told me every day for years? Don't be for sale, May Garth, he told me. He said, life's too short to be for sale."

"He sounds great." I didn't want to talk anymore after that. I didn't want to ask her if he was a traitor. She loved him. He was her father. "Go to sleep," I added. "Let's go to sleep now."

We went to sleep. At dawn I woke up still wearing my clothes and went back over to the dorm and typed up a copy of my skit. The Chi O's loved it of course. Our president called the president of the Sigma Chis and he agreed to lend us real Sigma Chi pledges to help put it on and even sent a sophomore to boss them around, a chubby good-natured young man named Hap Dumas. We started rehearsing every night and Hap and I became friends. He was studying sociology, a new subject for which there only seemed to be one book, *The Lonely Crowd,* by David Riesman. He was forever quoting from the book and trying to characterize everyone according to what kind of house they lived in. Middle class, upper middle class, lower middle class, and so forth. Of course everyone wanted to be in the upper middle class or nothing. When I described Mother's Victorian mansion on Wheeler Street, Hap immediately decided I was upper middle and fell in love with me. It was useful in getting the skit produced but it was impossible for me to get interested in a good-natured boy who loved me. I had been cathected by a narcissist. The only men who could interest me had to be completely unavailable or even slightly mean. I could love my English teacher or my lab instructor or someone with terminal cancer, but not just someone who wanted to love and have fun with me.

"Just go to a football game with me," Hap kept asking. "You can't understand Bama if you don't go to the football games."

"I don't like to see them knock each other down. When I was a cheerleader I never even looked out on the field."

"You could go to one game and see if you liked it."

"I might. When we get through with this skit maybe I will."

We won first place in the Derby. The entire Greek community of the university turned out to stand around the outdoor stage and watch the skits. After a series of very silly farces, "The Muses Come to Tuscaloosa" came on. It had a beginning, a middle, and an end. It had a story. It had allusions to the past and good costumes and I was fabulous as Mnemosyne. Afterward there was a party and Hap dragged me up onto the stage and danced with me. His big happy body had great rhythm. He was a happy man. He swung me in and out and twisted me around and made me look good. Afterward we necked on a sofa in the living room until the real housemother made him take me home. I slept that night in the guest room of the Chi O house. I was a celebrity. I had written the skit that won the Derby. I was a playwright.

I was awakened the next morning by our president.

"Rhoda, get up. The dean of women is furious about the skit. We have to go and see her."

"What about? What is she mad about?" I sat up in the bed and pushed the covers from my legs. "What are you talking about? How could she be mad?"

"She's mad about the language Slut uses. We have to go over there right now. You and me and the panhellenic representative."

"What in the name of God is there to be mad about? My God. This is the goddamnedest thing I ever heard of. Just because we won."

"She didn't like her calling the muses hussies. And the part where she keeps saying she'll drink all the G.D. whiskey she likes."

"Oh, Christ. Listen, Cammie, did you see the play? I mean, were you there? Were you listening? That's the best line in the play. She doesn't call them hussies. She says, 'Get out of here, you goddamn hussies, you hell damn incorporeal bodies.' My English teacher said it was a great line. He's letting me turn the skit in for a paper. Tell the dean to call Dr. Whitehead and see what he thinks."

"We need to go right after breakfast. You can have an excuse if you have to miss a class."

So after breakfast the president and the panhellenic representative and I went to the dean's office to argue our case. Or, more exactly, they went to grovel and apologize and I went to argue. "Good wins out in the end," I began. "It's a moral lesson, for God's sake. It's about civilizing men and stopping people from drinking whiskey. What more do you want?" The dean and I had had nice conversations in the past. She had interviewed me when I first came to the campus and since then I had gone by her office several times to talk about books. She had seemed to be an island of sanity and had even helped me change my English class to find one with a better professor. "Just calm down, Rhoda. No one's judging your play. Some people were bothered by your language."

"Who was?"

"I can't tell you that. Several students came in this morning to talk about it."

"They're just mad because I won. How can anyone get mad about language in a play? It's a free country, isn't it? Don't we have freedom of speech anymore?"

"Rhoda, please calm down." The president came around and stood beside my chair.

"I won the goddamn contest for you, didn't I? Did you even see it?" I asked the dean. "Or did some nasty little tattletale come in here complaining to you? Somebody who lost?"

"Rhoda, would you wait outside for us?" The dean came around her desk and took me by the arm. "I know you're upset. Artists are sensitive about their work. We'll work out something. Come on, come out here and wait in the outside room." She led me through a door and sat me down by her secretary's desk. She patted me on the shoulder. She patted me on the head. "I didn't see it," she said, "but I wish I had."

She went back into the office, leaving the door ajar, and I heard her ask the other girls to promise to submit future skits in writing before they were performed before an audience. The president and the panhellenic representative were satisfied but I was in a funk. I moped around all day and cut my classes. In the late afternoon I went for one of my long lonely walks. I walked past the Tri Delt house and thought about going in to see if May Garth wanted to swallow some iodine or get drunk but I didn't even feel like having May Garth for company. I wanted to wander around alone and figure out why every time I was happy something terrible happened next.

That Saturday I agreed to go with Hap Dumas to a football game. After all, a good-natured boy who loved me was better than no boyfriend at all.

We ran into May Garth at the game. She was with her cousin Sheffield Catledge from Guntersville. "Hi, Rhoda," she called out, stooping before I even came in range. "Come here a minute. Come meet my cousin Sheffield." He hove into sight, a good-looking blond boy about her height. He was carrying two hot dogs and shook his chin at me to make up for not being able to shake hands. "Sheffield is down for the weekend from Sewanee," May Garth said. "We're going tonight to see the Harlem Globetrotters. He just got here last night. He's going to stay all weekend." She was ecstatic to have her cousin there. I guess it was the first time she had had a date all year with a boy as tall as she was. He smiled and looked straight at me. A very fine good-looking boy to squire her around all weekend. I was glad for her. Hap began to talk to Sheffield about people he knew at Sewanee and I complimented May Garth on her outfit. She was wearing a pale gold suit with a matching blouse and a pillbox hat. I looked down at her feet. She had on heels. Not three-inch heels like everyone else was wearing, but at least they were heels.

"I'm so glad I saw you," she said. "I want you to come over again. Come play. We had a great game last week. We had six people. We played all night. We had two pints of whiskey and we had some cheese straws my mother sent. You think you can come sometime?" She held me with her hand. The conversation between Sheffield and Hap was waning. The crowd was filing into their seats. The band was playing. The Crimson Tide were taking the field.

"We'll miss the kickoff," the boys said.

"I might," I whispered to May Garth. "I'll come if I can." Hap took my arm and we parted. May Garth kept looking back over her shoulder at me as she walked away. Not stooping, with her cousin Sheffield at her side, but still longing. I was only a little half-baked nineteen-year-old girl, how could I have filled her longing? I had longings of my own.

"Who was that?" Hap asked.

"May Garth Sheffield. Her family owns a bunch of banks. She's brilliant, but she's very eccentric. She's always trying to get me to come to a poker game she has in the Tri Delt house. But I barely know her. I don't know her very well."

"It's a shame she's so tall. She has a pretty face, a really pretty
face."

"She does crazy things." I stopped at that. "I mean, she's nuts
about this poker business. I don't know why people want to play
games for money. When I played with my brother I would always
lose. Every game I ever played for money I would lose." I leaned
into Hap's soft jacket. He was getting more and more valuable to
me, dangerously valuable, in the cold fall weather, underneath the
stands.

"Let's go sit down," he said. He pulled my arm into his arm,
he was so kind, so loving, it embarrassed me to death.

"I hope they have some whiskey," was all I could think of to
say. "I love to get drunk at football games."

We went to our seats in the stands. The Sigma Chis had a section
of seats together. Hap's fraternity brothers were all around us with
their girlfriends. They slapped us on the back and offered us some
whiskey. We drank the whiskey, then stood up for "The Star-
Spangled Banner." The football players ran out onto the field. The
whiskey crossed the blood-brain barrier. I dug my hands into Hap's
arms. I buried my face in his jacket sleeve.

"What's wrong?" he asked. "Is something wrong with you?"

That night I necked with him on a bed in the fraternity house.
Wearing all our clothes we struggled against each other for several
hours. "Do you want my new pin when I get it?" he asked me. "I
lost the one I had last year, but I ordered a new one. If you want it
you can have it."

"Wait till you get it. When you get it, I might take it." I sat up
on the bed, straightened my sweater, looked down at him, ran my
hands across his fine soft face, caressed his soft brown hair, pushed
his shoulders down upon the pillows.

"Something terrible happened to me last summer," I began.
"And now I keep thinking about death all the time. I think I'm the
only one who thinks about it."

"No, you aren't." He sat up beside me. He took my hands.
"My grandfather died last year. He was the greatest man. I went to

sit by him while he was dying. He told me a lot of things. He said it was okay to die because he had all of us. He said he'd had a good life. He was the newspaper editor in Hope. He'd gone to a war. But I didn't see him die. I was asleep when he died." He pulled me back into his arms. "You're a funny girl, Rhoda. I can't tell if you like me or not."

"I like you. I'm just in a funny mood right now. I'm so mad about the dean saying all that stuff about my play. She made me so mad." I lay back down against his chest. I stretched my legs down beside his legs. I thought about a boy in junior high who had put his hands inside my pants one night. The silky wet memory of that night overwhelmed me and when Hap put his hand beneath my sweater I did not move it. Later, when he lay his hand across my stomach, I let him leave it there. "I love you," I said finally. "I think I love you to death."

The next day was Sunday. I woke up in my dorm room and thought a long time about the events of the day before. I had let Hap Dumas put his hand inside my bra. I had let him lay his hand upon my stomach. I was as good as married. It scared me to death to think such things. I rolled my head down underneath the covers. I made a tent of the covers and rolled myself up into a ball and thought as hard as I could think about it. It was like the summer before last when I had been engaged for three weeks. From the moment I took the ring until I gave it back I had been in a state of perpetual trauma. I had no dream of marriage. I had no desire to run a house or be a wife or live forever with a man. I wanted to be popular and have dates and act like I was normal, but I didn't want to belong to anyone. I belonged somewhere else. Somewhere I had never been . . . I rolled my head down into my arms. I stretched my arms and legs until they stuck off the ends of the bed. I belonged somewhere in laboratories full of men and women looking through microscopes . . . I belonged somewhere where people talked of poetry and didn't have to have things they read explained to them. I was going to be an old maid. I was a bluestocking and an old maid. No one understood me but Charles William and he was in Atlanta.

I was getting up now. The thought of how I had suffered made

me feel better and I began to think of what I would wear to the Chi
O house for lunch. I had a brand-new red cashmere sweater set I
had charged to my father the day before. I would wear my red
cashmere sweater set and my tweed wraparound skirt and my
pearls. I made up the bed and began to dress. I had forgotten all
about Hap Dumas. He belonged to Saturday night. Now it was
Sunday and I was going to concentrate on biology all day. Who
knows, my redheaded lab instructor might be falling in love with
me. He might ask me to marry him and we could go to Chicago and
split open atoms or invent vaccines.

All the way to the Chi O house I worked on my plan to marry my
lab instructor. I had us in a convertible driving up the road to
Chicago, Illinois, as I turned from the sidewalk and began to walk
up the path to the Chi O house. "Oklahoma," I was singing. "Every
night my honey lamb and I . . ."

"Rhoda." It was my big sister in Chi O, Donie Marsh.

"What's up?"

"Isn't May Garth Sheffield a friend of yours?"

"Sort of. Why? What happened? Why do you look that way?"

"She's had her appendix out. They had to take her in the
middle of the night. She almost died. They barely got her there in
time."

"It's iodine. I should have told someone. I shouldn't have let
her do it. People are dying all around me. Where is she? Can I go
see her?"

"Come in and eat lunch first. Sure you can. I'll go with you if
you want me to. We're supposed to visit people if they're sick. You
can get blue points if you go."

"That's okay," I said. "I can go alone. I don't need anyone to
go with me."

That evening I went to the hospital to visit May Garth. She was
propped up on the pillows wearing a blue nightgown with little
flowers embroidered on the yoke. "I guess it was the iodine," I
said. "Did you tell them you'd done it?"

"It wasn't the iodine," she said. "My appendix burst. It happens all the time. Where have you been? You never came back to play cards. I thought you were coming."

"That was only yesterday when I saw you. Are you okay? Are you sure you are all right?" I pulled a chair up closer to the bed.

"I've got a crush on a football player," she said. "This great big guy. He's from Guntersville. He's in my English literature class and the teacher asked me to tutor him. He came over to the house the other day." She drifted off, her hands played with the tubes going into her arm. "Listen, this guy is so crazy about me. Look here." She pulled the sheets down across her legs. "I bet I lost ten pounds having this operation. You should have seen the blood. You never saw so much blood in your life."

"How'd you see the blood? You weren't awake, were you?"

"I was wide awake. They doped me up, then they stuck a needle in my back, then they rolled me in and started cutting me open. There were people all over the place, they were screaming."

"Where's your mother and daddy? Aren't they coming?"

"They can't. They're in Europe. My aunt's driving down. She'll be here tomorrow. Listen, I found out where the football players go in the afternoon. You know that Quonset hut that has a bookstore in it? Over by the married dorms. That's where they hang out. I'm going to meet him there the next time I tutor him. You can go with me if you want to."

"I don't want to. I'm scared of them. They're too big. They act like animals."

"I'm thinking about getting some arsenic." She waited for that to sink in. "I read about it in this book called *The Moor at Midnight*. Women used to do it all the time. You take arsenic and it makes you pale. You get really thin and pale. It can make your bones thinner even. But you have to take the right amount. You have to be careful how much you take."

"You wouldn't do that, would you?"

"I might. If I can find out the right amount." She lay back against the pillows. "It's really nice of you to come by, Rhoda. My sorority sisters came this afternoon, but they all left together. I'm glad you're here." She reached out with the hand that didn't have tubes in it and I stood up and put my hand on top of hers.

" 'My life closed twice before its close,' " I began. "That's the beginning of a poem."

"It's beautiful. 'My life closed twice.' You should have felt it when they sewed me up. I could feel them make the stitches. They were pulling through the thread." She was fading now. Her hand relaxed beneath my hand. It lay upon her stomach in the exact same place that Hap Dumas had laid his hand on mine. "I better go," I said. "I better let you sleep."

"Come back tomorrow," she said. "Come back tomorrow if you can."

I left the hospital in a strange mood. The sky was dark and overcast, no sun or stars or celestial light. I started walking toward the campus. Then I changed my mind. I wanted a hamburger. I wanted a hamburger and some french fries and I wanted to talk to someone who was normal. I went back to the hospital and found a pay phone and called Hap. "Come and pick me up," I said. "I'll buy you a hamburger if you'll take me to a drive-in."

"Sure," he said. "I have to get dressed though. Why did you call me? Why did you think of this all of a sudden?"

"I'm at the city hospital. Someone I know almost died. We could die, Hap. Do you realize that? I mean, do you really know it?"

"You want me to change clothes or come right now?"

"Come right now. I'll be walking down Halley Street in the direction of the campus. Come as fast as you can." I hung up the phone and put my billfold back into my pocketbook and took my gloves out of my pocket and put them on. I pushed open the door leading out onto the dark street. I began to walk. I was thinking about hamburgers. I was thinking about juicy hamburgers with lettuce and tomato and mayonnaise and mustard and salt and pepper. I was thinking about chocolate milkshakes and how much I loved to suck them down through straws. I was going to kiss old Hap Dumas until he didn't know what day it was. I was going to kiss and neck and let him put his hand on my breast and then I was going home and write some poems about it. I was going to get out my dictionary and find some great words to go in poems. Words like *dark* and *rain* and *omnipotent* and *transported*. Like *blood* and *breath* and *food* and *cerulean blue* and *sapphires* and *atomic theory*. Words like *die* and *live* and *profound* and *mysterious* and *art*.

Chapter

9

The next week I moved into the Chi O house. A girl from Anniston had gone home so there was a small single room available on the second floor. I piled all my stuff in the car and hauled it up the stairs and put it away. Now my dream had come true and I was living in the Chi O house. The first night I was there my big sister in Chi O, Donie Marsh, called me into her room for a chat.

"I think you're gaining weight, Rhoda," she said. "I want you to start watching it. What have you been doing?"

"Going to the Waffle House at night. I get hungry, Donie. I can't eat all this stuff they cook here."

"Well, stop eating waffles and get your hair cut. I've got some exciting news for you. A very big man on campus is interested in you. A law student. He saw you somewhere and called and asked about you."

"Who is it?"

"His name's Stanley Mabry. His father's the lieutenant governor. He thinks you're cute and he wants to take you out to dinner."

"Why did he call you? Why didn't he call me?"

"Because he doesn't know you. Well, look, go on and get to bed. We'll talk about it in the morning. You look like you're tired."

"I'm not tired. I have a lot of things to read. I've got a lot of work to do." I left her and went back to my room and lay down on my bed. I had only been there one day and already I was thinking it was a mistake to move into the house. Already I was feeling claustrophobic. I got up from the bed and began to pile things in my closet. In thirty minutes I had my room looking the way I had always liked my rooms. Everything put away and a plain bedspread on the bed. I took all the powder boxes and junk off the dresser and set my typewriter up on it and moved the lamp beside it. I opened the drapes and pushed open the window. I turned off the light and lay back down on the bed. Some old law student in a dark suit was coming to take me out to dinner. He was dark and tall and cold. He never smiled. He wanted me to act like a lady. He wanted me to be beautiful and thin. Sophisticated and aloof, quiet and soft and perfect. He was my father. He had come to get my mother. Together they walked down the path from the Chi Omega house to the car. They were going out to dinner. They were irritated and very sad.

After a while I got up and took off all my clothes and put my pajamas on. I lit a small oil-filled lamp I had bought at the dime store. The smell of perfumed oil filled the room, a strange foreign smell. I turned on the radio. "Moonglow with Martin" from the ballroom of the Roosevelt Hotel in New Orleans. Every night my long-lost love, Bob Rosen, listened to that program. No matter where I was or how far away from him, if I was listening to it, so was he. *Radio waves.* "It must have been moonglow, way up in the blue. It must have been moonglow, that brought me near to you."

On Monday afternoon Stanley Mabry called me on the phone. I was upstairs in my room reading *Henry IV, Part II* out loud. I was walking around my room reading the king's death scene.

> "My day is dim.
> Thou hast stolen that which after some few hours
> Were thine without offense, and at my death
> Thou hast seal'd up my expectation. . . .
> Thou hidest a thousand daggers in thy thoughts,
> Which thou has whetted on thy stony heart,
> To stab at half an hour of my life. . . ."

"Rhoda." It was Donie at my door. "Come on. Stanley's on the phone. He wants to talk to you."

"Okay. Hang on. I'm coming." I stuck a bookmark in my book and laid it on the bed. Then I went out into the hall where the phone sat upon a shelf in an old phone booth painted blue.

"Hello," I said. "Hello. Who's this?"

"It's Stanley Mabry, Rhoda. Donie said she told you about me."

"Oh, yeah. Well, hello."

"What are you doing?"

"Reading Shakespeare. I'm reading the king's death scene from *Henry the Fourth*."

"That's boring."

"No, it's not. It's beautiful. It's poetry. It's iambic pentameter. It's wonderful. I could read it all night. I love poetry. I read it all the time."

"Well, look. I wondered if I could come over and meet you."

"Now?"

"Sure. Why not? Donie said you wanted to talk to me before we could go out." It was a laconic voice, dark and full of sarcasm. Where had I heard a voice like that, dark and full of challenge? Why did I think I was about to hear a lecture?

"Okay, come on over. I'm not dressed. I'll have to put on some clothes."

"I've seen you. Do you know that? Guess where?"

"I don't guess. Where did you see me? Either tell me or not."

"I saw you in the bookstore at the Quonset hut. You were reading books and eating potato chips."

"So what? When was that?"

"Last week. You looked so cute. You had some pink scarf around your coat."

"Oh, yeah. My great-aunt made it for me. She knitted it. It has some gloves. Did I have on the gloves?"

"I don't think so. You were eating potato chips. So you couldn't very well have been wearing gloves."

"So what? What's wrong with that?"

"Nothing. I didn't mean anything was wrong with it."

"Well, come on over if you want to. Are you coming now?"

"Yeah. Go down and wait for me. Be waiting at the door."

"Don't tell me what to do."

"I'm asking. I'm not telling. Will you do it?"

"I guess I will. Okay. I will."

I hung up and went back to my room and combed my hair and put on some pink lipstick and a pink blouse and a navy blue cardigan sweater. I wiped off my shoes. I combed my hair again and put on some L'Emeraude perfume I saved for special occasions. Then I went downstairs and began to wait at the door.

Forty minutes later he arrived from two blocks away. He came walking up the sidewalk dressed in a dark suit. He was large looking, not fat really, just large and soft. From way down the sidewalk he walked toward me. His soft laconic face, his fleshy cheeks, his spoiled bored eyes. I opened the door. He came into the house and we squared off and went into the living room to talk.

The living room of the Chi Omega house looked enough like my mother's living room to be its twin. A rose-colored sofa sat against one wall, a brocade one against another. An oriental rug was on the floor, bookcases, windows with a window seat and long brocade drapes that puddled to the floor. There were brocade tie-backs on the drapes with golden fringe. Behind the drapes hung curtains of white Belgian lace. The afternoon light filtered down through the trees outside the windows, took a turn through the lace, ended on the floor, fell down through the woolen threads some Asian hands had woven God knows where, God knows when. It was all a piece. The world was one, but I did not know that yet and certainly Stanley Mabry didn't know it.

"So you're from Dunleith," he said. "Do you know the Kellers there? My brother went to school with Shine Keller. Do you know them?"

"Of course we do. But we're not from Dunleith. My father's family is from Aberdeen. They own Aberdeen, to tell the truth. They own the whole town."

"Well, not all of it."

"They do too. They own all the houses. So your father's the

lieutenant governor? I'm sorry I never heard of him. I wasn't raised
in Alabama."

"Where were you raised?"

"In the Delta. Everywhere. I've lived a lot of places. Anyway, I
don't want to talk about that. So, where did you see me?" We were
still standing in the middle of the living room. I sat down in the
window seat. He hesitated, then drew a small armchair up beside me
and sat on that. He looked very uncomfortable but he pressed on.

"I saw you at the bookstore in the Quonset hut. I told you that.
I like that. I like smart girls." He smiled, an imitation of a sweet
seductive smile.

"I can't help it if I'm smart. I'm glad I'm smart. Well, Donie
said you wanted to take me out to dinner."

"I want to take you to this steak house on the river. It's in the
country. We go there on Friday nights."

"Who does?"

"The law students. Would you like to go?"

"I guess so. Sure, I'd like to go." He kept his hands folded on
his open knees. There was something I didn't understand about
him. I couldn't get comfortable somehow, but I kept trying.

"I won the Sigma Chi Derby with a skit I wrote. I guess you
know that. Did you know the dean called us in? She had a fit
because this character named Slut . . . it was about the Sigma Chis
and in it they have this housemother named Slut. Anyway, she said
goddamn a few times and the dean went crazy. I'm never writing
anything else to put on here. How dare she tell us what to have in
plays. I hate her. She's so ugly. I bet she never had a boyfriend in
her life."

"She's married to the head of the engineering school."

"What?"

"The dean of women, Shirley Lang. She's married to the head
of engineering. They have two kids. I've been to their home for a
reception. I think you'll like this place I'm taking you to, Rhoda.
It's rustic. They have a big fireplace and they cook the steaks inside.
We all go there now."

"Donie said you were from Birmingham. I know a girl from

there. May Garth Sheffield. Her family owns the bank. Anyway, she started drinking iodine in milk to make her bones thinner. Can you believe that? Can you believe anybody would do such a thing? Do you know them, the Sheffields?"

"Cal Sheffield? She's Cal Sheffield's daughter?"

"I don't know. I just know her. I don't know her father's name."

"He sold us out. Of course he thinks he'll sit on the big court for it. Yeah, I know who they are. My father knows him."

"I don't know her very well. I just saw her twice. Well, that's everyone I know in Birmingham." I watched his face. Surely I could make him smile. Surely something made him smile. But no, he just kept watching me with that laconic expression. I guess my pride kicked in because I began to want to make him like me.

"I'm probably going back to Vanderbilt after this semester. I just came down here to please my dad. He gave me a car to try going to school in Alabama but I don't think I'll stay. The classes are so easy I don't even go."

"You can get an education anywhere. Who do you have? Who are your teachers?"

Donie came into the room. "Dinner's ready," she said. "We'd love to have you stay, Stanley. The housemother said it was all right. You want to eat with the girls?" She gave him a flirtatious look, then a pat on the shoulder.

"Thank you, but I can't. I'm swamped with work." He stood up. "I'll pick you up at seven o'clock Friday night, if that's all right, Rhoda. Is that all right?" He put his arm around Donie's shoulder. He smiled. "You Chi O's can collect them, can't you? I love Chi O's. They're all so fat and jolly."

"I'm not fat and jolly," I said. "Who would say such a thing? Donie's not fat and jolly. Did you know that whenever people say something about other people they are really just talking about themselves? I learned that the other day in psychology." I faced him down. I moved back into the hallway with my hands on my hips, not intending to give him a chance to reply.

"I thought you said you weren't learning anything. I just meant that as a joke. I meant it as a compliment. Listen, Rhoda, are you going to be ready on Friday? Are you going with me?"

"Of course she is," Donie put in. "She's going to go, aren't you, Rhoda?"

"I'll be ready. I don't have anything else to do."

When he was gone Donie and I went in together to the dining room. "I think he liked you," she said. "I think you did all right."

"With that fat morose guy. You must be kidding. I had ten boyfriends at Vanderbilt that were cuter than that."

"His father's the lieutenant governor. He was vice-president of the student body when he was an undergraduate. He's a very big man on campus."

"People in my family are governor if they run for office. Not vice-president or lieutenant governor. You know what Stanley reminds me of? You know what I was thinking while I was sitting there? A line from T. S. Eliot. 'Will do . . . to advise the prince . . . Deferential, glad to be of use.' I don't know why I said I'd go out with him. Why'd you get me into this?" I stared off into a corner.

"Because I'm your big sister, Rhoda. I'm supposed to guide your career. You can be somebody here if you make the right connections."

"Oh, my God. Listen, Donie, I can arrange my own life, okay? I don't need anybody watching over me. I don't need a big sister. I'm a sophomore. So just stop being my big sister. Find a pledge to oversee."

"We always assign big sisters to transfers, Rhoda."

"Not to me. Not anymore. I don't want any help from you." I walked into the dining room and began to help myself from the buffet. I piled a plate high with scalloped potatoes and meat loaf and took it down to the end of the table where my pledges from Montgomery were eating quietly by themselves. Their names were Spooky Douglas and Imogene Sayre. Imogene was the one who was the niece of Zelda Sayre. "Can I sit down?" I asked.

"Oh, Rhoda," they said. "Oh, please do. Please sit with us."

"Did you read that book I lent you yet?" I asked Imogene. I had loaned her a copy of *This Side of Paradise*.

"I started reading it," she said.

"Your aunt inspired that, Imogene. She was a great writer's muse."

"I'd read it," Spooky said. "Can I read it when Imogene gets through?"

"Sure you can. Listen, we can't let the Supreme Court tell us what to read. My cousin in Mississippi is reading William Faulkner and I've got two copies of Tallulah Bankhead's autobiography. They'd kill me if they knew I had it."

"Oh, Lord." Imogene paused with a forkful of green peas delicately balanced in the air. "I wish I could read faster."

"Well, hurry up," Spooky said. "So I can read it too."

"Listen," I added, just to take the meal a notch higher. "We are going to get a copy of *Lady Chatterley's Lover* this summer. A boy we know is bringing it from Paris."

"What is that?" Spooky asked.

"It's a book about a woman who does it with her gardener in the woods. I don't know what all is in it. This English lady whose husband is a lord. It's banned everywhere but we are going to get a copy." I sat back, let it sink in. Neither of them knew what to say to that. They grew quiet. Their eyes shone out above their careful silverware and dinner. I had inspired a full measure of awe and fear in my sweet pledges and I was satisfied.

"She's going out with a law student on Friday night," Spooky said. "Aren't you, Rhoda?"

"Where'd you hear that?"

"Donie told everybody. She was really excited about it. They like us to make contacts."

"He isn't very cute. He's kind of fat and he thinks he's God Almighty."

"But you're going, aren't you?" Spooky's eyes were wide with interest. "You're going to go?"

"I guess I will. I might need the experience for something that I write. Besides, I have a new suit I want to wear. It just hangs in my closet. I never get to wear it."

"How old is he?"

"I don't know. I already love a boy who's older than he is. I've been in love since I was fourteen with a boy who's out of college." I hung my head, took a bite of meat loaf, decided to tell the story once again. "I was fourteen years old and it was the end of summer. We were having a dance at the Coca-Cola bottling plant on the tennis courts, and I was in charge of it. We had cases of Cokes in big tubs of ice and we had the courts all cleared and I was helping put the records on the record player. Then he was standing there with his back against the backboard watching me. He watched me all night. Every time I would look at him he was laughing. He thought everything I did was funny. Then he took me home in his car. He told me about the stars and infinity. He told me so many things. When he kissed me I grew up that night. He used to direct my career at Harrisburg High School until my daddy made me move. He has cancer. He's going to die. I will never love another man, not really. The rest is marking time." They had stopped eating. Spooky sat with her fork on the plate, her head bowed. Imogene was biting her lip. "There's nothing to be sad about," I added. "It's just what happened to me. Someday I'll write a book and dedicate it to him. I hope I write it before he dies. Anyway, I have to go upstairs and study now. He likes for me to study and be smart. He likes me to make good grades. He hears about me. Everything I do gets back to him. Thanks for eating supper with me."

"Oh, Rhoda," Spooky said. "We love you, don't we, Imogene? We love you more than anyone we know."

Friday afternoon was terrible. The heat had returned. After two weeks of cool weather, a heat wave had moved in and turned the air back into mush. If the heat continued into the evening, I would burn up in my new suit. Still, I would wear it anyway. When we costumed ourselves in 1955 we looked good at any cost. If it meant sweating all over the armpits of silk blouses and the silken linings of Daviedow suits that was the price we had to pay. We did worse things than wear wool suits in hot weather. We wore Merry Widow corsets, girdles that reached from our rib cages to our thighs, thick silk hose, three-inch heels, hats and gloves in every weather.

"You're going to burn up," Spooky said. She was sitting on my bed. "I've got a cotton shirtwaist you can wear. It came from Black's. It's very pretty."

"No, I'm wearing this. I'm only doing this to meet some other people. So I have to look good."

"I don't like to go out all the time. I like to stay around and rest up on the weekends. My boyfriend from Washington and Lee might call tonight. He's fixing it so we can go to Fancy Dress in the spring."

"Why are you so happy, Spooky? You're always happy."

"I don't know. I just am." She laughed a charming bell-like little laugh. She was the only child of a wealthy family in Montgomery. Her parents liked her so much they came down nearly every weekend to take her out to dinner. They brought her dog to visit. A cocker spaniel the color of her hair. The dog was very old and coughed all the time from distemper and Spooky and her mother hugged it while it coughed.

"I'm so glad you pledged Chi O." I turned from the mirror, went over to the bed, and hugged her. She was the epitome of what a girl should be. A small blonde girl with a pretty face who was satisfied to wait till spring to go to a party. A girl who was content to have her love life consist of long-distance phone calls from a boy she had gone steady with since the sixth grade. It was a level of emotional detachment that was beyond my ken. Still, I sensed its power and was mildly, sadly, longingly jealous of it.

"You don't have to go out with this Stanley," Spooky said. "Tell him you got sick. The Sandwich Wagon's coming by later. We can get some pork and pickle sandwiches and have a room feast. We can find some girls and play bridge."

"No. I have to go. He's taking me to dinner at this place where all the law students go." I went back to the mirror, added a string of pearls and small pearl earrings to my outfit, put on my shoes, navy leather pumps that were at least a size too small. I stuffed my feet into the shoes and turned back to Spooky. "How do I look?"

"You look perfect. I hope you don't burn up."

"I'm sweating all over this goddamn blouse." I stooped and

gave her a kiss. "Okay, wish me luck. I'm going downstairs and wait for him."

I went downstairs to the parlor, holding the handrail as I got my balance in the shoes. It was ten to seven. At seven forty-five, fifty minutes late, he picked me up.

This time he was bearing flowers but they were not for me. They were for Donie. I could smell the whiskey as soon as he came in the door. A dank unclean smell of cleaning fluid and whiskey. A thought crossed my brain. A terrible memory of the summer before. Lights coming out of nowhere. A two-lane highway in the dark and Clay's body being lifted on a stretcher. Most of the time I managed to forget that night. I had stuffed it so far back into my mind that whole days went by when I never thought of it. Then something would trigger it and I would think, Death is all around us. We walk around as though we will live forever, we won't live forever, we could die at any moment. At any moment death is stalking us, stalking our friends, anyone we love, anyone we could meet. It snuffed me like a light to think such thoughts and took my power away.

"Well, you're mighty dressed up," Stanley said. "I hope you can wear those shoes where we're going. It's out in the country. It's very rustic."

"I can wear them. I don't have any flat shoes that match this suit."

"You could change clothes. Do you want to change?"

"No. I want to get out of here. It's almost eight o'clock. Can we go now?" My power returned. I looked him in the eye. Wearing heels I was almost as tall as he was. I was in no danger from this soft laconic law student. I had been fighting better men than he was all my life. I had fought my brother Dudley, who had won the Junior Olympics in the four-forty and the hundred-yard dash. A big soft law student couldn't threaten me. Especially one who smelled like cleaning fluid. "Let's go. Come on, I want to get out of here."

"What about these flowers? I wanted to give these flowers to Donie."

"Give them here." I took the flowers and walked into the hall and handed them to a pledge. "Okay," I said, coming back into the living room. "Let's go. Let's get out of here."

We walked awkwardly down the sidewalk to his car and he held open the door and I got in. It was dark and cooler now. The suit would be all right. I would make it through the night in my Daviedow.

"I love the stars," I began. "They remind me of infinity. A boy I used to go with told me about infinity. He's dying of cancer. He has about two years to live."

"Well, look, you want a drink? There's a bottle in the glove compartment. As soon as we get to the Ferry I'll stop and get something to mix it with. It's this place we always stop at on the way to Big Momma's. Fiddler's Ferry, it's this old place."

"He plays the saxophone. He taught me to listen to jazz. Do you like jazz? My absolute favorites are Coleman Hawkins and John Coltrane and Illinois Jacquet. Mostly Coltrane, of course. Coltrane's the master. Jazz is like infinity if you think of it. It's like the art of fugue because it never stops or gives you a cheap thrill and makes you think you got somewhere. That's why jazz artists take a lyric and do riffs on it. So you're never finished or satisfied."

"You want a drink or not? Get the bottle out." I opened the glove compartment and got out a pint bottle of whiskey. I opened it and took a drink, then passed the bottle to Stanley.

"Infinity goes on forever," I continued. "It might go on forever in both ways. Have you ever thought of that? I mean, inside your head might be the whole history of everyone who ever was kin to you all the way back to the beginning of time when people began to think. Every single one of them and all their memories could be inside your head. In the other direction is infinity of the stars. I told a psychiatrist my brother brought home last summer about that and he said he thought so too. This psychiatrist who went to school with my brother. He isn't finished yet. He's just in medical school. It was about ten o'clock in the morning and I was sitting on the arm of his chair. This blue chair my mother loves. I can remember exactly when he said he thought so too. I looked at my watch so I'd know exactly what time it was."

"You want another drink? Have another drink."

"How far is it to this place?"

"About ten minutes more to the Ferry. Do you always talk this much? Have another drink."

"Jesus Christ. Well, look, tell me about your dad. He's the lieutenant governor? Where do you all live?"

"Just in a house in Montgomery. We don't live in the mansion. The governor lives in the mansion."

"Big Jim Folsom?"

"Yes."

"My dad showed him to me at a football game. He was drunk. Two men were having to lead him up the stairs."

"We don't see him much. If you aren't going to drink that, pass it back to me." I handed him the bottle and he took a drink and kept it. I stared out the window at the stars. I lit a Parliament. They were my favorite cigarettes but usually I didn't buy them because they cost fifty cents a box. I had bought these several weeks before and they were stale. I inhaled, blew the smoke out the window. We drove in silence, past darkened hills and banks of trees.

"We're almost to the Ferry," he said at one point. "We're almost there."

I followed a high white star into a reverie. Bob Rosen was beside me on the seat. He pulled me over close to him and held me in the crook of his arm. He took the cigarette I lit for him. He kissed me with his soft sweet mouth. He laughed and began to tell me stories about jazz. He told me about the time his mother cursed out the vice-mayor of Chicago. He told me about Illinois Jacquet and Jo Jo Jones and Sarah Vaughan. He sang for me. "If I should write a book for you, that brought me fame and fortune too, that book would be, like my heart and me, dedicated to you." You can do anything you want to, Rhoda, he had told me. Don't let anything stop you. Don't let anything get in your way.

"There's the Ferry," Stanley said. "I don't see any cars there. I guess everyone's gone on to Momma's." He stopped the car beside a wooden building and turned off the lights. He laughed happily. He had successfully completed phase one of his date.

He got out and came around and opened my door and escorted me into a plank-floored room. An old country man was standing beside a stove, drinking a beer. There was a bar with glasses and bottles and jars of pickled eggs and pickled pig's feet. There was a display rack of cigarettes and one of potato chips.

"This is my date, Miss Manning," he said. "Could you fix us a drink? A scotch and water."

"Sure can. You want anything else?"

"A pickled egg. You want one, Rhoda? They're great."

"God, no. I wouldn't eat one of those in a million years. You know what this place reminds me of, Stanley? It reminds me of this place I went to where the Ku Klux Klan has its meetings. In Warwick County where this friend of mine took me to a cockfight."

"Hey. Don't talk so loud. He might hear you." The proprietor had gone behind the bar and was making the drinks. "You sure you don't want an egg? You don't want anything to eat?"

"I guess I'll have some potato chips. Get him to give me some potato chips."

"That'll ruin your dinner."

"You asked me if I wanted anything." I went over and sat on a stool by the bar and took down a sack of potato chips and opened them and started to eat. The bartender handed me the drink. I sipped it. It was bitter and I shuddered at the taste but I kept on sipping. I finished the potato chips and drank some more. Meanwhile the bartender had supplied Stanley with his egg. He was holding it in a napkin and biting it. "This is great," he said and finished it and asked for another one. He drank his drink and I drank mine and we got into a better mood. He ate a third egg. The smell and boring dark dead-end feeling of the Ferry lifted. I began to like the place.

"This psychology teacher I have was telling us all about how people date someone who reminds them of their father. Or else their mother. Their opposite parent. They have this ideal they're trying to meet so they can make up for not being able to take their father away from their mother. I mean, they don't want to marry him. They want him to always be looking at them so they won't get sucked back into nothingness. You know what happens to baby bats? If they fall off the ceiling of the cave the bugs on the floor eat them up in about two minutes. They never have a chance. Well, we used to be like that when we were evolving. We were in danger all the time and babies are still in danger so they want somebody looking at them every minute. I was a pretty bad little girl. I'd do anything to get attention." I stuffed a potato chip in my mouth and chewed it up. The bartender was leaning back against a counter listening intently. Stanley was staring down into his drink. "Of course a lot of people don't believe in evolution. My father doesn't believe in it. He says he isn't descended from any monkeys much less bats. I argue with him all the time about it. Well, I sure don't believe there's some big God up there bossing everyone around. If he was there, there wouldn't be death. Who would invent death? Who would hold something that they made responsible for itself? That's what I'd like to know."

"Rhoda." Stanley had gotten up from the bar stool. He was putting money on the counter. He and the bartender were looking at each other. "Let's be moving on."

"Of course the world will always be full of stupid people. They don't want to know anything. I'm getting up some study periods for the Chi O's. To teach them Shakespeare. I'll say this, once you read it to them they start getting interested in it. I had one the other night and everyone thought it was great. We're doing *Henry IV, Part Two,* but I told you that. It's all about how Henry betrays his friend when he gets to be king. At first it's okay to run around with Falstaff and get drunk with him, but after Henry gets his crown, he betrays him and won't let him come to the palace. It kills Falstaff for him to stop hanging out with him. 'We have heard the chimes at midnight. Oh, the times that we have seen.' That's what Falstaff says to his other friend, this guy named Shallow. It's about how they used to get drunk with each other and get in trouble."

"Well, let's be moving on." Stanley had my arm. He was leading me to the car. "Three more miles. I can't wait to get to Momma's. Everyone goes there on Friday nights. You can hardly get in the place."

"Do you want to hear the rest of the play?"

"Save it for later, will you? You can tell it to me another time."

* * *

Big Momma's was an old farmhouse that had been turned into a restaurant. It sat on top of a hill surrounded by maple trees. The trees stood like sentinels in the dark. Light from the windows made a mosaic on the porches and the yard. Wind moved the leaves, the light became a kaleidoscope. Inside, fires raged in the old brick fireplaces, black servants in white coats cooked and served the food, high hilarity reigned. We were greeted at the front door by a tall black man in a dinner jacket. "Oh, Mr. Stanley, we're so glad you made it. Come on in. Who's that lovely lady you got on your arm?"

"This is Miss Manning, Archibald. This is Archibald, Rhoda. He's named for a brand of whiskey, aren't you, Archie?" Stanley laughed and handed Archibald a dollar. "You got a table ready? Is anybody here? Any of my friends here yet?"

"There's a whole table of them in yonder. Not any room left at that one. You want one in that room? Table for two?"

"Well, I guess so. Sure, that will do." Archibald led the way into a crowded parlor filled with tables covered with white tablecloths. Drunk fraternity boys were eating steaks at every table. It looked very grand to me, crowded and noisy and smoky and impenetrable. Exciting. I pulled in my stomach and stood up straight and tucked in my chin and smiled and smiled and smiled. Archibald led us to a table and I sat down and continued to smile.

"What do you want?" Stanley asked. "What do you want to eat?"

"I don't care. Whatever you want."

"Well, make up your mind. Read the menu. You want a fillet? The girls usually get fillets."

"Sure. That's fine."

"How do you want it cooked?"

"I don't care. However you have yours."

"A fillet," he told the waiter. "Medium rare, for the lady, and I'll have the ten-ounce strip, rare. And bring us a martini. Doubles. Two of them."

"With olives," I said. "I want a lot of olives."

"A lot of olives. Give her lots of olives."

* * *

The table next to us had noticed us at last. The young men called over to Stanley, teasing him and asking who I was. I guess I was very beautiful, with my golden skin and hair, in my Daviedow, the suit of all suits, my face soft and golden in the candlelight, my terrible innocence and golden youth. Sometimes I knew that I was lovely. Sometimes I knew it and drew strength from the knowledge. Sometimes I even knew that I was smart, smarter than almost anyone I knew, smarter than the rest of them. But mostly I thought I had to work to make them like me.

"We ought to be sitting over there," Stanley said. "Archibald should have saved me a place at the big table."

The martinis came. We drank them. Talk flowed back and forth from our table to the next. I was introduced. A boy who knew my brother got up from the big table and came to ours and kissed my hand. "Dudley's sister," he exclaimed. "This girl is Dudley Manning's sister. Her brother's famous. Her brother's the craziest boy in the South."

"I didn't know you had a brother," Stanley said. "You didn't tell me that."

"He trained for the Olympics in the four-forty," my hand-kissing admirer said. "He's a god. He beat me in every meet last year."

"He's good at sports," I said. "He's a genius. He has a photographic memory. He lost his eye. He can only see out of one eye but he was great at basketball anyway. He turns his head to shoot. Still, he had to be a guard. He would have been a forward."

"He could spark a team," my admirer said. "I played against him when he was at CMA. You let me know if you get rid of this guy," he added. "When you get tired of him, let me know."

"What's your name?" I looked up at him. He was sandy haired and blue eyed and laughing. He was a boy you could get to know. "Where did you go to school?"

"Get out of here, Shelby," Stanley said. "Stop bird-dogging on my date."

* * *

The steaks came and we ate them and had another martini and I guess one after that. We got up from the table and danced on the crowded dance floor. We talked to people. We smoked. My girdle was killing me. My shoes were killing me. The room was hot. I was burning up. I wanted to find Shelby and talk to him some more. Instead I was dancing with Stanley. A deliberate two-step. His hands clenched me around the waist. The flesh on my waist was squeezed in by the elastic top of the girdle, then covered with my slip, then my blouse, then the jacket of my Daviedow, then Stanley's hand. I felt his heaving breath. I felt his legs soft against my legs. When I danced with Bob Rosen we were music. Each other and laughter and music. This was heaving ego and sorrow.

"Rhoda." It was May Garth, touching me on the shoulder. "Oh, Rhoda, I'm so glad you're here. Look here, my cousin's with me. You remember him, my cousin Sheffield Hughes. Sheffield, it's Rhoda." She had me by the arm. Sheffield was right behind her. There would be no escaping her. Everyone would know she was my friend. This girl whose family was not received.

"This is May Garth," I said to Stanley. "This is her cousin Sheffield."

"Is your father Cal Sheffield?" he asked.

"Yes."

"This is Stanley Mabry," I said. "I've got a date with him. We're with all those people over there."

"I couldn't believe it when I looked out and there you were." She kept on trying. She stretched her hand out to me but I backed away. I wasn't going to ruin my chances of being somebody by being seen with May Garth out in public.

"Well, I'm glad you're here," I answered. I looked at Sheffield. He was very quiet, very thoughtful. He would grow up to be the president of a great university. He would fulfill his genes. But on this night he was only a twenty-year-old boy. Gangly and unfinished and out with his first cousin trying to figure out how to act at a nightclub.

"Come sit at our table," he said. "Come and talk to us."

"We can't," I answered. "We were just fixing to leave. I have to get back or I'll be late for curfew."

"I'm staying in town," May Garth said. "Sheffield's momma came with him. We're staying with her. I can stay out all night if I want to."

"Well, that's good."

"Nice to meet you." Stanley took my arm and began to lead me back to our table.

"Let's get out of here," I whispered to him. "I want to go home now."

We paid the bill and walked out into the cooling night. We got into the car and I rolled down my window and looked up at the stars. He began to talk. "So that's Cal Sheffield's daughter. God, she's ten feet tall. I guess the Hughes boy is Burdette Hughes's son. They're rich as Croesus but that whole family's looney. They send them up North to school. I used to wish they'd send me to a prep school. Now I'm glad they didn't. It's better to stay in the state and get to know everybody. Well, the night was okay, wasn't it? I think you passed muster. You looked great in that suit."

"She isn't ten feet tall. She's just tall."

"What did you say?"

"Nothing. It doesn't matter." We drove along in silence. I felt bad. Everything was going wrong. The night had gone downhill. I could have stayed with Spooky and ordered sandwiches from the Sandwich Wagon. I could be lying in my bed reading a book or listening to "Moonglow with Martin." Nothing was going right. My whole life was a flop.

"Yeah, I think the night was a success." He turned from the highway onto a dirt road.

"Where are you going? Turn the radio on, will you? Can you get New Orleans? There's a station I like to listen to."

He stopped the car beside a pasture. He turned to me. "Come here," he said. "Come over here to me."

"I wish you'd turn the radio on. What time is it anyway, Stanley? I have to be back by twelve, you know that."

"I'll get you back. I'll get you in. Donie's going to let you in."
He reached for me and pulled me to him. He was surprisingly
strong for someone so soft looking. He pulled me to him and held
me there.

"Stop it," I said. "Leave me alone."

"No, we're going to get that blouse off you." He had his hands
almost up my blouse. His hand had pulled my blouse out of my
skirt and was now half on my skin and half on the elastic top of my
girdle. I was fighting him. Fighting him the way I fought my
brother Dudley. Deadly, ferocious, biting his hand, clawing his
face, kicking, cursing. I was a deadly fighter, a consciousless biter
from way back. I bit his knuckle down to the bone and he screamed
and let go of me and I opened the car door and kicked off my shoes
and pulled up my skirt and began to run. I ran down the dirt road
in the direction of the highway. I heard the motor start behind me
so I crossed a ditch and climbed a wooden fence and began to run
across the pasture. I could see the lights of Big Momma's in the
distance. It was a beacon on a hill and I ran toward it. I had torn
my skirt up the side by then. I pulled what was left up around my
waist and ran through the pasture in my nylon hose. I ran without
looking behind me. I ran until I was sure I was alone. Dark and
alone with only the lights of Big Momma's in the distance. I
stopped and caught my breath. My heart was pounding in my chest,
my adrenaline at its finest, most divine. The darkness was around
me. And something else. Dark fragrant shapes. Moving nearer.
Moving their heads up and down. *Cows.* I was in a cow pasture. I
was surrounded by cows and more were drawing near me. *Cows or
bulls.* Oh, God, it was the pits of hell, the end of time, the living
dream. This time I would not wake up, this time I would die. "Get
away from me," I screamed. "Don't come any nearer." The shapes
moved back from me. Slowly, deliberately, the tide of shapes
seemed to move away, to make a path for me. They were not bulls.
I would not die. I walked through the shapes, waving my hands to
keep them away. I could smell them and hear their breath. I could
feel their breath around me, fragrant and fine and rich with grass
and earth and hay. Slowly my anxiety shifted from being gored to

stepping in cow manure and I began to worry about my feet, which were cut and scratched from running on the stubble. Tetanus. I would get tetanus.

A horn was honking on the highway. Stanley was calling me. "Rhoda, come back. Please come back. Tell me where you are. Call out where you are."

"I'm over here, for God's sake. I'm in a bunch of cows. I'm going to kill you for this, Stanley. My brother will kill you dead."

He crossed the fence and came toward me. Then he was there and picked me up and carried me to the car and put me in the front seat and tucked a blanket around me and apologized and offered me some whiskey.

"Just drive me home," I said. "Just get me home so I can fix my feet."

"Please don't tell on me, Rhoda. Say you won't get me in any trouble."

"I'll get my brother to kill you, Stanley. I'll let Dudley come down here and beat you to death. So just go on and drive me home and don't drink anything else. Just drive the goddamn car. No, wait a minute. I changed my mind. Turn around. Take me back to Big Momma's. I'll get May Garth to take me to a doctor. Turn the car around. I mean it. Do what I told you to."

"Oh, God. I don't want to do that. I can't go back up there."

"You'll do anything I tell you. My brother's going to come down here and beat you to death. You ask Shelby about my brother Dudley. Just ask him. Take me back to Big Momma's right this very minute."

"You can't go in there looking like that."

"Take me back there. I said to drive me there." I was screaming at him now, scrunched up in the seat with my bleeding feet tucked up under me. "I'm probably getting lockjaw right this minute. My uncles are doctors. I know all about things like this. Turn this car around. Take me back up there."

"They won't be there now. It's probably closed."

"It is not closed. You take me up there or I'll have you put in jail."

He turned the car around and went back up the hill to Big Momma's. He parked the car and went inside and found May Garth. In a few minutes she came running out the door with Sheffield right behind her. They tore open the door to Stanley's car and May Garth climbed inside and held me in her arms while Sheffield went across the parking lot and got his Chevrolet and drove it to where I was. Then he picked me up and put me in the front seat and May Garth got in beside me. All this time Stanley was standing by the open car door not saying a word. "I'm sorry," he said finally as we were getting ready to drive off. "Don't tell anyone else about this, Rhoda. Please don't go spreading this around. It will only make us all look bad."

"Just shut up, Stanley. And you're going to pay for this suit, remember that. It cost seventy-nine dollars. I'm going to get a tetanus shot. Get out of my way. Take your hands off this car." I sank back into May Garth's sturdy arms. Sheffield began to drive toward Tuscaloosa. "He's just white trash," May Garth said. "He comes from real trashy people."

"I want to go to the hospital," I answered. "I want a tetanus shot."

"What are you going to do?" Sheffield asked. "Are you going to tell on him?"

In the end I didn't tell on him. It wasn't done to tell on people in 1955. That is to say I didn't tell on him to the grown people. I didn't tell on him in the emergency ward of the Tuscaloosa General Hospital and I didn't tell our housemother when May Garth and Sheffield finally got me back there. "I was frightened by a bunch of cows," I told her. "We went out into a pasture to look at some things for a science report and these cows chased us and I lost my shoes."

"Where was this?" the housemother asked. "Where's your date, Rhoda? Where's the boy you checked out with?"

"He had a flat tire," May Garth put in. "So we brought her home. I'm taking her upstairs now, Sheffield. You stay here with Mrs. Clark." May Garth held on to me as I hobbled up the stairs. They had cleaned out the cuts on my feet and bandaged them at the hospital but it hurt to walk. "You want me to stay here with you?"

she asked, when we had arrived at my room and she had tucked me into my bed. "I'm so glad I was there, Rhoda. I think there's a reason I was there tonight. I think we will always be friends and be there to help each other. The minute I met you I knew you were going to be my friend." She sat down on the edge of the bed. She held my hand. She stroked me like a mother. "Oh, May Garth, I don't know if I deserve a friend. I barely even came to see you when you had your appendix out."

"You came. Don't you remember you came that night? You've been a friend to me, Rhoda. I think you're the best friend I have on this campus." She kept on patting my arm, looking down as if she couldn't stand to meet my eyes. Couldn't bear to think it might not be true that I liked her as much as she liked me. How lonely her life must have been in those years, I think now. "I might not be coming back next semester," she said. "My dad may put me in a school in Washington, D.C., so I can be near him. Or he might send me to England or something. He came down to see about me last week. He's really busy but he still has time to worry about me."

"I bet he loves you to death." I turned my hand over and began to pat her. "Thanks again for saving me. Thanks for staying up so late."

"I guess I better go. Sheffield's down there with Mrs. Clark. I guess she wants to get to bed."

"Goodnight, May Garth. You call me tomorrow, will you? Call and see how I'm doing."

"Sure. Maybe you can go somewhere with us tomorrow. If you're feeling better."

"I might. Go on then. Save your cousin." She moved her hand from under mine and stood up. Stood all the way up to her full height. Then she stooped and left the room.

When she was gone I turned off my lamp and lay for a long time looking out the window at the moonlight. I didn't deserve to have a friend. I was always turning into a Judas. Always denying people that I loved. I denied Charles William all the time. I was always half ashamed to be with him, half afraid it might injure me when people found out what he did. Now I had denied May Garth. I had told Stanley two or three times that I barely knew her and didn't like her. Yes, three times, just like Peter. Then in the end she saved me. It was disgusting. I just pretended to be wonderful. I wasn't wonderful. I had killed a boy in a car wreck. I had killed Patricia Morgan's only living son. That's what came of making friends with me. I'll do better, I decided. I'll change the way I am. The next time a friend needs me, I'll be there. The next time something scares me, like things Charles William does, I'll face it down. I won't be a coward to my friends. I won't be a Judas. And I won't tell on Stanley Mabry although I should. What a terrible dopey jerk he is. What a sloppy mess and he sure better pay me for my suit.

A long time ago when I was happy, Bob Rosen held me in his arms outside a drive-in and laughed at everything I said and told me what to do, told me what the world meant and how to live in it and then we moved away. I wish "Moonglow with Martin" was on tonight. I wish I could send my mind across the miles to touch him. Somewhere, wherever you are, I'm thinking of you. And I still love you. I will love you until I die. I'm a mess right now, Roberto, but I won't always be. Te amo, mio caro. Te amo, my one and only love. I'm going to get better. I'm going to grow and make you proud of me. And you will know it. You will know it even if you're in a grave.

After a long time I slept. After a long terrible time my body curled down into the position it had known inside of Ariane and took its rest.

Of course Stanley never paid for the suit. Actually, I never heard from him again although I passed him several times on campus and we both looked away. The cuts on my feet healed in a week. Things heal on nineteen-year-old girls with the swiftness of divinity. If I were to envy the young for anything it would be for that. The way an injury can seal and cure itself almost overnight.

My feet healed and my heart pumped its miraculous message to my cells and the days began to unfurl the flag of the future. Irise came by to deliver an invitation to Georgia Tech and somewhere in Atlanta a boy with green eyes and better genes than Stanley's was getting ready to be there when my panties finally began to fall. Was waiting to help me fulfill my destiny or seal my fate or just plain get laid at last, however you like to phrase it, whatever you think it means.

Deeper than the mass, Anna once called it, more profound and much, much older. That mysterious time was almost upon me. And something else to ponder, the strangeness of Charles William. Queer duck, my father called him. Oh, Charles William, my brothers said. The Waters boy, the men sighed and lifted their eyebrows. And yet, there was hardly a house I visited in Dunleith that had not been changed by his genius, a flagstone path by pear trees, a porch painted green with a French blue ceiling and white wicker furniture he collected and painted, a dining room with Chinese screens, recessed lighting he created before you could buy such a thing, freestanding lamps with rice paper shades, walls painted red. Paint covers a multitude of sins, he was fond of saying, and the metaphor could have been his life. He left beauty and charm everywhere he passed. Also, drunkenness and a strange apologetic darkness. You would have been careful to leave a teenage boy alone with him. Still, I had no other friends my own age who were deeply truly interested in literature and art. Perhaps if I had been allowed to stay at Vanderbilt I would have found them soon, but Daddy had closed that door. "Goddammit, Sister," he kept saying when he called me on the phone. "Thank God you're down there with some white people. This place is going crazy. It's about to explode. I thank God every day I got you away from those liberals in Nashville. Are you all right? How's your car running? Do you need any money?"

Part Three

THE PISCEAN ODYSSEY

Ruled by the magical and mysterious Neptune,
Pisceans operate on their own wavelength.
Because Pisces is often considered the "lonely
heart" sign, Pisceans are susceptible to illusions.
They become either masters of their fate or life's
most unwilling servants. In the most extreme
interpretation, Pisces is the sign of the purest
spiritual expression and, conversely, that of the
most degraded or lost soul. This sign is
symbolized by two fish; one swimming upward,
toward heaven, and the other heading down, into
the depths of despair.

Linda Goodman

Chapter

10

After the night with Stanley I decided to settle down. I had had all the blind dates and sorority bullshit I could bear. Sorority meetings were held in a hot cramped attic room with everyone sworn to secrecy at the door. After we swore we sat around and talked about appointing people to committees and how to raise the grade-point average. Then we voted on things and planned the initiation ceremony.

I had been going to meetings regularly ever since I moved into the house but finally one night I couldn't take it anymore.

"Look here," I said, getting up from my chair. "The best way to raise the grade-point average is to let me go downstairs and study. I'm behind in two subjects."

"You're out of order," the president said, looking around for help. No one ever asked to leave a meeting. The girls looked embarrassed.

"I'm behind in biology lab. I need to work."

"Well, go on then. We're almost through anyway. We're almost to the prayer."

"Okay. I'm leaving." I made my escape and went down to my room and found some change and bought a couple of Butterfinger candy bars out of a machine and tried to settle down to study. I worked on biology for a while, memorizing the classifications of animals. Then I decided to work on world history. I was writing a paper on the Great Ages of Man. "The great ages of man all began with political organization. There has to be a leader, whether he is a pharaoh, a king, a caesar or a pope. The problem comes in when the leader starts thinking he is God and can do whatever he likes. That's why democracy was invented. If the leader has to be voted on by the people, he has to keep in touch with them and give them what they want."

"Rhoda." It was Irise. I hadn't seen much of her in the past few weeks as she belonged to a different sorority and didn't go out much except to classes.

"Irise. Where've you been? I haven't seen you in so long. I have a thousand things to tell you." I got up and went to the door and pulled her into the room.

"Charles William said to tell you he's got it all fixed up for Homecoming. He got you a date with a wonderful boy. You're going to go, aren't you? Are you still going to go with me?" She sat down on a corner of my bed. She was all dressed up in a green corduroy jumper and a soft white blouse with puffed sleeves. Her face smiled out from her short brown hair. I had forgotten how much I liked her, how much it brightened up a room to have Irise around.

"God, I'm glad to see you. Everybody's driving me crazy."

"Can you go? He wants us to call him tonight and talk to him about it."

"When is it?"

"Weekend after next. Can you go? Will you go? He's building the Wreck again, this thing they build out of old cars. His won last year. It was a mountain made of beer cans with a goat on top."

"God, yes, I'll go. I'm dying to get away from here. I shouldn't have moved in the house, Irise. They're driving me crazy. I have to study in the middle of the night. So what's his name, my wonderful date?"

"His name's Malcolm. Charles William sent me a picture to show you. Isn't he cute? Charles William said he was a Greek god." She produced a photograph of a young man with a crew cut that

stood straight up on end and big features and a somber smile. I took
it from her and stared down into the paper eyes. Paper and silver
oxide, black and white and shadows, icon, omen, prophecy? Do the
genes know what they are seeking? Do our ends seek our beginnings?

"Don't you think he's cute?"

"I guess so. What's wrong with his hair?"

"He was Charles William's roommate last year. Charles William says he's a Greek god."

"Well, I want to go. You know I want to go."

"You have to buy an airline ticket. It costs twenty-six dollars."

"That's okay. How old is this guy?"

"The same as us. He's a sophomore."

"He looks like a baby."

"I think that was taken last year. We can get the airline tickets
at the airport. Oh, Rhoda, you can wear your green dress we bought
at Helen's."

"I hope it fits." I got up from the bed and rummaged around
in my crowded messy closet for the dress. Right before we had gone
back to school in September Charles William and Irise and I had
gone shopping. Under Charles William's tutelage I had bought an
emerald green satin dress cut down so low in the bosom my nipples
almost showed. It had a bustle of green satin in the back and was
so tight I could hardly zip it.

"I think you're going to like this boy," Irise giggled again.
"Charles William says you're going to like him a lot."

Prophetic. Twelve days later on a Friday afternoon Irise and I
boarded a Southern Airlines plane and flew from Tuscaloosa to
Atlanta. The plane bobbed up and down in the clouds, gained and
lost altitude without warning. Passengers clutched their airsickness
bags, wrote mental wills, prayed to be forgiven, prayed to live. But
I was too excited to be scared. I sat by Irise and thought about my
luggage. I had three pieces of luggage and a hat box. In one suitcase
was my green satin dress and some silver slippers and a pair of
elbow-length white gloves and a Merry Widow and a girdle and
some nylon hose. In another I had three sweaters, three skirts, three

blouses, six pairs of underpants, three brassieres, four pairs of socks, some penny loafers, and a suit. I was carrying the third piece of luggage, a cosmetic kit with my cosmetics and a fitted jewelry case and a book. *The Complete Poems of Emily Dickinson.* I took out the book and began reading it as the plane dropped fifty feet, then recovered, then dropped again. I tore off a piece of airsickness bag to mark a poem.

> I died for Beauty—but was scarce
> Adjusted in the Tomb,
> When One who died for Truth, was lain
> In an adjoining Room—

"Betrayed at length by no one but the fog whispering to the wing of the plane," I said out loud. "Edna Millay. How do you feel?"

"I feel okay. There's nothing to be afraid of. Birds fly, don't they?" She put her hand on top of mine. "We're going to have so much fun. We're going to have a wonderful time." The plane lurched again, then seemed to settle down. Outside the window were fields of clouds. Like a recurrent dream I had when I was small of being rolled in layers of clouds. I would wake from the dream dripping with sweat and run and jump into my mother's bed.

"How long does it take? I forgot what they said."

"An hour and forty minutes. I think forty have gone by, don't you? At least forty."

" 'The young are so old. They are born with their fingers crossed. We shall get no help from them.' That's another part of the poem."

"You always tell me poetry. Tell me the one about your children are not your children." She snuggled her shoulders down into the seat. I leaned toward her and began to recite *The Prophet.* " 'Then said, Almitra, speak to us of love. And he raised his head and looked upon the people, and there fell a stillness upon them. And with a great voice he said: When love beckons to you, follow him, though his ways are hard and steep. And when his wings enfold you yield to him, though the sword hidden among his pinions may wound you. And when he speaks to you believe in him, though his voice may shatter your dreams as the north wind lays waste the garden.' "

"Oh, it's so beautiful. That's how it is."

"When did you start loving Charles William?"

"I always did. We went to kindergarten together. His momma would take me in their car. He's always lived right there on the corner and I lived in my house. I haven't ever had another boyfriend. I wouldn't know what to do with anyone else." She turned her face to mine. Her freckles stood up on her nose. Her beautiful small hands lay in her lap. The motors roared outside the window. The propellers turned. "He always takes care of me."

"We're going to have a wonderful time," I said. "I bet it's going to be the best weekend there ever was."

"Do you know the part about the children? About your children are not your children?"

"Oh, yeah. 'Your children are not your children. They are the sons and daughters of Life's longing for itself. . . . You may give them your love but not your thoughts, . . . for they dwell in the house of tomorrow, which you cannot visit, not even in your dreams.' Is that the part?"

"I love that. I love to hear you say it."

"What time is it?" She looked down at her dainty little platinum watch and told me the time. "I'm going to sleep," I said. "I'm going to sleep until we get there." Then I closed my eyes and went into a dream of Almitra standing before the assembled people of some ancient village. The people moved their heads and swayed back and forth to the wisdom of his language.

Fifty-seven minutes later Irise woke me and handed me a piece of chewing gum. "We're almost there," she said. "You can see the city." The plane lurched toward the ground. We stuck the gum in our mouths, chewed furiously. A baby screamed. Our ears popped, the motors roared. We slammed into the ground and rolled down the runway.

"There they are," she said. "They're waiting for us." The plane came to a stop near the end of a board-floored covered walkway. Charles William and a tall boy in a blue shirt stood at the very edge of the walkway. Charles William was waving his hands in the air.

"What do you think?" Irise asked. "How do you think he looks?"

We climbed down the stairway from the plane and the young men walked out to meet us. Then we walked back down the boardwalk four abreast. I had barely glanced at Malcolm. I was having a hard time remembering his name. "Oh, God," I said. "You should have seen this baby on the plane. It screamed all the time. I wouldn't have a baby for all the tea in China. If I had a baby, I'd give it away."

"When's the Wreck Parade?" Irise asked. "Are we going to be on time?"

"It's in the morning," Charles William answered. "All we have to do this afternoon is get you settled and go eat dinner. Oh, Dee, there's this fabulous record shop I want to take you to. Then we're going to dinner at Cotton's Gin. Then there's a party at the house."

"Oh, God. I can't wait. Where are we going to stay?"

"At Putty LaValle's apartment. She's from Dunleith. She's gone for the weekend. She's letting you have the place."

"Oh, God. I can't wait." I stepped in a crack between the boards and caught my heel. "Well, goddammit." I threw my pocketbook down and tried to extricate my foot. Malcolm knelt down beside me and took hold of my ankle and pulled it out of my shoe. Then he pulled the shoe up from the crack and put it on my foot. He kept his hand on my calf. I stood very still. Charles William and Irise faded into the background. I looked down into his face. He stood up beside me. "I'm glad you could come," he said. "I'm really glad you're here."

We collected the luggage and piled it into Charles William's car. Two of my suitcases had to go in the backseat. Because of that I ended up riding into Atlanta on Malcolm's lap. Talk about libido. Talk about desire. I didn't understand what we were into but I guess he did since he had been raised on a cattle farm. "You sure do smell

good," he said at one point. "That's nice perfume." More profound, Anna said she should have written. And much, much older.
"It's Nuit de Noël. My mother always wears it on her furs."
"Dee," Charles William was saying. "Did you bring the green
dress? I can't wait for you to see this record shop. The owner is a
friend of mine. He's dying to meet you. Malcolm, you're going to
have to give her to me for a while. I have a surprise for her." Irise
leaned into his arm, happy that he loved me too. What a strange
and gentle girl she was and without jealousy. A girl who could
believe that she was loved.

We drove down into the neighborhoods near the Georgia Tech
campus. The fraternity houses were decorated and boys and girls
were in the yards drinking beer and putting the finishing touches on
the Wrecks.

"What are they about?" I asked. "What do they have to do?"

"They have to run." Malcolm laughed and moved me from
one side of his knees to the other. I was sweating in my wool suit.
My body was suffused with heat and I squirmed around and pulled
off my jacket. The smell of the starch in his shirt, the smell of
shaving lotion and the fine hard line of his head beneath his crew
cut. His green eyes and thick lips *so near to me I could hear him
breathing*. "What are you going to do with all those suitcases?" he
said. "What do you have in all of them?"

"We have to have them." Irise turned around on the seat and
smiled her bright freckled smile. "Wait till you see this green dress.
Then you won't mind carrying them for her."

"There's the shopping center," Charles William called out.
"There's the record store. There it is." He pulled into a parking
place and we all piled out and went into the store and were introduced to the owner. Then Charles William took my arm and pulled
me around a corner and into a soundproof room with a turntable
and bins full of classical records and Caedmon recordings of poets
reading their poetry. At that time customers were allowed to play
records before they bought them. "I've been dying to play this for
you," Charles William said. "I can't wait till you hear it." He took
a recording out of its cover and put it on the turntable. "Listen, Dee,
just listen to this." He dropped the needle into its groove and

Siobhan McKenna's incomparable voice began to speak the Molly Bloom soliloquy from *Ulysses*. "Yes because he never did a thing like that before as ask to get his breakfast in bed with a couple of eggs since the *City Arms* hotel when he used to be pretending to be laid up with a sick voice doing his highness to make himself interesting to that old faggot Mrs. Riordan that he thought he had a great leg of and she never left us a farthing all for masses for herself and her soul greatest miser ever was actually afraid to lay out 4d for her methylated spirit telling me all her ailments she had too much chat in her about politics and earthquakes and the end of the world let us have a bit of fun first God help the world if all the women were her sort down on bathingsuits and lownecks of course nobody wanted her to wear I suppose she was pious because no man would look at her twice . . ." I was gasping with delight. It was the book Sarah Worley's sister had studied at Wellesley. It was the book about Ireland. "Oh, God, Charles William, I've been looking for that. I can't believe it's on a record. Let me see the cover."

"It's Siobhan McKenna, Dee. Someday we'll go to London and hear all these people and see them on the stage. We'll go and spend a summer and hear all the great people of the world and talk to them. We won't always be here, in this little place where we were born. But, listen, listen to it."

". . . O, tragic and the dyinglooking one off the south circular when he sprained his foot at the choir party at the sugarloaf Mountain the day I wore that dress Miss Stack bringing him flowers the worst old ones she could find at the bottom of the basket anything at all to get into a mans bedroom with her old maids voice . . ."

"Oh, God, I can't believe you found this."

"Isn't it beautiful? Isn't her voice the greatest thing you ever heard?" He drew near to me. His sweet embattled face above his wide soft powerful body moved in to tell me once again what he needed so desperately for me to know. "Davie discovered it. He brought me here. I want you to meet him while you're here, Dee."

"Who is Davie?"

"A boy who's very special to me. A freshman from Valdosta. I'm gay, Dee. You never listen when I try to tell you that. I love

Irise. I'm going to marry her. But I like Davie too. He wants to meet you. You're going to love each other. I know you will."

I spun around, pulled a record out of a bin, shook my head, tried not to hear it. I did not want to let it in. I wanted the world to be something I could understand. I was not safe enough to grow into a larger understanding. If I changed my spin I might disappear, be dissolved, sink back into sand, heat, broom, air, as Anna would later write. "Stone walls do not a prison make, nor iron bars a cage." Where had I heard that? Why couldn't I forget it? How did I know it was true so long ago and so encapsulated and so lost?

"What are you all doing in here?" Irise came into the room. "What are you listening to?"

"I thought we were going out to eat." Malcolm had followed Irise into the room. He came and stood by me. "I thought we were going to eat and then take you to where you're staying."

My eyes met Charles William's around their heads. I didn't smile or frown. I couldn't react because I didn't know what to think. It was very dangerous, what he had told me, and I didn't want to be involved in danger.

"Well, let's go then," I said. "Bring the record, Charles William. We'll buy it and take it home." I took hold of Malcolm's arm. His arm was as strong as my daddy's. I leaned into his arm, into his one hundred and twenty-five I.Q. and his normalcy. What passes in the world for normalcy. I decided to ignore what Charles William had been telling me. I didn't see what I could do about it. I didn't want to be involved in it. So I turned my attention to Malcolm Martin and his perfect body and decided to forget it. "Not that I care two straws who he does it with or knew before that way though I'd like to find out so long as I don't have the two of them under my nose all the time like that slut that Mary . . ." Charles William lifted the needle from the groove and picked up the record and slid it into its cover and handed it to me. Then he pulled a second recording out of a bin and laid it on top of the first one. It was Edna St. Vincent Millay. My favorite poet. A recording of her voice. No one else gives me such presents, a poet would later write, and I would think of Charles William when I read it.

We paid for the records and left the store and went across the

street to a restaurant called Cotton's Gin and went inside and were
seated at long plank tables. We ordered beer and salads and platters
of french fries. "Tell about the Wreck," Irise said. "Tell us what it
looks like."

"It's hidden." Charles William waved his beer glass in the air.
"Over by the engineering building. We finished it last night. It's a
surprise. You'll see it in the morning."

"It's the best one we've ever had," Malcolm added. "One of
our alumni saw it. He said it was the best one he'd ever seen. It's
sure to win."

"I wanted to decorate the house to match it but they made me
stop." Charles William laughed again. "Davie and I started on a
sofa, making it match the Wreck decor but they all came in and
stopped us."

"You wouldn't believe what he did." Malcolm finished his
beer and moved closer to me. He put his hand on my arm as he
talked. Later he put his hand on my leg and I let him leave it there.
This was what I had been waiting for. Poetry and music and wild
conversation. Yes, I said in Molly's voice. Yes and yes and yes and
yes. I forgot the disturbing elements of Charles William's life. I
forgot everything but Malcolm's hand on my leg and the way it
made me feel. By the time we finished lunch all I wanted in the
world was to let him kiss me. Later he did kiss me, on the way to
the apartment in the car and on the couch in the living room while
Charles William and Irise did whatever they were doing in the
bedroom.

The green dress, that's part of what happened next whether
anyone wants to believe it or not. Last week, when Charles William
called me from the hospital to talk for seven hours, the first thing
he wanted to talk about was that dress. "Do you remember that
green dress, Dee?" he asked. "That you wore to Homecoming with
Malcolm?"

"Of course I do. How could anyone forget that dress? I would
never even have tried it on if you hadn't been with me."

"You were gorgeous in it."

"I was, wasn't I? Or anyway I thought I was and I guess that's
the same thing."

A green satin dress, the green of Irish hills, so very green, so shiny and tight and short, cut down so low in the bosom that my nipples almost showed. Only Charles William could have found that dress and made me believe I was beautiful in it. Only Charles William could have talked me into wearing it. I put it on that night with my gold high-heeled sandals and wore it out to vamp poor Malcolm Martin who was already thoroughly vamped from my having sat on his lap all the way into Atlanta. Poor Malcolm Martin, a boy as vain and cold and unloving as my father, a perfect match for my animus.

Later, much much later, we locked ourselves into the bedroom of Putty LaValle's apartment and I took off the dress and we did it. Whatever I had thought doing it would be, this was more terrible and exciting and interesting and endless than anything I could have imagined and even if I was doing it wrong I wanted to go on doing it.

"You might get pregnant," he said at last. "I have to get some rubbers if we're going to keep on doing this."

"Are we going to?"

"I don't see why not. I hope so."

"Do you love me?"

"I guess so. Sure, I think I do."

"Well, I love you. I can tell you that. I think I love you to death." I had pulled the sheet up around my breasts. Doing it was bad enough. Letting someone look at my breasts was going too far. "Where are Charles William and Irise?"

"I don't know. Are they in the living room? I don't know if they came in or not. I wasn't listening."

"How will we find out?"

"We better look. God, we're drunk, aren't we? What time is it?"

"It's four-fifteen."

"I'm going to look out the door." I got up and found a bathrobe and put it on and looked out the door. Irise was asleep on the sofa. Charles William was nowhere to be seen. A light was burning in the kitchen.

"Come back to bed," he said. "Let's get some sleep."

"Okay. I guess it's too late to worry about them anyway." I lay back down beside him and covered us with the bedclothes. Then I curled up into his arms and fell asleep. I had done it. I was as good as married.

The next morning Charles William introduced me to Davie. We were at the KA house waiting for the Wreck Parade to begin. Our Wreck had already been hauled by truck to the starting line on Shaw Street. It was a surreal room mounted on the chassis of a yellow jeep. Walls melted down into the wheels. Windows curved down into the seats. The steering wheel was an ellipse of melted stars. A fake motor was mounted on the side. Colored smoke poured out of the motor, red, yellow, blue, green. An engineering major was driving the thing. All Charles William had to do was stand on the street and watch it go by and wait to pick up his award as the designer.

"Dee, come here a minute." He was drinking a Bloody Mary from a silver mint julep cup. "Come back here with me, I want you to meet someone." He took my hand and led me into the kitchen where a boy with golden hair was polishing glasses with a cloth.

"This is Davie," Charles William said. "Davie, this is Dee. I want you two to love each other." The young man put down the cloth and held out a hand to me. He was shorter than Charles William, not much taller than I was, but he was very beautiful, as beautiful as a girl. He smiled at me and held out his hand. Charles William bent down and kissed him on the cheek. Light poured in the kitchen windows onto the brass pots hanging above the stove. Light rang out against the brass and fell down onto the painted cabinets and spotted our arms and hands.

"I'm so glad to know you, Dee," Davie said. "He talks about you all the time. He thinks you're wonderful."

"I need to go find Malcolm," I said. "I want to walk on down and see where the parade is going to start."

"Davie's in architecture," Charles William went on. "He's my assistant this semester. We're building a cathedral all of wood, aren't we, Davie?" He still had his arm around him. He was holding him as he would a girl. Their bodies melted into each other. Surreal.

"So you and Malcolm hit it off." He giggled. "I tried to talk to him this morning, but all he would say is that you're pretty."

"What did he say?"

"I said, Don't you think she's gorgeous? and he said yes."

"What else did he say?"

"Not much. He doesn't talk much, haven't you noticed that by now?"

"I think I'm in love with him. I mean it." I took Charles William's hand. I forgot Davie was there. "Do you think he likes me? Did he say he did?"

"I told you, he said you were gorgeous. And you are, isn't she, Davie?"

"She sure is. I've been dying to meet you, Dee. He talks about you all the time."

"Well, I'm going to go and find Malcolm." I stood in the circle of the two young men. The three of us were perfectly safe at that moment, safe in each other's good graces with the sunlight pouring down through the windows and the morning of the world all around us. "I think I'll get a Bloody Mary," I added. "Is that a pitcher of them over there?"

"I'll pour you one." Davie took the glass he had been polishing and filled it with ice and poured in vodka and Bloody Mary mix. He handed it to me.

"Thank you. I'm going to find Malcolm. Are you sure I look all right?"

"Wait a minute," Charles William said. "Get me a comb." I took a comb out of my pocketbook and then, as if it were the most important thing in the world, Charles William combed my bangs down across my forehead and stood back to admire his work. "Perfect," he said. "You look absolutely beautiful."

"She does," Davie added. "You're gorgeous, Dee." I took my Bloody Mary, and, believing I was beautiful, I went back into the living room and found Malcolm and made him believe it too. We walked out onto the sidewalk and started down the hill toward the engineering school. The sidewalks were lined with young men and women in bright fall clothes. The sky was a brilliant blue. The sycamore trees golden in the clear fall air. An incorruptible mirror that cannot be contaminated by experience, Anna once wrote, meaning life. So I suppose whatever price Malcolm and I were going to have to pay for that day's ecstasy would be the proper price. "I love you," I said and took his arm.

"I love you too. You want to go back to Putty's apartment after a while?"

"I have the key." His leg brushed against mine. A marching band began to play. The first Wreck hove into view, a vehicle with a bed mounted on top. On the bed were two young men dressed as women. They were wearing pantaloons and huge balloon breasts and they were locked in an embrace. Now even the trees seemed sexual, locked in the ground by their roots. The sycamore leaves made golden beds upon the grass. Light coming down between the buildings seemed a sexual thrust. I looked up into Malcolm's face. There were specks of gold in his green eyes. Gold on the freckles of his arms.

"Let's go now," he said. "We don't need to see this damn parade."

There was a party at the house that night and Malcolm drank gin martinis and danced a crazy dance he learned from his mother's gardener. "I call it the hootchy-cootchy," he would yell, and laugh uproariously and do it again. His legs and feet moved like liquid. I could barely keep up with him. "Yes, it's me and I'm in love again," he kept singing. "Yes, it's me and I'm in love again."

At intermission I went out into the backyard. One of Charles William's projects had been turning the backyard of the KA house into a garden. There were rows of holly bushes and flower beds and a goldfish pond. Charles William and Davie were standing by the pond. As I watched, Charles William took Davie in his arms and kissed him on the mouth. He knows I'm watching, I thought. He knows I see him doing that. I was in a strange conflicted sensual mood anyway. The things that Malcolm and I had been doing all afternoon were all over me. I didn't feel guilty about doing them, just surprised and interested and amazed. I turned away from the pond. I thought of the weight of Malcolm's body on mine, the smell and taste of him, how I had thought I could kiss through his shoulder to the bone and taste the birth of blood. I had melted into his body and he into mine and that was what was meant by love. And that was what Charles William was doing now to Davie.

"Rhoda, where are you?" It was Malcolm, coming across the patio looking for me. "Come dance with me," I said. "I want to dance some more."

"What's going on?" He looked toward the pond. "Oh, that. Well, he won the Wreck Parade for us, didn't he?"

"Why is he kissing Davie?" I took his arm. "Why is he kissing him?"

"Don't you know, Rhoda? You really don't know?"

"No. And I don't want to stay here anymore. I want to leave. I'm sick of this party. Sick of people getting drunk. Let's go back to Putty's. I want to leave right now."

"I can't leave right now. Come on inside. Don't worry about other people." He led me back into the crowded living room. The KA's and their dates were becoming sweaty and wrinkled and incoherent. I saw Irise in a corner dancing with her cousin from Dunleith. A harsh yellow light filled the hallway near the front door, fell down the stairs into the darkened room where everyone was dancing. "I have to get out of here," I said. "I'm very sensitive, Malcolm. Sometimes I can't stand to be in crowds."

We found my coat and my sequined scarf and my white gloves with rhinestones sewn around the cuffs and got into the car and drove back to Putty's. "I have to leave in the morning," I said. "How can I go home after this? How can I leave you?"

"You can come back up. You can write to me. We can write each other letters. Come sit by me. Come over here. Put your hand back on my leg."

"I can't leave you. I won't be able to leave after this." I began to cry. Terrible tears rolled down my cheeks. I held on to his sleeve. "Why did we start doing that? We shouldn't have done it. What did we do it for? Now I have to leave you. How can I go away?"

"It's all right. We'll see each other again. You can come up any time you want to." He patted my leg. He drove the car. We were going back to Putty's. We would do it again and then I would go away and never see him. It was the same thing always with my life. If something was valuable to me it would disappear. No one would ever be there to hold me in their arms when I needed them. I would always be wandering through strange houses, through unknown rooms. Malcolm pulled the car over to the side of the street and turned off the motor and pulled me into his arms. He held me while I cried. "It's all right, Rhoda," he said. "We'll see each other again very soon. It isn't only you, you know. I'm in this too." He held me away from him. He began to laugh, a wonderful boyish happy laugh. "Yes, it's me and I'm in love again," he sang in a crazy voice. "I'm in love in Georgia. Hootchy-cootchy's in the air."

It was a full moon. We did it again that night and when he left I slept and dreamed of horses racing down hills toward the water. In the middle of the night Irise came in and got in bed with me and put her small sweet hands on my back and patted me awhile. In the morning I started menstruating. Rich red blood poured out of my body so I didn't even have to fear that I was pregnant.

At eleven Malcolm and Charles William came and got us and took us out to breakfast and then took us to the airport and put us on the plane.

"You fell in love with him, didn't you?" Irise asked, when we were high above the city, rocking our way south and west to Tuscaloosa.

"Why are people always leaving each other? It seems like a dumb thing to do."

"It's just when you're young. When you get older I think you stay."

Part Four

ATLANTA

Chapter
11

Dear Malcolm,

I'm so glad you liked the teddy bear. I made it out of my black cashmere sweater. The one I was wearing the night we were in Putty's apartment. It is named Errington. Oh, Malcolm, I miss you so much but I'm happy and I'm busy with schoolwork. I told my parents I was going to Emory to summer school next summer. Are you sure you're going to be at Tech? If you are, I'm going to make the applications.

I wish I could apply you to my shoulder and my arms and around my waist and so forth and so on, et cetera, et cetera, et cetera. Ad infinitum.

I love you. More later. I have to go to class and I want to mail this from the student union.

Love and more love,
Rhoda Katherine, her mark

Dear Rhoda,

My roommate said he was going to take Errington for a swim and almost got him out but now I have him tied to the bed. Phinias, not Errington. Are you sure you want to write that paper for me? It would really help. It has to be a thousand words. You can write on any modern American poet. I have to tie his feet.

Love always,
Malcolm

Dearest Malcolm,
Here is the paper. It's on Dorothy Parker, my absolute completely favorite poet now. She was speaking at Randolph Macon when I was at Southern Seminary but I was campused for smoking and they wouldn't let me go. Can you believe that? Anyway, I hope you get an A. Anyway, I love and miss you so much. Are you really coming with Charles William in *ten* days? It seems like nothing and it seems like a million. I will kiss you a thousand times and then a thousand more.

Love,
Rhoda

P.S. Please bring Errington with you. I am lonely for him. He wants to see his old sleeves which I have made into pillows for my bed.

Te amo,
Rhoda

Dear Malcolm,
Now it is seven days. One week. The way we divide up time but time seems different in different times. Now it seems like water that never moves or waiting for rain.

We had the most amazing English class yesterday. The new teacher the dean got me is the best teacher I've ever had anywhere. His brain spins out in six or seven directions and he asks the most amazing questions. He's been around the world twice. He quit everything he was doing when he was twenty-one and bummed his way around the world. He said he couldn't *presume* to teach until he knew where he was in space and time. Now I think the only reason I moved to Dunleith and came to Tuscaloosa was to be in the presence of this man. Yesterday he spent the whole class on one poem. First he passed it out to us and let us read it. Then he read it out loud twice. It is called "Thirteen Ways of Looking at a Blackbird." I think you could keep on thinking about it the rest of your life and never completely understand it. Mr. Whitehead said he reads it every year and each year it seems to be about something entirely different but the images stay exactly the same. Here is a line from it, "Once a fear pierced him, in that he mistook the shadow of his equipage for blackbirds."

There is another part that goes, "A man and a woman are one. A man and a woman and a blackbird are one." "Among twenty snowy mountains the only moving thing was the eye of the blackbird." I am going to write my term paper on Stevens. God, he might be the only poet I read all winter. "One must have a mind of winter to regard the frost and the boughs of the pine-trees crusted with snow; and have been cold a long time. . . ." God.

Thirty minutes have gone by. I just want to hold you in my arms forever. Maybe this is too much for you. I don't know any other way to be in love.

Hurry, love,
Rhoda

Dear May Garth,
Thanks for the note and the picture of Randolph Macon. I'm sorry you got shipped off there and I'm sorry you almost got raped by a football player from V.M.I. I really miss you and think of you when I walk by the Tri Delt house.

I am so much in love I am almost crazy. His name is Malcolm Martin. Charles William fixed me up with him for Homecoming at Tech. They are coming here in twenty hours. I haven't been asleep in days. Durrell says there are eight people involved in any love affair but he doesn't tell who they are. Maybe they are all the other boys you liked and the girls they liked. I don't know who Malcolm liked except this girl I went to camp with named Pepper Allen who is a perfect little angel goody-goody whose grandfather owns Atlanta.

We will all be in Dunleith for Christmas for Irise and Charles

William's wedding and we can tell our stories then. In the meantime stay away from those gray uniforms and write when you have time.

Yours in the western world,
Rhoda

P.S. Later

I'm going crazy waiting for him to get here. I think he won't like me after all or will think I'm fat or think I'm silly or think my hair is too short or maybe I'll really get lucky and my face will break out for the first time in my life. I made him this teddy bear out of a cashmere sweater. In short, I am in love. More later. Don't let the bastards get you down.

Dearest darling Rhoda,

You want the whole story? He pulled off my underpants and took them home. When he called up to apologize he said he had them in his hand while he was talking on the phone. He said he would be satisfied with the underpants but I said, no, come back over Saturday night and we'll try it again.

I mean it. I went out with him again. He's from a really poor family in some town in West Virginia. If he wasn't playing football he couldn't even go to school. He's three inches taller than I am. His hands are very crude and he's tough looking. He looks like someone your mother would have over to paint the house. His name is Iler. It's his mother's maiden name. I'm glad you're in love. I am too. I can't write you any more details. They read our mail. They feed us saltpeter in the potatoes but I never eat in the dining room anyway. My parents are still getting a divorce. It will keep my father from ever being on the federal appeals court. My mother did it on purpose because she hates him. She hates me too so I'll probably go live with him when I get out of school here. Fuck this place. Iler says fuck all the time. I do too. I love to say it. Read between the lines if you want to.

Love,
May Garth

Dear Rhoda,

Charles William and I will leave Atlanta at four o'clock on Friday afternoon. He wants to leave sooner but I have to see my adviser at three. Thanks for all the letters last week. My roommate is in love with you. If we let him off the bed for more than five minutes he gets your letters and reads them. He is a birdwatcher and used to keep bees but I played football with him at Darlington so I have to keep him around. See you Friday night.

Love,
Malcolm

P.S. He wants to write a note.

Rhoda, oh, Rhoda, why are you wasting yourself on Monk Martin when I am here. I am five feet eight inches tall and will read Yeats to you while you languish in pools of aquamarine water. I will bring you oranges and tangerines and take you away from all this. He won't introduce me, but he is letting me write this note because he ran out of things to say. People call me Kayo but my name is Phinias Kernodle. Errington likes me more than he likes Monk. I don't hang him from the light fixture during the night.

Dear Malcolm,

It will never be Friday. It will never never never never never be Friday. Let's say it finally gets to be Friday. And you leave Atlanta and start driving here. Then you will have a car crash and die a fiery death or I will fall into a hole and end up in China. You'll be in Tuscaloosa and I'll be in China. But there is no way we could be together in the same place. That would be too good to be true. I love you. Me.

Rhoda

Chapter

12

After an eternity of hours it was Friday afternoon and I could really begin to wait for him to come. It seemed a dream that I had taken off my clothes and made love to him. In another way it seemed like the only real thing that had ever happened to me except for sometimes when I was reading poetry or sometimes when I wrote it. Maybe, at last, after all these years, since I was fourteen years old, maybe I was really going to be in love again. In love with a flesh-and-blood person who loved me back and wasn't going to die. "Do not project unmet developmental needs onto the current love object via the vehicle of romanticism." There was an idea I could have used but it would be many years before I would hear that and many years before I knew what it meant. For now, I was a nineteen-year-old cauldron of unmet needs and ecstasies and hopes and fears and desires.

At five o'clock I went over to the KD house to wait for him to come.

"They're going to be so late," Irise said. "We won't get to see them for more than two hours. If they don't hurry up we won't get to see them at all."

"I'm going to see Malcolm all night. I signed out to spend the night over here with you. I'm sneaking out as soon as we sign in."

"You have to tell our housemother."

"I already did. I told her when I came in."

"How will you get out?"

"I don't know. How do people do it?"

"I don't think they do."

"There has to be a window somewhere on the ground floor. All I have to do is climb out and climb back in. I used to do it all the time at Southern Seminary."

"What would you do when you got out?"

"Sleep on the ground or in the stables. Nobody's keeping me locked in. Dudley and I've been sneaking out of our house at night since we were twelve years old. There's nothing to it, Irise. You just do it."

"There's the car. It's Charles William's car. It's them. Oh, Rhoda, here they are."

Charles William's car drove up and Malcolm got out and came up on the sidewalk and put his arms around me. I had forgotten how big he was, how powerful he was. I had forgotten how much I loved him. I only thought I had remembered. Irise and I signed out and we went to a drive-in and ordered things and talked. "I'm applying to Taliesin West to study with the Wright foundation," Charles William said. "They have summer apprenticeships. If I get one Irise and I will go next summer. It would be the greatest thing that ever happened to me. He built houses that fit the earth. He's revolutionized architecture."

"What time do you have to be in?" Malcolm whispered. He was holding me between his legs in the backseat. His tweed coat, the muscles of his arms, the power of his legs and hands.

"I don't have to go in," I answered. "As soon as we sign in, I'm coming back out."

"I'll get us a motel room," he whispered. "Charles William said I could take the car. Where will you be? What time can you get back out?"

At eleven o'clock Irise and I signed back into the KD house and the housemother turned out the lights and the house settled down. The only sound was the furnace and the fans on the back of the refrigerators in the kitchen and the girls dreaming in their beds. At 12:15

I got out of bed and put on my clothes and walked down the stairs to the kitchen and opened the kitchen window and climbed out. I dropped down into the spirea bushes. Then I walked across the yard and out onto the sidewalk and Malcolm was waiting in the car. We drove to a motel and went inside and took off all our clothes and lay down on the bed. Then for timeless unforgettable hours we did it. For timeless unforgettable hours nothing seemed to exist but that room and the strange light coming in the closed curtains and the bed with us on it. It seemed to mean something so vast and endless, as though our arms and legs and bodies were made of marble and each instant was recorded somewhere forever.

"I can see the face of our grandson," I said to him. "We will be very old and still in love with each other and our grandson will come and visit us and we will tell him about the way we fell in love."

"God. Don't say that."

"Don't say what?"

"About us being old."

"Everyone gets old." I pulled my body away from him. "Why are you getting mad? Why do you care what I say? What's wrong? What's wrong with you?"

"You just say the weirdest things. What time is it? See if you can find my watch over there." I got out of the bed and pulled the sheet off the bed and wrapped it around my breasts and tied it. Then I hobbled over to the dresser and found his watch and went into the bathroom and turned on the light and read the time.

"It's four-thirty."

"We've got to get you back. It will be light soon. Get dressed. Come on. Let's get dressed." He got out of the bed and pulled on his pants and I turned on the light and went into the bathroom and put on my clothes and came back out into the room and tried to look at him but now he was a stranger. He was scared to death of what we had been doing. He was scared to death of me. He thought the things I said were weird and I was tired of the things we had been doing and I was getting angry and tired of trying to figure out how to please him.

*   *   *

I climbed back in the kitchen window and closed it and found a loaf of bread on a cabinet and some mayonnaise in a refrigerator and made a couple of mayonnaise sandwiches and ate them and then I drank some milk and then I went upstairs and got into Irise's bed. "What happened?" she said. "I've been worried to death. I bet I hardly slept all night."

"I wish you hadn't introduced me to him. He thinks I'm weird. He got mad because I said we were going to get old some day. He always gets mad at things I say. He gets mad when we're making love. What do you and Charles William do when you make love? What does he say to you?"

"I don't know. He just tells me things. About things he's interested in."

"No, I mean when you make love to him. What do you do? What do you say? I have to talk to someone about it. I have to know what to do."

"We just lie around and laugh about things and listen to music if we can be at his house alone. When Eula goes to play bridge. Then he just tells me things or I put on his kimonos and he ties them around my waist and we tell each other things. Maybe we can go to sleep now, Rhoda. Let's go to sleep." Her soft little hands patted my back. Her sweet voice soothed me and I slept.

The next day we went to a party at the Beta house and then to a football game and then to a party at the Kappa Sig house and then to a party at the SAE house and I got drunk and threw up for about an hour and went to sleep on a sofa. Somehow they got me home.

On Sunday morning Malcolm came over alone to the Chi O house to tell me goodbye. I felt so bad I could hardly get dressed and go downstairs to talk to him.

"I'm really sorry," I kept saying. "I'm sorry it happened."

"You aren't the only one who got drunk. We all got drunk."

"I thought you would give me your pin."

"What?"

"I thought when you got here you would give me your pin. If you want to ever do it with me again you have to give me your pin."

I was standing beside a brocade sofa in the living room. He was sitting on a chair. He was wearing a white oxford cloth shirt and a pair of khaki pants and a sweater. Monk, they called him at Darlington. He looked like a monkey to me at that moment, like a great beast or orangutan or chimpanzee. "Are you going to give it to me or not?"

"Not today. Not like this."

"Then forget it. Forget the whole thing." I walked out the front door of the Chi Omega house and left him standing there. I walked out into the front yard and went over beneath a tree and started counting the leaves that were piled up underneath the tree. Atoms into molecules, molecules into bases. One, two, three, four, five, six, seven, eight, nine, ten, eleven. He walked out the front door and started my way, but I turned around and waved him off. I was so angry I thought I might go crazy.

"Rhoda. Talk to me a minute."

"You better go on. Charles William is waiting for you, isn't he?"

"I wish you'd talk to me."

"I talked to you." He was standing on the sidewalk. He turned away from me then and walked on to the car and got in and drove away. I leaned over and began to pick up the leaves. It was a maple tree and the leaves were the shape of my hand. I tried to find the largest leaves I could find. I tried to find the ones that were the same size as my hand. My hands were shaped like my father's hands. They were very large for my size. My arms were very long and my hands were big and a long time ago I had used them to pull my body through the water. A long time ago I had been a great swimmer. I was training to swim the English Channel and the only reason I quit was because I hated to be smeared with grease to swim it. I had to gain a lot of weight and be fat and let them smear me with grease. Then, at night, in the black night, I would be swimming against the waves. My father was beside me in the rowboat. He would never let me drown. Swim, Sister, he coached me. One, two, three, four, five, six, seven, eight. Keep swimming. You can make it. I'm right here. You can do it, Sister. Let me see you swim. Pull, pull, pull. Pull your heart out.

Chapter

13

Dear May Garth:

So much for love. That was the worst weekend I ever spent in my life. Sunday afternoon, after they were gone, I went over to the pool and swam for about three hours. I have to get back in training. Maybe next week I'll see about getting on the team here. I hope I never see him again. His roommate calls him Monk. It's because he looks like an orangutan. He really does, now that I think about it. He lifts weights all the time to make his body bigger. There isn't a single soft place anywhere on his whole body. He cuts his hair off so short he looks like he is bald. He doesn't even have soft hair.

Well, three more weeks and it's Christmas vacation and we'll all be back in Dunleith and Charles William and Irise will be getting married. The dresses are waiting for us. I hope your diet goes well so you'll fit in yours. I'm as thin as a rail. I got so I don't care if I ever eat.

I'm writing this paper on Stevens now. It's all I can think about. "Among twenty snowy mountains the only moving thing was the eye of the blackbird."

Irise and I will be home on the eighteenth. When do you get there? Are you coming on the train? They are going to have lobster for the reception and all the champagne anyone can drink. "Three be the things I shall never obtain. Envy, content, and sufficient champagne.''

Hurry home,
Rhoda

Dec. 15, 1955 (unmailed)

Dear Malcolm,

I have tried to write this letter about a hundred times. So this time I will mail whatever I write. I am not writing it of course. I am typing it on my Royal portable typewriter I have had since I was thirteen. I learned how to type in three days. Did I ever tell you that? I am a very smart girl. Did you ever realize that? What do I know? Nothing. ''Once a fear pierced him, in that he mistook the shadow of his equipage for blackbirds.''

Dec. 16, 1955 (mailed)

Dear Malcolm,

I am going to mail this no matter what it says. I'm sorry that last weekend was so horrible. I'm sorry I got drunk. I'm sorry that we got into an argument in the motel. I'm sorry it's so hard to know what to do every day of our lives.

Charles William called me last week and said you were really sorry about all of it too. He said you looked like you were unhappy so that's why I'm writing to you.

I started menstruating so at least I'm not pregnant. Charles William and Irise are getting married at Christmas. I'm the maid of honor. I guess you know that. I think we'll really have a great party. I'm helping Irise plan the wedding. Charles William wants everything perfect as you can imagine. Here's a poem I wrote while looking at the photograph of you Charles William sent me (was that two thousand years ago, turning and turning in a widening gyre) to get me to go with you to Homecoming. Things get started in the world and they seem so fresh and white and hopeful and then they usually end up like this. Well, onward, as they used to say when the wagons headed west.

Yours in the human race,
Rhoda

POEM IN JANUARY
The rain, the rain, is kind to come
It sings its song, dumb, dumb,
It sings that things aren't what they seem
And love, my love, is still a dream
And so I have to sit and stare
At a tiny little two-inch square
A photograph of a dream I had
Like one who is entirely mad.
There might be life outside this place
Where I worship your tiny paper face.

Dear Rhoda,

My roommate thinks he is going to get to read the letter you wrote me and read the poem but he won't get to read that one. I have read it a lot. I think it means a lot. I think we should forget about that weekend.

I wish I could come to the wedding but I have to stay home at Christmas. My parents need me there. My father is in a lot of trouble now about money and I'm going to be helping him.

I got an A on the paper. Then my teacher asked me to stay after class. He said, Mr. Martin, I would never have picked you out to be a fan of Dorothy Parker.

I love you,
Malcolm

Dear Rhoda,

Did you get the letter I wrote to you before Christmas? I mailed it to your address in Dunleith? I thought you would write back to me if you got it. Let me know if you got it.

Yours truly, love,
Malcolm

(unmailed)

Dear Malcolm,

This letter will not be mailed. I don't think I can get back into that stuff we were doing. I'll get back into it and I'll be so happy I

think my feet don't touch the ground and the whole world will be
so beautiful it's like a place I never saw before except heard about
in Wallace Stevens' poetry or maybe Wordsworth's or maybe Hous-
man, or "Wild Peaches" by Elinor Wylie:

> When the world turns completely upside down
> You say we'll emigrate to the Eastern Shore
> Aboard a river-boat from Baltimore;
> We'll live among wild peach trees, miles from town,
> You'll wear a coonskin cap and I a gown
> Homespun, dyed butternut's dark gold colour.
> Lost, like our lotus-eating ancestor,
> We'll swim in milk and honey till we drown.
>
> The winter will be short, the summer long,
> The autumn amber-hued, sunny and hot,
> Tasting of cider and of scuppernong;
> All seasons sweet, but autumn best of all.
> The squirrels in their silver fur will fall
> Like falling leaves, like fruit, before your shot. . . .

This is how my mind works. Things like this are part of my
psychological makeup. I don't think you can deal with this. I don't
think you have the slightest idea who I am. You know what May
Garth said when she was here at Christmas. She said, anyone who
could study math could never understand a poet. She said, anyone
can count. I got so mad at you for hurting me that I started thinking
evil things about you, about the way you look and trashy stuff like
that. I guess I'll just go on and be a bluestocking and an old maid.
If you were someone I should love I could mail this letter to you and
you would know what it meant. I can't and you can't.

Sayonara.
Rhoda

Dear Rhoda,
We got back to school in a snowstorm. I wrote to you before
Christmas and I wrote to you on January 2, 1956. Now I am writ-
ing to you on February 7, 1956. I am sorry you got mad at me and

I don't blame you. When you started that stuff about us having a grandson I felt like I was getting sick at my stomach. My parents are real old people. They were forty years old when I was born. I am afraid of getting old. I'm afraid I'll never get out of Tech and get a job.

Please write to me. I have a lot of things on my mind right now. My brother is coming home from Europe and my mother hates his wife. They have three kids who were born over there. We have never even seen them. My brother's wife is almost six feet tall. She was the valedictorian of Agnes Scott. She is really crazy. She drives my mother crazy. They have been letting the children run around with Greek people and send us pictures of them wearing weird clothes. It drives my mother crazy. Now they are coming home. We don't know why Gray married her. She is really crazy. She wrote my mother and told her they put flowers in their toilets. She says anything that comes into her head.

I'm drinking beer. I was drinking it all afternoon and then it started to rain and I started thinking about you so I decided to write you. I don't think I'm ever going to get out of this school. I have to get a degree because my father has lost all his money. He is working in a hardware store in Martinsville now. His ancestors built Martinsville and now he is working as a clerk in a hardware store. That is very hard on my mother.

I found Errington the other day. He was in my sock drawer so I got him out and let him drive around in the car with me. Please, come up here one weekend and let's talk this over. I want you to come to Emory for the summer. I want you to do anything you want to do. I just have to study harder. My folks are spending a lot of money to keep me here and they can't afford it anymore. I have to make better grades than I have been making.

                                        I love you,
                                        Malcolm

Dear Malcolm,

I have written you about a hundred letters since that weekend when I saw the face of your grandson (and mine) smiling at me from the ceiling of the room where you were making love to me. I have written you at least a hundred letters and at least twenty poems. What would you like to have first, a letter or a poem? I threw most of the letters away. But I will put one or two into this packet. Along with this tie which I bought for you for Christmas. That seems about a year ago. So here are four poems. If you read them and think you can keep on writing to a person with a mind this weird write back and I'll send you a letter I wrote to you in January. It won't scare you to death.

Love,

Rhoda

ONE THING ABOUT THE LIVING
EVERY NOW AND THEN ONE OF US
STOPS DYING FOR A MOMENT

After forty days it came back in December while the wind blew like Baltimore around this southern city. It came back. It walked around talking to gardeners, waving at football players, luring me back to your bed. It came back, colder, deeper, more terrible than I remembered. I knew the route it took to find me, the detours it made, the washed-out bridge, the dangerous ferry crossing. I pretended it was a cat wailing on another roof.

Later I took it to lunch. I fed it bread and wine. I gave some to Spooky and some to Irise and some to the football players and poured some into a letter and went upstairs and got into bed and held it while it took my arms and legs. I closed my eyes it grew heavier. I held still it grew heavier.

All afternoon I dreamed of Uncle Piljerk Peter. He lives on cloud nine. He ties his pill to a ten-pound test line and drops it down the first child's throat and jerks it back up and drops it down the second child's throat and jerks it back up and so on so forth until the pill loses its strength and no one can be saved anymore. This is a story out of a southern children's book. It's all about the black people and how funny it is when their children die. It's all about dying and love and how there isn't enough strength to go around. It's about how you weren't strong enough to love me but I don't care. Why should I care? It's not your fault my father ruined my mother's life.

AUBADE

There was one night knowing all my songs
you came to me
and all night long you crossed my body
with your music

Oh, I can still sing every note
of all the songs you taught me
Every gaudy jaybird
Every yellow warbler

THE FLIES AND THE HONEY POT

A pot of honey having been upset in a grocer's shop
the flies came around it in droves to eat it up nor would
they move from the spot while there was a drop left.
Finally they became so clogged in it they could not
fly. Miserable creatures, who, for the sake of a
moment's pleasure, had thrown their lives away.

This is the wisdom of white-haired ladies
on verandah swings,
my early warners,
my corseted teachers.

Stifled in luscious sweets
all things are timeless.

Did my ladies know the honey
dripping on the floor?
The white necessity of love?
Or only bear its burdens.

I am caught forever in those summer mornings,
reading their books,
smelling their coffee and their powder,
hating their warnings.

GUEST

Tied to memory's plumbline the night
like a long dark road leads on and on
into the silent spaces of the heart

The days lengthen
This is the season the surveyor
doubles his team to take readings
it is dawn go on

February 10, 1956

Dear Rhoda,
They are the best poems I have ever read. I don't know what they mean exactly but I know I want to read the letters too and I want to make love to you more than anything in the world. You can have my goddamn pin and throw it in the river. Here it is. Either wear it or throw it away.

Love,
Malcolm

February 13, 1956

Dearest Malcolm,
I took it out and then I cried. Then I pinned it on the inside of my bra and wore it there awhile. Then I pinned it on the outside of my bra. After supper I pinned it to my sweater. I walked around the house but no one even noticed it. I'm glad. I can't talk about this yet. I love you. I could never love anyone this much again if I lived a thousand years. You angel.

Love,
Rhoda

February 14, 1956

Dear Malcolm,
Happy Valentine's Day. HERE is the letter I wrote to you in January.

Dear Malcolm,
   It was the worst Christmas I ever spent. All I did all day was drink sherry and walk back and forth from our house to Charles William's house to Irise's house. Their wedding was so beautiful. I had a red velvet bridesmaid's dress and the church was full of candles and I cried like a baby when they pro-

nounced them man and wife. I got your letters but I can't seem to answer them. Do you mean it that you love me? I have never stopped loving you a second. No matter where I was, I was thinking about you dancing that first night I went to Homecoming with you.

I don't know what else to say.

I love you,
Rhoda

Dear Rhoda,
I have to see you. Can you come here at Easter? I know that seems like a long way away but if I could look forward to that, it would change things for me. I could come to where you are if you can't come here.

Love,
Malcolm

Dear Malcolm,
I will come at Easter and I will write to you every day until then. What difference does time make anyway? Time is just a way we measure eternity. We don't even know if time is true. I love you,
Me

Dear Rhoda,
Errington and I are going to keep Phinias tied to the bed until you get here. I told my folks I had to stay in Atlanta to study. My aunt is going to be out of town and she said you could stay in her apartment if you wanted to. It's a nice house out in Ansley Park and we wouldn't have to be with Charles William and Irise all the time. Don't take that to mean anything. I like Charles William and I am really sorry I said that about him to you. You better call me when you get this letter so we can make plans. She is my mother's sister and she lives by herself. She's my favorite aunt. I told her I was in love with you and she wants to meet you.

Love always,
Malcolm

Dear Malcolm,

I can't think of anything I'd rather do than stay at your aunt's apartment. I want to be in a place where someone in your family has lived. I want there to be ions and atoms of your gene pool everywhere. I want there to be artifacts and pictures and clothes and furniture and memories of all the life you had before me. I am jealous of every day on the earth you spent and I wasn't there to watch you and love you. I love you, did I remember to tell you that? I want to reach down into your mother's womb and caress you in your beginnings. I was conceived in a tent on the banks of the Mississippi River when my father worked for the Corps of Engineers. Where were you conceived? I want to visit the room and bless it and be blessed by being there. See, this is what you get if you let a poet love you.

                              I love you,
                              Rhoda

Chapter

14

It wasn't easy to get permission to go to Atlanta alone to see a boy. But it was possible. First his aunt wrote the Chi Omega housemother and asked if I could stay with her. Then the housemother called my mother. Then my mother called me.

"You can trust me, Mother," I told her. "You can trust me. You can trust me."

"You're flying to Atlanta all alone? Why don't you stay with Irise? Why do you want to stay with some aunt of his you don't even know? We've never even met this boy, Rhoda. Your father isn't going to like this."

"He's from a nice family, Momma. He used to go with Pepper Allen who went to camp with me. He used to be Charles William's roommate. My God."

"Why can't you find someone to go out with in Tuscaloosa? Why do you always have to be running all over the country? I thought you had all that work to do for the newspaper there. You told me you couldn't come home for the weekend because you had all that work."

"Momma, it's for Easter. They have all these dogwood trees I want to see."

"Rhoda."

"Yes, ma'am."

"Don't chase men, Rhoda. Let him come to see you."

"I don't want him to come here. I want to go to Atlanta."

"All right. All right. I give up. If your father says it's okay. How much money do you need?"

"A hundred dollars will be enough. The airplane ticket cost twenty-six."

"I'm trusting you, Rhoda. Remember that."

"I will. You can. Well, thanks, goodbye."

So the money was sent and I packed a bag and flew to Atlanta. Malcolm came and got me at the airport. I hadn't seen him in five months, but the chemistry was still working. As soon as I saw him I started thinking about finding a bed. "I have to go by the laundry and pick up some shirts," he said. We were leaning up against the rickety supports of the walkway. He ran his hand up and down my back. I ran my hand up and down his back. He touched my waist. I touched his waist. He kissed me on the mouth. November, December, January, February, March disappeared like wild geese into the stars.

"Okay. That's okay."

"I forgot to take them until yesterday. If I don't pick them up I won't have anything to wear."

"That's fine. I want to get your shirts. That's great." We walked out through the airport and collected my luggage and got into his car and started driving into town.

"Where'd you get the car? I thought you wrecked your car. Charles William said you wrecked your car."

"I ran it into a brick wall." He laughed out loud. "This is Aunt Gaye's. It's her apartment you're going to." He turned off an exit that led down into the neighborhoods near Georgia Tech. We went past the KA house and the engineering school and parked in the shopping center with the record store Charles William had introduced me to.

"I wish we had time to go to that record store," I said. "They have stuff no one else ever has."

"I have to get those shirts before the place closes and we have to get over to Aunt Gaye's. She wants to meet you before she leaves for the weekend."

"Oh, God. I look terrible. I'm so wrinkled. I wish I could change clothes before I meet her."

"She doesn't care. She just wants to show you how to feed her cat." He turned off the ignition key and pulled me into his arms again. He put his hands on my breasts. I put my hands on his chest, then on his arms, then on his back, then on his legs. It was devastating. It was divine. It was crazy.

"Not now," he said. "We have to wait."

"I can't. How long. Let's stay here. Hold on to me. Never let me go."

"She's leaving this afternoon. We'll have her place to ourselves. Let's get my shirts. It won't be long. We have to go on over there."

"Kiss me again. Say you love me. I can't get close enough to you."

"I love you too."

"How much. Say how much. Say you'll always love me. Forever and ever and ever. Say you'll always love me and you'll never die."

"Come on, Rhoda. I have to get out of the car. Let go of me a minute."

Malcolm pushed me away and got out of the car and stood beside it with a terrible expression on his face and wouldn't look at me. I took a lipstick out of my pocketbook and began to put on lipstick in the rearview mirror. "Wait a second," I said. "I'll go in the cleaners with you."

We collected the shirts and drove down into Ansley Park and stopped before a brick and stucco duplex. We got out of the car and started up the walk. Before we could ring the bell, the door opened and a beautiful tall woman came out and drew us in. "Oh, Malcolm, you angel," she said. "Oh, this is Rhoda. Oh, I'm so glad to have you here. Is your friend with you? I thought you were bringing a friend."

"She's coming later," Malcolm said. "She had to do some shopping."

"Well, come on in. Look around. I'm not settled yet. Everything is still in disarray." I looked around me. Everything in the apartment was very old. Old furniture and old paintings in gilt frames and dark Turkish rugs on the floor. A huge cat the color of faded gold sat on top of an upright piano. "I love your apartment," I said. "It's so nice of you to let us stay here."

"The cat won't bother you, will she?" She threw back her head as if to clear her mind, then fixed me with a harassed worried smile. "All you have to do is make sure she has food and water. She knocks the water over. Well, let me take you upstairs. Malcolm, bring her bags. I made you a pineapple upside-down cake. It's his favorite cake." She turned back to me, took my arm. "I always make it for him. I never forget to make his cake."

We followed her up the narrow stairs. Malcolm left my bag at the door of the guest room, then disappeared. The room was small and every inch of it was stuffed with furniture. In the center of the room, with barely enough room to walk around it, was a four-poster bed with a pink canopy. The walls were covered with flowered wallpaper. Roses seemed to leap from the walls. Hanging from the center of the room and threatening to tear the canopy was a hand-painted wrought-iron chandelier with pink roses around each teardrop light bulb. The windows were closed and the blinds were drawn. What oxygen there was in the room seemed to be concentrated around the bed. The rest was buried in furniture, snuffed out by furniture, overpowered by furniture.

I lugged my suitcase into the room and put it down on a luggage rack, which was squeezed in between two huge dressers. The drawers of the dressers were stuffed full of sweaters and jewelry boxes and table linens. The closets were stuffed full of wool suits and cocktail dresses. The closet shelf was stuffed full of hatboxes and leather handbags. The floor of the closet was stuffed full of shoeboxes. "I'm sorry everything's so crowded," Aunt Gaye said. "When Marvin was alive we had a big house in Buckhead. I couldn't live there after he passed away." She was behind me in the doorway. She put one hand against the door frame and the other to her brow. "We had a wonderful marriage."

"How did he die?"

"He had a heart attack. At his office." She sat down on the bed. Looked down at her hands, then up at me as if to beg forgiveness. "I didn't get to say goodbye. He died before they got him to the hospital. It's been three years. I should throw all this away." She pulled open a drawer of one of the dressers and began to take out stacks of table napkins and put them on the dresser top, which was already crowded with framed photographs and shepherdess lamps and china powder boxes. The photographs were of Aunt Gaye and a man, at the races, on a sailboat, under a tree, in a studio dressed in dark city clothes, holding hands.

"Is that Marvin?" I asked.

"Yes."

"You don't have any children?"

"No. Thank goodness for Rose's boys. They're so dear to me, especially Malcolm. Are you in love with him, Rhoda?"

"Yes, I am. I broke up with him and we didn't see each other for a long time but I never stopped loving him. I guess he loves me too. He asked me to come here. I guess we're made up now."

"What did you get mad about?"

"I can't remember now. I think it was my fault. I don't remember. We got drunk and had a fight. That's what really happened."

"He told me he was in love with you." She put the stack of napkins on the bed and turned and took my arm. She was so beautiful, I had never seen a woman that old who was that beautiful. It was frightening almost. A frightening, hesitant beauty. She was so gentle and so worried and so beautiful.

"Where are you going?"

"To the Carpegian gardens with a Mr. Day. A man I play duplicate with. We're going to a tournament with some other couples. I haven't been out of town with a man since Marvin died. We're going to be chaperoned, of course." She sighed, sat back on the bed. "I don't think Malcolm's mother, Rose, approves. I think Rose is worried about it. Don't say anything if you talk to her."

"I've never met her."

"We're going to play in a tournament. He has so many master points. He's within a hundred points of being a life master. Oh, dear." She put her hand up to her head. For a moment I thought she was going to change her mind and stay in Atlanta with Malcolm and me.

"Go on and have a good time," I said. "You know what Dorothy Parker said, don't you? 'Drink and dance and laugh and lie. Love the reeling midnight through. For tomorrow we shall die! But, alas, we never do.' It's called 'The Flaw in Paganism.' Well, anyway, go on and have some fun. You need to get out and have fun."

"Oh, you're right, I guess." She hung her head.

"Of course I am. If anybody doesn't like it, they're just jealous. Listen, Aunt Gaye, you're the best-looking woman your age I ever saw in my life. You could be in the movies. You can't just stay home with your cat. My great-grandmother had three husbands. As soon as one would die, she'd marry another one."

She seemed to brighten up at that. "You're right, of course. Life goes on. Marvin would be distressed to see me shut up in this dismal place. Well, I'll go freshen up before Mr. Day gets here." She went into the adjoining room and sat down at her makeup table. I opened my suitcase and took out a dress and hung it over the chair. Then I took out my high-heel shoes to see if they were squashed from the plane ride. Then I opened a compact and began to put on lipstick. I looked at my watch. It was almost six o'clock. When was she going to leave? I walked to the door of the room. She was sitting at a dresser powdering her face. "I'm going downstairs and look for Malcolm," I said. "I don't want him to be alone."

I found him in the dining room looking at paintings of his ancestors. "I love your aunt," I said. "I love meeting her." I tried to put my arms around his waist but he pulled away.

"Not now," he said. "You'll get lipstick on me. Let me get you a Coke. Let me cut you a piece of cake."

* * *

The doorbell was ringing. We ran for the door. It was a tall uncomfortable man who looked as if he was full of secrets. I immediately took an intense dislike to him. He reminded me of my mother's cousins in the Delta, bloodless, proper, scared.

"I'm Tom," he said. "I've come for Gaye."

She came down the stairs. She had changed into a pink wool suit. She was very elegant in white leather shoes and gloves. She was carrying a small suitcase in her hand and Malcolm ran up the stairs and took it from her. We made hasty embarrassed conversation for a minute. Then Tom and Aunt Gaye left the house and left us there. We closed the door. We went upstairs and lay down upon the bed and began to heave and sigh against each other. Time passed. Darkness fell.

"You're supposed to do something about it," he said at last. "You're supposed to use some jelly or take a douche."

"I don't have any. I forgot to get it."

"Look in the bathroom. Maybe Aunt Gaye has something."

"I will. In a minute. I don't want to get up yet. I don't want to let go of you."

"Okay. Come here. Get back on top of me. Like that. Oh, yes, just like that."

Much, much later, around three or four in the morning, I got out of bed and went into the bathroom and found a douche bag still in its cardboard box and read the directions. Beside the box was a bottle of dark green liquid called Betadine. I filled the douche bag with water, added the liquid, and lay down in the bathtub and tried to stick the plastic nozzle up my vagina. I held the nozzle in with one hand and the bag above it with another. It was awkward, but I managed. When most of the water had run out into my body, I stepped out of the tub. The bottle of Betadine was sitting on the edge of the small washstand. I knocked it off and it fell to the floor and broke and the antiseptic spread everywhere, a deadly green lake on the white tile floor. I grabbed a towel and threw it down upon the mess. I grabbed all the towels in the room and began to mop it up.

The smell was suffocating. I stepped gingerly around the pile of towels and pushed open the window. Then I knelt down and began to pick up the glass.

"What happened?" Malcolm said. He had come to stand in the door.

"I broke the goddamn douche stuff. Go get a mop, will you? Help me clean this up." He disappeared down the stairs and returned with a mop and a pail and we cleaned up the mess as well as we could and rinsed the towels in the bathtub. "I can't believe it," I kept saying. "I can't believe I spilled this goddamn stuff all over the goddamn floor."

"You can still smell it," he said. "We'll never get this smell out of this room."

"I'm starving." I had found a bathrobe on the back of the bathroom door and was tying it around my waist. "Let's go downstairs and eat that cake. She wants us to eat that cake."

We went downstairs and found the cake and plates and forks and poured glasses of milk and began to eat. It was the first time since I had met him that I felt that Malcolm was even in the same species with me. He had seemed a dream or a field to cross or a mountain to conquer. Now he just seemed like my brother, cleaning up the house before my mother got home and eating all the cake as fast as we could eat it.

"They always make this cake for me," he said. "They make lemon meringue pie and upside-down cake. All my mother's sisters make the same things for me. My brothers were away at the war when I was little. I was the only boy they had."

"How many sisters does she have?"

"Just two now. There used to be five of them, counting my mother. They lived in Rome, where I went to school. Their daddy was a doctor."

"What are we going to tell her about the smell?"

"I don't know." He laughed. "We can say your friend spilled it. How about that?" He cut us another piece of cake. I poured us each another glass of milk. Then the phone began to ring.

"What time is it?"

"I don't know. Answer it."

"You answer it."

"I'm not supposed to be here. You answer it."

"Okay." I picked up the receiver. A woman's voice was on the other end. Very frazzled, very frantic, very high and musical and terrible. "Miss Manning, is this you? This is Mrs. Martin, Malcolm's mother. I hate to bother you so early in the morning. Do you know where Malcolm is? There's been an accident. Is your friend there? Perhaps you should wake her up."

"What is it? What happened?" There was a sob on the other end, a sound like crying. Then a man's voice was on the line. "This is Mr. Martin, my dear. Malcolm's father. There's been an accident. Aunt Gaye died. Do you know where Malcolm is?"

"He's right here. He came to take me out to breakfast. Wait a minute. Here he is." I handed him the phone.

"They're coming here," he said, when he hung up the phone. "They'll be here in two hours. We have to clean up this place."

"She's dead? Your aunt is dead? How could she die?"

"She had a heart attack. Come on, let's get dressed. They're coming here."

"We have to clean up that bathroom. We have to get that smell out of here."

"Where's the cat?" he asked. "Have you seen that goddamn cat this morning?"

Two hours later we were dressed and standing by the door. We had made up the bed, packed my bags, mopped the bathroom floor a dozen times, thrown the stained towels in the outdoor shed, emptied the wastebaskets, and fed the cat. We were very quiet as we did these things. Even I could not think of anything to say in the face of this enigma. One minute she was standing in the hallway telling us goodbye, the next minute we were making love in her bed. A moment later I had spilled her douche stuff all over the bathroom floor. I had stuck the nozzle of her douche bag up in my body at the moment of her death perhaps. Maybe she knew what we were doing and it killed her. No, she wouldn't care. She just died to keep from being lonely. And I was going to be lonely too when Malcolm left. This weekend would be over and I would be alone again. Not the whole Chi Omega sorority or my momma or daddy or brothers or Charles William or anyone at all would do now. Only one touch could save me. This tall cold boy whose body had entered mine. This boy I had to have.

"Malcolm." I looked up at him. I had been putting water in the bowl for the cat. "I have to be where you are. I'm coming here this summer and go to Emory. I really am. Say you want me to. Say you want me here."

"I want you here. I said I did."

"Say it again. I have to hear it every fifteen minutes. I'm scared of death, Malcolm. When someone dies, it's like it happens to me. I've been scared of it all my life. It's too horrible. How can people disappear? We were talking to her. She could have died while we were in her bed making love. Think of that." I moved near to him. I touched his sleeve.

"Let's wait outside for them," he said. "I think we ought to wait outside."

"I feel like we've been in this house a month. Oh, Malcolm." I put my arms around him. Tried to pull his body into mine.

"Not now. Don't mess up my shirt. We have to go to the funeral home. We have to go see about the body."

"I'm going too?"

"You don't have to go. You can stay here. My cousins will be here."

"I'll go with you. I want to help you. I want to do anything I can." I touched his arm again, ran my hand up and down his sleeve. He looked down at me, a strange puzzled look, a look I would never penetrate or understand. All the years I would sleep with him and breed with him and eat and drink and fight with him were yet to come. All the painful days and nights when we would struggle to grow up beside each other, all the cigarettes and whiskey and feigned gaiety and feigned remorse and jealousy and passion would not teach me who he was, would not tell me what he was thinking or what he dreamed or feared. I would never know this man.

"Let's go outside," he said. "They ought to be here any minute."

They drove up in a blue Ford. His mother, Rose, was riding shot-gun, her hands clutching her purse. The worries of the world were always on her head and now she had a full-blown tragedy. Behind the wheel Malcolm's father held down his corner of western civilization. He was the oldest son of an old Georgia family and in true aristocratic fashion he had lost the plantation in the Depression. It was the assailing metaphor of Mrs. Martin's life. Mr. Martin didn't care. He had rented an empty mansion on the main street of the little town of Martinsville and he liked the rented one as much as the one he left behind. He got a job in the hardware store and became adept at helping his fellow citizens repair screen doors and small appliances and choose shutters or paint for their houses. Every morning he put on a white shirt and a bow tie and left his rented mansion and walked down to the store. At noon he walked back home and Mrs. Martin fed him vegetables and cornbread and tea. Then he walked back to the store and worked all afternoon. On weekends he and Mrs. Martin drove to other small towns to visit people they had gone to school with or their wealthier relatives in Monroe and Madison and Griffin and Forsythe. Some Sundays they drove out to Martinsrest and sat in the car, looking at the lost plantation. Wealthy Yankees had turned it into a showplace. Mrs. Martin began to believe it had always been that way, but Mr. Martin remembered the leaking roof and rotting timbers and how hard he had had to work when he had owned it. "This is where you were born," Mrs. Martin would say to little Malcolm, when he was a child. "By rights this should be yours. Your great-grandfather built it."

"It was in disrepair," Mr. Martin would add. "It was a great deal of trouble to keep up."

They got out of the car. Mr. Martin smiled at me and took my hands. "My dear, we are so concerned about the shock to you. We want you to call your parents."

"A terrible thing happened," I answered. "There was a black widow spider in the bathroom and I tried to kill it with some medicine and I broke the bottle. The smell is everywhere. Some medicine Aunt Gaye had."

He had my hands in his. "That's not important. Don't worry about that now. Are you all right?"

"We'll get a maid over here," Mrs. Martin put in. "Malcolm's cousin Minx is coming. I'll have her bring a maid." She turned to Malcolm. "Oh, son, they're bringing her body up this morning. We need to go to the funeral home. Oh son." She tried to put her arms around him. She clasped his waist, but he didn't hug her back. His arms stayed at his sides. The impenetrable expression did not leave his face.

"Let's go in," Mr. Martin said. "Let's go inside." We walked into the house. I could smell the Betadine from the front hall. The smell was everywhere.

"Can you smell it?" I asked. "I'm so embarrassed. I'm sorry I broke the bottle."

"Don't worry about anything," Mr. Martin answered. "You're a fine brave girl. A fine brave girl."

"I have to stay another day," I told my mother, when I got her on the phone. "I've already called the college. They said I could stay. I have to stay and help them, Mother. His aunt died in her sleep. She was this gorgeous woman. They're really nice people, Mother. Wait a minute. They want to talk to you." I put Mr. Martin on the phone and he introduced himself and they talked awhile. Then Mrs. Martin took the phone from him. The doorbell was ringing. It was Malcolm's first cousin, Henry, and his wife, Minx. Henry and Minx were very chic, very popular young Atlantans who were dedicated to reliving the lives of F. Scott and Zelda Fitzgerald. They came sweeping in carrying flowers and wiping tears with ironed handkerchiefs and immediately took me to their bosom. "We heard all about you," they said. "We heard you had a column in a newspaper when you were only a child."

"It's true," I said. "I am a prodigy, I guess you'd call it."

"This is terrible," Minx said. "This is the worst tragedy I've ever seen. Henry's mother just died last year. There are only two sisters left, out of five. Malcolm's mother and Aunt Lily in Monroe. Imagine that. Oh, it's steeped in tragedy."

"We're going to the funeral home with you," Henry said. "We came to see the body."

"What is that smell?" Minx asked. "What is that terrible smell?"

The day passed as if in a dream. We drank sherry and Mrs. Martin cried. We stood in the dining room and talked about the paintings. We went to see the body. We talked about what the body should wear. We decided on a pale blue suit. We dug it out of the crowded closet. The smell of Betadine was everywhere.

Later, Malcolm and I went off with Minx and Henry to their apartment in Buckhead. Henry put on a velvet smoking jacket and mixed martinis and we drank them. Malcolm fucked me in the guest room with his cousins in the next room and I let him. We drank more martinis. We cried and listened to phonograph records and I told Minx and Henry the story of my life. We went back over to Aunt Gaye's. We smoked and smoked and smoked. We cried and talked and touched each other's arms. We were engaged in timeless ritual. We were burying our dead.

About twelve Malcolm took me back to Minx and Henry's to spend the night. He left me at the door. For the first time I realized the inconvenience of not being married. Here I was, with a dead body in my brain, and I was going to have to sleep alone in a dark room. "You aren't going, are you?" I asked. "You aren't going to leave me?"

"I have to go back over there," he answered. "I have to spend the night with them."

"With your momma and daddy?"

"I have to. I told them I'd come back. I'll see you in the morning." He was standing in the door. He was leaving.

"Jesus Christ. I can't believe you're going to leave me here."

"I have to. They wouldn't like it. I'll see you in the morning."

"Okay. Go on. Who cares? Who gives a damn?" I walked away and he didn't move to follow me.

"I'm sorry," he said. "I'm sorry I can't stay."

"It doesn't matter. Go on and leave. Get out of here." I walked across the room and turned and looked at him. He shook his head and left me there. I went into the bedroom and tore off my clothes and got into the bed and rolled up in a ball. Who gives a damn, I told myself to lull myself to sleep. He's not even very cute. I don't really even like him.

The funeral was the following morning. Malcolm came over at nine and we drove to the funeral home with Minx and Henry. "The story in the papers made it sound like she'd been in bed with him," Minx said. "Has Miss Rose seen it yet?"

"If she did she didn't talk about it. All she's been doing all morning is crying." Malcolm paused. "She's been crying all her life," he added and turned and looked out the window of the car. It was an amazing confession from him, the only time I ever heard him criticize his parents. "She cried the whole time my brothers were in Europe. Then she cried when they came home."

"They're jittery people, those Tucker women," Minx began, then changed her mind. "I mean, they're very sensitive people, extremely sensitive and bright. They're lovely women. Henry's mother was an angel. I adored her."

"They're jittery." Henry laughed out loud and laid his hand on Minx's leg. "My mother was a nervous wreck."

"I wonder if Aunt Gaye was in bed with him," Minx said. "I'd like to think she had some happiness before she died. She was a slave to her husband. He bossed her around like a slave."

"Don't talk about it." Malcolm had recovered his demeanor. "What difference does it make? She's dead. Let's talk about something else."

"What's his name? What is this man's name that she was with?" Minx was pressing it. She had had two glasses of sherry with breakfast and she was on.

"His name is Tom. I don't think we should talk about it anymore." Malcolm was getting mad. He moved away from me.

"Oh, God. Like in *Gatsby*. Wouldn't you know it, Henry."

"Fitzgerald," I said. "You know Scott Fitzgerald."

"We worship him," in unison.

"Oh, I do too. I worship him."

"Have you read 'A Diamond As Big As the Ritz'? It's Henry's favorite story."

"No. What's it about? Tell me about it."

"It's about this man who has a diamond as big as the Ritz-Carlton Hotel and he builds a castle on top of it and mounts anti-aircraft guns on the roof so he can shoot down anyone who tries to take it. It's this fantastic story."

I leaned up into the front seat. Minx and Henry and I began to all talk at once, about Scott Fitzgerald, Dorothy Parker, the Algonquin Round Table, going to New York, going to live in Paris. We lit cigarettes. Smoke filled the car. We drove and talked. We pulled into the driveway of the funeral home and got out of the car, still smoking.

Mr. Tom Day was waiting on the steps. We introduced Minx and Henry. Then Mr. Martin appeared and took Tom's arm and Mrs. Martin began to cry again and we went inside. A man in a dark suit greeted us and took us to a waiting room with brocade chairs in a line against a wall. The smell of gladiolus was everywhere. Huge sprays of pink and yellow glads were on every table. "The hairdresser is almost finished," the undertaker said. "I hope it suits you. We did all we could. We're so sorry for your sadness. So sorry for all this." He took Mrs. Martin's arm and led us into the chapel. Soft organ music was playing. A stained-glass window shone colored light down upon an empty platform. Two men in suits came out rolling a casket and lifted it and sat it on the platform. They raised the lid. One of the men reached inside and adjusted Aunt Gaye's blouse. They stepped back. They bowed their heads. The music rose. "I come to the garden alone, while the dew is still on the roses. . . ." The undertaker motioned to Mrs. Martin and she left her seat and walked up to the coffin. Mr. Martin came next, then Tom, then Malcolm and I, then Minx and Henry. We stood in a circle around the coffin. Mr. and Mrs. Martin and Tom had the head. Minx and Henry, the midsection, Malcolm and I, the feet. The body was wearing the blue suit. There was a corsage of orchids pinned to the lapel. I tried to look at Malcolm, but he would not return my look.

"I hope that suit's all right," Mrs. Martin began. "She was so fastidious. She never had a hair out of place. Oh, my baby sister. Oh, I'm losing my little Gaye." Mr. Martin put his arm around her and led her to a pew. The rest of us continued to stare at the body. Aunt Gaye's beautiful cold face commanded the room. Her lovely high cheekbones, her ice-cold mouth, her forever-lidded eyes.

"Dust into dust," Henry began.

"Into the grave, the lovely, the gentle, the brave," quoted Minx from an elegy she was composing. We all started crying at that. Minx started it and I joined in. Even Malcolm had a few stingy little tears falling down his cheeks. Henry took out a handkerchief and began to weep into it. Tom burst into a paroxysm of grief. A pair of undertakers appeared and led us back to the parlor.

After the funeral we had lunch at a cafeteria in Buckhead. Then we went back to Aunt Gaye's apartment and I collected my suitcases and Mrs. Martin made me a little supper of peanut butter sandwiches and carrot sticks and a boiled egg. She packed it in a tiny hatbox she found on a shelf. A very small hatbox that must have contained an elf's hat or a veil for church. All the way to Tuscaloosa from Atlanta, as the DC-8 bumped up and down through the clouds, I would look at the little box beside me and shudder, thinking of the crowded bedroom and the brooding presence of all those clothes. Occasionally I thought of what Malcolm and I had done on the bed, of the deep cavernous adventure. "Do it harder," he kept saying. "Think about it. Try." Where had he learned how to do it? I wondered. How did he know how to tell me what to do?

Once I slept for a while and when I woke, sweating and surprised, jolting up and down with the plane, I thought perhaps I had been doing it in my sleep. "Do you love me?" I had asked him at the airport. "Are you sure you love me?"

"Sure. Sure I do."

"When can I see you again?"

"I don't know. I don't know what's going to happen." We

were standing with our backs against the rickety uprights that supported the canvas roof of the airport walkway. Minx and Henry were a few feet away, talking to the ticket agent.

"I'm coming to Emory to summer school," I said. "I really mean it."

"I'll be here." He pulled my body into his. *Fire,* a black singer would later call it, and I would know what she meant. This was love, wasn't it? Surely this was love.

"I hope we'll see you again soon," Minx said, coming to stand beside me. "The next time you're in Atlanta, come and stay with us. You bring her to us, Malcolm. And make it soon. Don't let this darling girl get away from you."

"I won't." He smiled a dazzling happy smile. Unless he was drinking, he was stingy with smiles. I decided he was relieved that I was leaving.

"Come on," Henry said. "He wants your ticket now." I kissed them all goodbye and walked out onto the runway. When I was almost to the plane, I turned and waved to them again. "Goodbye," I called. "Goodbye again. I'm going to miss you."

"Come back to us," Minx called out. She jumped up and down and waved her hands like a signal man on an aircraft carrier.

"Come back immediately," Henry screamed. "Don't stay away."

Malcolm stood with his hands in his pockets. He didn't even wave. God, I love him, I told myself, and started up the stairs into the cockpit. God, I've never loved anybody that much in all my life. God, I hope he loves me. God, I hope to God I'm good enough for him.

This ice-cold Georgia aristocrat with his fierce libido. I know something now no twenty-year-old girl could have known. He could feel emotion but he couldn't let it show. Actions speak louder than words, a wiser, older lover would one day tell me and I would remember Malcolm and wish I had known that then.

This passion and that dead body in that coffin ended any debate I may have had about education or art or going to the big world. I wanted only one thing now. To be rolled up in Malcolm's arms. Whatever light I followed took me straight to where the only defeat of death we know of lies.

"When I'm with him I think I will never die," I told Charles William when I got him on the phone to tell him about the weekend. "When he's with me I forget the bad things. If he touches me I'm not afraid. It's all I think about. I don't think of anything but him."

"Then go be with him this summer. You can talk them into it. Ariane is scared to death of you."

"Do you think he loves me?"

"He had a fight over that teddy bear. You didn't know that? He didn't tell you? Someone said something about that bear and he almost killed them."

"You should have seen his aunt lying there dead. I can't forget it. That's where we're going, Charles William. Sooner or later we will be there too."

"But not this summer, Dee. This summer I'll be at Taliesin and you'll be in Atlanta. We'll be talking and breathing and the earth will be in orbit if we're lucky."

"Oh, God, Charles William. I love you so much. Why can't I love someone like you?"

"We love each other, Dee. It's just a different kind of love."

"I have to be with him. I don't care what I have to do."

"Then go to Atlanta. Make them let you go."

Chapter
15

So I went to Atlanta for the summer. I enrolled in summer school at Emory University and moved into a dorm overlooking the medical school. It had been reasonably tricky talking my parents into the plan but I persevered and they were so caught up in their new life in Dunleith with their seven hundred admiring friends coming over to get drunk on the porch every night that they weren't as wary as they had been in the small world of Franklin, Kentucky. Also, they were sick of my sarcasm and tired of my refusal to be polite to their endless stream of visitors. They were probably relieved to think I would be somewhere in summer school. They could say to their relatives, Oh, yes, Rhoda's in summer school at Emory. She's such a bookworm, yes, she's a mess but what can we do. A mess, that's the word my north Alabama relatives used to describe me. They had had other messes to contend with, my fox-hunting grandfather being one and Tallulah Bankhead another, but in my generation I was the main mess. So I got to do what I wanted that summer, while my daddy made money and my momma spent it and my brother Dudley and his wife, Annie, tried to make a marriage out of a real mess and my little brothers threw basketballs through the hoop and shot at each other with B-B guns and chased goats through the woods at Finley Island and the porch filled up at night with whiskey drinkers. When I read the *Odyssey* I thought of Dunleith. How the suitors filled our porches and drank our wine and ate our meat.

I had hardly been in Atlanta a week when I started wanting to get married. It was too hard to do it if we weren't married. It was impossible to do it in the car. It just wasn't big enough. And it was hard to do it in Malcolm's room in the KA house because people kept slamming in and out the front door and scaring me to death and because half the time we had to sneak out the kitchen door when we got through. Don't get me wrong. Doing it was worth it. Doing it was divine. The more we did it, the more I wanted to do it and the more he wanted to do it. All we wanted to do was do it. It was what we had in common and it was plenty.

"Don't you want to get married?" I asked him finally. We were parked outside the Echo Hot Dog Stand, The World's Largest Drive-In. The place was a great favorite with Tech boys and their dates. On any given night we would see two or three couples we knew. Couples coupling in their cars, couples eating hot dogs and drinking Cokes, couples in varying stages of emotional excitement and disarray. I'll say one thing for Malcolm and me, we were up to the task. We didn't have enough guilt or depression between us to fill an ashtray. "Everyone's running away," I added, taking a Parliament out of a box and lighting it with the car lighter. "We wouldn't have to tell anyone. We could keep it a secret."

"I don't know."

"Why not? You love me, don't you? Then we could rent a little apartment and have a place to do it. God, it's driving me crazy not to have anywhere to do it."

"Where would we go?"

"To South Carolina, where Avery and Mary Adair ran away. Ask Avery where they went."

"They told their folks last week. They just moved into the married dorm."

"We don't have to tell anyone. I've got enough money to get us an apartment. Let's do it. Please let's do it." I moved over to his side of the seat, put my hand on his leg, moved my hand up and down his thigh. "Oh, please, Malcolm. I want to have a place to live with you. I want it so much."

"I don't know. I guess so. I guess we could. When do you want to go?" He put his hot dog down on the dashboard and turned around to me. My hand was still on his leg. Now there wasn't any hot dog or steering wheel or drive-in or car. There was only desire. I had to get some bonding energy to keep from thinking I was going to die and he had to get some pussy to keep from being in pain, so there we were, in love in Georgia, being bounced around like the electrons and protons of which we are in all probability composed.

"Next weekend. On Saturday. We could go on Friday and get married and spend the weekend. Oh, let's do it. Say we can."

"All right. If you really want to. If that's really what you want to do." He honked the horn for the waiter to come and take the tray from the window of the car. He put the half-eaten hot dog on the tray.

"I'll have to get a wedding ring," I said. "I guess we can go buy one tomorrow."

"I guess we can."

"Let's go to Stone Mountain," I added. "Let's go do it on a blanket on the ground."

Four days later, on Thursday morning, I cut all my classes and drove down to Rich's department store and went shopping. I bought a white piqué dress with pearl buttons down the front and a white satin slip and a long white negligee and a gown. I bought some white satin slippers with fuzzy white balls on the toes. I bought a book on how to have sexual intercourse. I bought a gray and white striped sundress with a jacket and some red Capezio sandals and a tube of contraceptive jelly. I went downstairs to the coffee shop and bought two doughnuts and a cup of coffee and ate the sugar off the first doughnut while I read the book. It looked as though we had been doing it right. But the stuff about getting pregnant sounded bad. I polished off the doughnut and thought it over. The redheaded black girl behind the counter came over and stood beside me looking at the cover of the book. "Is that any good?'' she asked. I was the only customer in the shop so she had time to chat.

"I guess so. Except about the contraceptives. It keeps saying something works fifty percent of the time or ninety percent of the time. But it doesn't say which one is best.''

"What you been doing?''

"Nothing. I'm getting married tomorrow.'' I looked around to make sure no one had come in. "We're running away. My boyfriend and I. We're going to Walhalla, South Carolina. So I thought maybe I should be finding out what to do.''

"Better late than never, I suppose. You better get you some rubbers and start to pray. Them babies have a way of finding their way into the world.''

"Have you got any?''

"I got three. Three more than I got any use for but I love them. Don't be doing any of that rhythm business. That doesn't work. Nothing works but rubbers and they don't work too good. You ought to get you a pessary or a diaphragm.''

"There's a part in here about them. I guess I could go to a doctor after I get married and get one, couldn't I?''

"Honey, you don't have to be married to get one. They give them to anybody.'' She reached behind herself and got the pot of coffee and refilled my cup. "When's the wedding going to be?''

"We're going to drive up tomorrow and get married Saturday. You have to get the license, then you have to wait twenty-four hours before you can get married. Some friends of ours did it. So we know where to go.''

"Well, I wish you luck. What you got in all them packages?''

"A wedding dress and a trousseau. I thought I ought to have a trousseau.''

"Honey, I sure am glad you came in today. I'll be thinking about you tomorrow and I'll be thinking about you on Saturday. What time you think you'll be getting married?''

"About noon I guess. High noon.'' I giggled. "Shoot out in Carolina.'' The waitress laughed with me. We kept on laughing harder and harder and she filled my cup one more time and I gobbled down the second doughnut and drank the coffee while I laughed.

Chapter

16

A boy and girl walking into a gray stone building to get married. It is very early in the morning. He is wearing a pair of chinos. She is wearing a long white dress with tiny pearl buttons down the front. They are holding hands. Her hand is beautiful and plump and the color of apricots. His hand is large and bony and covered with fine brown hair. They look like brother and sister. Neither of them has slept in days.

"What if we can't get it?"

"We'll get it."

"Did you bring the blood tests?"

"I told you I did."

"Oh, Malcolm. I can't believe it. I can't believe we're doing it."

"I bet they aren't open."

"Yes they are. People are going in." A man wearing suspenders walked up the steps and disappeared into the heavy polished doors. Walhalla, South Carolina, June 25, 1956. Malcolm and I are going to get married.

The night before we had made love all night in a small motel room on a lumpy bed. The motel was on a rise of land surrounded by pine trees. All night the wind sang in the trees and pine needles fell on the asphalt roof above our heads. All night long we moved our hands up and down each other's bodies and told each other secrets and said a hundred times, Are you awake, are you still awake, are you asleep yet? I love, love, love you, I said a hundred times. I love you too, he answered. Get on top of me. Stay like that. Do that some more. Don't move until I tell you to.

So it went until the sun rose above the hills and we slept awhile. At eight o'clock I woke up and looked at my watch. "Get up," I said. "It's eight o'clock. Let's get up and go get married."

"Let's sleep some more. Come get back in bed."

"No. I want to do it now. I'm afraid you won't marry me. I have to do it now."

"Oh, Rhoda."

"I can't help it. It's how I am. Come on, get up, I want to be the first person married today. I want to be the first person in the world to get married on this Saturday."

"Let's sleep a little longer."

"No, I can't wait. Please get up. Please let's do it now." I picked up a pair of cotton underpants from the floor and put them on. I picked up a white satin slip and pulled it over my head. He reached out and pulled me into the bed and climbed on top of me. "Move," he said. "See if you can move."

"I want to have ten sons who look like you. Ten tall sons to carry my coffin to the grave."

"Why do you always talk about dying?" He got up and stood beside the bed. "You're only twenty years old."

"I can't help it. That's how I think."

"Don't get your feelings hurt. I'm getting dressed. Come on, see if you still have the license. You didn't lose it, did you?"

"No, it's right here. I have it here." I pulled the license out of my pocketbook and read it. He came and stood beside me. We moved into each other's arms. Electromagnetism, Aphrodite, sunspots, whatever explains such things.

"Do you want to get breakfast first?"

"No. I want to be the first person married today in South Carolina or in the world."

"Okay, get dressed. Let's go."

* * *

The sheriff of Milan County had bought a pickup truck and a motorboat with the money he had made performing marriages on weekends, he later told us. Ten dollars here, five dollars there. It added up.

"Come on in," he said. "Have a seat while I round up the bailiff. He likes to be my witness. Well, you got a pretty day for it. I'll say that. How old are you?"

"I'm twenty," I said. "He'll be twenty next month."

"Marrying an older woman. You both from Atlanta?"

"We go to school there." Malcolm shook hands solemnly with the sheriff and handed him the license.

"That will be twenty-five dollars," the sheriff said and Malcolm got out the money and handed it to him.

"We could let Denise witness it, if we can't find Bobby. There he is. Come on in, Robert. They're chomping at the bit to say the vows. Come on in. Stand by her, boy, that's the way. Take her hand. You got the ring?"

"I've got it," I said and produced it from my pocket and gave it to Malcolm. I had been wearing it off and on for days.

"Let's go then," the preacher said. "Dearly Beloved, we are gathered here in the presence of this company, to join together this man and this woman in Holy Matrimony, which is an honorable estate, instituted of God and like unto the union between the church and our maker. Therefore, let no one enter into it lightly, but reverently, soberly and in the sight of God. . . ." I looked at the book he was holding, at the light coming in the dusty window, at the suspenders, the chairs, my shoes. I did not believe I was worthy of such a moment. I could not bear such happiness.

An hour later we were back at the motel packing to leave. We had stopped and eaten breakfast at a small café and endured the stares of the patrons. Every Saturday at least two or three couples found their way to Walhalla to get married. We're turning into the runaway capital of the world, the citizens must have told themselves. Old Bud Halbritton's getting rich marrying kids from Atlanta. We ought to build a new motel, now that Walhalla's finally on the map.

* * *

I didn't have to wait long for the reaction to set in. We had hardly driven fifty miles back toward Atlanta before we had an argument. God knows what it was about. Maybe I touched his leg and he told me not to. Maybe he started desiring me and it embarrassed him. Maybe he was sorry he had done it and I picked that up. I am deeply intuitive about other people's reactions and there was plenty to react to that day. My mania was rising to a fever pitch. I am married, I kept saying to myself. Now I will never be alone, never be afraid, never be sad again. Isn't that true? It must be true. If getting married doesn't work, nothing will. If getting married doesn't work, I'll never be happy. Never, never, never, never, never.

"What will we do tonight?" I said finally. We were leaving the mountains and turning onto the four-lane highway. "We could go get some Italian food and celebrate. I'd really like to drink some Chianti."

"I'm going back to the house and study," he said. "I've got classes all day on Monday."

"You're going to the house? You're going to leave me?"

"We've been gone two days. . . . I'm taking ten hours, Rhoda. I have to do some work."

"We could go up to Stone Mountain and have a picnic. You can't just take me home."

"I have to take you home. I'll be up studying all night as it is."

"Okay. Never mind. It's okay. Take me back to Emory then. What difference does it make." I stared out the window at the ugly midsummer road. I looked down at my ugly wedding ring. I was married. Well, I wasn't giving up. I would keep on trying. I wanted to be happy so much I would do anything, even keep on looking out the window, even keep from crying.

Chapter
17

My mother went crazy when she found out. She went upstairs and shut the door to her room and wouldn't talk to anybody. "I can't believe it," she kept saying later. "I can't believe you'd do this to me."

"I had to do it. I wanted to marry him. I didn't have time to talk to you. I was too busy talking him into it."

"Calm down, Ariane," my father said. "We'll fix it. We'll send them to school. Come on, Sister, tell us how to call his parents. We have to call his parents."

"He's telling them right now," I said. "We said we'd both tell you at ten this morning. Here's the number." I handed my father a piece of paper with Malcolm's parents' phone number on it. My father dialed the phone and began to talk. In five minutes he and Malcolm's mother had found a common ancestor on my paternal grandmother's side and a meeting had been arranged in Atlanta. "Oh, God in heaven," my mother sobbed, coming back into the room with her tear-stained face. "Oh, Dudley, how did we ever have this child?"

"Ariane, calm down. She fell in love with this kid and she married him. He's from good people. My grandmother's sister married a Percy Martin from Monroe, Georgia. It's some of this boy's people. Now stop that goddamn crying. Come on, Sister, you come with me.'' He winked at me. Winked and smiled the old smile that meant, Don't pay any attention to her. She's too weak and silly to be involved in the real work of the world, making money, being headstrong and passionate, winning, running away to marry whoever you damn well please.

"It's just like Little Dudley," Momma cried. "First Little Dudley and now her. I think you do this, Dudley. I think you put them up to this."

On Saturday we flew to Atlanta and got into a taxi and went to a hotel and sat around the room waiting for Malcolm to arrive with his parents. The hotel had given us a suite with a balcony overlooking a parking lot and my mother had set up a table so we could have lunch when they arrived.

"Just try to keep your mouth shut, Sister," my father said. "Just let me do the talking."

"It's my marriage, Daddy. It's my husband that I married who's coming here."

"Well, we have to get things arranged. We have to get this sorted out and decide where you're going to live."

"We're going to live in Atlanta and I'm going to get a job and support us. That's what everybody does."

"You can't support anybody," my mother began. "You can't quit school . . ."

"Shut up, Ariane," my father said. "Just let me handle this."

Finally the phone rang. It was the Martins. They were in the lobby. "Come on up," my father said. "Come on up. Ariane's got lunch waiting." He hung up. "Call down there and have them bring the food," he said. "Tell them to hurry up." Then Malcolm and his mother and father came in the door and Daddy fixed drinks and everyone sat around and drank their drinks and Daddy told them what was going to happen.

"He can go to school all year and I'll get them a place to live and give them an allowance and when summer comes they can come and stay with us and he can work for me." He refilled the drinks. He charmed Miss Rose. He charmed Mr. Percy. Mother charmed Malcolm, then she charmed Mr. Percy, then she charmed Miss Rose. I got up and went to stand in the bedroom. They had done it again. They had taken my life away from me.

"Rhoda." Malcolm had followed me into the room. I turned around and pulled him to a corner behind the door. I put my mouth on his mouth and began to touch his dick. If they stole my life, they could not steal this. This was mine. This belonged to me. I had found him and I had taken him and he was mine. "I want to fuck you so much I'm going crazy," I said. "We have to get out of here. We have to go somewhere and do it."

"All right. There's no one at the house. It's vacation. We can go there, I think. Do you want to go and do it at the house?" He put his hand on top of mine. I had him. I had made him love me, want me, need me. It was okay. I wouldn't be alone anymore. I had a husband and he wanted to do it with me.

"I have the car keys," he said. "We can take our car."

"Good. Yes. Let's go."

We walked together out into the living room where our four parents sat on four chairs talking. Waiters were putting food on the table. Miss Rose still had her pocketbook in her hands. Mr. Percy had started smoking. Mother was dealing out the charm and Daddy had put on his patrician posture. They all knew what they were doing and I, Rhoda Katherine Manning Martin, knew what I was going to do. "We're leaving," I said. "We want to be alone. We're going over to the campus to the KA house. You talk all you want to. We're leaving."

"Lunch is ready," Mother said. Horror overwhelmed her, horror lined her brow. I was leaving the room with a man. I was going off and do it. Right there with her watching and Daddy not doing a thing to stop me and two strangers for witnesses and the waiters laying silver beside the napkins. All the years she had bathed me four times a day and shuddered at the slightest hint of my sexuality and covered me up with clothes and underpants and stockings and brassieres and girdles were disappearing before her eyes. "Don't you want to eat your lunch?"

"Let them go, Ariane," Daddy said. "They're young. They want to be alone."

"We'll be back pretty soon," Malcolm began, but I grabbed him by the sleeve and pulled him out the door. We went down the hall to the elevator and pressed the button a dozen times and when it came we got aboard and began to kiss as hard as we could kiss. When the elevator doors opened in the lobby we were still kissing and the desk clerk and a couple checking in got a whiff of twenty-year-old, not-fucked-up-yet desire and they smiled as though the sun had just come out after a rain. We found the car and drove out to the deserted Tech campus and went into the empty KA house and broke into the manager's room and moved a dresser against the door and then we did it. We did it with him on top and with me on top and standing up and then we did it some more on our sides and then lying down some more. That was the day we discovered doing it on a chair. He would sit on the chair with his fabulous desire which was endless and terrible and painful and impossible to satisfy or conquer. He could not conquer it and I could not end or satisfy it. Then I would sit across his legs and we would laugh and talk while we drove each other crazier and crazier. We were so sheltered we did not even know what to say but we made things up. Anything we said seemed evil and sinful and made us crazier. That feels so good. Don't do that. I can't stand it. It hurts. I especially loved to say it hurts, although it didn't hurt at all. Nothing hurt, we were tree and roots and earth and bird and song and music and water and divine young bodies in love with ourselves and maybe even each other. Oh, God, that's so good. Over there. Over here, do it some more, make it last, make it last forever. Oh, yes, yes, yes, yes, yes. It may have been that day that I finally learned to come. It had happened before once or twice, but without warning. Now I began to understand that I could make it happen. Most wonderful of all, *that I could think it up.*

"Will you go home with us?" I asked. "Will you go back to Dunleith and stay with me until school starts?"

"I don't know if I can. You stay with us. Go home with me. You've never even seen Martinsville. You've never seen where I live."

"You haven't seen where I live either. I don't have any clothes to go with you."

"I just have the things I'm wearing."

"I want you to go with me. I can't leave you. All I do is leave you. All you do is go away." I was starting to cry. I was crying so hard I could hardly talk. It was always the same thing. He always went away. He was always leaving. It was all so sad. All he did was leave. It was never long enough. The days went by too fast, the moments, hours, minutes.

"We'll be together all the time as soon as we find a place to live," he said. "We'll see each other every night. We're married, Rhoda. What else do you want?"

"I don't know. I don't know what I want. Why is it so terrible? Why is everything so hard?"

We got back to the hotel at five o'clock. We had left our parents without a car for five hours. We hadn't even called to tell them where we were. But they weren't mad at us. They had drunk a fifth of scotch whiskey and told each other their genealogies and decided they were good enough for each other and moved on to the problem of where we would live and how much they hoped I wasn't going to get pregnant. "Oh, Rhoda," Miss Rose said. "We love Ariane and Dudley so much." "Oh, Malcolm," my mother said. "We love Rose and Percy like they were our own. Now you're our very own, our own little son-in-law." "And Rhoda's my daughter," Miss Rose added. "Not my daughter-in-law, but my very own daughter. The daughter I dreamed of. The one I never had."

"Can Malcolm sleep here with me?" I asked. "Can he spend the night?"

"Of course he can," my father decreed.

"How will he get home?" Mr. Percy put in.

"You all spend the night," Daddy said. "Tomorrow we'll drive down and see this town your ancestors built. I want you to come to Aberdeen and see our town, Miss Rose. You'll have to come in the fall when we have our Aberdeen stew parties. Or come up to the field trials. That's the ticket. You need to see the field trials my daddy started."

"We can't stay," Miss Rose began. "We didn't bring our things." But Momma and Daddy persisted and Momma lent Rose

a nightgown and Daddy lent Mr. Percy a razor and they called down
and got another room and we all had dinner in a Chinese restaurant
and then Malcolm and I went to bed and did it until we fell asleep.
Outside in the living room, Daddy and Miss Rose were at the
genealogy again. They were back to the seventeenth century when
the Mannings came across the North Sea to Scotland from Norway
and when the Martins and Barretts were building their empire in
the south of England. Mr. Percy had gone to sleep in a chair and
Mother was in the bedroom creaming her face.

Oh, the dear lost years when we were twenty. We woke up about
three and did it a couple of times and then we didn't do it any more
until dawn.

After breakfast we drove the sixty miles to Martinsville and took a
tour of the antebellum homes the Martins' ancestors had built.
Then Rose and Percy had an impromptu cocktail party. The town's
doctors and lawyers and the mayor and the newspaper editor and
several widowed cousins and a bachelor uncle came over and talked
to Mother and Daddy about genealogy and Malcolm and I got drunk
on Drambuie and walked around town in the dark and then sneaked
back in and went upstairs and did it while the guests sat on the
porch smoking and drinking bourbon and talking about the dances
they used to have and how Miss Rose was the most popular girl in
Georgia.

"Swear you'll go home with me tomorrow," I said. I was
holding on to his back. "Swear you'll go. I can't leave you. How can
I keep on leaving you?"

"I don't know," he said.

"We have to find an apartment. You have to go back to Atlanta
with me and find us a place to live."

The next morning Malcolm and Mother and Daddy and I drove
back to Atlanta and rented a garage apartment and then the four of
us got on a Southern Airlines prop plane and flew back home to
Dunleith. As soon as we got home, I took Malcolm up to my
bedroom and lay down with him on my very own little cherry

four-poster bed. "We will sleep in this bed forever," I said. "We will always sleep in this bed."

"It's not very big," he said. "It's too high off the floor."

"We'll take it with us to Atlanta and put it in our apartment. I want us to always sleep in this bed."

"It won't fit in that bedroom. We need to get a springs and mattress and put them on the floor."

Chapter
18

My maternal birth control lecture took place in a blue Oldsmobile in front of Momma's brown mansion on a brilliant sunny afternoon. Momma and Aunt Celeste were in the front seat of the car. I was in the backseat. Across the street Aunt Celeste's daughters were playing badminton on her lawn. Even from the car I could see how perfectly their shoes were polished. Aunt Celeste was a perfectionist who could even put my mother to shame. The three of us had been to the beauty parlor to have our hair turned into football helmets. Aunt Celeste's dark hair was sprayed and shining. Mother's platinum blonde hair was backcombed into a beehive. My red hair was cut into a bob that made me look as if I were twelve years old. Our nails were freshly polished. Momma's were Windsor Pink. Aunt Celeste's were Pink On Pink and mine were Fire Engine Red to match my lipstick. I had been married for ten weeks. I was not pregnant yet. This was some sort of miracle of which I was not aware. I was still laboring under the misapprehension that I couldn't get pregnant unless I wanted to.

"Momma," I said, as she turned off the ignition key and rolled down the car windows to let the air conditioning out and the heat of August in. "Momma, I need to do something about birth control. What should I do?"

"I told you to get some rubbers and some Lysol suppositories," she said. "I told you in Atlanta what to do."

"You need to use the suppositories," Aunt Celeste added. "The rubbers don't do any good without them."

"We don't like to use rubbers," I said. I sat back against the backseat, watching Momma's face contort into a terrorized mask. It was torture to make her realize I was doing it in my bedroom with my husband.

"I'll talk about it to you later," she said. "Celeste, let us help you carry in those groceries. Here, I'll open the trunk." She jumped out and hurried around to the back of the car to open the trunk. "You have to use the rubbers," Aunt Celeste said. "Whether he likes it or not. There isn't any other way, Rhoda. It has to be that way."

"Celeste," Momma called. "Come here and show me which bags are yours. Violet, Charlotte, Aimee, come over here and help your mother." Then my teenage cousins came flying across the street in their polished shoes and began to lift the grocery bags from the trunk of the car. Overhead the huge branches of the live oak trees shaded us with their leaves, poured down oxygen and golden pollen upon our hair. The sun shone down between the leaves and spotted the arms of my cousins and made a mosaic of Wheeler Street. I looked toward the house and saw Malcolm coming out the door to look for me. His wide shoulders, his worried smile, his long skinny legs, his great big lips and crew cut and green eyes. He wasn't perfect, he wasn't what I had intended to marry, but he would do. At least I was finally getting to do it and at least I wasn't going to be an old maid.

He left a few days later to get ready for the fall semester. The first of September I moved to Atlanta to join him. I hadn't seen Charles William or Irise all summer. They had been gone to Taliesin West where Charles William had an apprenticeship with the Wright foundation. I had postcards from them and a letter saying they were glad we would all be together in Atlanta in the fall. Malcolm was still in Dunleith when the letter came. "I hope we won't have to see much of them," he said. "I hope we won't be hanging around with them all the time."

"Why not? Why don't you like them?"

"I don't want to talk about it." We were in the yard. My little brothers were shooting basketballs at the hoop over the garage. My brother Dudley's little girl, Ariane, was playing in the sandpile beneath a tree. I reached for Malcolm but he shook me off.

"I don't want to talk about it, Rhoda. Just forget it. But don't think we're going to go around with Charles William all the time when we get to Atlanta, because we aren't."

"Why not?"

"Because he's queer. He tried to do something to me one night. We're married now, Rhoda. We have to settle down." He was turned away from me. When he got mad the veins stood out in bas relief on his forehead. I couldn't bear it when I made him mad. I couldn't bear for him to frown at me. "Okay," I said. "We won't see them. I promise we won't. If you'll stop being mad. If you just stop being mad at me."

"I can't help it, Rhoda. Charles William is too much. He goes too far."

"Okay. You're right. We won't see them. Come here. Let's go up to my room. Please go up there with me." Then he agreed to fuck me and we went up to my room and I used my fabulous imagination to make myself come and gave him credit for it. The bonding energy had kicked in and I was growing more and more in love with this cold unloving Georgia boy. I had to have him love me. This poor little twenty-year-old boy with his burning ambition and terrible fear of failure, with his overbearing mother and his gentle weak father was going to be called upon to love me twenty-four hours a day, morning, night, and noon. If he so much as frowned at me, I was going to have to blame someone, wasn't I? For a while I would blame myself, but sooner or later I was going to figure out how much more pleasant and easier it was to put the blame on him. At first, however, I was going to be good and try to please him.

It was easy when I first got to Atlanta. I was enthralled by our garage apartment and stayed busy trying to "fix it up." I covered lampshades with burlap and painted wastebaskets and shoved

cheap unpainted furniture around from wall to wall trying to find
a satisfactory arrangement. Also, I had gotten a job selling clothes
in the French Room of J. P. Allen's and that used up my days. Every
morning Malcolm dropped me off on his way to school and in the
evenings he picked me up. Charles William called several times but
I was cool to him. Then one day, a bright clear day in early October,
Charles William came downtown and found me.

"What are you doing here?" he asked. "Why are you working
in a store?"

"I'm putting him through school. It's fun. You get to see all
the new clothes come in."

"You aren't going back to school?"

"No. What for? It's boring. I hate to go to school."

"Oh, Dee."

"Oh, Dee, what? Look, do you want to go to lunch? I can leave
in a few minutes. You want to wait for me?"

"Sure. Sure I do." He went over and took a seat on the uphol-
stered sofas where husbands sat while their wives tried on clothes.
I tallied up my morning's sales and turned in my sales pad and then
I collected Charles William and we rode down the elevator and
walked out onto Peachtree Street. It was a beautiful fall day, cool
and clear. Dressed up men and women hurried up and down the
crowded streets. I had meant it when I said I loved to work. I had
never lived in a city. It was wonderful to me to be downtown all day
with city life going on around me. We found a small restaurant on
a side street and went inside and sat down at a table.

"Tell me what's going on," Charles William said. "Are you
happy? Do you like it?" He giggled, trying to establish our old
repartee, but I would not go into it with him. The things Malcolm
had been saying about him frightened me. Still, I could not resist
him. He was so funny, so honest, so intelligent, insightful, imaginative, clever, *so much fun.*

"Oh, Charles William. I've missed you so much."

"He doesn't like me anymore, does he?"

"No. He told me not to see you. He won't let me ask you over."

His face fell. He was quiet for a moment. It was the only secret we ever had between us and it wasn't a secret really. It was just something that stayed unspoken. I loved him too much to talk of it, to take a chance on hurting his feelings.

"You could come see us. We have a marvelous place. It's below Putty's apartment, in the basement. We've made a grotto, with sconces everywhere. It's divine really. You must come and see it. Can't you slip away? Doesn't he ever go anywhere?"

"He's refinishing a cobbler's bench. He does it every night. If he has to study sometimes he stays at school. He takes my car."

"We can come and get you."

"Okay. I'll come over soon. Maybe I'll come tonight if he stays at school." The waiter appeared with our grilled cheese sandwiches. We ate our lunch and Charles William told me stories about people we knew.

"May Garth's here," he said. "She's living with her father and she's working in a bank."

"A bank! My God."

"She said she was only going to take about twenty dollars a day to start with and work up to larger amounts. She tells the greatest stories about it. She's dying to see you. Oh, Dee, we've found this fabulous place to go. A black nightclub down in the section where the wealthy black people live. Passen Blanc, they call them in New Orleans. We've been three times. We saw Stan Getz the other night and they say Coltrane's coming. If he does, do you want to go?"

"A black nightclub? They let you in?"

"Sure. Judge Sheffield's a hero to them. If May Garth's with us they let us right in. They gave us a ringside table at the Getz concert. You should have seen May Garth. She was dancing with the drummer at intermission. He was about a foot shorter than she is. It was hilarious, Dee. God, I wish you'd been there with us."

"I don't know. I don't know if I could go to a black nightclub. I don't think Malcolm would do it. I want to, though. I wish I could."

"Go with us. He doesn't have to go, if he doesn't want to. You don't have your hand sewed to him, do you?"

"I don't know. I might. I can't stand for him to get mad at me."

"Well, I wish you could go sometime. Davie's been asking about you, by the way. He goes with us." He paused, looked down, began to slip his napkin in and out of his fingers, folding it into a fan, then slipping it very very sensuously between his fingers. I took a package of cigarettes out of my purse and lit one. I began to smoke furiously. "I have to get back now," I said. "I really have to get back to the store."

We paid the bill and walked arm in arm back down Peachtree Street toward the store. Malcolm wasn't completely fucked up yet. He still could feel the excitement of the city and it was fun to be downtown with him. But it couldn't compare to being downtown with Charles William. Charles William *really* knew how marvelous the city was. Charles William laughed at everything and hugged my arm into his arm and stopped and peered into store windows and stopped to inspect a pigeon on the sidewalk and added his gaiety to mine in a way that Malcolm never could. Malcolm was too worried to live fully on the sidewalks of a city. Malcolm was too worried to live fully anywhere. He was on his way to power and money and all the things fear swears will end fear. Fear lies, fear always breaks its promises. Fear feeds on fear and on the things we think will end it. Nothing can conquer fear but love. Charles William and I had loved each other from the moment that we met. When my hand was slipped into his arm there was nothing in the world but light and laughter. We walked slower and slower as we neared the store. A radiant world was all about us.

At the revolving doors he took my hands and held them and kissed me on both cheeks as the French do. "Come and see us, Dee. We miss you. I want to show you the designs I did this summer, the photographs of Taliesin. Davie wants to see you and so do Putty and Irise. I'm sorry Malcolm doesn't like us anymore but surely we can still see you."

"I'll come tonight, if he goes to study and I can get the car. I'll come over if I can. I really want to. I'll try." I put my arms around his big soft body and held him close to me. What did it matter if he kissed Davie? Why should anybody care? How could anyone stop loving Charles William? "Oh, Dee," he said. "I love you so much. You're so important to me. There's only friendship in the world, you know. It's the only thing that lasts." We pulled away from each other then and I stood a long time in front of the revolving glass doors watching his fine ample back stroll away. His flat feet splayed out in front of him, his shoulders swayed, his big fine head with its thick wavy light brown hair was held at a bright angle. I thought of the first time I had seen him from the window of my bedroom in the chocolate-colored house. Of how sad I had been that day and how fast he and Irise had worked to salve my pain.

I rode home that evening with Malcolm in the car. He did not speak except to curse other drivers as he moved his shoulders into the seat.

"What's wrong?" I asked. "What's wrong with you?"

"Nothing. Look, are we going to have anything for dinner? I'm starving. Have you got something to cook?"

"I don't know. Stop by the store and get some French bread. We'll make garlic bread and salad. Go to the Piggly-Wiggly in Maywood." We turned off the highway and found the store and Malcolm went in with me and we bought bread and salad things and took them to the counter.

"We're spending too much money," he said. "We can't spend this much money every day."

"Yes, we can. Daddy doesn't want me down here in Atlanta starving. Go get some ice cream. I haven't had any ice cream in a week."

"You go get it if you want it. I'm tired, Rhoda. I've been studying all day when I wasn't in class. I don't want to spend all night in this store." I left him in the checkout lane and went back to the freezer and found some chocolate ice cream. On the way back, I stopped in the liquor department and got a bottle of sherry. I can't stand it, I was thinking. It's terrible. All he does is fuss at me. I can't stand it here. I've been working all day and now I have to cook dinner for him and he still won't love me. He won't even go get ice cream for me. He's the most selfish person I ever met in my life. He never thinks about me. All he thinks about is himself. He thinks I'm his slave.

I walked back to the checkout counter and added the ice cream and sherry to the things in the cart. "Oh, God," he said. "Now you're going to start drinking. It's Tuesday night, Rhoda. We're not going to start drinking on school nights."

"I just want a glass of it. I'm tired too, Malcolm. I'm worn out." And suddenly I was worn out. I had been full of gaiety when I left the store. The excitement of being with Charles William had continued into the afternoon and I had sold three dresses to a pretty woman my mother's age to wear to chaperon a fraternity party in the mountains. Now I was just a married lady arguing at the grocery store with her husband. The salesgirl totaled up our purchases and I wrote a check and then we left and got into the car and drove to our apartment. A skillet from three days before was in the sink. Plates and glasses and silverware from breakfast were piled on top of that. The ashtrays were full of cigarettes. The bed was unmade. Several tubes of contraceptive jelly were lying on the floor. "This place is a goddamn mess," Malcolm said.

"Well, help me clean it up." I opened the bottle of sherry and poured some into a glass. I tied an apron around my waist and began to move things gingerly from the sink to the counter. I was still wearing a wool skirt and sweater I had worn to work that day and I was trying not to get them dirty. Another thing Malcolm and I had started arguing about was the cleaning bill. We both threw everything we wore down on the floor and once a week we picked it all up and took it to the cleaners.

I drank the sherry. Then I began to try to clean the skillet. Three minutes went by. It was six o'clock. "Have you started dinner?" Malcolm asked. "Stop doing that and get the food in the oven."

"Do what?" I turned around and dropped the skillet on the plates in the sink. "What did you say to me?"

"I said I'm starving to death. Get the chicken in the oven before you start on those dishes." I reached behind me and untied the apron. I walked out of the kitchen. I could see the car keys lying on the coffee table. "You know how to do the chicken better than I do. Fix it and put it in the oven and I'll do the rest. I want to go upstairs and take off these clothes. The salesladies said I'd ruin my feet if I wore shoes this high all the time.'' I started up the small narrow stairwell that led to the bedroom. I can escape from anywhere, I told myself. I am Dudley Manning's daughter. No one can make me do anything. No one can conquer me. No one can keep me from getting into my own car and going to see my friends.

"Okay," Malcolm called from the kitchen. "I'll put it in and then I have to study while you do the rest.''

I stood in the narrow stairwell and finished my wine. I sat the glass down on the stairs. Then I walked into the living room and grabbed the keys and ran out the door. I had the ignition on by the time he came out the door behind me. I backed the car around and took off down the driveway at top speed. I turned out onto the street and started in the direction of Putty's apartment building. I was exhilarated and I was terrified. I felt as though I had stepped onto another planet leaving behind *the very air I breathed.* Still, I had to get to Charles William. I had to get somewhere where someone loved me.

I parked the car in Putty's parking lot and looked around for the basement door. Down a flight of concrete stairs was a door painted Chinese red. The door handle was a huge brass elephant with a third eye in its forehead. Only Charles William would have such a door. I rang the bell and in a moment the door opened and there was Irise in a blue-and-white kimono. "Oh, Rhoda," she said. "Come in. We were hoping and hoping you would come. May Garth's here. Oh, May Garth, hurry up. It's Rhoda. She's here.''

"I left him," I said. "I hate him. I had to run away. Can I spend the night? Can I stay here with you? Oh, my God, this place is fabulous. What did you do?''

"Of course you can. Come in. Come and see what we did.'' She drew me into the room. It was a grotto. For seventy dollars a month Charles William had rented the entire downstairs of the building except for the furnace rooms. He had painted the walls red and covered the floors with cork squares and straw rugs. There were sconces everywhere, some holding candles and some holding lamps. Christmas lights were strung across the ceilings. Two wide black leather sofas faced a coffee table made of mosaic tiles. "It's our grotto," Charles William said. "Do you like it, Dee? What do you think?"

"I love it. It's divine. May Garth's here? She's here now?"

"Here I is, Miss Rhoda." She emerged from the kitchen wearing a pink kimono with red hibiscus on it. "You want to wear a kimono? We have another one. My aunt brought them back from Japan." She giggled and held out her hands.

"My God, May Garth, you're thin as a rail. I heard you were working in a bank."

"I've got a prescription. Look at this. It's called Dexedrine. I've got black ones and black-and-white ones. Which one do you want?" She reached into a pocket of the shorts she had on underneath the kimono and produced two bottles. "You can have some if you want them. I can get all I want. You want one now? You stay awake all night if you take them."

"Let me see." I took the bottles from her and looked at them. They didn't look like the pills I had taken that summer. Still, it might be the same thing. "I might take one. Which one's the best?"

"The black ones last longer. Take a black-and-white. Here." She opened the bottle and handed me a pill. I walked into the kitchen and got a glass of water and swallowed it.

"Let's have a drink," Charles William said. "I've got some fabulous scotch whiskey."

Three hours later we were still drinking scotch and talking. "I want to go to the Continental Club and dance with the band," May Garth kept saying. "Rhoda has to see it. Just you wait, Rhoda. You never heard music like this in your whole life."

"I used to love a saxophone player," I kept answering. "I still love him. I should never have married Malcolm. If Malcolm calls, tell him I'm not here. I'm never going back. All he does is yell at me. He thinks I am his slave."

An hour later I was dancing with a black musician in a black nightclub. We had been given a table on the edge of the dance floor. Black men in tuxedos came by the table and spoke to May Garth and held her hand. It was very powerful and strange in the room.

It was the closest I would ever come to a revolution. I was in the center of the power base of black power in the American South but I was too drunk and high to register anything but fleeting images. Lights on the bandstand, a sweet pink drink in a tall glass, Charles William standing by the table laughing and joking with the men in tuxedos, elegantly dressed black women who never spoke to us, the small black man who led me out onto the dance floor and tried to dance with me. I could almost follow him but not quite. Every time I thought I had figured out what we were doing the step would change.

Later I was lying on a sofa in the manager's office and May Garth was fanning me. Later still I was in a car being driven to the ''grotto.'' Then I was sleeping in a soft clean bed with sheets that felt like the ones at my mother's house.

In the morning we ate breakfast on trays and told the stories of the night and May Garth called the bank and told them she could not come in. No one went to work and no one went to school. The night moved on into the day. I was among friends.

At three o'clock that afternoon I returned to my apartment. I had no idea what was going to happen. I had never run away from a husband before or gone home to be forgiven. I was going to have to make it up as I went along. I took May Garth with me for a shield.

Chapter
19

The apartment was empty when we got there. It looked as if it had been deserted for weeks. Now that I had been gone for a day the whole place had lost its charm. The gravel driveway seemed rutted and poor. The yard with its wildflowers seemed overgrown and tacky. The half-finished cobbler's bench sitting in the yard seemed embarrassing. Who would be married to someone who refinished furniture in the yard? (Of course, if Charles William had been doing it, I would have thought it was artistic.) I opened the door, and May Garth followed me into the living room.

"That's our sectional sofa Momma bought us," I said. "I used to like it but I hate it now. I hate that color green."

"When do you think he will be home?" She sat down on the sofa and began to play with her eyes. She had a brand-new pair of contact lenses, the first any of us had ever seen, and she seemed to take them in and out at least every other hour. "I think I better get these out. They're starting to bother me." I sat down on the other half of the sofa and watched as she dug around in her eye and finally retrieved first the left and then the right lens. She laid one on top of the other and put them on the edge of a crystal ashtray.

"I ought to empty those ashtrays," I said. "I have to clean this place up before he gets home, May Garth. You want to play some music while I do it? I've got a lot of records but no forty-fives anymore. I burned them up driving home from Vanderbilt. I won the freshman writing contest there, did I ever tell you that?''

"There's a car," she said. "I heard a car." She stood up and looked out the window. A dark blue Pontiac was pulling up beside my car. "Is that him? Is that Malcolm?''

"Yeah. And his old roommate, Phinias. I guess Phinias brought him home." Malcolm and Phinias got out of the car and came walking up the path. They were talking to each other with their heads bowed. I went to the door and opened it.

"Where were you?" he said. "I thought you'd gotten killed.'' I looked up into his face. With his old roommate beside him he looked like the boy I had loved such a short time ago. He looked like someone who was valuable and to be desired. He was my husband. Or, at least he used to be. How could anyone as terrible as I was deserve a man this fine? "I'm so sorry," I said. "I don't know what came over me. Oh, God, don't be mad at me. This is May Garth. Her father owns some banks. This is Phinias, May Garth. Phinias Kernodle, our friend." I dissolved in tears and ran up the stairs to our room. Malcolm followed me, leaving Phinias and May Garth to amuse one another as best they could.

Chapter

20

Nature does not waste such emotion. After we made up, and Phinias and May Garth had left together, Malcolm made love to me and then he fussed at me and I apologized and begged to be forgiven. Then we made love some more and he asked me if I wanted to go to the mountains for the weekend.

We left on Saturday morning. Malcolm and I and Avery and Mary Adair and Charlie McVey and his wife. The six of us in a Chevrolet, all the camping gear stuffed into the trunk of the car. THERE WAS ONLY ONE TENT.

We drove all the way up into the mountains. It was almost dark when we got there. We built a fire and started cooking dinner and then we cut the cards for the tent. Malcolm reached out his hand and plucked the ace of spades from the deck and neither of us had remembered to bring a rubber.

"Where are you going?" he asked. It was morning and I was pulling on my pants and boots.

"I'm going to the bathroom. Let me up. Unzip the tent." He reached above me and undid the zipper to the front of the tent and I climbed out and stood up and looked around. On three sides were tall granite cliffs. In front was a mountain lake. I struck off in the direction of the sunrise and soon had climbed a hundred feet above the lake. I found a large boulder and relieved myself and then I climbed another forty feet and sat down on the path to look down on the dark green tent and the sleeping bags that held our companions. "Well, I think I'm pregnant," I decided. "I bet I am. I know I am." I looked off into the distance. For once in my life I was content. I didn't want a thing. I knew exactly where I was and how I fit into the scheme of things. I wasn't hot or cold. I didn't want anyone to talk to me or need me or tell me anything. I just wanted to sit there and look down on the lake and think about how absolutely hysterical it would be if I was pregnant. I thought it was hysterical. I thought it was the absolutely funniest and most amusing thing I had ever heard of in my life.

After a long time I saw Avery get up from his sleeping bag and go over and start poking around in the fire. Then Malcolm came out from the tent and joined him and I decided to go on down. I wanted to climb farther up and maybe build a lean-to out of vines but I decided they'd get mad at me, so I started back down the path to the camp.

Chapter

21

Eight and a half months later I woke up in the surgical recovery room of the Dunleith General Hospital and it was over. I woke up screaming for my baby. "Where's my baby? I had a baby inside of me. A great big baby. I saw it on the X ray. Where is it? Why don't they show it to me? Give me my baby. Granny, make them give it to me." My father was outside a glass window and there were tubes and wires and I was going to die of thirst. "Give me a drink of water. Make them give me some water. I have to have some water and I want my baby. I want to see my baby. Somebody better bring my baby to me." I tried to meet my father's eyes. I screamed louder. Surely he could hear me. Then a second nurse came in and laid a piece of wet gauze across my lips and lifted my arm and gave me a shot. Then the terrible thirst disappeared and the terrible backache that had lasted for days and I slept and woke again in the late afternoon. This time I was more cunning. I decided to beg. "Please let me see my baby. I only want to look at him. Let me look at him. He's dead, isn't he? There's something wrong with him. If he was okay, you would let me see him. Put a piece of wet cloth on my lips. I won't suck the water out. I swear I won't. Please give me some water. Is my father here? Where did my father go? Where is Doctor Freer? Is he coming to take care of me?" The light passed away from the high windows of the room. It seemed I had

been on that bed for several days. It seemed so many hours had
gone by. Why didn't my father return and save me? Where had my
grandmother gone? Why wouldn't they give me any water?

I drifted down into a dark sleep and nurses came and put wet
cloths on my lips and when they turned away I would suck the
moisture out.

Malcolm and I had come back to Dunleith in June to wait for the
baby to arrive. He was supposed to come in August, but he couldn't
wait. One Sunday in July he began to be born. Upside down and one
foot first, my body began to push him out into the world. We were
at a picnic on Finley Island and my mother and my sister-in-law
took me to the hospital. At eight o'clock that night Doctor Freer
called in a surgeon and they rolled me into an operating room and
put me to sleep on sodium pentothal and cut him from my womb
and put him in an incubator.

They had asked me if they could. After hours of pain, Doctor
Freer had come into the room and said, "Rhoda, we're going to
have to take the baby. We're going to do a cesarean section."

"Does that mean I'm going to sleep? Does it mean it will stop
hurting me?"

"Yes. In a few moments you'll be asleep."

"Good. I don't care. Do anything you want to do."

Then, what seemed an eternity later, I was alone in a gray room
begging for water. By the time that night came I was sure the baby
was dead. If the baby was alive they would have let me see him,
wouldn't they? Wouldn't they? Then my mother was beside the bed
and they moved me onto a stretcher and rolled me through the halls
and Malcolm appeared and took my hand and kissed me and they
lifted me onto a bed and someone tucked the sheets around my legs.
Then a huge black woman appeared in the door with a tiny little
bundle in her hand. She held it out to me. She put it into my arms
and I looked down into the face of my first son. A little boy, so
beautiful and perfect that forever afterward the thought of him
could break my heart. A little five-pound preemie with a face so
beautiful and perfect, with black eyes and golden hair, with such

perfect little feet and hands, that I trembled with joy to touch him and I put him to my breast and let him suck. My milk came in very quickly. It seemed there was always milk for him and he knew how to suck it out. Later, with the others, I would have to coax and teach them, but not with this first perfect little boy. He knew what he wanted and he got it. He would suck fiercely at one breast, then at the other, and lie in my arms so quietly I was not certain he was breathing. He ate and slept, ate and slept.

"I didn't know anything could be so beautiful," I said to him. "How could you be so beautiful? Aren't you glad we lived? We almost died, Little Malcolm. We almost died, you and me, but we didn't, did we? We wouldn't die. We wouldn't let anything destroy us." I whispered to him as he fed. I was overwhelmed with tenderness and a strange terrible unknown joy.

Everyone who came to see him said he was the most beautiful child they had ever seen. "That's the prettiest baby I ever saw," my mother said, and Aunt Celeste, and Aunt Roberta, and even old Doctor Freer, who should have retired years before, was jealous of the surgeon he had called in to do the operation and took the stitches out himself a few days later. He would come into my room every morning on his rounds and sit beside the bed and watch the baby. It was out of fashion to breast feed babies in 1957 but Doctor Freer had insisted I do it because he was so small. "You must feed him at your breast," he kept telling me. "I don't know why the women have stopped doing this. It's the best food for him. We can't take a chance on him losing weight."

"Isn't he wonderful?" I would say every morning. "Isn't he the prettiest baby you've ever seen?"

"He's a fine healthy boy. You gave us a scare, Rhoda. You sure gave us a scare."

"He's gained three ounces. He's gaining every day. He's getting bigger. When can we go home?"

"Wait until Saturday. You can go home then." He patted my hair, patted the baby's matching hair. "I almost tried to deliver him but it would have caused you too much pain. It might have broken his leg. You're a fine healthy girl, a strong girl. The Mannings all are tough. I knew you'd make it." He bent over me to watch the

baby nurse. The smell of A&D ointment was everywhere. In a fury
of mothering I rubbed it on my nipples by the handfuls. In all
probability the baby was drinking about a fifty-fifty mixture of
breast milk and A&D ointment. "Be sure and clean that ointment
off before you feed him," Doctor Freer said. "Did the nurse show
you how?"

"I do. They showed me."

"What does his father think of him?"

"He likes him. He won't pick him up though. He's afraid to
pick him up."

"He'll get braver. When you get him home."

"Well, I don't care. Dudley picked him up. He went into the
nursery. Did you hear about that?"

"Your brother?"

"Yeah. He has two girls now. He wants a boy so much."

"Did you name him yet?"

"He's named Malcolm, of course. He's named for his father.
We always name boys for their fathers." I bent down to the baby.
Touched his hand, touched his cheek.

"Don't wake him up. Let him sleep." Doctor Freer kissed my
cheek, kissed the baby's head, kissed my hand. "I'm proud of you,
Rhoda. You're a fine girl. A brave girl."

"I just wanted to go to sleep. I didn't care what you did if you
put me to sleep. I love you for taking care of me. For saving us. I
really love you. I really do."

"I have to go and make my rounds. I'll stop back in tomorrow.
Be sure and wash the ointment off."

"I will. I do." He left the room and left me there. The sun came
in the windows onto baskets of flowers. Everyone had sent me
flowers. And I had given birth to a boy. An heir. A grandson for my
father. I sank back into the pillows. The only thing wrong was the
way Malcolm was acting. He only came to the hospital late in the
afternoon after he got through working. He was working for my
father on a road job and he would go home and bathe and dress and
not get to the hospital until almost seven o'clock. Then he would
only stay a little while and he wouldn't touch the baby. "He sure is
little, isn't he?" he kept saying. "He sure is small."

"He's beautiful," I would answer. "He's perfect. He's the prettiest baby I've ever seen in my life."

And every night after he kissed me gingerly on the cheek and left the room and went away I would turn over into the pillow and cry for a long time. My stomach hurt at night and I was still fat and my husband didn't even want to kiss me.

Chapter

22

The day after I got home from the hospital we had a real fight. I was set up in my mother's bedroom with the baby crib beside me and a nurse at my beck and call. My parents had moved into the guest room until I was "on my feet." It was a Saturday morning and Malcolm was standing at the foot of my bed buttoning his shirt. Charles William and Irise had just called from Arizona where they were spending a second summer at Taliesin. Charles William had told me a joke on the phone and I was repeating it to Malcolm. "Poontang," I said, laughing uproariously at the punch line.

"Don't say that," Malcolm said. "Don't talk like that."

"What's wrong? You didn't think it's funny?"

"I don't think it's very attractive for a woman to say words like that. Especially when you have a baby." He finished buttoning his shirt and began to adjust his belt. His body was perfect. His body looked like a Greek god. He wasn't lying in a bed with his stomach hurting all night every night and fat all over the sides of his waist.

"Where are you going?" I asked. "Why are you getting so dressed up?"

"I'm going to play golf with Dudley. I'm not dressed up. These are the only clothes I have."

"You're going to play golf? I only got home yesterday. I

haven't even seen you. You're going to go off and leave me here?''

''I'm only going to play golf, Rhoda. I've been working sixteen hours a day on a road job, for God's sake. This is my day off.''

''Your day off. I'm lying in this bed and you won't even stay here and keep me company. My God, I can't believe it. You haven't even picked up the baby yet. Jesus Christ.'' I kicked off the covers and started getting up. It still hurt to go from sitting to standing but I was so mad now it didn't matter. ''Then I'm going somewhere too. I'm sick and tired of staying in this goddamn bed all day taking care of a baby.''

''Rhoda.'' It was my mother, hurrying into the room with the cook, Fannin, right behind her. ''Rhoda, are you all right? Is something wrong? Is anything wrong with you?''

''I want to go somewhere. Where are my clothes? I want my clothes. I want to go somewhere. I want to go to the beauty parlor.'' I was starting to cry. All of a sudden I decided I was the ugliest person in the world. Fat all over the sides of my waist and milk dripping out of my nipples and my goddamn stomach hurting all the time. Malcolm was backing out of the room.

''Oh, honey,'' Fannin said and came around and held me in her arms. She wrestled me back into the bed and the nurse was right behind her. ''I got you a little quail under glass that Mrs. Waits sent up from Aberdeen and your momma made you a devil's food cake. Come on, honey, get back in the bed. You'll curdle your milk getting upset like that.''

''She's right,'' the nurse said. ''We're not out of the woods yet with this tiny baby. Get back in the bed, Rhoda.''

''You can go somewhere tomorrow,'' Malcolm said. He was to the door. He was leaving. ''I'll take you somewhere in the car tomorrow. I promise that I will.'' Then he was gone and Momma and Fannin and the nurse got me back underneath the covers and Fannin brought up a tray with the quail and some ice cream and mashed potatoes and the cake. ''It's a shame it's Saturday,'' she said. ''We got to wait till Monday to see some more of the story.''

''I can't wait to see what happens next,'' I answered. We were talking about *As the World Turns*. Fannin and I had been watching it together all summer. ''Ellen found out where her baby is. Did you know that? I saw it Thursday in the hospital. They have a TV in the lounge and they took me down in a wheelchair and let me see it."

"Yeah, I saw it yesterday when she went over to hide outside their house and look at it."

"You all were watching in the kitchen?"

"We sure were. On that little television set your daddy got from Sears."

"That was so sad when she saw them carry it in the door. I was crying like a baby. God, it was sad. I think she'll steal it back though. I'd steal it if it was mine. If anybody tried to take my baby, I'd kill them. I'd stab them in the heart."

"Why don't she tell her daddy? Her daddy works at the same hospital."

"They can't. They don't want anyone to know. They think it's a disgrace because she wasn't married."

"She ought to tell her daddy."

"She ought to go over there and grab her baby and take it home. If it was Lisa's, nobody would keep it from her."

"You're right about that. That Lisa don't let anybody mess with her."

"I wish it was on on Saturday. I wish they had it every day."

"So do I. Well, I guess you can read some magazines. Set over there and eat while I make this bed up for you. Then you can get back in and I'll get you some magazines." She moved my tray to a card table and helped me over to it. Then she pulled the covers off the bed and made it up with blue sheets and a pale blue satin blanket cover with lace on the edges. She fluffed up the pillows and tucked me back in and brought me a stack of *Good Housekeeping* and *Redbook* and *Better Homes and Gardens* magazines. Then she closed the blinds and drew the curtains. The nurse had gone to sleep in a reclining chair. The baby had slept through everything. "You get you a little sleep now," Fannin said. "That baby'll be waking pretty soon. You sleep so you can make some milk. Sweet little baby, sweet little ole boy." She closed the last curtain and pulled the switch on the ceiling fan to slow it down. "You rest now, Rhoda. You too high-strung this morning for your own good. You got lots of time to be on your feet. All you got to do now is rest up so you can feed this baby.''

I closed my eyes. The mahogany blades of the fan turned above me. The baby stirred in his crib, sighed, breathed. How large were the breaths he was taking? About the right size to fill a piece of bubble gum, I decided. I closed my eyes, imagining little bubble gum–sized breaths going in and out of his lungs. I slept awhile and woke up with him crying and picked him up and put him beside me in the bed and let him find a breast. The long pull started in my nipple and traveled all the way down to my vagina. It felt wonderful and he was wonderful and I patted his tiny head.

I'll get out of here before long, I told myself. I'll get well and I'll feel good and I'll be myself again. It's okay. I'm glad I had him. He's so beautiful and perfect and now I have a son and Daddy has a grandson and even Dudley can't give him that. Yes, it's all right even if I have to be fat a few more days. As long as I NEVER NEVER NEVER do it again. If I get pregnant again I'll stick a Coke bottle up my body and kill it. I'll read that book again. What was it? *An American Tragedy*. All the ways to do it are in there but I didn't read it closely enough. If I read it again I'll figure out what it is you do. I think there's something you can drink. Something you make out of vinegar or something and you drink it and it makes you start. I'll ask Fannin. I bet Fannin knows. Someone knows. Well, it doesn't matter. I'll just be so careful. I'll always use the jelly and I'll make him use a rubber and we'll never take it off even if it doesn't feel as good. He could make me come with his mouth if he wanted to. He could do it with his fingers. If he wasn't so goddamn selfish all the time. He's so mean. I can't believe he went off with Dudley to play golf. I bet he's out there with girls talking to them. Girls in bathing suits without any fat on their bodies. Well, I don't care if he loves me or not. Who cares? He's just a nobody. His daddy works in a hardware store. If it wasn't for my father we would starve. Oh, God, now we have to go back to Atlanta and live in an apartment. Well, we'll get a bigger one this time. I'll tell Daddy to give us some more money. I want to go to sleep. I'll just lie here beside my baby and I'll sleep and tomorrow I can get up and ride my bike and start to get this goddamn fat off my waist.

Chapter

23

It was three weeks later before I went on and said what I had been thinking about every day. It was the last of August. Almost time for Malcolm and me to pack up our baby and go back to Atlanta, Georgia, so he could finish school. It was late in the afternoon, a Saturday. My parents had gone to Aberdeen for the day and left us with the children. The baby was asleep in the crib. My little brothers were outside shooting baskets. Malcolm and I were entwined in each other's arms. We had been making love for an hour with the fan slowly turning above the bed and the sweet hot August air blowing the curtains against the window frames. I had made him come twice and he had made me come three times and we were tired now. "This is it," I said. "That's the last baby I'll ever have. You know that, don't you?"

"What? What do you mean? What are you saying now?"

"That's the only baby I'm ever going to have. If I get pregnant, I'll have an abortion."

"No, you won't." He sat up in the bed. "Of course you won't. What would make you say something like that?"

"I can't stand it. Every time we do it I think I'm going to get pregnant. It scares me to death. I'm not getting cut open again, Malcolm. I can't stand it. There was blood everywhere. You've never seen so much blood. I keep dreaming about it." He got out of bed and began to search for a cigarette. His body was so goddamn perfect. He could walk around a room naked and let anyone look at him from any angle. He found the cigarettes and lit one.

"You say the goddamnedest things, Rhoda. Of course you won't abort our child. It's against the law. You could go to jail."

"People do it. There are ways. Hand me a cigarette, please." He lit a second cigarette and handed it to me. "I mean it, Malcolm. If I get pregnant again I'll have an abortion. I can't stand it. I just can't stand the idea of swelling up and dying. Why should I die? I'm only twenty-one years old, for God's sake. What do you want? You've got a son. That's all the goddamn babies I'm ever going to have." I was out of bed now, looking for my clothes. I found a pair of underpants and pulled them on, then retrieved my shirt from the floor and shook it out. The baby began to cry. A small cry at first, then a scream. "Go see about him," Malcolm said.

"You don't have to tell me to. Let me get my shirt on, for God's sake." I pulled it over my head and walked into the next room and picked up the baby.

"He's hungry," Malcolm said. "You need to feed him, Rhoda."

"I know he's hungry. Jesus Christ." I sat down cross-legged on the bed, pulled my shirt up, and gave the baby a breast. "Oh, God, I love him so much. Look at him, Malcolm. Look how hard he sucks. Isn't he wonderful? Isn't he the prettiest baby you ever saw in your life?" I bent over him, caressed his head with my hand.

"Then how can you talk about killing one? Goddamn, Rhoda. Sometimes I think you're crazy."

"I'm not crazy. I just don't want to die. You try getting your stomach cut open sometime and see how much you like it. I'm scared to death I'll get pregnant."

"If you do, you'll have the baby. I'm telling you that much. You aren't killing any baby of mine."

"Stop being mad. Don't be mad at me. Look, he can't eat now. He's getting the hiccups because we're fighting."

"Well I guess he ought to get used to that. I'm going out. I've got to get out of here." He was at the door. He had the car keys in his hand. I got up from the bed, carrying the baby, and moved in his direction. "Leave me alone," he said. "I've got to be alone for a while. Your family's driving me crazy, Rhoda. You aren't the only one who's going crazy. I can't wait till we leave for Atlanta. I don't know if I can take another week."

"Then go on," I screamed. I went into the other room and put the baby back into his bed. As soon as I put him down he started screaming. I went back into the other room and stood in front of Malcolm. "Goddammit. Leave if you hate it so much. I can bring the furniture alone. I'll bring Fannin to help me. Go on. I don't care. Pack your clothes and go on now. Leave today."

"Okay, I will. But don't leave the baby in there crying just because you're mad at me."

"You're going?"

"Yes, I am. I need to start getting ready for school." He was back in the room. He pulled a suitcase out of a closet and started throwing clothes in it. He threw in three ironed shirts, two pairs of ironed and folded khaki pants, some underwear and socks and T-shirts, and went into the bathroom for his shaving kit.

I went into the baby's room and picked him up and brought him back to the bed and sat down upon it and gave him a breast but he wouldn't take it now. He was hiccuping from crying. I watched Malcolm packing.

"Be sure and see Pepper Allen when you get there," I said. "You can take her out and buy her some peppermint ice cream. Her little cutey favorite."

"Oh, for God's sake, Rhoda. What are you talking about now?" He had the suitcase in his hand. He was leaving. I bent my head down over the baby and began to cry. Tears were rolling down my face and falling on the baby's head. I was about to drown my tiny little baby in my terrible, terrible tears. "Please don't go," I sobbed. "I love you so much. I can't stand it if you leave. We'll go tomorrow together. Tomorrow we'll go to Atlanta and start our life. Oh, Malcolm, please don't leave me." He put the suitcase down upon the floor and came back to the bed and put his arm around my shoulder. With his other hand he began to touch the baby's back with his finger. "I won't get an abortion," I said. "I swear I won't. I don't know what made me say a thing like that."

"I'm sorry I got mad. I really need to get out of here, Rhoda. I can't work for your daddy another day. I'm so goddamn sick of being dirty."

"Okay, we'll leave tomorrow. We'll leave as soon as we get packed in the morning. Call Minx and make sure the apartment's ready."

"It's ready. It's a new development they just finished building."

Malcolm's cousins, Minx and Henry, had rented us a larger apartment in a new development near their house. We had talked on the phone about it a dozen times but I was still worried. I had begun to worry about all sorts of things since the baby came. The slightest little ailment would send me into paroxysms of hypochondria. I had never been sick in my life until the operation. My body had always been able to tolerate anything I did to it. Now I began to imagine that things could go wrong. They had kept me on Demerol for many days in the hospital, even after I began to nurse the baby. I have always thought that played a part in the hypochondria. Also, the private duty nurse who sat with me at night was full of superstitions and dire warnings. By the time she left she had instilled a full measure of caution in my unlettered little twenty-one-year-old mind. She had once taken care of an infant who died mysteriously in the night and she told me the story a dozen times. After she left I would get up every hour or two and go to the crib to see if the baby was still breathing.

"Call Henry and make sure they moved the beds into the bedrooms," I said. "They weren't sure when they could deliver them."

"They moved them in. Minx said they did it Tuesday. You want me to call them again?"

"Yes. I want to make sure things are ready before we leave here. I won't have anyone to help me when we get there. I won't have anyone to help me take care of him. You sure aren't going to help. I know that much."

"Oh, God, you're going to start that again."

"You won't even pick him up. You can't even change his diaper. Did Minx say they got the diaper service? They know where to come?"

"She said they did."

"We have to get a washer and dryer put in as soon as we get there. Daddy said to get anything we need." I sat back against the pillows. The baby was calmer now. He had begun to play with the nipple. He was going to settle down and eat. I stroked his head. As long as he was still and didn't cry I adored him. But when he cried and wouldn't eat, I didn't know what to do. I rocked him and walked around the room and sang to him and danced with him but sometimes he just kept right on crying.

"You don't have to go to Atlanta," Malcolm said. "You can stay here with your mother's maids. You can do anything you want to do, but I have to go back to school. I have to go and finish my degree."

"I know you do. I want you to. I love you, Malcolm. I just want to make sure everything's going to be all right."

"It will be all right. The apartment's ready. Minx and Henry are waiting for us. So tell your folks we're leaving. Because I'm leaving here tomorrow, Rhoda, whether you go with me or not." He turned and looked down at me and I had to choose. Either I packed up my baby and went to Atlanta to be a wife or I would never be loved again. I was ruined now. I had a baby and fat around my waist and it was Malcolm or no one. Besides, I had never had any real attention or tenderness from my father. Why would I expect it from any other man?

We had rented a trailer a week before to carry the furniture my mother was giving us for the apartment and the paraphernalia for the baby and the boxes of books I took everywhere. The trailer was half packed already. As soon as we woke up the next morning we finished packing. We unscrewed the pieces of the crib and put that in. We folded up the bassinet and the bathinet and the high chair and the stroller and stuck the books underneath and closed the back and locked it. We stuffed the suitcases full of clothes in the trunk of the car and locked the trunk. We put the wicker baby basket in the backseat and then we got into the car and began to try to leave. My parents were hanging on the windows of the car trying to give us advice and money and some more furniture and the phone numbers of doctors in Atlanta and begging us to stay another day. We drove off finally with them still calling after us and drove down beside the park and out onto the highway leading north and east to Atlanta. Hotlanta, Georgia, where we were going to be happy forever and ever and ever, amen.

"Are you going to hold him all the way to Atlanta?" Malcolm said. "Can you put him back there in that bed?"

"In a minute I can. As soon as he falls asleep. Why?"

"Because I want you to sit over here and put your hand on my dick. Because I want to see how it feels to be alone with you."

"That's the most romantic thing I've ever heard you say. What made you say that?"

"I don't know. I just feel good. Roll down the other windows, will you? It's going to be so hot today. It's going to be ninety-five all the way to Atlanta."

"I hope we have everything we need. Are you sure the apartment's going to be ready?"

"Minx is going there this morning to have it cleaned up and make sure the lights and water are turned on." He reached across the seat and found my hand and held it. "Come over here. Bring him too. Get over close to me." I moved to his side. The highway opened up before us, two lanes of beautiful new asphalt highway that led all the way to Guntersville Lake and on to Atlanta. All the way to our new home. I looked down at the sleeping baby. The most beautiful baby in the world. I stood up on the seat on my knees and very very carefully laid him down in the basket in the backseat and turned back to my husband and cuddled up beside him. "Yes, it's me and I'm in love again," he started singing. "Ain't had no loving since I don't know when." He was laughing and singing and driving our blue Chevrolet down the highway as fast as it would go.

We got to Atlanta in five hours and went straight to the new apartment. Minx and Henry were waiting for us with two bottles of champagne and the floors waxed and flowers on a table Malcolm's mother had sent up for the hall. There was a small living room and a dining room and a modern kitchen with lots of shelves. There was a staircase that led to an upstairs hall and two bedrooms and a bathroom. It was a palace compared to the garage apartment where we had lived the first year of our marriage. The master bedroom was already furnished with a new bed and a beautiful hooked rug that Minx had made for us. We plugged in the record player and drank the champagne and Minx carried the baby everywhere and would not put him down. She and Henry had never been able to have a child although they had been married for twelve years. "I will be his fairy godmother," she kept saying and Henry went out for more champagne and we drank that too.

Later, when Minx and Henry left, I fed the baby breast milk now abundantly laced with alcohol and he went to sleep and Malcolm and I went into the bedroom and lay down upon the bed and made him a baby brother. "I love you," I kept saying. "I love you to death. I love you so much I can't stand it."

"Do it like that," Malcolm said. "Do it harder. Like that. That's the way. That's what I want."

"Do you love me? Say you love me. Swear you love me. You have to love me."

"Of course I love you. Don't move. Make it last, Rhoda. I want to make it last."

So now and forever afterward it would be Malcolm and Jimmy Martin, my little boys. Malcolm and Jimmy this, Malcolm and Jimmy that. Don't fight, stop fighting, stop yelling, stop tearing everything up, you're driving me crazy. My sons, my glorious sons, whom I am doomed and blessed to love. What wild little boys, people would say. Those are the wildest little boys I have ever seen. Are they twins? No. How far apart are they? Ten and a half months, I would answer. We weren't very good at birth control.

Strangely enough I was good-natured about the second pregnancy. Because of it Daddy sent us enough money to get a nurse for Little Malcolm so my life was easy and except for worrying about the coming operation I was peaceful for the next eight months. We had planned on going to Dunleith for the birth but again my body could not wait and began to push the baby out a month too soon. I began to have pains one morning right after Malcolm left for school. I called a taxi and went to the hospital and was rolled into surgery all alone. A wise doctor shot me full of drugged courage so I had the illusion I was brave. I was so drugged I thought it was hilarious. Hilarious when they gave me a spinal. Hilarious when they cut me open and pulled Jimmy out. I looked down beside the operating table at the huge pads soaked with my blood and all I thought about was how much weight it would make me lose. I won't even be fat this time, I remember thinking. How great. I get the baby out of me and get my figure back at the same time. Sew me up tight, I kept muttering to the doctors. Make my stomach flat.

"Do you like him?" I asked Malcolm, when he appeared at my bedside that evening. "Do you think he's beautiful?"

"He looks like a monkey. Where'd he get those ears?"

"I'll tell you one thing," I said, sitting up. "If I ever get pregnant again I *will* get an abortion. I mean it this time. I'll never do that again as long as I live. You ought to see the blood. Sheets full of my blood were on the floor. My blood was everywhere."

"Well, you're all right, aren't you? They said you were fine."

"You didn't even bring me flowers. Why didn't you bring me flowers? When is my momma getting here?"

"She's driving here now. I would have brought some flowers, Rhoda, but I barely got here. I was taking a test in calculus when they found me. I had to go home and shave. I hope to God I passed it. I guess they'll let me take it again."

"Get me some water," I screamed. "Get out of here. He does not look like a monkey. He's a beautiful baby. I hate you. Get out of here. Don't you ever touch me or talk to me again."

A week later they released me from the hospital and I packed up my babies and went home to Dunleith to live. "I can't stand him," I told my mother. "He doesn't love me. He won't help me. All he does is get me pregnant. He's going to kill me if I stay with him."

"Come on home," Daddy told me. "We'll take care of you. Leave that little bastard. I never did like the little son-of-a-bitch anyway."

*   *   *

Now I was going to be home for a long time. I would be a child
again, in my mother's house with maids taking care of my babies.
Meanwhile, in Atlanta, Charles William was building houses while
he finished school and Irise had a job working for the chancellor of
Georgia Tech. May Garth was also in Atlanta now. She was living
in a black neighborhood and going out with a Justice Department
lawyer. The only thing I had left in common with them was that we
all still loved to drink. Irise and Charles William came home fre-
quently to visit their parents and those visits became the high
points of my life.

"Look at this, listen to this, did you hear about this?" They
came in from Atlanta bringing records, books, magazines from
Italy, surreal cartoons from France, ideas, gossip, excitement. I
began to live for their visits. The rest of my mind was at bay,
trapped, shut down, on hold.

"Come play with your babies," my mother was always saying
to me. "Come take them for a walk, Rhoda. They want you. You
should spend more time with them." And I would dutifully go into
their room and open books and read to them out loud sometimes for
hours. I liked to look at them and I could read to them or push them
in their strollers but I could not stand to be alone with them. My
mind could not tolerate their incessant demands. I wanted to be in
Atlanta dancing with my friends, reading, thinking, learning, ex-
panding into the world. Instead, I was rolled in the hot sweet taffy
clouds of family. On one side my mother and my father and their
suffocating cloying love. On the other my wild demanding little
boys. Sometimes in the fall afternoons I would put on a skirt and
sweater and saddle oxfords and walk the streets of Dunleith trying
to be happy, trying to think, trying to understand, but there was
nothing to understand. I was bored to death, that was all. Deeply,
dangerously, tragically bored.

Part Five

CRY SORROW, SORROW, SORROW, YET LET GOOD PREVAIL

Chapter

24

Momentous events had been happening in the United States while I struggled with my personal demons. And I had moved back into the heart of the struggle. North Alabama, nineteen hundred and fifty-nine. The Montgomery bus boycott was over, the Little Rock crisis, the integration of the New Orleans schools, the rise of the White Citizens' Council, the creation of a whole new school system in the South. It was the most divisive thing that had happened in the United States since the Civil War and there was no middle ground. You were for civil rights or you were against it. I didn't know where I stood. I was for it when I was with my friends and against it when I was with my father. "Now the niggers will be all over us," he said. "They'll take us over. They'll mongrelize the races." He held forth every night, drinking scotch and water on the porch with his cousins. "You turn the niggers loose and the women will be right behind them. Well, I got home just in time to stiffen up your backs," he would yell at them. "What you boys going to do, Cousin Larkin? You just going to let them take you over or you going to fight?" He would wave his glass in the air and furrow up his brow. Cousin Noisy, his cousins called him behind his back but they could not stay away. The scotch was free and, besides, he was saying everything they were afraid to say, everything they wanted to hear. "I got these grandbabies coming along," he would say. "I bought some land for the new academy and gave it to them. What you going to do for them, Larkin? How about you, James MacDonald? You going to pitch in or you going to let your little girls go to school with niggers?"

I listened to it and I would get caught up in the language. He could hold forth with the best of them and debate you into the ground but I did not believe everything he told me anymore. I had come to believe he could be wrong. He had encouraged me to leave my husband and here I was, as miserable as I could be, getting drunk every night to salve my loneliness. Besides, for every fearful statement I heard on the porch at night, I had a different stream of information pouring in from Atlanta. Charles William had given me a terrible book to read, *Native Son,* by Richard Wright. It made me see the black people around me with different eyes. No matter what they said or how obsequious they pretended to be, they cared. It mattered to them what we thought of them just as it would have mattered to me. The thought cut me like a sword. The thought pierced my heart.

Then May Garth sent me a book of poetry by Langston Hughes. "Oh, shining tree! Oh, shining rivers of the soul." I kept the books in the bedside table where I hid journals and the copy of *One Arm and Other Stories* Charles William had given me the summer we met. In that little cherry bedside table were all the secrets my culture meant to keep from me, everything they feared and wanted me to fear. I did fear the books in that table but I could not keep from reading them and I did not throw them away.

Meanwhile, Malcolm had gotten his degree in engineering and was working in a small milling town in South Carolina. He did not call me and after I called him drunkenly several times in the middle of the night he got an unlisted phone number. "My sons are virgin births," I had started telling people. After a while I began to believe it.

"I'll build Sister an apartment in the side yard," Daddy had said, as soon as he got us back again. "I've already called the builders. We ought to adopt those babies, Ariane. They're Mannings, Manning boys. We ought to change their names."

"Don't encourage her," my mother answered. "Don't encourage her to leave her husband."

"To hell with the little bastard," Daddy said. "I never did like the little son-of-a-bitch anyway." It was all he said now if anyone mentioned Malcolm's name.

So the carpenters had appeared and built a room onto the side of Momma's house and Daddy hired two more maids. "Sister can go back to school," he decreed. "She can go to business school and learn about the markets." I dutifully signed up for business school and went out and bought a wardrobe of businesslike dresses and even went to the classes for a week or two. I went until they had a spelling bee. One morning I found myself standing with my back against a blackboard spelling simple words in competition with a dour-looking man in a short-sleeved shirt. I lost on some simple word, picked up my pocketbook, and walked home in a rage. What in the name of God was I doing in a business school? I stopped a block from my mother's house and sat down on a low stone wall and wept like a child. I couldn't even win a spelling bee at a goddamn business school. It was clear my mind was gone, my life was over.

Meanwhile, Daddy's lawyers were getting me a divorce and custody of my children in exchange for Malcolm not having to pay me any child support. He had agreed to the proposition but he had not signed the papers yet.

"I ought to adopt those children," Daddy kept saying. "You ought to let your mother and me adopt them, Sweetie. If anything happened to you, those sapsuckers up in Georgia could come down here and take those little boys away and raise them any way they liked."

"Oh, Daddy." I was shocked by the ferocity of the idea. He was always doing that, cutting right to the heart of the matter, coming out of nowhere to say what no one else would say.

"They're Mannings," he went on. "And it looks like Dudley's never going to have a boy. We ought to adopt them and change their names to Manning. That little husband of yours doesn't care anything about any of you."

"I couldn't let you do that. I couldn't do that to Malcolm."

"Well, you go on and have a good time with your friends. I'm
sorry it didn't work out about business school but we'll think of
something for you to do. Maybe you can go up to Florence to that
branch of the university next year. You could stay up there with my
cousin, Ellen Moore, and come home on the weekends."

"I might. I need to do something."

"Well, go round up the boys and we'll take them out to Finley
Island to see the goats. I'm going to have them a little goat cart
made. It's time for them to start learning to control animals." We
rounded up the babies and the maids and piled into Daddy's car and
went out to the river to see the goats. "We'll get them a pony next
year," he said. "By next year they ought to be big enough to ride.
I swear, that Little Malcolm's a wild one. He's the strongest little
boy I've ever seen." Then he would sweep my children up into his
arms and laugh with delight. He had forgotten they were mine. He
thought they belonged to him.

In the world outside, momentous things continued to go on. The
public schools of Memphis, Atlanta, and Dallas desegregated in the
fall. White people were building their academies, sending money to
the Klan, joining the White Citizens' Council, digging in. The part
of my father that did these things and bragged on doing them was
his Achilles' heel. It would keep him from greatness and in the end
would take away the riches he had been so proud of making.
EVERY DAY THE WORLD TURNS UPSIDE DOWN ON SOMEONE
WHO THOUGHT HE WAS SITTING ON TOP OF IT was a saying he
had pinned to his dresser mirror. It should have said, HE WHO
HATES IS LOST.

Some fortunate star, some bright crystalline piece of luck had given
me Charles William and Irise as a counterweight to all of that. If it
was new, they wanted to see it. If it was interesting, they had to be
there. If it was revolutionary, they were for it. So when they came
home for Christmas vacation the first thing they wanted to do was
go down to Montgomery and visit his cousin who had married a
Yankee journalist and was getting crosses burned in his yard.

"Come with us," he said. "Come on, Dee. There's nothing to be afraid of."

"She brought the cross inside and built a pond around it," Irise added. "An architect from Sweden designed it for her. It's got goldfish in it."

"It's in their house. In the living room." Charles William waved his hands in the air. "I have to see it. Come on, Dee. Go with us. You haven't got anything else to do."

He was right. All I did all day was watch the maids take care of the babies and go shopping and walk into the kitchen to see what time it was.

"Momma," I said that night. "Charles William and Irise want me to go to Montgomery with them to see a house with a pond inside it. Can I go? Will you take care of the babies?"

"For how long?"

"Just a weekend. We'll be back on Sunday. We're going to stay with his cousin Charles."

"Let her go, Ariane," Charles William said. "She needs to get away."

"We'll be back Sunday," Irise put in. "We'll come right back, I promise."

"Oh, I don't know," she began. "I don't know if you should go off and leave these babies."

"Please, Momma. I'm so lonely. I'm so tired of everything. I never get to have a bit of fun."

"All right," she said. "Okay. You can go, but have her back by Sunday, Charles William. I don't want to be alone with these babies past Sunday night."

On Friday afternoon we piled our bags into the trunk of Charles William's car and started driving. It was a hundred and eighty miles to Montgomery, a four-hour drive.

"She used to be a reporter in Washington," Irise said. "She went to jail for something that she did."

"Cousin Charles is a brain surgeon," Charles William added. "He lets her do anything she likes. He built her the most modern house in Montgomery. He doesn't care what she does."

"They had to send their children off to Arizona to go to school," Irise added. "They sent them both away."

"What's her name? Where are we going to stay?"

"Derry. Her name was Derry Maitland, but now it's Derry Waters. Wait till you meet her."

"I don't know if we should do this. We're going to get back so late." I sank down into the backseat. I was getting scared. Going to see a woman who went to jail for helping Negroes sit up front on buses.

"You want some of these cookies?" Irise turned around in the seat and handed a basket of cookies to me. "Eula made them for us. They're pecan and chocolate chip. Try one."

We stopped in Birmingham to go to a liquor store and get some wine. "I want to go to the bookstore too," I said. "If it's still open. Let's go and see if it's open."

"The liquor store closes early. We better do that first."

"Drop me off at the bookstore. Then you can go get the wine." Charles William drove down the main avenue, then turned onto a side street and stopped the car beside a small hidden bookstore with dirty windows and a door with peeling green paint.

"We'll be back in fifteen minutes," he said.

"Okay. I'll grab something and come back out and meet you here." I ran inside and hurried back to the poetry section. I read the titles, T. S. Eliot, Emily Dickinson, E. E. Cummings, Wordsworth, Edna Millay, Shakespeare's sonnets. I already had all of them.

"Can I help you?" The owner had come to stand beside me.

"I want some poetry that I haven't read. Do you have anything new? I was in here a couple of months ago. Charles William Waters brought me."

"Oh, I know Charles William. Where is he? Is he with you?"

"He's at the liquor store. I only have a minute. We're on our way to Montgomery." I lowered my voice and looked around. "We're going to meet a civil rights worker. His cousin is married to a civil rights worker. We're going to meet her."

"Oh, Derry Maitland that married Dr. Waters. I know her. She orders books from me. Look, I didn't get your name."

"Rhoda Manning, well, it's Martin now but I'm divorced, I think. I guess it's final. Do you have anything new in poetry? Anything I haven't read?"

"And what have you read?"

"Well, everything that's up there I guess. Millay is my favorite and Wordsworth and Elinor Wylie but I only have five poems by her. Do you know 'Wild Peaches'? I love 'Wild Peaches.' And that one that goes, 'I can not give you heaven; nor the nine Visigoth crowns in the Cluny Museum; nor happiness, even.' God, I love that poem."

"Have you read the Greeks? Do you know this?" He reached up and took a small brown book from the shelf, *The Oresteian Trilogy*. "This is poetry," he said. "It's a play. This is a new translation."

"Oh, let me see it." I opened it to the introduction and began to read out loud. "A proper introduction to these plays . . ."

"No, not the introduction. Turn to the beginning. It's a play written in Greece at the beginning of civilization and recorded time. A chorus opens it. They're three men on the towers of a palace. It's the last watch before sunrise. Picture a palace of stone with statues of Zeus and Apollo and Hermes before it. The men are sleeping on the roof. See, it has an opening like *Hamlet*. Listen." He began to read from the book:

O gods, grant me release from this long weary watch. Release, O gods!
     Twelve full months now, night after night.
Dog-like I lie here, keeping guard on this high roof of Atreus' palace.
The nightly conference of stars,
Resplendent rulers, bringing heat and cold in turn,
Studding the sky with beauty.

"Well, you can see the parallels to *Hamlet*, can't you? It's the same story, an adulterous queen and a murder. In *The Oresteia* you're going to see the stabbing, of course. I love this new translation. It's by Philip Velacott. I heard him speak once in London."

I was transported. This was the life I longed for, the person I wanted to talk to, the things I wanted to talk about.

A horn was honking. "That must be Charles William," I said. "I guess I have to go. How much is the book?"

"Ninety-five cents. And tax. I'll have to ring it up." He

walked with me to the front of the store. The horn honked again.
The owner opened the front door and waved at Charles William
and Irise. They had parked the Buick by a fire hydrant. "She's
coming," he called out.

"Donald, it's us," Irise said. "We're going to Montgomery to
see Derry Waters. Come with us."

"I already know her. Here, Rhoda, take this book as a present.
No, I want to give it to you. Go on, they're waiting. No, I insist. I
want to introduce you to the Greeks." He followed me outside. "I
gave her *The Oresteia*," he said to Charles William. "I don't suppose
you've read it either. I can't depend on anyone to educate any of
you anymore. What do they teach you in those colleges? I'll send
you some poetry, Rhoda. When I decide what I want you to read,
I'll mail you something."

"You won't know my address. How will you know where to
find me?"

"Park the car," Donald said to Charles William. "Come in the
store. This is too uncivilized. This terrorizes me. Park the car. Take
something to Derry and let me get this child's address. Here, my
dear." He reached in and helped Irise out of the front seat. "Drive
around back through the alley, Charles William, and park by the
back door. I can't imagine this. Using a bookstore for a drive-in.
Come along, we'll call Derry and tell her where you are." Charles
William shook his head, smiled, and obeyed. Donald took Irise and
me back into the store. "Now, my dears, look around the store
while I call Derry and see if there's anything I can send her while
you're going. Let me get that back door for Charles William." He
disappeared to open the door. Irise and I giggled and began to look
at the art books. Irise found an Italian monograph on Giotto and a
book of English gardens and I wandered back into the poetry department and began to read. Charles William came in the back door
and was loudly directed to the art section to see a new book about
the French Surrealists. "Life is the urge to ecstasy," Donald mut-
tered. "I don't know if they're educating you at Georgia Tech or not,
Charles William. I worry about you. And you all drink too much.
Well, let me call Derry and see if there's anything she wants." He
went over behind the desk and rang a number and began to talk on

the phone in a loud voice. "They're here with me. Yes, I'm loading them up before they leave. Rhoda, yes, she reads poetry. Clutch them to your hearts, the ancients said, every strand of hope. What happened? The old *Jet* magazine article about Till? I might have one somewhere but send it back. Of course I saw it. Imagine them writing that. Bragging about it. All right, I'll send it on then but mail it back to me, Derry. Well, you never returned that article from *The Guardian*. All right. That's fine. Good. Say hello to Charles. Fine. Goodbye.

"At least you've been to Taliesin," he continued, returning his attention to Charles William. "When I saw it, I thought, the second movement of Beethoven's Sixth. Turns out to be one of his favorite pieces of music, naturally. They were awfully kind to me. A genius. Well, bring the books up here and let's get them wrapped. Education. How can they call what they're doing education. Nursemaids and sycophants. Villains and cutthroats, greed and ambition in the academy. I knew it would come to that, but what can you do? Milk toast instead of Latin. There won't be a Sanskrit scholar left in the world by the time I die. It's gone out of favor in India. That's what happens when the class system poisons a culture. Too many people everywhere." He was wrapping the books.

"I took Latin," I said. "I took it for four years. They made me go to three high schools but I still got educated. I educated myself. I took anything hard they had wherever I went to school. I love Latin. I translated the whole Gallic Wars I think. I still have the books."

"A shaft of light. Well, let me add this up." He took the books Irise and Charles William had and began to add up the prices on a pad of paper. He continued to talk and mutter as he added. "Take this phonograph record to Derry. It's Debussy, something I'm lending her. And this." He handed a magazine to me. It was *Jet* magazine, a magazine about black people. I opened it curiously to a page with a bookmark in it. There was a photograph of a child whose face had been beaten and disfigured. I stared in disbelief at the photograph. Charles William and Irise were looking over my shoulder. No one said anything. We just looked at the photograph and read the words. *Emmett Till.* "The men who did that got off scot-

free," Donald said. "They gave an interview last month and told
how they did it. They sold the interview for four thousand dollars.
Take it to Derry. She needs a copy for something. This is where we
are, children. This is the dark side of our coin. Go on, look a long
time and remember."

"It's a terrible picture," Irise said at last. "Why did they do
this, Donald?"

"He was accused of flirting with a white woman. He was
fourteen."

"Rhoda and I saw the Klan," Charles William said. "I wanted
her to see it. She knows it now, don't you, Rhoda?"

"Isn't it against the law?" I asked. "They don't arrest them?"

"They let the men who did that off scot-free. Well, it's getting
late and I've kept you too long. Come along. Let me help you into
the car. Read *The Oresteia*, Rhoda. When you finish it, let me know
and I'll decide what's next. Education, they call it. They call it
educating people." He opened the back door and put us into the car
and closed all the car doors and stood in the alley waving as we
drove away.

"Read the book he gave you," Irise said, as soon as we were
on the highway heading south. "Read it out loud. I love to hear you
read."

"Open the wine," Charles William added. "Let's drink wine
and hear Dee read the play. Donald went to school in New England,
Dee. He put himself on a train when he was thirteen and went up
north to Exeter and Harvard. Then he came back to live in Birmingham as though he'd never been away."

"He likes selling books to us," Irise suggested. "He's from an
old old family, Rhoda. A lot of his people are pretty crazy."

Irise opened the wine and poured it into paper cups and passed
the cups around. Charles William drove the car. I read out loud
from *Agamemnon*. "Zeus, whose will has marked for man the sole
way where wisdom lies; ordered one eternal plan: *Man must suffer
to be wise*."

"He sacrificed his daughter to make his ships sail," Charles
William said. "I remember now. They had this huge army assem-

bled on the beach, all the chieftains and their soldiers and their ships. But the winds didn't come so they just sat there with the soldiers getting restless. Then the priests told him to send for his daughter and they sacrificed her. They told her mother she was coming to Aulis to be married to Achilles."

"Oh, God, this is so much fun. I'm so glad we're doing this. So glad we got away." I leaned back in the seat. The barren winter scenery seemed beautiful to me. Charles William and Irise in the front seat. Wine to drink, books to read, strange new poetry to enlist my dreams.

"So you're really divorcing Malcolm?" Charles William asked. "You aren't going to change your mind and go back to him?"

"I can't. He's so mean to me. He never lets me have any friends. And he told me I was fat. I'm not fat. You know I'm not fat."

"It's all he knows how to say," Irise suggested. "He's not a very happy person." She took my cup and filled it from the bottle, which she was holding between her legs. "You want ice in it or not?"

"Put some in. There, that's enough." She added ice from the ice chest, then closed the lid, and put her feet on the top. Her skirt slid up her legs. I could see her lace-edged petticoat. I giggled.

"Hand me a cigarette," I said. "I smoked all mine. I'm out." Irise handed me the package of Pall Malls and I lit one and sat back against the cushions of the backseat and inhaled. Charles William lit up and added his smoke to mine. The smoke curled around the ceiling of the car. The plains of Alabama rolled by. "Let's don't drink too much before we get there," Irise said. "Then we won't have any fun tonight."

"One more drink before Union Grove," Charles William decreed. "Then one at Clanton. Then we'll quit until we get to Montgomery."

Derry's house sat at the end of an old boulevard. From the driveway all you could see was a long bluish green roof and banks of azalea bushes. Charles William helped us from the car and we walked down a stone path toward a wooden overhang that led to an indoor garden. "It's Japanese," Irise said. "Oh, Rhoda, isn't it a dream?" I wasn't sure. I had never seen anything so subtle. I couldn't take it in. I stopped to admire a lantern built into a stone wall.

"Come in. Come in." A tall woman with curly black hair came flying out the door and began to embrace us. "I'm so glad you're here. So glad you could come."

"Look at the roof, Dee," Charles William said. "It's made of copper. Have you ever seen one?"

"It's blue."

"Copper turns blue. It oxidizes. It will last forever."

"Come see the inside," Derry said. "Did you notice the azaleas? Charles has been planting them. Forty azaleas and twelve Japanese magnolias. We call him the mad tree planter." She smiled widely and I decided she was beautiful. And something more. Some kind of power I had never seen in a woman. I would not have wanted to cross her or make her mad.

We went past an indoor garden into a room with a vaulted ceiling. A creek ran beside the garden and ended in a pond. In the center of the pond was a charred cross with flowers growing around it. There were walls of glass and skylights in vaulted ceilings. The floors were polished stone. There were Indian rugs and comfortable chairs and tables covered with books and pieces of sculpture. Stacks of papers and legal folders were everywhere, piled under tables, stacked up beside a fireplace, underneath a baby grand piano. Derry led us into the kitchen. She began to lay out cheese and crackers.

"Tell me about yourself," she said to me. "Charles William said you were a writer. That you wrote for a newspaper once."

"I'm not a writer. I just had a column in a little weekly newspaper. That was a long time ago. I'm nothing. All I do is take care of my children. Do you have children?"

"They're gone. They're away at school."

"How old are they?"

"Fifteen and seventeen. We sent them away when the trouble started. I'm lonesome for them. It's killing me to have them gone." She opened wine, found glasses, threw open the refrigerator, got out salad things, began to cut up salad for our supper. Servants walked in and out of the living room. She talked to them. She answered the phone. Every time she put the phone down, it rang again. "It's all fear, Rhoda. Beware of fear. Tell me what books you got in Birmingham. Tell me about yourself."

"I haven't always lived here. I just moved to Alabama. I thought it would be so wonderful. All my life they told me my life would begin when I lived back in the South but it bothers me now. I saw that magazine Charles William brought you. I can't believe people do things like that. How can they do it?"

"Ignorance and dogma. Fear, always fear. They grow up with fear and they live with fear and they impart it to their children. They are so unhappy they have to have an enemy. So the Negroes are the enemy."

"We saw the Klan. They had their capes on and this flaming cross. The cross was the worst thing of all. It was worse then the cockfight. I don't believe in God. It wasn't terrible because it was sacrilegious. One of the things I hate about the church is that goddamn cross. Imagine worshipping an instrument of torture. Every time I see one of those things I think about Jesus being crucified. I don't think about him rising from the dead or any of that. I just think about him being nailed up there. Do they nail black people to the crosses?"

"They hang them mostly, or drown them. Or beat them to death."

"How did you get involved in this? Why did you come down here?"

"I was a reporter in Washington. Then Charles wanted to come home and I came with him. We got here in nineteen fifty-four, right before the movement started. A woman who worked for me came to me when the bus boycott started and I got involved in it. One thing led to another. Her sister works with me now. Her name's Aurora. You'll meet her."

"What are all these servants doing? You're cooking dinner." I filled my wineglass. I was completely comfortable. I could say anything.

"They aren't servants. They're working in the office. There's an office in the back of the house. We've been very busy the last month. Whenever a new semester is beginning there's a lot to do. We're trying to get some children ready for the schools in Arkansas. It isn't easy to talk the parents into letting them go." She put down a spoon she had been using to stir a pot of rice. "I wouldn't let mine go. I don't even have them. Charles won't have them here."

"I'm sorry you are sad."

"There is a price for everything, Rhoda. Nothing worthwhile is free."

" 'For each ecstatic instant/We must an anguish pay.' "

" 'In keen and quivering ratio/To the ecstasy.' " She smiled into my eyes. "Where did you grow up, Rhoda? If not in the South."

"In a small town in Illinois. I was a cheerleader and I wrote the school play. Then they dragged me to Kentucky but the schools there weren't good enough so they sent me to a girl's school in Virginia. Then they sent me to Vanderbilt, then I went to Tuscaloosa, then I ran off and got married and had two babies. So that is that. I want some more wine if it's okay. Is there plenty?"

"What do you mean? That is that?" She filled my glass. She leaned into me. "Go on."

"So now I'm home again. I live with my parents and they give me everything I want and they take care of the children. I don't know what to do with myself. I don't have anyone to talk to who's interested in the things I am. Well, at least I'm here today. I want to look at your books if I may. I've never seen so many bookshelves."

"My father's library is in the hall. And my books and Charles's are everywhere else. Daddy had poetry from all over the world. Find some. We'll read it out loud. Donald said you were a reader. He said he spotted you the minute you came bursting in his store."

"I read all the time. I've been reading all day all my life. Unless I was swimming or asleep or something." The phone rang. It was Hodding Carter calling from Greenville, Mississippi. It was Roy Reed of the *New York Times*. It was Anthony Lewis. It was

Stokely Carmichael. It was Constance Baker Motley. It was her husband, Charles, saying he'd be late for dinner. It was her youngest daughter calling from Arizona. "She's only fifteen," Derry said. "She isn't adjusting. She's overweight right now. What can I do to help her? What would you suggest?" As she talked on the phone she had kept on fixing dinner. The salad was prepared. French bread was sliced, buttered, slipped into an oven. A roast was pulled from a second oven. A black woman came into the kitchen. "Let me help you, Derry," she said. "Go sit with your company. Let me take over in here."

"All right. Thanks, Aurora. I think everything's done. Constance called again. She wants Roy to come if he can leave Florida." She put her hand on the black woman's shoulder. They looked into each other's eyes. The black woman reached up and covered Derry's hand with her own. I had never in my life been in a place so charged, so energized. It seemed momentous things were going on around me as dinner was being prepared. It seemed I had waited all my life to be sitting in this room with Derry. But there was nothing I could do to be worthy of it. There was no way I could earn the right to even drink her wine but I kept on drinking it.

"Let's go find Charles William and Irise," she said. "They went in the bedroom to look at the Wyeth. He lived in our apartment building in Washington. He gave us a painting for keeping his cat. Well, come along. Let's find them before anyone else calls." She swept out of the kitchen and through the beautiful open rooms. I followed carrying my wine. She stopped in the living room to answer the phone and talk to Roy Reed again. Then to someone named Thurgood Marshall.

"Who is that?" I asked. "I've heard of him."

"A lawyer, a very brave man. It's grown dark outside. Let me turn on these lamps." She began to move around the living room turning on the lamps. She stopped in the middle of the room, became very still, rapt. "Charles will be home soon," she said. "He's so glad Charles William came to visit. We've been so cut off, you know. It's been hard on him."

"Does he care what you're doing?" I looked up into her beautiful troubled face. Except for Patricia Morgan, she may have been the first truly grown woman I had ever known, a full and complete woman who was free to act. I could not have expressed her fascination for me then. I only knew that I was drawn to her and for some reason she was allowing me to draw near. I had no idea that there was something in myself that could call up an answering love in such a creature. I thought of myself as a half-baked, not dry behind the ears, slightly overweight, pretty much ruined forever person. I could hide in books and I could pretend to love myself but it was a chimera in which I did not believe. If Derry allowed me to draw near to her, I thought it was some mistake or momentary lapse.

"Does he care?" I repeated. "Does he care what you're doing?"

"I don't know." She reached down and took my face in her hands. "I don't think so, Rhoda. He loves me, you know. He wants me to do what I have to do. He wants me to be happy."

I didn't answer. It was too large an idea for me. I could hear the words but I could not understand them. I could not imagine such a thing being true.

The phone rang again. It was Roy Reed again, calling to talk to her about Orville Faubus.

We found Charles William and Irise in the master bedroom kneeling on an unmade bed, looking at a painting above the headboard. It was a painting of autumn leaves beneath a tree. "It's a Wyeth," Charles William said, and I shook my head. "There's a catalogue of his things," Derry added. "I'll show it to you. He's a northern painter. You might not have heard of him."

"Come here, Dee." Charles William pulled me onto the bed and I knelt beside him and looked as hard as I could at the strange painting. It was so simple and so compelling. I examined the details, the seemingly messy brushwork. I think now it was the first real painting I had ever been close to. I had never been in an art museum. I felt small and uneducated and dumb but Charles William put his arm around me and brought me into the field of his pleasure. "It's egg-based acrylic, Dee. It has the feel of oil but it lets him work fast. I read an article about it. I've been dying to see one."

"It's great," I said. "I love it. Where's the book? I want to see the book."

We went back into the living room and Derry gave me a catalogue from a Wyeth show and I pored over it while she opened more wine and put a record on the record player. We sat back on the beautiful white sofas to wait for Charles to come home. "What is that music?" I asked. "What is that wonderful music?"

"Toscanini and Heifetz," Derry answered, giggling with delight. "Ludwig von Beethoven. Everyone said they could never work together, then they made this. It's the Violin Concerto."

"I want to live here," I answered. "I want to live and die on this sofa." Derry came and sat beside me. Her face grew still. She reached out and touched my arm. Charles William and Irise were cuddled up together on the facing sofa. Someone had built a fire in the fireplace. I could hardly speak for joy, some joy I could not begin to sound or understand. Aurora came in and joined us. "That roast's going to be ruined if Charles doesn't hurry up," she said. "What do you want to do?"

"If he doesn't come in fifteen minutes we'll go on and eat." Derry stood up. The phone hadn't rung in fifteen minutes. I guess that made her nervous, as she went over and picked it up and dialed a number. Then the front door opened and Charles William's cousin Charles came in. He was a handsome man, tall and intense with sandy reddish hair and powerful dark eyes. He embraced Charles William and spoke to everyone, then disappeared into the bedroom to take off his coat and tie. When he came back he sat down by Derry and kissed her and laid his hand upon her leg. After he arrived she began to talk in terms of him. Charles does, Charles thinks, Charles believes, was how she prefaced her statements when he was in the room. Derry says, Derry thinks, Derry wants, is how he prefaced his. The thing that was between them was like a force field and we were all drawn in. We moved into the dining room to take our places at the table. "Hold hands," Derry said. "Let's hold hands and say a blessing."

"Lord make us thankful for these and all our many other blessings," Charles said. It was my mother's old blessing. If she had said it I would have sniffed and been contemptuous, but here, with these people, I was caught up and said amen as though I meant it.

"Jim Phillips called and said he's coming over," Aurora said. "He was leaving the courthouse when he called."

"Good," Derry answered. "Did you ask him to dinner?"

"I ask him anytime he calls. I love to feed that man."

"Jim Phillips is a lawyer from Washington who's helping us." Derry smiled at me. "He's originally from Minneapolis. He worked for Hubert Humphrey. He's a fabulous man. I'm glad you'll get to meet him."

"Is he married?" Irise giggled. She was drinking wine, sitting very close to Charles William.

"I don't think so. No, of course he's not." Derry smiled back at her.

"Pass those plates," Charles said. "I am now serving this roast."

We were having dessert when the missing member of our party appeared. He was a short man with a smile as wide and eager and open as Derry's own. He took the empty seat next to mine and turned the smile upon me. "Southern belles," he said. "Where do you beautiful girls come from? What do your mothers do?" He was turned around in the chair toward me. His shirt collar was rumpled. His tie was rumpled. His jacket was rumpled. He needed a shave. His hair needed combing. He was an utterly adorable and charming and disarming man.

"Well, I'm not a southern belle," I said. "I have two children. I wouldn't be caught dead being a southern belle. I've lived half my life in the North."

"Where in the North? How far north?"

"Southern Illinois. I lived there from the sixth to the ninth grades. It is my favorite place in the world. Where I was happiest."

"You have children? You're only a child."

"I have a baby face and two little boys. But I'm not married anymore. I don't think I am, anyway. My father's lawyers are getting me a divorce. I don't know why it's taking them so long."

"I'm a lawyer. Did Derry tell you that?"

"How's it going by the way?" Charles asked. "At the courthouse?"

"Not well. But there will be appeals. There will be many trials and many appeals. It seems a damned long road. God, I'm tired tonight."

"First you eat and then we'll talk about it. Derry, get this man some roast beef, please." Derry got up and in a minute she and Aurora had put plates of bread and salad and roast beef and potatoes swimming in butter before Jim Phillips and he began to eat. I watched all this with great attention. Suddenly I became very conscious of the clothes I was wearing. I had on a short pleated plaid skirt and a navy blue sweater my babies had almost ruined by spitting up on when I burped them. I had had it cleaned several times but I imagined I could still smell the sweet decaying smell of thrown-up breast milk. I raised my fingers to my pearl necklace and ran my fingers around it.

"What is the case about?" I asked.

He stopped with a forkful of potatoes and lay the fork down and turned back to me. "A black man accused of raping a white woman. We have to proceed so carefully. But let's not talk about that. Do you live here, in Montgomery?"

"She's visiting from Dunleith," Derry said. "She loves poetry, Jim. Isn't that your forte?"

"I got this great book today," I said. *The Oresteia.* I just started reading it. It's a new translation."

The Oresteia," he repeated. He ate the potatoes, then lay his fork down again. "I read it one night to cram for an exam. I remember getting about two-thirds of the way through it and thinking, damn, this stuff is good. I wish I had read this when I could pay attention to it."

"You could read it now. I would let you read it." He smiled at me again. He was not paying attention to anyone at the table except me.

"Charles William hasn't told us about Frank Lloyd Wright

yet," Derry said. "Is a building like a play, Charles William? Can
we learn our secrets from it?" The talk drifted into architecture and
the summers Charles William had spent at Taliesin. We finished
our dessert and coffee. I helped Derry take the plates to the kitchen.
Anytime I glanced his way Jim Phillips was looking at me.

After dinner we went into the living room and drank brandy and
listened to Nina Simone and the phone continued to ring. Lawyers
called and politicians and reporters. Derry would listen very intently, then answer in a low voice, then hang up and the phone
would ring again. Around eleven o'clock I remembered to call my
mother and give her the phone number. "Have you been drinking,
Rhoda?" she asked. "Have you been drinking again?"

"No, I haven't been drinking. Are the babies all right?"

"Malcolm called you twice. Your husband. He wanted that
number but I didn't have it to give to him. Do you want the number
he gave me? Do you want to call him?"

"No."

"Wait a minute. Your father wants to talk to you."

"Sister."

"Yes, sir."

"That boy's been calling here all night. Now, Sister, Judge
Pointer's about got these papers ready. They got it all straightened
out so your mother and I can adopt those children while we're at it.
Now wait a minute, it won't change your rights. It's just so if
anything happens to you in an accident we could have them to
raise. I wrote and told that boy about it so that's probably why he's
calling you. Just leave it alone until you get home and we'll call him
together. Don't go calling him on your own."

"What's the phone number, Daddy? Where is he?"

"Just wait until you get home and we'll straighten all that out.
You don't need to go calling him up late at night when you've been
drinking."

"I want the phone number, Daddy. Give it to me."

"I'm not going to do that, honey. I know what's best about this
now. Don't go getting in a hurry. Don't—"

"Daddy, give me the number Malcolm gave you. I have to call him back."

"We'll see you Sunday," Daddy said and hung up the phone. It was always how he ended conversations he didn't like.

"Excuse me," I said to Derry. I had been talking on the living room phone. "I have to go and make a call. I'll use the phone in the bedroom." I went into Derry's bedroom and called Malcolm's mother in Martinsville and got his phone number in South Carolina and called him. "Daddy said you called me," I said. "What did you call me for?"

"Where are you?"

"I'm in Montgomery with Charles William and Irise. We came to see his cousin."

"Oh, my God. You're with them."

"They're my friends. We came to see a house. An unbelievable house with glass walls and a pond that runs through the living room. They're my friends, Malcolm. I love them. What did you call me for?"

"Your father's lawyers sent me some goddamn papers. I'm going to sign them, Rhoda, because my father's sick and my mother and father can't even pay their rent. I have to help my parents. I can't pay child support to you and help them so I'm going to sign this goddamn thing. I just want to make sure you know why. Whatever your old man's up to."

"I wish I could see you. I wish I could talk to you. Little Malcolm asks about you. He said—"

"Rhoda."

"Yes."

"This is your divorce. You're the one who wanted to divorce me."

"Why shouldn't I? You don't love me. You don't care a thing about me. What do you want me to do? What are you doing? You're fucking someone, aren't you? I know you're fucking someone. That's why you don't care what happens to the children. You never even picked them up."

"I'm hanging up. To hell with it. To hell with you." He hung up the phone. I sat with the phone in my hand and listened to the operator come back on the line. "If you are finished with your call, please replace the receiver on the hook. This is your operator. If you are finished . . ." I put the receiver down on its cradle. I looked around the room. A room where a man and woman slept together and loved each other and made love. I will never have that again, I thought. Now it is all over for me. Now I will be alone forever.

"Rhoda. Is anything wrong?" It was Derry. She came into the room and sat down beside me on the bed.

"Everyone's hanging up on me." I looked up at her and laughed. "My father hung up on me and now my husband did. I don't know what to do, Derry. I'm so confused all the time. I never should have married him. We don't have anything in common. We don't even like each other, but the children belong to him. The oldest one asks for him all the time. He says, where's my daddy? When's my daddy coming back? I don't know what to tell him." I looked up at her. I had never had a grown person listen to me with such intensity. She moved into me.

" 'I spit on the grave of my twenties.' H. L. Mencken. I think it was Mencken who said that. These are hard years, Rhoda. They are hard for everyone, no matter what they're doing."

"How old are you?"

"Thirty-eight. It's better later. It really is. It smoothes out."

"I wouldn't think your life was very smooth. Not with the things you're doing."

"But that's my work. Work is the main thing, Rhoda, if you can find something worth doing, something that adds to the good of the whole. It's how you define yourself, how you create your meaning. No, I mean my emotional life is smoother now. Charles and I have gotten through the hard parts."

"I don't think Malcolm and I could get through the hard parts. I don't think it would ever work. He won't talk to me. But I miss him. I want to, well, I'm tired of sleeping by myself."

"Do you go out with other men?"

"I can't. My mother won't let me. She won't let me do it until I'm divorced."

"Do you feel like going back with the others? I think Jim has to leave soon. Would you like to tell him goodbye?"

"Sure. I'm okay. Thanks for coming in to see about me." I covered her hand with mine. Our hands lay together upon the counterpane. Her long thin fingers, scrubby unkempt fingernails. My fat smooth young hands, one wearing a class ring, one still wearing a diamond engagement ring that had belonged to my grandmother and the plain gold band I had bought for myself so we could get married.

"We'll talk some more later," she said. "After Jim leaves and the others go to bed. I have something I want to show you. A book of poems I think you might like to read." She took back her beautiful busy hand. A hand that cooked and typed and planted flowers and touched a man she loved, a hand that was being used up and consumed. We got up from the bed and went back out into the living room. Jim was standing by the fireplace. "There's a Celestron telescope mounted on the roof of this house," he said. "Has Charles shown it to you?"

"No."

"Take her and show her the moons of Saturn." Charles laughed. "Jim can't stay away from that telescope. I think that's all he comes over for."

"I do not. I come for Derry's cooking. Come along, Rhoda, come see the stars. Charles William, you and Irise come too."

"Not me. I'm going to bed."

"Me too," Irise answered. "I didn't sleep a bit last night. I was so excited. I never sleep before I go on a trip."

"I never sleep anyway," I said. "My mother says I've never been asleep in my life." Derry and Charles looked at each other. A strange dark look passed between them.

"The unsafe child," Derry said. "Charles is writing about that."

"Tell me, Rhoda," Charles asked, "was your mother sick when you were small?"

"She almost died having me. She had uremic poisoning. She said I almost tore her up being born. They had to give her something to make me come fast."

"I want to talk to you some more about that, if you'll let me. Well, take her up on the roof, Jim. Make him let you see the moons, Rhoda. He never shows anyone the moons."

"Charles is obsessed with the moons." Jim took my hand. "Stars behind stars behind stars. A zillion light-years of celestial lights and he looks at the moons of Saturn." He pulled me from the room and up a flight of circular iron stairs onto a balcony overlooking the living room. A door opened from it onto a covered porch with a telescope set up. He removed the cover and made adjustments in the lens and pulled me over close to him. He adjusted the lens again and showed me how to look through it. "That's the universe," he said. "We're only a dot in all that wonder. It looks like we would learn something from that after all this time, doesn't it?" He took my hand and held it. He was very close to me. "What can you see?"

"Infinity. It's all so cold and far away, and beautiful. But we're not nothing in all of that, Jim. I think our minds are very much larger than we know. Much much larger. I think our minds have the memory of everything that ever happened to the human race. Every one of us has the entire memory back to the first spark of electricity that started life. Why would we lose it? Why would we forget? Just because we didn't always have words for it doesn't mean that knowledge isn't there. If it isn't there, how can we recognize truth when scientists find it? Or writers write about it? How can we know what is true unless it's in our brains waiting to be said. I told my English teacher at Vanderbilt that, and he said it made sense to him. Well, he said it was brilliant, to tell the truth. I shouldn't have quit Vanderbilt. Now I'll never finish college, I don't guess. I'll just have to be illiterate."

"You aren't illiterate. Here, let me adjust that. You can make it reach farther back in space on a night this clear." He played with the telescope for a few minutes, then directed my head down to the opening. "See that? I don't have names for any of that. Look at the myriads. It seems more of that light should reach us, doesn't it? Once I dreamed it was coming our way."

I looked at the vast clusters of stars, the unbelievable space and beauty of the universe. I looked as long as I could bear so much truth, then I stood up and turned to Jim. He put his hands very very gingerly on my waist and moved nearer to me and finally I was standing very close to him and we were both completely still. After what seemed like a long time I raised my head and kissed him on the lips and he returned my kiss. Shyly at first, like a very young boy, he very very carefully began to kiss me. I had never imagined kissing another man while I was married. But I was doing it. It was very strange, very gentle and hesitant, very different from the passion I had with Malcolm. It was as hesitant and quiet as a question about the stars.

"I want to see you again if I can," he said. "I have to be in court all day tomorrow but if you'll be here tomorrow night I'll come back. When do you leave?"

"Sunday. Come tomorrow night. I'll be waiting for you. I want to see you too."

"As soon as I can get away. A man's life depends on me right now, Rhoda. I'm in over my head down there. So I don't know what time. It might be late."

"That's okay. Whenever you get here." I moved back, I was still in his arms but already I felt the cold encroachment of parting. Always it was this way. Love drew me near, then whatever I loved went away. Sometimes I just pushed it away and got it over with.

But Jim Phillips wouldn't be pushed away. He kept hold of me. "You're a very special girl, Rhoda. There's a light inside of you, a vibrancy."

"I don't know what to say. I've never had anyone talk to me like that."

"You don't have to say anything. Everything doesn't have to happen all at once. We have this night and these stars and then tomorrow night we'll have something else."

"Jim."

"Yes."

"Kiss me again please. I want you to kiss me."

Later that night, after Jim left and everyone else had gone to bed, I sat in the guest room with Derry and talked to her alone.

"What do you think of Jim?" she asked.

"He's so nice. I don't think I've ever met a man that kind. God," I started giggling, "he's so messy. Is he always that messy?"

"Ever since I've known him. This is a critical case he's trying, Rhoda. He'll probably lose it here, but we hope it will go to the Supreme Court. The courts are our only real hope. The people can rise up and they can march but only the courts can create justice. We can't win justice on the streets."

"He's coming back over tomorrow night."

"I know. I'm glad. I want to give you this book to read when you get in bed." She reached behind herself to a shelf of books and took down a very small gray book and handed it to me. "It was written by a young white girl who helped with the boycott. She died in an automobile accident shortly after that was over. We published this as a memento. I think you'll like it." I took the book and held it in my hand. *I Play Flute,* the title said. I opened it and read.

> I am yellow crocus
> In the morning fog
> I am ball and socket
> Of your shoulder bone
> I am breath and if you kiss me
> I am universe
> and water
> All flowering springs
> This intense cool fragrance
> "So complete is happiness."

"What a strange beautiful poem. You knew her, the girl who wrote it?"

"There are fourteen poems. We printed a hundred copies. Well, I'd better get to bed. It's wonderful to have you here, Rhoda. I hope you'll want to come again."

"I want to live here. I told you that." I settled back against the pillows, the book in my hand. "I meant it. I'll just move in."

"I think you have enough parents," Derry said. She stood in the doorway looking down at me. I think now how much it must have pained her to watch me suffer and be dumb, to know how very far I had to go to even begin to understand. She came back into the room and kissed me on the head and said goodnight. After she left I settled down to read the book, which made me sick with jealousy. I could write these poems, I was thinking. There's nothing to this. I could do this anytime I wanted to. I could write poems a thousand times better than these.

I woke at dawn and went into the kitchen and sat at the table and began to write. "Alabama is not a place you're from," I wrote,

> Not a shadow you roll up in a drawer
> It will follow you to Boston on the train
> You are my brother whether you want to be or not
> Gandhi said. Sometimes I think I am underneath
> A song, looking up.

Derry appeared at the door. "What are you writing?" she asked.

"An answer to the book you gave me."

"Let me see." I handed her my poem.

"Oh, Rhoda, that's lovely. Very lovely."

"It's because of the book. It's only an answer, that's all it is."

"Where did you learn about Gandhi?"

"At Vanderbilt. I was going to write a paper on him when I went back. Well, that was a long time ago."

"Let's have breakfast. I haven't had young people in the house in so long. Oh, this makes me happy." She began to pull bacon and eggs and bread and butter from the refrigerator and the pantry. She went into what I would always think of as Derry-gear, very very fast and hot and busy. I sat back and watched her cook.

That afternoon Charles William and Irise and I went antique shopping all over Montgomery. He was looking for new things to make into sconces for the grotto. At five-thirty we got back to Derry's house and she said Jim had called and said not to wait dinner on him. "He said to tell you he was sorry," she said. "He said he'd be here as soon as he could."

At seven we ate dinner without him. At seven-fifty he called and said he'd be there as soon as he could. At ten-fifteen he showed up at the door with a Justice Department lawyer in tow and bad news about the trial.

"Did he do it, Jim?" Derry asked.

"He says he didn't."

"What do you think?"

"It's going to be hard to get it reversed if they convict."

"This one's too hard," the Justice Department lawyer said. "This isn't the one we want to take all the way."

"He lied to me," Jim said. "Ten convictions I didn't know about. We were blindsided all day."

I waited while they talked. Several times Jim looked at me as if to say, I'm sorry, so sorry the evening turned out this way. Finally we got away from the others and walked out on the porch. It was colder than it had been the night before. I stood shivering beside him and he took off his coat and put it on my shoulders. "I'm so sorry," he said. "You won't trust me after this."

"Why would I need to trust you? I'm married. I shouldn't even have kissed you. I shouldn't be out here."

"Oh, Rhoda."

"You should have been here for dinner. We had baked red snapper. Fresh fish from down on the coast. We went to a fish market to get it." He took my arms and pulled me into his body. "It won't always be like tonight," he said. "My life isn't always this way."

"I don't let people stand me up. My mother was the most popular girl in the Mississippi Delta. My aunt was Maid of Cotton. I don't get stood up, even by Yankee lawyers who went to Harvard." I was half serious, half joking, completely scared to death. I was pulling away from him, away from his strange gentle power, but he wouldn't let me go. He kept on holding on to me.

"I need you, Rhoda. Stay with me tonight. Talk to me. Stand by me."

"I'm married to someone, Jim. I have a husband and two children." I pulled away from him then and went back into the house and told everyone goodnight. Then I went into Derry's bedroom and tried to call Malcolm, but his line didn't answer. It was Saturday night. He's out with someone, I decided. He's screwing someone somewhere. This goddamn Yankee lawyer stands me up and Malcolm's got another girlfriend, or two or three or four. He's representing a black man who raped a white girl. My daddy will kill me if he finds out I'm with these people. They'll put me in a jail. I went into my bedroom and put on my nightgown and took a sleeping pill. Doctor Freer had given me a bottle of tranquilizers and a bottle of sleeping pills to counteract the sleeplessness caused by the diet pills he was again supplying me with. I climbed into the bed and waited for the drug to reach my brain.

Irise and Charles William came to the door of the bedroom twice to try to talk to me but I wouldn't talk to them. I was tired of this adventure now. I wanted to go home.

On Sunday after a late lunch we started back to Dunleith. It was late afternoon when we got there and the town was frosted with a snow. I walked up onto the porch and the front door opened and Momma was standing there with my little boys by her side. They were dressed in the red velvet suits we had bought for them to wear for Christmas. There were bells laced into their carefully polished white leather hightop shoes. They ran out of the door fighting and screaming to get into my arms. I swept them up and carried them into the room Daddy had built for me. It was finished now, decorated in beige and gold. Everything in it was fine and new and expensive and beautiful. Still, I had been lonesomer in that room than anywhere I had ever been in my life. Lonesomer and more confused. Part of the confusion was caused by alcohol and all the pills Doctor Freer gave me. Part of it was caused by the children and their incessant demands. All of it was made worse by the fact that I never for a second doubted that everything was my fault. If I stopped thinking I was to blame, Daddy was always there to remind me.

Still, on this snowy night, Charles William and Irise followed me into my lovely spacious new room and Mother brought in a tray of tea and cookies and the children ran around and let us talk about how beautiful they were and the world seemed possible and full of warmth and friends.

"Malcolm's the golden child and Jimmy is an apricot," Charles William was saying. "They're angels, Dee. They should be painted in those suits. We'll get Mimi to paint them. Do you want me to ask her?"

"She only paints people she wants to paint," Irise said, "but anyone would want to paint them."

"Sister." Daddy had come into the room. "James Myers delivered these divorce papers to me today. You better come on and sign them so we can get this settled." He was standing in the door, looking so kind and charming, holding two sets of legal papers. He lay the papers down on my desk. "Your friends will excuse you a second. Hello, Irise, hello, Charles William. How you doing? How was your trip?" He stood by the desk waiting. I went over and sat down in the desk chair and he opened the papers to a page and held out a pen.

"You want me to read them?" I asked.

"There's no need for that. One is about the divorce and the other is about custody for your mother and me. You can read it if you want to."

"I don't. Where do I sign?" I took the pen and wrote my name in two places on each brief, then dated the signatures and handed them to Daddy.

"You aren't reading it?" Charles William asked.

"Of course not. Who wants to read legal papers. They're so boring. I never read contracts. That's what lawyers are for, isn't it, Daddy?'' I looked up at him. He was smiling at me. He loved me. He had given me this beautiful new room and let me buy new carpets and drapes and all the new furniture I wanted. He loved me and he had his important lawyers get me a divorce and I didn't even have to go to court. I moved near him and put my arm around his waist. "We're mighty proud of you, Sweet Sister,'' he said. "You're settling down to be a fine little mother.''

"Momma and Daddy are going to be the adoptive parents if anything happens to me,'' I explained to Charles William and Irise.

"It's to make sure the boys are safe,'' Daddy added.

"They'll be his heirs if anything happens to him,'' I laughed. "Just think how mad it would make Dudley to have to share the money with my children and with me.''

"Charles William, you and Irise want to witness this?'' Daddy said. "Then James Myers can go on and get it filed in the morning.'' He held out the pen. Charles William and Irise stood up.

"I don't know if we should,'' Charles William said. "Malcolm was my roommate, Dudley. It might not be a good idea for us to sign it.''

"I want you to,'' I said. I held on to my father. "I want you to sign it. It doesn't matter anyway. I promise you I'm not going to die.''

"I don't know if I should.''

"For God's sake you're only witnessing my signature. You don't have to like what it says.''

"I'll sign it.'' Irise took the pen and began to sign her name below mine on all the pages. Charles William stood with his head bowed looking at his feet. When Irise was finished signing the papers he took the pen from her and signed them too. Then I showed them to the door. "I hope you know what you're doing, Dee,'' he began, but I would not listen to it.

"My daddy knows what he's doing,'' I said. "He's the one who takes care of us, Charles William. He's the best friend I have. Besides, I don't want Mrs. Martin to get hold of my children. She might ruin them.'' I stood in the doorway looking out at the snow. Whatever person I had been six hours ago in Montgomery, Alabama, had disappeared. I was back in my father's house. I was my daddy's indulged and happy little girl. All I had to do from now to the end of time was eat from the bowl he held.

Chapter

26

My children had bad colds they had caught playing in the snow so I was busy with that and didn't get to see Charles William and Irise before they left to go back to Atlanta. They called at ten that morning and made me promise to come and visit. "Come on up to the city," Charles William said. "This time I'll fix you up with an architect. I think our mistake was in getting you an engineer. We need to move in the direction of the arts."

"Is May Garth still going with that lawyer?"

"No, it's a musician now. He plays drums for a black band. She's dancing to a different drummer."

"Thanks for taking me to Montgomery. It was really nice."

"Have you heard from Jim?"

"No, why should I?"

"Oh, Dee," Charles William began to laugh and I could not resist it.

"Okay, well, hell no, he hasn't called me. I was rude to him when he was late that night."

"I bet he'll call you."

"He doesn't even know my number. He doesn't know my parents' name."

"You call him. Call Derry and find out his number."

"I'm not calling a man. Of course I'm not. Besides, it scares me, all that stuff they're doing."

"Well, I love you. We have to go now. Irise is standing by the door. She wants to get back and see if the parakeet died. May Garth was supposed to be feeding it but Irise doesn't trust her."

"I love you too. Write to me."

"I will. Goodbye. Call him, Dee. Life is as interesting as you let it be." He hung up and I stood by the phone thinking about the things Charles William was always saying to me. "There is no security," was his latest mantra. I went into the children's room to see how they were doing but Fannin had them on the floor building a fort with Lincoln Logs so I wandered upstairs and went into the bathroom and took off my clothes and weighed myself. I had gained three pounds. I reached up in the medicine cabinet and surveyed the different bottles of diet pills Doctor Freer had given to Mother and me. There were black ones for all day, black-and-white ones for half a day, and some pink tablets that Mother thought "were quite enough. The others make me talk too much," she said. "I talked Sara Redding's arm off at bridge the other day after I took one of those black ones." I took down the bottle of black-and-white pills, then I put it back and took a black one. Might as well go on and get the three pounds off in a hurry, I said to myself. Fat is so insidious. And I'm a divorcée now.

Half an hour later I poured myself a glass of sherry and went into Momma's study and called Derry Waters's house in Montgomery. Aurora answered the phone. "It's Rhoda Manning," I said. "How are you? I'm calling for Derry."

"She isn't here. She's still in the hospital."

"What? What are you talking about?"

"You don't know?"

"No, tell me what's going on. What are you saying, Aurora?"

"Don't you read the papers? It isn't in the papers up there?"

"What. Tell me what."

"She was cut. They got her. They finally got her."

"Tell me what happened, Aurora. What are you saying? What are you talking about?"

* * *

It took a while to get the story out of Aurora because there was so much going on behind her in the house. Doors opening, doors slamming, other phones ringing. "She was attacked coming out of a restaurant with a lawyer from Washington. He ran away and left her there and they got her. They cut her. Charles got a doctor from up North to come and fix her face but they can't fix her arm. They cut an artery in her arm."

"What arm?"

"The right one. The one she uses. They don't know what's going to happen. They're talking about taking her somewhere. To a different hospital."

"What can I do?"

"Nothing. You can't do anything. I have to go now, Rhoda. There are a lot of people to be taken care of. Write her a letter when she gets home. I really have to hang up now."

"What hospital is she in? I want to call her."

"Don't do that now. She's had too many visitors already. Wait and write to her." Aurora hung up and I was left with this tragedy to contemplate all alone. A tragedy that came from a world I did not belong to. A world of action and courage and life, a world where men and women were fighting and dying for a cause. Justice, Derry called it.

There was no way I could call Charles William and Irise for another hour or two. There was no way to find Jim Phillips as he was living in a black neighborhood and didn't have a phone. I hated to call Charles Waters. If I told my parents they would be mad at me for even knowing these people. In Montgomery, Alabama, momentous things were going on but they did not include me. They had nothing to do with me.

I wandered back into the playroom and sat down on the floor with my children and wiped their noses and felt their foreheads. Fannin was sitting on a chair watching over them. "A friend of mine who is a civil rights worker was cut with a knife today," I said. "She was cut down the face and on the arm. Her arm was really hurt. They severed an artery in her arm."

"That's big trouble everywhere now." Fannin's face closed up like a fist. Her eyes would not meet mine. She turned her eyes away. She did not trust me, and with good cause. I did not know whose side I was on. I was too powerless to have a side or to be trusted to say what I meant. "Lot of folks going to get hurt."

"I stayed at her house last week when we went down there. She had a cross burned in her yard. Now they've cut her up."

"Well, I got to go get supper started." Fannin stood up. "You take care of these babies for a while so I can get my work done."

"Is Ifigenia coming to help?"

"She'll be here at five. You going to stay and watch them now?"

"I said I would. I tried to take over an hour ago and you said you didn't need me."

"Well, I need you now." She left and went into the kitchen and I sat on the floor with my little boys and helped them build a fort for the Indians to attack. We had fifty soldiers and eighteen Indians and ten horses that either the Indians or soldiers could ride. We had enough Lincoln Logs to build a big fort with a wall around it and we also had some Marines and a few tanks and planes from a different set but we almost never brought them in when we played Lincoln Logs until the very last when we had used up all the rest of the stuff.

The next afternoon was Friday. The children were better and I decided to go downtown and buy them some books. "I'm going to start reading to them every day," I told my mother. "I'm going to start really paying attention to them. I bet I could teach Little Malcolm to read if I really tried."

"Sure, honey," she said. "Go on. But don't be back late. Get back before Fannin leaves."

"I'm only going to the bookstore."

"I know. Don't go by anyone's house on the way home. Don't start drinking with anyone. Promise me you won't."

"I won't."

"You really should stop drinking, Rhoda. You've been drinking too much lately."

"I can't help it. There's nothing to do. I'm so bored all the time."

"Well, go on to the bookstore but come back by five. Promise that you will."

"I already did."

"Well, keep it this time." I walked away without answering. It was driving me crazy to have her watching me all the time. Sometimes I just got into the car and drove aimlessly around town trying to put off the moment when I walked back into the house and back into her power. Daddy had the money power but she had the maid power. She had the power to make me take care of the children. He had the power to make me rich or poor. What did I have? Well, I had the bookstore.

The only bookstore in Dunleith at that time was connected to a gift shop in the old business section of town. They had cookbooks and gardening books and leatherbound classics and children's books and a few new novels, three or four at a time. I bought a children's book about the Arabian Nights and one about a little boy who loved horses and paid the saleslady and drove slowly home through the cold winter day. There was hardly a leaf on a tree. The dead of winter. The winter of my darkest discontent.

As I neared my mother's house I saw Malcolm's car parked by the entrance to the side porch. It was the old blue Chevrolet Daddy had given me for quitting Vanderbilt. That seemed a million years ago. The sight of my husband's car burst upon Wheeler Street like a storm. As I drove nearer I could see him standing on the side porch. He had Malcolm in his arms and Jimmy was holding on to his legs. I parked the car and got out and ran up the steps and put my arms around him and began to cry. I wanted him. I wanted him back. I wanted to take off all my clothes and fuck him and tell him I was sorry. I wanted to be guilty and punished and I wanted him to fuck me. It was the first thing that had happened to me in months that I could understand.

"I'm moving to Alexandria, Louisiana," he said. "I've got a new job. It's a promotion and a raise. I'm going to be the plant engineer. I want you to go with me, Rhoda. I want us to go there together."

At dinner we told Mother and Daddy we were making up.

"I wish you'd leave those boys here with me," Daddy said. "You and Rhoda go on down there and get settled and I'll bring them later."

"No, I want them to go with me." We were all at the dinner table. Mother and Daddy and Malcolm and I and my two little brothers and the boys in their high chairs. Usually we made them eat in the kitchen with the maids but sometimes we spread plastic cloths over the oriental rug and let their high chairs be at the table.

"Your mother and I could take care of them while you get your lives straightened out," Daddy said. "I don't mind Sister going off with you again, son. I'm glad you want to get this straightened out, but don't go taking the boys off. You haven't even got a place to live."

"We're going where he goes," I said. "That's it, Daddy. That's settled. They're our babies. They belong to Malcolm and me."

"My new boss is finding us a house," Malcolm said. "His wife found us a brick duplex with a fenced-in yard. He said they'd have it ready. All we have to do is move in. I talked to him again this afternoon."

"When are you leaving?" Daddy looked very old suddenly. Fannin and Ifigenia were serving vegetables and roast beef. Mother was passing biscuits. My brothers were talking to each other and fighting with their forks under the table. In Daddy's desk were the adoption papers signed, sealed, and delivered. Malcolm had signed them and I had signed them and old Judge Butts had put his stamp on them. They said that Mother and Daddy had custody of my children in case I was incompetent. Neither Malcolm nor I had the slightest idea what we had done or what had been done to us.

But this night, at this dinner table, Daddy was sad and suddenly old. It was clear he had lost a skirmish. I was going to pack up my babies and go off and live anyway I liked in a place where he could not control me. I was going to go off and ruin his grandchildren. His hope of renewal, his survival, the survival of his genes. Manning boys, he was always saying when he showed them off. They're perfect little Mannings.

"When do you have to be there?" he asked Malcolm.

"We need to leave tomorrow. I have to start work on Monday."

"I'm going with him, Daddy," I said. "I'm going where he goes."

"Well, you're going to need a bigger car. We'll go out in the morning and get you a station wagon." He cut a very small piece of his roast and chewed it. He took a sip of tea. Malcolm sat up very straight and ate my mother's food. My mother looked grim but also happy. She was going to get rid of me. She was always glad of that. My little brothers began to fight above the table. She ordered them to go outside. The babies began to fuss and squirm in their high chairs. I got up and took them out on the porch. I was leaving this goddamn place. I was going to get the hell out of here. There was one good thing about moving around all my life. Packing up and leaving meant nothing to me. I could do that all day long.

Chapter
28

So we made up and this time we were going to have a chance. We were twenty-three years old and we had suffered. Even the Greeks knew you had to suffer to be wise. Aeschylus knew that and put it in the mouths of the chorus in *Agamemnon,* the play that Donald had given me to read. We had suffered and I had met some people who weren't crazy and Malcolm had begun to make a small success in the world. People had begun to talk about him in his profession. They said he was a comer, they said he was after it. He still had to spend nine and ten hours a day inside of manufacturing plants but at least people had their eyes on him.

"I talked to my boss about you," he said to me. "He let me have extra time to come and get you. He's really a nice guy. I'm really going to like working for him, I think. It's going to be a damned hard job though, Rhoda. You have to help me. You have to start acting like a wife. You can't drink all the time and act like you're crazy."

"I will," I swore. "I can. I want to. I love you. Come here, get closer to me." We were in bed, waiting to get up and buy our new station wagon and drive it down to Alexandria and begin our life.

"I mean it, Rhoda. You have to help me. You have to do your part. I mean it about drinking. We can do it on the weekends but not during the week."

"I won't. I swear I won't. I won't do it at all." I snuggled my head down into his chest. I was so glad to be in his arms. So glad not to be alone. I had a vision of the bottles of diet pills I had hidden in my suitcase. If I took them they made me want to drink. But if I didn't take them I would get fat and he would never love me, never touch me, would be disgusted by my body.

"Don't you think I look good?" I asked. "Did you notice how thin I am? Do you think I feel good?"

"You're a lot thinner. You look better. You're fine." He lay back against the pillows. "We'd better get up now. I want to get packed. I want to leave as soon as we can."

"Do you think I'm thin enough?"

"You could lose a little around the hips. That wouldn't hurt." He got out of bed and began to put his clothes on his perfect flawless body. I hated him. I hated his goddamn little girlfriend, Pepper Allen, who was as thin as a boy, and I hated his perfect body. I got up and began to put on my clothes and get ready to leave. His body might be better than mine but my face was prettier and my daddy was richer and they were my babies.

"I'm going to be making six hundred dollars a month," he said. "We have to make a budget. We have to live within our means."

"I'm going to get the babies up and feed them before we leave. I'm so excited, Malcolm. I can't wait to get there."

"They've never had a plant engineer. I'm going to do the first time-studies ever done in this plant. If it works, they'll use the program in the other plants. I'll be gone a lot. You'll have to amuse yourself. I won't be there all the time."

"I'll do anything." I went to him and put my arms around him. "I'll be so good. I'll be good at everything. I love you so much. I love you more than words can say."

"We have to make a home for these boys. We have to go to church and stay home with them and have a real home."

"I want that too. It's what I want. I want it more than anything."

"Okay, go get them up. Let's get out of here."

* * *

I wanted to stop in Montgomery and see Derry on our way to Alexandria but Malcolm didn't want to spend the time. He did let me stop and call from a pay phone at a gas station. "Are you better?" I asked her. "Are you okay?"

"I will be. The arm's pretty bad. I may not be able to type but I think my face will be like new. Can you come over? I'd like to meet your husband. I'm glad you made up with him, Rhoda. You were so sad when you were here. It made me sad to watch you."

"No, he's impatient to get there. He's just getting gasoline. Oh, Derry, I can't believe this happened. I can't believe it happened to you."

"I have bodyguards now. Two bodyguards from the Justice Department. They're very nice. They live here, even at night. It's driving Charles crazy, of course. Well, I'm sorry you can't come by. Keep in touch with me though."

"Derry."

"Yes."

"Have you seen Jim?"

"Not in a few days. He's going back to Washington next week. He liked you so much."

"Tell him hello for me, will you?"

"Of course."

"Take care of yourself. Maybe I'll get to see you someday. I hope I do. I hope I see you again."

"There's an organization in Alexandria you might want to get in touch with, Rhoda. The American Friends Service Committee. They're doing studies to start a tutoring program for poor children. If you have some time on your hands, call them up. They'll find work for you to do."

"Oh, I will. Thanks for telling me that. Well, I'd better hang up. Malcolm's having a fit. He wants to go."

"Where will you spend the night?"

"I have to go. I really have to go. He's getting mad." I hung up the phone and walked back over to the station wagon and got in and tried to quiet the boys down and my husband revved up the

motor and pulled out onto the highway and we continued on our
way.

At twelve the next afternoon we drove up into the yard of our
new house, a small brick duplex across the street from an apartment development. It was clean and the walls were painted white
and although the rooms were small they would do. What furniture
Malcolm had managed to salvage from the apartment in Atlanta
was arranged haphazardly around the room. A moving van was
coming that afternoon from Dunleith with the baby beds and furniture from my room. It was not going to be much compared to the
life I had been leading but it would do. It would do as soon as I
found someone to take care of the babies. It wasn't that I didn't like
them or resented them coming unbidden into the world. I just
didn't like to take care of them. It bored me to take care of small
children because it's a boring job. Nature never intended a young
woman to be alone in a house with small children. In any simple
natural culture women gather in the daytime in groups and the
older women care for the children and the younger women find
work to do. Nowhere in nature is there anything like the boring life
I was fixing to lead in Alexandria, Louisiana. Of course, by the time
I had been there forty-eight hours I had found Klane Marengo and
for forty dollars a week she was going to come at breakfast and stay
until supper and take my boring work off my hands. Daddy had put
two thousand dollars into a checking account for me to use for
emergencies. The way I figured it, at forty dollars a week I could
keep the wolf of motherhood from my door for at least six months.
If that wasn't an emergency, I didn't know what one was.

"How do you like it?" Malcolm asked. He was standing in
the middle of the half-empty living room holding Little Malcolm in
his arms.

"It's great. It's really nice. It was nice of them to get this ready
for us. Nothing's going to happen, Malcolm. We're going to be
okay now. We're going to love each other from now on."

"I hope so. I really hope so. I can't take much more of this,
Rhoda. I can't take another year like the last ones."

"Momma," Jimmy said. "Hold me, Momma. I'm hungry. I

want to eat." I pulled his fat little happy body into my arms. I kissed his face and arms. We had been in Alexandria for an hour. Who knows, he may already have been bitten by a dozen mosquitoes.

Part Six

ALEXANDRIA

Chapter

29

Then it was spring and the town of Alexandria was heavy with the smell of Cape jasmine. Fat white flowers washed clean by rain. Rain fell nearly every afternoon in that tropical plane beside the Quachita River. Torrential rain full of salt from the Gulf of Mexico. It washed away the smell of the paper plant where Malcolm was raging away his days. The smell of jasmine and rain and the babies asleep in their beds and Klane Marengo's brilliant black skin appearing at my door each morning on her way home from her conjugal visits to the jail.

"Hi, Klane," I would say. "How's it going? What's going on?"

"I'm doing okay. How's the baby?"

"I don't know. He's still asleep."

"Was he okay last night?"

"I guess so. We had a party. God, I got so drunk. We made grasshoppers. You ever had one? Well, he slept all night. He's still asleep."

"You want me to stay late today?" She filled the door frame. She was six feet tall; she must have been of Watusi stock. She was the only maid I had ever had who could control Little Malcolm. In return I put up with her undependable hours and let her borrow money from me.

"You want me to stay late tonight or not?"

"Yeah, I do. You want to go home first? You could eat breakfast here and sleep awhile."

"Nah, they'd wake me up. I'll come back around noon. Where are they?"

"They're still asleep. Come on in. You want some coffee?"

"I want a ride home. I don't feel like taking no bus."

"Okay. Come on in. I'll take you as soon as they wake up."

"I don't know if I want to wait around." She was in the kitchen now, pouring herself some coffee, looking around to see what kind of messes we'd been making. "Where'd you go last night?"

"We went over to Karla's to make beef Stroganoff. We made grasshoppers. God, I bet I drank a million of them. You want to do the floors this afternoon? I got to get some more wax if you want to do them."

"I might. If I get time."

"Well, I got to get the wax if you think you might. Here, have a biscuit. Get some of that jelly over there." I handed her a plate of toasted biscuits. "You want an egg?" I added. "Scramble you an egg."

"Nah, not now. I guess I might go on and stay the morning." She was stirring sugar and evaporated milk into her coffee. She was spooning jelly onto a biscuit. "But you got to let me get some sleep. You got to keep them off of me. Where's the baby? I want to look in on him."

"Don't wake them up. I feel terrible, Klane. I really have a hangover."

"You been drinking too much. You been drinking every night."

"No, I haven't. It just seems that way." I raised my eyes, looked out the kitchen window to where the sun was coming out from in between the clouds and lighting up the branches of the crepe myrtle tree. Sunlight glistened on every gray-green branch. How could anything so perfectly balanced and cantilevered and shaded and luminous and gorgeous and beautiful and useful be created, over and over again, everywhere on earth. For a moment

I could see infinity, the window, branch, blossoms, clouds, sky, stretching up forever and ever, world without end. I shook it off.

"You leaving these babies too much. Miss Winchester tole me you was gone all weekend and she didn't even know where Malcolm was."

"He was mad at me. He went to a motel. He tore the phone out of the wall. You know about that."

"Well, I'm going back and look in on the baby." She finished off a second biscuit, folded the crumbs up into a napkin, and laid the plate on the sink.

"Don't wake them up."

"I won't. I'm just going to look in at the door."

She left the room. I sipped my coffee and thought about the night. Our new friends, Speed and Karla and Robert and Hilton, and Malcolm and me. Getting drunk on grasshoppers and dancing on the sidewalk in our midriff blouses.

"He's still asleep," Klane said, coming to stand in the door. "That medicine's not doing him no good. You ought to have them change it. You better take him back."

"I took him Wednesday. They said he's doing okay." She shook her head. "It's them mosquitoes," she said. "It's them mosquitoes that did it." She came into the room. She began to pick up the plates from the table. "You ought to take him to a different doctor."

A wave of melancholy passed through me. Melancholy and helplessness. I took him to the doctor nearly every day. I waited in the waiting room. I bought the medicine and gave it to him. Still he did not get well. He kept on running the fever in the afternoons. What else could I do?

I went out into the play yard and sat down on the swing. I looked up into the crepe myrtle tree. I considered calling my mother and asking her for something, some money, a new dress, a sofa for the living room. I swung for a while, trying to soothe myself. I began to remember scenes from the night before. Our new friend, Robert Haverty, dancing with me, in the living room, in the den, on

the patio and sidewalk. You know I'm in love with you, he said. I
have to have you. We were meant for each other. Maybe he was
right. Robert was rich. He had inherited a lot of money. He could
make the doctors pay attention to me. He could take me to the
Caribbean to live. We could leave these messes here and run away.
I leaned my head into the swing chain. I had to make it come out
right. I had to find some way to be happy.

"The phone's for you," Klane said, coming to the door. "It's
a man."

"We wanted to see how you are," Robert said. "Hilton wants you
to meet her in the park. Are your children up?"

"I'm fine," I said. "How are you?"

"I woke up thinking about you. Will you call me later, at the
newspaper?"

"Yes. Where's Hilton?"

"In the other room. Go with her to the park. I want our children to play together."

"All right." I put both hands on the receiver. It was so sexy.
So dangerous and scary and sexy. He was so bold, such a risk-taker.
He wanted us all to be together, then he wanted to be alone with me.
He was the man I should have married, the man I should have
waited for.

"Here's Hilton," he said. "She wants to talk to you. We're
glad you're okay."

"Oh, Rhoda," she said. "We had so much fun. Malcolm's so
much fun. He's the wittiest man I've ever met. Robert wants us to
go to the park. He thinks the children should have a picnic."

"Okay," I said. "Sure. As soon as I get them up."

I went into the babies' room to see if they were waking. Little
Malcolm was beginning to stir. I went over to the bed and touched
his head. "Get up, precious," I whispered. "We're going to have a
picnic in the park." He stirred, his beautiful little head bumped up
and down on the sheet. In the other crib Jimmy was curled up like
a snail, so deep in sleep I wasn't sure I could wake him.

I left the children's room and went into my bedroom and
opened my jewelry box and took out the bottle of diet pills and

swallowed one without water. Then I went into the bathroom and found some aspirins and took two of them and put my mouth under the faucet and drank.

In half an hour I was in the station wagon driving to the park, the children in the back dressed in blue and white sunsuits with sandals on their feet. I had on yellow shorts and a new white piqué blouse. You never could tell, Robert might decide to come with Hilton to the park. He owned the newspaper. He didn't have to go to work unless he wanted to.

That afternoon I took the baby, Jimmy, back to the doctor, a Jewish pediatrician who had gone to Tulane. He was overworked and had little patience with young mothers. He always kept me waiting for at least an hour and never spent more than five minutes with the baby when he finally saw him. This time, however, I made him talk to me.

"My maid says it's the mosquitoes." I took his arm, holding his sleeve so he couldn't leave the room. "She said he got something from the mosquito bites."

"What bites?"

"He got covered with mosquito bites right before he got sick. He got impetigo from them. Don't you remember? You gave me some medicine for it. It was in February. Right after that first warm spell. My maid said to tell you it was from the mosquitoes." He shook my hand from his sleeve, took the chart down from the door, began to read it again. Then he took Jimmy out of my arms and carried him to the examining table and began to stare into his eyes. "I want to put him in the hospital this afternoon and run some tests," he said. "I may want to do a spinal tap."

"A what?"

"A test for encephalitis. There was an epidemic of it in Monroe last month."

"We were in Monroe. We went to see my cousin play the organ."

"Could you bring him to the hospital this afternoon? Could you spend the night there with him?"

"Sure. I can do whatever you want me to. I'll have to call my husband and my maid. Can I use your phone? You want me to go to the hospital right now?"

"No. By five is plenty of time. They can do the blood work and if we need to do the spinal tap I'll do it in the morning." He picked up the baby and held him in his arms. He seemed to sniff him. He put his head down next to the baby's chest.

"I told you there was something wrong with him," I said. "He sleeps all day and he always has that fever."

"We'll find it," he said. "We'll find what's wrong." He looked at me. He met my eyes. Hope filled the room like snow. All the repressed terror and dismay of my young motherhood scrambled to leave me. Light was everywhere. Light and snow. The doctor had my baby in his arms. The doctor would save him.

"Do you know the Havertys?" I said. "Robert Haverty, who owns the newspaper here?"

Two hours later we checked into the hospital. Klane had agreed to stay with Little Malcolm and Big Malcolm had come home from the plant to stay with me. The baby slept in my arms. Now my elation was gone and dark worry had come to take its place. Encephalitis. My medical dictionary said it could injure the brain. My baby's brain could be injured, harmed, maimed. While I was out dancing with my friends my little baby's brain was being eaten by mosquito-borne germs. While we were listening to my cousin Sally play the organ, mosquitoes had risen up from the swamps and stuck their nasty needles full of poison into my child. I should never have left him for a second. I should not have taken him outside. I should have gone home to my mother where a halfway decent doctor would have found out what was wrong weeks ago. Oh, God, don't let anything be wrong with his brain, I prayed. If you will get him well, I swear to God I'll believe in you. I'll go to church every Sunday until I die. I'll give them money. I'll teach Sunday school.

"Rhoda." It was Malcolm. He was filling out the entrance forms for the receptionist at the admitting desk.

"What?"

"See if you've got that insurance card in your purse. The one I gave you last month."

"I've got it. Here, take the baby, will you? Don't wake him up. Oh, well, never mind." I handed Jimmy to him, a warm sleepy heavy precious little bundle. I looked down into his beautiful warm face. Oh, God, I began again. If you let anything happen to him, I'll kill you. Goddamn you for doing this to my baby. I hate fucking mosquitoes so much. I hate this goddamn mosquito-ridden town . . .

"Rhoda."

"Yes."

"Hurry up, will you? She's waiting on us." I produced the insurance card and the receptionist finished filling out the forms and directed us to a room on the third floor. We followed a yellow line to the elevators and got on and rode up to the third floor and went down a long hall and into a large rectangular room with a single bed and a crib. All this time Jimmy had not awakened. When I laid him down into the crib, I began to cry. "It's going to ruin his brain," I wept. "For God's sake, Malcolm, call my uncle, will you. Why don't the goddamn bastards hurry up."

A nurse came in and dressed the baby in a hospital gown. She was joined by two male nurses carrying a portable scale. They drew blood and weighed and measured him and took his blood pressure and his temperature.

"What is it?" I asked.

"It's ninety-nine," one answered, but the other frowned and I knew they weren't supposed to tell me. I walked over to where Malcolm was standing by the window with his face drawn up into a knot. He was blaming me for this, that much was clear. He was hating me and blaming me.

"This isn't my fault," I said, walking toward him. The nurses were still in the room. Jimmy was allowing them to do whatever they liked with him. Jimmy always trusted people. He always let people hold or touch him. He was the opposite of Little Malcolm who wouldn't even let *me* cuddle him. Little Malcolm was like his father, made of ice and stone. A beautiful golden stony child.

"Nobody said you did it. I will say this, if that goddamn Jew sends me another bill after this, I'll stuff it in his mouth. Where is he? I thought he was going to meet you here at five."

"I don't know. He said he'd come."

"Well he better get his ass on over here or I'm calling another doctor. That kid's been sick for weeks. Why did it take so long for this guy to figure out what's wrong? I told you not to take him to a goddamn Jew to begin with." He turned back to the window, his face going into one of its silent tirades.

"He's the best doctor in town. Everyone said to go to him. It's your fault we're in this goddamn town where we don't know anyone, where nobody knows who we are. You're the one that had to come here and work for that goddamn paper plant. You could be working for my daddy. It's your fault that we're starving to death in this goddamn mosquito-laden swamp. If anything is wrong with him, I'll never forgive you for this." I was near him now. I was in range and he turned and took my wrists in both his hands.

"Don't start anything in this hospital, Rhoda. Don't start a fight with that sick baby over there."

"We're through here," the nurse said. "You can feed him now. I called and told them to bring a tray."

"I'm starving," Malcolm put in. "I haven't had anything to eat all day. I'm going downstairs and get a sandwich. Do you want me to bring you anything?"

"No. I'm all right. Well, I guess I might like some coffee if they have any." I went over to Jimmy's bed. He was standing up with his hands on the rail, his bright little black eyes looking from his father to me and back again. "Oh, darling," I said. "Oh, my precious little baby boy."

The doctor came while Malcolm was downstairs. Dr. Klein, Dr. Samuel Klein. He took Jimmy out of the crib and sat on the bed holding him. "We'll do a spinal tap in the morning," he said. "Then we'll know."

"What will you know?"

"If the virus is there."

"Then what will you do?"

"There isn't much we can do. We'll do what we can. When he begins to respond we can test and see what happened."

"What could have happened?"

"Nothing he won't outgrow, I think."

"You think. What does that mean?"

"Let's don't get excited until we get the tests back." He handed me the baby. He was leaving. I couldn't bear for him to leave. I began to weep even harder than I had the first time. Tears rolled down my twenty-four-year-old cheeks. My Revlon pancake makeup ran down all over my linen blouse. Then the baby began to cry. Doctor Klein stiffened, seemed almost to tremble. He called out the door for a nurse, then came to me and began to pat me on the shoulder and the hair. The baby screamed even louder. My makeup and my tears rolled down onto my yellow skirt.

A man appeared in the door. It was an angel, yes, a godsend from the church of my mother's father's. Actually, it was my obstetrician, a tall, gray-headed man my father's age who was a lay reader at the Episcopal church which I sporadically attended. He was my kind of doctor, a good-looking Christian man who flirted with me and kept me supplied with diet pills. "Doctor Williams." I ran across the room and threw myself into his arms. "Oh, God, thank God you're here."

"I saw your name on the admittance list. I just came by to see what's going on. Hello, Sam, nice to see you."

"He might have encephalitis," I said. "It will destroy his brain. He's going to be an idiot. It's the baby, Jimmy, not Little Malcolm. We went down to Monroe to see my cousin Sally play the organ and he got it there."

"Oh, now, don't get excited. I'm sure it isn't all that bad. What's going on, Sam?"

"We're going to do a spinal tap in the morning. He's been running a low-grade temperature. I don't think it's critical if he did pick it up."

"His brain's being eaten by mosquito germs," I said. "I want my uncle here. I want someone to call my uncle and tell him what's going on."

"Her uncle's Carl Manning down in Mobile. He's doing that

heart transplant stuff with De Bakey." The doctor stood up. He directed his conversation toward the pediatrician. Then Malcolm appeared in the door with several nurses hurrying around him into the room.

"Why don't you take Rhoda somewhere and get her a drink and calm her down?" the older doctor said. "The baby's going to be fine, Rhoda. I'll call your uncle tonight if you want me to."

"Not a drink," Malcolm said. "For God's sake don't anyone give her any whiskey."

"Well, then take her out to eat." He turned to me. Took my hands, was so sweet I wanted to cry some more. "Take her somewhere and get her some dinner. The baby will be fine with the nurses, Rhoda. I'll be in the hospital another hour. I'll check back by before I leave. Go on, honey, get your pocketbook. Go on down the street and get some dinner."

Things settled down after that. Malcolm and I went down the street to a restaurant the hospital staff frequented and had a steak sandwich and some french fries and I even ate some ice cream. The diet pill was beginning to wear off. The food tasted good.

By the time we got back to the hospital the staff on the third floor had changed. A skinny blonde woman my mother's age was now in charge. She seemed more benevolent and kind. Maybe Dr. Williams had told her to be nice to me. Maybe he had told her I was crazy. Malcolm left to go relieve Klane and I played with Jimmy for a while on the single bed, then he fell asleep again and I lay down with my clothes on to read. I was reading *A Farewell to Arms*. I had already read it twice or three times, but I liked Hemingway so much I could read his books over and over, turning to any page to begin. "We had a lovely time that summer," I began reading. "When I could go out we rode in a carriage to the park. I remember the carriage, the horse going slowly, and up ahead the back of the driver with his varnished high hat, and Catherine Barkley sitting beside me."

"Rhoda." It was Klane, still wearing the dirty slacks and striped cotton blouse she had appeared in from the jail so many hours ago that morning. "I come by to see if I could do anything to help." She stepped gingerly into the room. Then walked straight over to the baby's bed and looked down at him. "What did they find out?"

"Nothing yet." I put a bookmark in the book and laid it down upon the bed and got up to go stand beside her. "They don't know anything . . . if he's got it, it might injure his brain. It's an inflammation of the brain. That's what it means. If he's got it, there isn't anything they can do. Just hope for the best." I took Klane's arm. I began to cry again.

"Don't wake him up," she said. "Don't cry, Rhoda. It's done now. His brain's okay. He couldn't be hurt. He's too sweet. He's the sweetest little boy I ever saw in my life." Now tears were in her eyes too. She led me over to the bed and turned it down and fluffed up the pillows. "You get on your nightclothes and get in bed. You're going to need your strength in the morning. You go on and get into the bed. I'll sit by him. That's what I come down here for."

"Don't you have to go home?"

"No. Delmonica's there. She'll take care of things."

"I thought you didn't like her anymore. I thought you said she was flirting with your husband." Delmonica was Klane's younger cousin from the Delta who had come to live with her. Last I had heard Klane had kicked Delmonica out for making out with her husband when he got the weekend off from jail and came home to patch the roof.

"I got Delmonica on my hands whether I like her or not. She ain't got no place to go home to. Her folks got kicked off the place for voting. They got mixed up with that mess at the Greenville Air Force Base."

"I don't know about that."

"Well, don't go talking about it now. Go on to sleep. You needs to get your sleep before the morning. No telling what the morning's going to bring." She went over to my suitcase and got out my nightgown and handed it to me. She watched while I undressed and put it on, then she put me into the bed and pulled the covers up around me. "Go on to sleep," she said. "I'm right here." She turned off the lights and pulled the lounge chair up beside the crib and sat back in it and folded her hands. "What about your children?'' I asked. ''Who's taking care of your little girl and boy?''

''They gone up to the country for the summer. They won't be back till almost school.''

''Who'd they go to see?''

''They went to stay with my momma up on Cockleshell. There's work for them up there hoeing cotton. You go on to sleep, Rhoda. Don't talk to me no more.''

''Okay,'' I said. I curled my legs up into my stomach and fell into a deep sleep.

I woke up once in the night to go to the bathroom. Klane was still there, asleep in the chair beside the crib. I suppose the nurses came in and out, checking on us, but I don't remember hearing them.

''Lethargic,'' I heard a male nurse say. It was sometime in the early morning. I sat up in the bed and realized I had a nightgown on. I wrapped the sheet around me and got up and began to look for my robe. Two nurses and a resident were hovering over the crib.

''Your maid said to tell you she'd gone home to see about your husband and your other child,'' the resident said. ''She said to tell you she'd check with you later.''

''What are you doing?'' I went to stand by the crib. Jimmy was awake, basking in the attention he was getting.

''You might want to get dressed,'' the resident said. ''They'll be in before too long to prep him.''

''Sure,'' I said. ''Sure, as fast as I can.'' I reached toward the baby but the resident was listening to his heart so I retreated and found my clothes and went into the small bathroom to put them on. The room was large for a hospital room but the bathroom was closet size. Once inside, with the door shut, I could barely get on my underwear. I pulled things on as well as I could and went back into the room. Jimmy was standing now, cooing and being charming to the nurses. The resident was letting him play with his stethoscope. They turned my way. They were all waiting for me.

''It won't take too long,'' the resident said, ''but you probably won't want to watch. They have to hold him very still, but it won't hurt him. Just scare him.''

"What are they going to do?"

"Prep him for the spinal tap."

"Just get him ready."

"Yes."

"Then what? Put a needle in his spine?"

"They have to take some fluid out of the spinal column to see if its infected with the virus. That's all."

"How much?"

"A very small amount."

"Okay," I said. "Whatever you have to do."

The resident and the nurses left. It was almost an hour and a half later when the next set of nurses came in to the room. By then Jimmy was screaming with hunger and the anxiety he had picked up from me.

The new nurses came in and lay him down on the crib and began to try to get an intravenous drip into his arm. A small blonde nurse stuck needle after needle into the fat flesh of his small perfect arm but she could not find a vein. On the fourth try, I was starting out of the room to complain at the nurses' station when Klane's huge frame reappeared in the door. She was dressed up now, in her Sunday school clothes, a long dark green gabardine dress with a white lace collar and white stockings and polished shoes. She had on long crystal earrings and several bangle bracelets. I had never seen her so dressed up, not even the time she had to go to court.

"Klane," I said, and threw myself into her arms. "Thank God you're here. They keep putting needles in him and they can't find a vein. They haven't even started on the spine yet." She glanced at me, then went to the crib. She reached down into the bed, through the sea of arms, and picked up Jimmy and held him. "You can do it now," she said. "I'll hold him. Do it fast if you have to do it. I can hold him still. I know what to do. I worked here all the time when I was young."

"Klane Marengo," one of the nurses said. "Sure. I remember you. You used to be in E.R. on the weekends."

"He's my baby," she said. "I takes care of him. Go on. Get back. I can hold him. What arm you want that drip in?"

Then she whispered to him and cuddled him down into her dress and picked up his left arm and held it out for the nurse. She immobilized it somehow and the nurse took the needle and directed it into the vein and strapped the sustaining board on the arm and taped it down. Jimmy was screaming, then sobbing, then still. "I got you," Klane was saying. "I got you right here at my heart. Ain't nothing going to hurt little Jimmy. Nothing ever going to hurt my baby."

She lay Jimmy down on the bed and the nurses tied him down, and then, suddenly, I had not known it was going to happen, they began to roll the bed out of the room and down the hall toward the operating room. As they went through the door the suspended bottle of intravenous solution fell and broke all over the floor. "Oh, God," I screamed. "No, you can't do it again. Don't do it again." I began to fight the nurses, fighting to get to the bed but Klane had me in her arms and Malcolm was coming in the door. Somehow between them they got me to the bed and the baby left with his retinue.

An hour later he was back in the room and Klane was holding him and I was sitting on the bed. "You haven't been home," I said. "You haven't had any sleep. Who's been going to the jail to feed your husband?"

"Delmonica's looking out for him. She took him some food this morning."

"I thought you didn't trust her with him."

"I don't. Well, Jimmy looks like he's better this morning. I don't think he's as sleepy as he was last week. Look here, Rhoda. His eyes are brighter."

I got up and went to stand beside her chair. Jimmy looked up at me. He didn't look any brighter. He looked like my cousin, Baby Gwen Mayhew, with her big brown bedroom eyes we all said had come from her Mexican blood and distant kinship to Ida Lupino. Now I thought they had come from all the mosquitoes in Clarksville, Mississippi, from the long flat flooded Delta fields and the insect-burdened spring and summer air. Yellow fever, typhus, malaria, the scourges of our ancestors, now encephalitis to haunt the future. Inflammation of the mucous membranes of the brain, the cerebral cortex, spine, or brain stem.

The doctor had come into the room while I was lost in my morbid thoughts. "It's over, Rhoda. You can take him home this afternoon. I'm going to start him on some new antibiotics. I want you to bring the other child in tomorrow and let us do some blood work. Are you listening?"

"Yes. Then there's nothing you can do?"

"About what? We're doing everything we can."

"If his brain was hurt? You can't fix that?"

"I wish you hadn't read that medical dictionary." He stared away. "A little knowledge."

"A little knowledge what? He's my baby. I have to know what's going on. I don't know what's going on. I don't think you're telling me what you know."

"What else do you want to know? He's a fine baby, a fine child. There isn't anything else to know. The sleepiness will get better. It's going to take time. We do what we can, Rhoda. That's all we can do."

"All right. I'm sorry. I'm sorry I'm so bad."

"Thanks for your help." Malcolm put down his magazine and came to the doctor's side. "We know you're trying."

"Your baby's all right. This was just a test so we'll know what's happened."

"Give him here." I had turned to Klane. She got up and walked toward me. A flat clear light was all across the black marble floor. She walked across it in her majesty and handed Jimmy to me. I took him from her arms. "Thanks," I said. "Thanks for everything."

The next three months we watched and waited. June and July and August came and went. Malcolm got a raise. Hilton got pregnant and almost lost the baby and had to be put to bed for weeks. Karla and Speed went to Mexico for a vacation and came home with souvenirs and stories about tequila. My tan got darker. Jimmy quit sleeping all the time. He still slept too long in the afternoons and fell asleep in the high chair when I fed him, but he seemed better. Every day I said to Klane, "Do you think he's better?"

"He's okay," she would answer. "He's fine. Yeah, he's just fine."

It was sometime that summer that I discovered Freud. "Read Freud," Derry had told me. I had taken to calling her on the phone when I was especially unhappy or had a bad hangover or got in the mood to dream of wisdom or courage or a life that was not pervaded by Cape jasmine and sex and gin. "Read Freud, read Jung, read Margaret Mead. And don't drink so much, Rhoda. It clouds your brain. It makes you dumb. You'll never solve your other problems until you quit doing that."

"I'm going to. I'm really going to. I'm going to quit until my birthday. [I'm only going to drink on Saturday nights. I'm never never drinking again on Sunday afternoons. I'm only going to drink at parties. I won't drink before five o'clock in the afternoon. I won't drink until we go to the coast. I won't drink anything else after this one drink, this last night, this one final party.]"

I am going to find out about Freud, I decided one summer afternoon. I went down to the Alexandria Public Library and found the books and spread them out on a table and began to try to read them. Okay. There are three parts to the brain. The ego, that's the part that talks to itself. The id, whatever that was. The superego, that sounded like my daddy, maybe.

I sat at the library table, desperately trying to concentrate, to understand. What did it mean? I didn't know. I couldn't guess. I looked around me. A poor mangy-looking lot of people were in the room. There was one tall man with glasses who looked as if he might want to talk about Freud but I didn't think I should risk it. He might follow me home. No, I would figure it out for myself. I read it through again. It was beginning to make some sense. I envisioned a phenomenological head. A large ugly egg with veins in it. It was divided into three parts, this superego, like my father, this ego, like the thing I call I, whatever that meant. I was I, wasn't

I? Wasn't I? Anyway, the third part was the id. The id was like a fairy or something. It was the crazy part. I didn't like it. I closed my eyes, thought as hard as I could, trying to penetrate the mystery of the mind. All I could see were coils of flesh, flesh and maybe bones, so thick, like intestines, or liver. How could it think? What does it do? How does it do it?

All of a sudden I thought I was going to suffocate from the dusty smell of the books and the dust all over the library floor. The library was too hot, there were too many people and not enough air.

I closed the books and stacked them up on the table and made my escape through the door. I went out onto the sidewalk, out into the burning hot summer day. The sun beat down on me, a zillion bolts a minute. It poured down upon the cars and sidewalks and trees and camellias and Cape jasmine bushes and crepe myrtle trees. It poured down upon my hands and arms and sandaled feet. The same sun had shone on ancient Greece, on Italy in the time of the Caesars, on me when I was a small child in the Delta, on me when I was twelve and lost a baseball game by striking out. It had shone on Freud when he thought up all that stuff and on the dinosaurs and where I was standing for millions of years. It had shone on Malcolm and me the summer we ran away to get married. It was still shining, that much was sure, but all the rest was lost in myth. I did not know where I was, in any way. I want a drink, I decided. I'll talk Klane into staying and I'll go get Hilton and we'll go out to the country club and order some hot hors d'oeuvres and a gin martini. I have to have some fun. Life is short and then we die. We die and don't even know what's up there in our brains. It's just some stuff like gray toothpaste. We don't even know how we got here or what will happen to us. I don't have anyone to love me. I just have Malcolm and he hates me. He thinks my hips are big. He thinks I'm fat.

Chapter

30

"I wish you would go to a psychiatrist, Rhoda." It was Derry talking to me on the phone a few weeks later. "I gave you the name of that man. Did you lose it?" I could hear her losing interest in the conversation. She had started being short with me when I called her up. She kept telling me things to do and I never did any of them and she was getting tired of having me call her up all the time.

"I definitely am going. I don't know what I'd do without you, Derry. I know you're tired of me calling you up."

"I'm busy this morning, Rhoda. Call the doctor whose name I gave you. You can't figure it out by reading books. You have to have some help."

"I'm going to. I really am. I'm going to call him this afternoon."

"Call him now. Call him when you hang up."

"Okay. Goodbye. Thanks for taking time to talk to me. Derry?"

"Yes."

"Have you heard from Jim?"

"I'm going to be seeing him next week. We're going to a meeting in Washington. He'll be there."

"Tell him I said hello. Will you do that for me?"

"Of course I will. Call the doctor, Rhoda. Get some help."

"I will. I promise. I'm going to. I really am."

One morning in August I finally called him. Malcolm had gone to a seminar in Atlanta to find out new things about time studies and I had spent the week getting drunk with Robert Haverty every night. We had gotten so drunk the night before we had broken all the crystal water glasses filling them with scotch and trying to use them for a piano. Finally the card table we had them on had collapsed on the stone-floored porch.

As soon as I woke up the next morning I called the psychiatrist Derry had told me about. There was an opening that afternoon. I put on my best dress and went down to talk about myself. "I drink too much," I said. "I do things I don't want to do when I get drunk. I broke all the crystal water glasses. My husband's going to kill me when he finds out."

"If it causes you problems, you should quit."

"It makes me fight with him. We don't like each other very much anyway. Well, we like to sleep together, but that's about all. So I want to quit, because I want to make our marriage work."

"Yes."

"Besides, I broke all those glasses."

"Yes."

"And I almost drowned the other night. He's been gone for a week and I've been drinking with Robert Haverty. He owns the newspaper here. His father died and left it to him. He's so rich. He has a yacht. Anyway, we went out on Speed McVee's boat on the river and I almost drowned. I dove into the river to show off and I couldn't swim against the current. They barely saved me. I mean, I'm a great swimmer. I meant to swim the English Channel. It's all I thought about when I was young. I swam the two-hundred-yard freestyle in two fifty-nine point five in college once. I mean, I was really good."

"How did you almost drown?"

"I jumped in in my bathing suit at eleven o'clock at night. Speed is Robert's cousin. They both dove in and dragged me back. The captain was furious. He said he'd never take the boat out with me on it again. He was really mad at me and he was mad at Robert."

"Is Robert married?"

"Yes. But he's in love with me. Everyone's in love with me, except my husband. I think he hates me. He thinks I'm fat. No matter how thin I get, he still thinks I'm fat. He used to have this girlfriend in Atlanta. Pepper Allen, she looks like a boy. I bet she doesn't weigh a hundred pounds. I think he's still in love with her. I think he wishes all the time he'd married her. He only married me for Daddy's money." I was starting to cry. There was a box of Kleenex on the doctor's desk and I got up and got a piece and began to cry into it.

"Well, that sounds pretty bad. I don't blame you for feeling bad."

"I want to quit drinking. I read about this stuff in *Time* magazine. Antabuse. If you take it, you can't drink. I want you to get me some. I really need it. If I don't stop, it's going to ruin my marriage and I'll have to go home and live with my folks again. They drive me crazy."

"I'll give you some Antabuse if you can take it. You'll have to have blood tests done at the hospital and we'll have to wait for the results, but if you can tolerate it, I don't mind trying. You'll have to be sure all the alcohol is out of your system. Can you quit for two weeks for me, Rhoda?"

"Sure. I can do anything. I'm going crazy with things the way they are. I'm not an alcoholic. I only drink to have fun."

"Well, don't have any more fun for two weeks and get the blood tests done. Can you come back on Thursday?" He pulled a notebook out of his desk and began to look at his appointments. "My nurse is gone for a few days. I have to do this myself. Yes, Thursday at two. Can you come then?"

"Sure. Whatever you want me to do."

"What do you fight about besides him saying you're fat."

"He's jealous of me. He never lets me have any friends. He thinks I want to sleep with everyone."

"And do you? Want to?"

"No, of course not."

"Men are herd animals. They project their desires onto their wives. They think you want to do what they want to do."

"I don't think he thinks about anybody else, except Pepper Allen."

"Well, that's good. Here. Take this over to the hospital and get the tests made and I'll see you Thursday then." He stood up. He smiled at me. He was very old, at least fifty years old. I didn't even want him to desire me. I didn't even want to sleep with him.

I went by the hospital that afternoon and had the tests made and ran into Dr. Williams in the hall. He put his hands on my waist and told me to come by his office after work someday.

"What for?" I looked up into his balding bespectacled kindly face. "What would we do?"

"Just talk awhile. I like you, Rhoda, don't you know that?"

"Sure I do. I'll never forget you helped me when Jimmy was here." I backed away. His power was getting on me, drawing me in, a sort of smell of power. I usually found such a thing seductive but today I was concentrating on stopping drinking and being good.

"Is Klane Marengo still working for you?" he asked.

"Yes."

"Be careful of her. She's been in trouble with the law, you know that, don't you?"

"Well, she's the only maid in town who can keep Little Malcolm out of trouble. She's wonderful with my children. She loves them. She loves me. Her husband's out of jail. He got out last week. They can't help it if sometimes they have to steal."

"Just be careful. Well, call me sometime. Here's a number that will answer if the office doesn't. After hours or on the weekends." He handed me a card with a phone number written on it. I took it and put it in my purse.

"Thanks," I said. "Thanks for giving this to me."

I went home in a wonderful mood. Doctor Williams was in love with me. I was going to quit drinking. Robert was coming over. Maybe Speed was in love with me too. Malcolm was out of town and I didn't have to cook dinner for three more days. Best of all, I had a new mauve linen dress and there was a party at the country club that night to wear it to.

I pulled into my driveway, singing to myself. Klane came out the kitchen door with Jimmy in her arms. Little Malcolm was beside her carrying his guns.

"I got to get on home," she was saying. "I can't stay any longer today, Rhoda."

"Oh, I'm going to a party tonight. I thought you'd stay till the baby-sitter gets here."

"Not tonight. I got to get on home. We got a whist game tonight and I got to cook a roast."

"You could cook it here. Well, okay, go on then. I don't care." I got out of the station wagon and kissed the children and kept on talking as we walked toward the house. "Guess what, I'm quitting drinking. I really am. I'm getting these pills that if you drink while you're taking them you can die. So after that, I know I won't drink. But first I can't drink for two weeks. Malcolm, you little angel. Give your momma a kiss." I knelt beside him and hugged his powerful little body into my own. The shells from his bandolier cut into my skin. He let me kiss him on the cheek, then ran away. "What's wrong with him?"

"He's just showing off. Well, that's good news. If you stick to it." She was walking into the house, picking up her pocketbook off the shelf. "I'm leaving, Rhoda. I got to get out of here."

"Okay." I had hoped I could get her to bathe the children before she left, but there was no stopping Klane when she was set on leaving. I went inside and put a record on the record player and began to dance around the room. Jimmy began to dance with me. I picked him up and danced him around the kitchen table and out into the polished hall. Klane had done the floors. This day was getting better and better. This day was so good it deserved a drink. I started toward the kitchen cabinet that held the scotch, then stopped myself. I picked up the phone and dialed the newspaper office to talk to Robert instead.

"I can't have a drink for two weeks. What am I going to do?"

"We'll come get you early," he said. "What time can you get ready? We'll go out early and have dinner at the club before the party. Can you be ready by six?"

"I'll see."

I made it all night without drinking a single thing. It was the first party I had been to since I was fifteen at which I didn't get drunk or at least very tipsy. It was strange and made the evening stretch out into an eternity. At twelve we dropped Hilton off and took the Havertys' baby-sitter home. Then Robert took my baby-sitter home, then he came back over to have a drink with me. We put Errol Garner on the record player, "Concert by the Sea." I had never been to California, but I knew it from the music. It was beautiful cliffs with the sea below and Robert and me driving along a mysterious road in the moonlight, close together in the front seat of a Karmann Ghia. Both of us madly in love, no children, no problems, no doctors or mosquitoes or worries of any kind. Just Robert and me, rich and madly in love, driving forever up the California coast on our way to someplace great to drink wine and eat dinner.

In real Alexandria, Louisiana, I took off my clothes and we began to make love on the living room floor. "Oh, Robert," I said, "it's so good. It feels so good. You're so good at it."

Of course, it really wasn't good. It wasn't half as good as the passion Malcolm and I lavished on each other in the long sexy married nights. But the music was good and my imagination and the power of the money Robert had inherited was taking care of the rest.

"Let's go to bed," I said. "Let's go do it on the bed."

We moved into the bedroom and lay down upon the bed. About that time a mosquito bit me. I got up and turned on the lights and began to swat mosquitoes with a house shoe. For some reason Robert decided that was hilarious. He sat up and began to laugh uproariously while I killed at least ten mosquitoes, leaving their bloody carcasses all over the white-painted walls.

Then I turned off the lights and got back into the bed and began to laugh with him. We fell asleep still giggling.

* * *

At three that morning the phone rang. It was Klane. "Delmonica's dead," she said. "Delmonica's not moving."

"What? What's happening?" I sat bolt upright in bed, groping for the switch on the lamp.

"Delmonica fell on a knife I was holding. We was playing whist."

"My God. Have you called the police?"

"No. I was hoping Malcolm might come over. Is he there?"

"Mr. Haverty's here. Robert Haverty. You used to work for them. . . . (Robert, wake up. It's Klane. Wake up. Somebody's dead.)" I shook his shoulder. "Wait a minute, Klane," I said. "I've got to wake him up."

"Where's Malcolm? Is Malcolm there?"

"What's going on?" Robert sat up on the bed. I handed him the phone. "It's Klane Marengo. There's somebody dead."

"Klane, it's Robert Haverty. Tell me what happened." She told him and he listened, then he said, "I'll be right there. Don't touch anything. Tell everyone not to touch anything. Call the police, Klane. I'll be there by the time they are." He was out of bed, pulling on his clothes. I got up and turned on the overhead light. The mosquitoes I had killed were all over the wall above the headboard of the bed. The bedclothes were half off the bed, the candles were burned down into their saucers. I found a robe, put it on as Robert dressed. "What should I do?" I asked. "Is there anything I can do?"

"No. Yes, call Hilton and tell her I passed out on the sofa. Tell her I've gone down to the project to help Klane. What did she say to you? I couldn't understand the story."

"She said someone fell on a knife she was holding. It was a whist game."

"Who was it?" He was buttoning his shirt, tucking it in.

"Her cousin Delmonica. She's been flirting with Klane's husband." I stood by the door. He finished his shirt and put on his socks and shoes. Then he walked out into the hall. I followed him to the door. "Call me," I said. "Call me as soon as you find out what's going on."

When he was gone I turned on the lights in the living room and picked up the records and glasses and ashtrays. Then I went out on the porch and began to collect Coke bottles. I went in and out from the porch to the living room to the kitchen, cleaning up. When I was finished with those rooms, I went into the bedroom and gathered up the candles and took the sheets off the bed. I made the bed up with pink-and-white-striped sheets and pillowcases. I swept the floor with a broom. I hung up all my clothes. Then I went into the kitchen and put on a pot of coffee. While it was brewing, I took a shower and washed my hair and began to get dressed.

When I finished dressing, I walked out into the yard to see if the newspaper had come. Malcolm's car pulled up to the curb and he got out and walked past me into the house.

"Where'd you go last night?" he said. "I called at twelve-thirty and the baby-sitter said you were at a party. Who'd you go with?"

"How did you get home? I thought you had to stay till Monday."

"I drove home last night. They need me back here. Where'd you go? Who'd you go out with?"

"You better calm down and listen. Klane killed someone. Robert Haverty's over there. I think Klane killed Delmonica."

"What? What are you talking about now, bitch?"

"Klane killed someone. Someone fell on a knife she was holding."

"Where are the boys?"

"They're asleep. Don't wake them up. What are you mad at me for?"

"Because you've been running around all over town while I was gone. Dave saw you. He called and told me. I'm leaving this morning, Rhoda. I'm going back to South Carolina. I'm through with this shit. I'm leaving now."

"Don't you care about Klane? Don't you even want to know what happened?"

"Not particularly. I've seen nigger murders before. Every Saturday night in Martinsville, Georgia. I'm leaving, Rhoda. I mean it this time."

"Then go on. Who cares. You don't think I care, do you? I don't give a tinker's damn." I stood back from him, examining his head. In the front was the ego, on the side was the superego, on the back was the id. I could see it all so clearly. All three parts fighting against themselves. "You are so goddamn dumb," I said. "I hate being married to you. I don't care if you leave or not. I hate you. I hate being married to you."

He took a step toward me as if to hit me, then he backed off and turned and walked into our room. I heard the shower running. A long time later he came back into the living room carrying a small bag in one hand and his shaving kit in the other. "I'm taking the good car. Your daddy will get you another one."

"Go on then. No one's stopping you." The phone began to ring. "Answer the phone, will you. It must be Robert. He's gone down to the police station, I guess."

"You answer it. She's your maid. I told you not to hire her."

"She's the only one who can take care of Malcolm and I like her. She's a Watusi. She's supposed to be fierce."

"What does that mean? Never mind. I'm leaving. I'm going, Rhoda. I'm leaving now."

"Wait till I answer the phone, can't you? Can't you wait a minute?" I grabbed the phone and answered it. "Wait a minute, Robert. I can't talk. Malcolm's here." I dropped the receiver and walked to the door and took Malcolm's arm. "Help me. I need you to stay and help me. Klane killed someone. Don't you understand?" But Malcolm shook my hand from his arm and walked down the sidewalk toward the car.

"That's my car," I screamed. "Don't take my car." He just shook his head at that and got in and started driving. I walked back into the house and picked up the phone. "I'm sorry. What's happening? What's going on down there?"

"Malcolm's there?"

"He was here. He's gone. He's leaving me. Never mind. He doesn't know you were here. Tell me what's going on down there."

"They took her off downtown. Her kids are home and her sister's got them. I'm going to the police station. Did you get Hilton on the phone?"

"No, I never did. You want me to call her now?"

"No, I'll call. Just meet me at the police station as soon as you can. I'll call my cousin Edmund. He's a lawyer. He'll help, I think. There were five people there, Rhoda. They all witnessed it and they all say she fell on the knife. They swear she fell on the knife."

An hour later I was down at the jail with Robert talking to policemen and lawyers. "She always had a knife," I kept saying over and over. "She used it to cut up things. She needed it to cut up vegetables and things. She always had a knife."

"Did you know this Delmonica was having an affair with her husband?" This from a tall redheaded cop.

"How could anyone have an affair with him? He was in jail. Klane went down to see him every day. She spent the night on Sundays."

"Well, one of the neighbors said there was bad blood over a man. Maybe it wasn't a husband."

"She didn't stab her," I kept saying. "Klane wouldn't stab anybody. My little boys just love her. She's so good with children. She wouldn't kill someone. Delmonica fell on the knife. I want to see her. I want to talk to her."

Finally, I was allowed to talk to Klane. They took me down a hall into a concrete cell with iron bars. Klane was sitting on a cot. She looked so small, so frightened, her shoulders bent into her chest. "Rhoda," she said. "Oh, Rhoda, where have they put my children?"

"Your sister has them. Is that okay? Are you okay?"

"Where's she keeping them? At her house or my house?"

"I don't know. I'll go find out. Where do you want them to be?"

"At my house. I don't like her husband. He's not a good man. They shouldn't be over there."

"Klane."

"Yes."

"We're going to get you out of here. They're setting bail. We'll get you out by tomorrow. Robert said they'd have you out tomorrow. His cousin Edmund who's a lawyer is going to get you out."

''I can't stay here.'' She stood up and I put my arms around her. She smelled like the night, dark and forlorn. I held her gingerly at first and then something happened to me, maybe it was the hangover or the Dexedrine I had taken as soon as Malcolm left, maybe it was the whole blown-out-of-reality spring, maybe I just went crazy, but all of a sudden I was able to really hold her in my arms, all the whole long tall black body, all the history of her people, the majesty of the Watusi, spear and lion, ancient warrior race, God knows my wild genes had not come from peaceful men, maybe I admired her, maybe it seemed absolutely logical to let your enemy fall upon your knife.

''No one's going to keep you in the jail,'' I said. ''We'll get you out of here tomorrow. I'll go by your place and find your sister and tell her to take your kids to your house. I'll get someone to keep them there if I have to. Klane?''

''Yes ma'am.''

''Don't call me ma'am. You said you wouldn't do that, remember? Listen. This is going to be all right. I'm going to fix it. Robert and I will fix it. You understand that?''

''I hope so. I'll kill myself if I have to stay in here. I can't stay in here.''

''You don't have to. Tell me what happened. What happened last night?'' I led her over to the cot and we sat down on it.

''Delmonica and Shirley and Shirley's husband, Willie, came over to play whist. Shirley and Willie and Brown and I been playing whist for fifteen years on Saturday nights. Ever since we came up from Lafayette when we was young. Delmonica had been out drinking. She stepped in the door and right away started talking about my roast. That roast's not right, she said. She's always talking about my cooking. I said, Delmonica, don't come in here talking about my cooking in my own house. Then we dealt out the cards and Willie said, 'Open me a beer,' and I took out the knife to open his beer and she jumped at me. I hadn't said a word. I just took out the knife and she jumped me across the table and then she was on the floor and the knife was in her throat and Willie started crying and Shirley said, 'Call somebody.' I didn't kill her, Rhoda. I didn't kill anybody. You got to get me out of here.''

"Time's up." It was the sheriff. I hugged Klane again and comforted her as best I could and then I followed the sheriff back out to the office where Robert and his cousin Edmund were talking to a clerk.

"We have to get her out," I said. "She said she'd kill herself if she has to stay in there."

"We'll get her out," Edmund said. "But you'll have to put up bail. It might be five hundred dollars."

Robert walked me out to my car and opened the door and put me in. "Can I see you tonight?" he asked. "I'd like to kill some more mosquitoes." He grinned widely, holding the door for me, so sure of himself, so satisfied and vain. I started disliking him intensely.

"No. I don't know. I have to find out if Malcolm really left. What if he stays here and he comes over? It scares me, Robert, he was really mad. Look what happened at Klane's."

"Oh, Edmund will take care of it. No one minds if the blacks kill each other."

"I care. And I don't believe she did it. I talked to her. You should have seen her face. Why couldn't someone fall on a knife? Someone could fall on a knife."

"Oh, Rhoda. Really. Don't talk like a fool. Of course she killed her. Nonetheless, Edmund can handle it. Can you come up with the money?"

"Of course I can. Well, I'd better go now. I have a neighbor watching the children. I don't have any help. God, that's all I need with Malcolm running around God knows where."

"We'll get your maid back. Don't worry about it. Can I come over tonight if you find out he's left?"

"I guess so. I'll call you later. Where will you be?"

"Call the newspaper later. I'll be in and out all day."

"Thanks for helping. Thanks for getting your cousin."

"He's a lawyer. This is what he does. We have him on retainer for the paper, of course. Maybe he'll waive the fee." He grinned again and I could just imagine the conversation where he told Edmund he was fucking me. I was really getting irritated and the sun was beating down. It was past noon and it was hot.

"I'll call you later," I said, and drove off and left him standing there with his totally self-satisfied expression extending even to his wrinkled seersucker suit.

When I got home, Malcolm was in the yard playing with the children. He had gotten them from the neighbor and had even fed them lunch. He had made peanut butter sandwiches and put them on little plates with potato chips and pickles. He had poured milk. "I'm glad you came back," I said. "I love you. I want to fuck you. Let's put them to bed and go make love."

"I should go back to the plant. I talked to Dave, Rhoda. He said to come back over here and talk to you and give it one more try. If you want to try this again then I will too." He stood up beside the swing set, looking so old and so young, so worried and determined. My guilt over fucking Robert covered me like a pall. It spread up my arms and legs and into my face and I knew that at any moment I might confess and wait for him to kill me. "Let me make love to you," I said instead. "I'm so terrible, Malcolm. I'm so crazy and I drink too much but I'm going to quit. I'm getting some Antabuse and I'm going to take it. I swear I am. I won't drink anymore, ever. I swear to God I won't. I want you to love me. I want so much to be good." The children had stopped playing and come to stand between us. Little Malcolm was holding on to Malcolm's legs and Jimmy was pulling on me. "Let's try to get them to sleep," I said. "Let's take them inside." I looked up into my husband's face. Would anything ever make up for what I had done already? Could anything forgive and wash away my badness? I was so bad I'd be lucky if I lived another day. I picked up Jimmy and moved closer to Malcolm and laid my hand upon his cheek. "Please love me," I said. "Please try to forgive me and give me another chance."

On Tuesday morning Klane was back in my kitchen. Subdued, darkened, but back. The trial was set for late November, almost three months away.

"Are you okay?" I asked. "Are you going to be okay?"

"I guess I will," she answered. "I guess I'm doing okay."

"Everyone's testifying for you. Edmund said everybody was on your side. There's no way you'll be convicted."

"If I am, I'll kill myself. I won't stay in no jail."

"You won't be in jail. I swear you won't." She was putting her jacket in the closet. Setting her purse on the shelf. "Look, can you baby-sit for us on Saturday? The Havertys want us to go with them to their place up on the lake. Could you stay on Saturday?"

"What time?"

"Around noon. Until six or seven at night. Could you come then?"

"I'll try. I'll see if I can. How's the baby doing?"

"He's better. Go on in and see if he's waking up. He's been missing you. We've all been missing you."

"I'll wait till he wakes. I need me some coffee. I didn't get much sleep last night." She poured herself a cup of coffee and brought it over to the table. She bent over it, then she lifted her head and looked up at me. There was so much pain in her eyes I couldn't look at it. I lowered my eyes and she looked away.

Light was pouring in the windows. Pouring down upon the kitchen table with its blue and white china and its white-painted enamel top and the vase of lilies I had cut that morning.

Klane sipped her coffee, then set the cup down into its saucer and was still. Her hands lay in a streak of sunlight. I met her eyes again; the pain was still there, so deep and old and frazzled there was no way to untangle it.

"I know what," I said. "We've got half a bottle of wine in the refrigerator. This South African wine Robert got from his cousin. Let's drink some of it. I haven't had a drink in the morning but once in my life and that was at a hunt breakfast. I mean, early in the morning like this. Have you ever?"

"I don't know. You mean, when you get up, not staying up all night?"

"Yeah." I got up, opened the refrigerator, and took out the bottle. "This is so decadent. We'll just have one glass, then I'll help you do the floors. The floors are a goddamn mess. They

tracked in all that rain from yesterday and God knows what all."
I took down two gold-banded wineglasses and filled them with
wine and handed one to her. She took it and shook her head.

"Listen, Klane," I said. "I'm going over to the library later to
study something. It's by this man named Freud who discovered
everything about the brain. The brain's divided into three parts and
they are always fighting against each other. One part is the ego,
that's the part that's you and me. Like I think I'm Rhoda and you
think you're Klane. Then there's the superego, it's like your daddy,
and the third part is the id. I don't know what it does yet because
this stuff is so hard to read and you have to work real hard to figure
it out. I'm going back to the library this afternoon and read it some
more."

I lifted my glass and drank it off. Then I picked up the bottle
and filled my glass again and waited while she drank hers and filled
it. "We might as well finish off this little bit. What the hell, we've
had a pretty terrible week. God, I almost died when I had to come
and see you in that cell. Goddammit, Klane. I was so scared.
Weren't you scared to death?" She kept on looking at me. I reached
over and took her hand. "You never have to go back in there," I
promised. "There is no way on earth that anyone will put you back
into a jail." I drank my second glass of wine. Sun poured in the
window. "Listen, Klane," I went on. "Edmund said there was
nothing for you to worry about. He said there is no way on earth
they are going to put you in jail and leave your little children with
no one to take care of them." A very slight breeze blew in the door,
harbinger of rain coming from the Gulf. I felt very old suddenly,
mean and powerful and cynical and old. I could make too many
calls. I could pull strings. Robert owned the newspaper. My new
friend, Speed, owned all the real estate downtown. There wasn't
any justice anyway, or any law, there was only this, knowing
people and making calls and getting all the men to be in love with
you. "You're safe," I added. "I swear you are." I poured us a third
glass of wine. "You wouldn't believe how interesting it is to read
this stuff about the brain. We just walk around all day and we don't
even know what's up there. I mean, we all have a brain and we
don't even understand the parts of it."

"I believe I'll make Mr. Malcolm a gumbo for his supper tonight," Klane giggled. "And some of them little short biscuits from that recipe his momma gave us. You ought to be nicer to him, Rhoda. He's twice the man of Mr. Haverty. Mr. Haverty don't ever even go to work. When I used to work for them he used to stay in bed half the day."

"I'm nice to him. I'm nice as I can be. Well, I got to go take a bath and get dressed. I might go on over to the library as soon as it opens." I stood up. Drinking wine in the morning was a wonderful idea. Having Klane back in the kitchen was wonderful. It was a wonderful world and the sun was shining and would probably go on shining until two or three o'clock that afternoon. I bent down and kissed Klane on the cheek. The babies appeared in the door. They had climbed out of their beds and come to see what was going on.

"Cereal," Jimmy said. "Cereal, potato chips."

"Where's my gun?" Little Malcolm put in. "Jimmy put my gun somewhere."

"It's right here where you left it," Klane said. "Don't go blaming everything on Jimmy all the time."

"That's probably the id part." I was searching his skull for the divisions. "I bet that's the id that's always trying to start a fight. Yeah, that's the id, over there in the middle. It's sure not the superego. That's us, Klane, when we boss them around." I grabbed Little Malcolm on his way to get his gun from underneath the high chair and gave him a kiss and ran my hand across his head. Klane got up and went over to where Jimmy was standing in the doorway. She picked him up and cuddled his fat little body into her arms. She sat back down and let him hug her while she finished off her wine. I drank the rest of mine. Little Malcolm picked up his machine gun and went out into the backyard to look for targets.

"I don't boss them," Klane said, hugging Jimmy's soft fragrant little body to her. "It don't do no good to boss them, Rhoda. When you going to figure that out? All you can do is hug them and feed them and keep them out of trouble. Get trouble out of their way."

"I haven't finished reading it yet. I just barely got started."

"Well, I got to get on them floors sometime today so don't stay gone the whole time I'm here."

"I'll be back by noon." I walked over to the door and looked out into the yard. Little Malcolm was pushing his playhouse toward the fence. Every week or so he managed to get it all the way to the fence and climbed out and ran away but usually we pushed it back to the middle of the yard before he made an escape. "He's pushing his house," I said. "How far do you think we ought to let him move it?"

"Let him go awhile. He don't like being penned up. Nothing likes being penned up."

I walked over to her chair and took her shoulders in my hands. "You won't be penned up, Klane. Over my dead body will they put you in a jail."

Jimmy raised his eyes and looked from one of us to the other, then smiled and curled his head down into Klane's chest. The cerebral cortex was going down again. It was losing water. Its messages were stuck on sleep. Sleep, it was saying. Sleep some more. Everything's okay. There's nothing to worry about. Nothing to fear.

Chapter

31

Of course I was pregnant. Nature doesn't waste such weather, so much turbulence, so much heat. I was supposed to start menstruating on the Tuesday after Klane got out of jail. I didn't start. I had been late exactly three times in my life. Once when I had pneumonia and twice when I was pregnant. All day Tuesday I walked around the house remembering something that happened the night I slept with Robert. The rubber had come off while he was fucking me. We had laughed about it because I was also wearing my diaphragm and some new contraceptive jelly. Besides, a long time had gone by since I had Jimmy and I had begun to get careless. Maybe it was possible to keep from getting pregnant. Maybe there was a way.

So I didn't start on Tuesday and I didn't start on Wednesday and Thursday I began to have all the other symptoms. I couldn't smoke. I couldn't sleep. I was urinating all the time. There was nowhere to go, nowhere to turn. I was pregnant and that was that. I was pregnant and I didn't have the slightest idea whose baby it was. It was Robert's or it was Malcolm's. Either way I was not going to have it. There were abortionists somewhere in the United States of America and I would find one if it was the last thing I ever did in my life. I was not going to be cut open again for anything or anybody. I was going to live.

*   *   *

On Friday I didn't start so on Friday afternoon I found Dr. Williams's telephone number in my pocketbook and called him at his office and told him I had decided to take him up on meeting him for a drink.

"You have to take care of them for me," I said to Klane. "I have to go and meet this doctor and get the name of an abortionist. I'm pregnant, Klane. I can't stand it. You have to stay. You have to tell Malcolm a lie. Tell him I had to go talk to someone about a problem at the church. Tell him it's about raising money for the new pews."

"I'm here, Rhoda. You can count on me. Let me call my sister and tell her I'll be late."

Then I dressed up in my best silk dress and my best high-heel shoes and got into the old car and drove down to Dr. Williams's office. "Come down here after office hours," he had said. "Then we can go somewhere together."

When I got to Dr. Williams's office, he was waiting at the door and took me back to an examining room and took a seat on the table. I sat down in the chair and we began to gossip about people at the church.

"What I really came down here for was to ask you something," I said. "Do you promise not to tell anyone I asked you?"

"Of course. Anything you tell me is confidential. I'm a physician."

"Well, I think I'm pregnant and I want to get an abortion. I want you to tell me where to go."

"Oh, Rhoda. It's probably hysterical. Haven't you been wearing your diaphragm?"

"Yes, but a rubber broke the other night and I'm five days late."

"Wait a minute. I thought you were wearing the diaphragm."

"I was wearing the diaphragm and we were using a rubber too."

"You were using a rubber and a diaphragm?"

"I can't stand to be pregnant. I can't stand the idea of it. I'm scared to death of getting cut open again. I told you that the first time I came in here. Now it's happened anyway. I'm five days late."

"Five days isn't much."

"I'm never late. I'm usually a few days early. Besides, I think I am. I feel like I am."

"You couldn't have symptoms this soon. It's probably hysterical. Come in tomorrow and bring a specimen and we'll do a test."

"No." I had gotten up and was walking around the room. I opened the door to the hall. I walked out into the hall, then back into the room. "No, I know I am and I don't want a test. I don't want there to be a record of me being pregnant. Then if they find out they can put me in jail."

"Oh, Rhoda."

"Don't patronize me. I'm too tired and scared for that. I want the name. Will you give me the name?"

He hesitated. He shook his head. He spread out his hands.

"I'll fuck you if you'll tell me. I know you want to fuck me. You've been wanting to fuck me ever since you met me. You want to every time I come to church. Sometimes I get dressed up and sit in front of you just to make you want me. Well, will you? Will you or not?" I had started unbuttoning my dress. My bra was showing and my slip. "Tell me the name and I'll let you do it. I'll do it so well you never will forget it."

"Doctor Van Zandt," he said. "In Houston, Texas. I'll give you a phone number. He won't hurt you. He does it the way it should be done."

I unbuttoned the rest of my dress and let it slip to the floor.

Malcolm was standing in the carport with Klane beside him when I drove up. "Where have you been?" he asked. "It's almost seven-thirty. Have you been drinking again?"

"No, I have not been drinking. I went to a meeting and then I went to talk the doctor into giving me some Antabuse. I told you I was going to quit drinking and I'm going to. I had to have some more tests made. They have to be sure I can take it before they give it to me." I didn't look at him. I just got out of the car still talking and I kept on talking. "Thanks for staying so late, Klane. What an afternoon. Did you get anything out for dinner?"

"I made you some fried chicken and a pan of biscuits. Well, I'm going on if you're here." She looked at me from under her eyebrows.

"Go on then. I'm sorry it took so long. I'm sorry I didn't call you, Malcolm. Everything took longer than I thought it would. Besides, it's still light. I lose track of time this time of year. Come on in. If you'll watch them another minute while I change clothes, I'll get dinner ready." I swept by him into the house and went into the bathroom and pulled off all my clothes and grabbed a washcloth and washed off my body and stuck a tube of spermicide up my vagina and then put on some cutoffs and a loose shirt. I swept back into the kitchen and started setting the table and heating vegetables and getting out bread. I was pretending I was Derry Waters. I could do it all and do it all at once. I could cook and set the table and take care of babies and plan getting an abortion. I was Aphrodite and Athena and Diana. I was unstoppable and amazing and divine and I sure as hell wasn't going to have any more babies no matter who they belonged to or what I had to do.

"Come on in and put them in their high chairs," I called out to Malcolm. "I'm sorry you're having to take care of them but come on in here and talk to me. Tell me what you did today. Tell me what's going on at the plant." He came into the kitchen with the boys. He was still suspicious but he didn't know exactly what to be suspicious of. He knew I was up to something, but I was moving so fast it was throwing him off.

"Tell me about these tests you had done," he began. "I thought they'd already done them."

"They have to be very careful who they give that stuff to. It can kill someone if they use it wrong. I told you I wasn't going to drink anymore and I mean it. I don't care what I have to do. Don't worry about how much it costs. Daddy will pay for it if he has to. Don't worry about anything, Malcolm. It's all going to be all right." I put the platter of chicken on the table. I handed him a plate with green peas and carrots on it. "The biscuits will be ready in a minute. I know you're starving. Go on and eat. I can get the babies in their chairs."

"What if the tests don't work? Couldn't you just stop, Rhoda? Don't you have enough willpower just to quit?"

"I don't want willpower. I want something that can't fail." I smiled at him, a great kind powerful Athena-like smile. "I want to keep my promises to you, that's all I really want.

"I hope you mean that, Rhoda. God, I hope that's so."

As soon as Malcolm left for work the next morning, I put the babies in the car and drove home to Dunleith. I didn't even leave a note. Mother knew something was wrong but she couldn't figure it out and I wasn't telling her. I unpacked the car and moved our things into my room. "What's going on?" she kept asking. "Why did you decide to come home all of a sudden?"

"I'm tired. I'm worn out from everything that's going on. They charged my maid with murder. They said she killed someone. I can't talk about it now, Mother. I have to get some rest. I haven't slept in days." It was true. I was feeling terrible and I was so scared I hadn't slept in days. As soon as the children were asleep I fell into a bed and slept until three in the morning. I woke up with moonlight coming in the window and went upstairs and found my father in the guest room and woke him up and told him to come downstairs.

"I'm pregnant, Daddy. I have to get an abortion. You have to help me. I'll die if they keep cutting me open every year. I can't do it again. I just can't let them do it anymore." I was sitting on the sofa in the den. He was sitting in the brocade armchair, wearing his pajama bottoms and a cotton T-shirt, his old outfielder's body so strong and fine. I loved him so much. I was safe in his presence. He would not let me die. No matter what the world did, this man would save me. He would not let me die from anybody's madness.

"Oh, Sister, give me a minute. Let me think."

"There's nothing to think about. I know the name of an abortionist. A doctor in Houston who will do it. My obstetrician told me the name. He's a real doctor. But it costs five hundred dollars, Daddy. I'm sorry it will cost so much."

"Don't worry about that, honey. It doesn't matter how much it costs. Just for God's sake don't tell your mother. Don't tell her anything. Who's this doctor you know about? What's his name?"

"His name is Doctor Van Zandt. He's a real doctor and my obstetrician said he wouldn't kill me. I have to do this, Daddy. I can't carry another baby. I can't stand to be pregnant again. I'll kill myself if you don't help me."

"Calm down, sugar. Don't talk so loud. Of course I'll help you. You're my little girl. Go back to bed now. Go get some sleep. I'll have this figured out by morning."

"There's nothing to figure out. We have to go down there and have him do it. Malcolm will kill me if he finds out I did it. He got me pregnant on purpose, Daddy. He did it to keep me from leaving him."

"Oh, honey, please don't tell me all of that. I can't stand to hear all that. It doesn't matter now. Just let me think a minute." He put his head down into his hands. Oh, God, I thought, now he's going to talk to God. "It's not my fault," I added. "He did it to me on purpose. He did it to keep me from leaving him."

"All right, honey. You go back to bed now. In the morning I'll call Uncle James and have him check on this doctor and then we'll go there. Don't worry about anything tonight. Go back to bed."

"I could have a legal abortion but there isn't time. You have to have three doctors sign the paper and Malcolm would find out and stop me. You're going to do it, aren't you? You're going to help me?" I stood up. I was raising my voice.

"Be quiet, Sweet Sister. Just go to bed now. I'll take you in the morning. No one's going to make you have another baby." He stood up beside me and patted me on the shoulder. He was worried to death. That was as close as I ever got to having him adore me. I wanted him to adore me. I adored him. Why couldn't he adore me? Well, he was going to take me to get an abortion. That was as good as adoring me. It would suffice. It would do.

I walked on up the stairs and went into my room and got into my bed and went back to sleep. I was in my house. My mother and father were there. No one could harm me in any way.

In the morning we told my mother we were going to Kentucky to see Daddy's coal mines and then we got into the car and drove to Nashville, Tennessee, and got on an airplane and flew to Houston, Texas.

A taxi took us from the airport to the new Hilton Hotel. A bellboy took us up to our rooms. Daddy had rented us a suite of rooms with a balcony overlooking the swimming pool. "Look here, Sister," he said. "That's part of the Olympic team. The manager said they were using the pool to work out in the afternoons. It's an Olympic-sized pool. I want you to try it out later. I've always been sorry you didn't keep up with your swimming. You could have been right out there with them. Well, that's water under the bridge." He sighed, walked back into the room and gave ten dollars to the bellboy and sat down on a chair. I felt terrible. Not only had I failed him by quitting swimming, I had gotten pregnant and was costing him all this money.

"I'd go swim now but I didn't bring a bathing suit. I wish I had one with me."

"Go buy one. There's a gift shop down there." He reached for his billfold and found a hundred-dollar bill and gave it to me. "Go get a suit and a robe to go over it. I'll sit up here and watch you swim."

"We have to call the doctor. We have to make an appointment. We have to make sure he's there."

"Uncle James is taking care of all that. I'll call and check on it. You go on down and buy you a swimming suit." So I took the money and went down on the elevator and found the gift shop. It was a beautiful little glassed-in area that smelled of cool perfumes and was presided over by an elegant woman with her hair up in a bun.

"I want a bathing suit," I said. "Something really pretty."

"Here's the latest thing from the Caribbean." She handed me a one-piece black maillot cut very low in the back. I slipped it on and stepped out to look in the mirror. It looked great. I might be pregnant but at least I still looked like a human being. While I was admiring myself in the mirror, the saleslady handed me a black-and-white beach robe and I put it on. "It's the latest thing," she said. "I sold one last week to Debbie Reynolds."

"I'll take it. I want to leave this on. Cut the price tags off." She took my money and gave me change and found some scissors and cut the tags off the suit and robe and then I stuffed my clothes into a bag and walked out of the shop and down a hallway to the pool. I stepped out onto the blue-tiled patio. The Olympic team was just beginning to leave. I watched them gather up their things and put them in their bags. They looked so happy. So powerful and useful. I was a swimmer, I wanted to tell them. I can swim the five-hundred-yard freestyle in 6:53. I can swim the hundred-yard but-terfly in 1:28. If I hadn't quit I could have trained for the Olympics. I could swim with you.

I must have been staring at them because a boy in a pair of blue trunks walked over to me. "Do you need anything? Are you looking for us?" Two girls about my age were beside him. Their shoulders looked as powerful as my father's. They were deeply tan. "Come on, Robbie," the tallest one said. "We have to get back to the rooms."

"No, I was only watching you," I answered the boy. "It looks great. You looked like you were really swimming."

"It's a great pool. We're lucky to have it in Houston." He moved off with the girls. The rest of the team and their trainers left in groups. I looked up at the balcony. My father was leaning over it, watching me. I put the robe down on a beach chair and dove into the deep end and began to swim. I swam for an hour and then I went upstairs and we ate dinner and I fell asleep reading a book. *Across the River and into the Trees* by Ernest Hemingway. I turned to the place where I had stopped reading it that morning on the plane. "Then she came into the room, shining in her youth and tall strid-ing beauty, and the carelessness the wind had made of her hair. She had pale, almost olive colored skin, a profile that could break your, or anyone else's heart, and her dark hair, of a thick texture, hung down over her shoulders.

" 'Hello, my great beauty,' the Colonel said."

                                *   *   *

When I woke the next morning, Daddy was dressed and talking on
the phone to his mine foreman in Tennessee.

"I love you for doing this for me," I said. "I'll never forget that
you did it."

"Well, let's just don't talk too much about it, Sister. We're
going down there at ten o'clock and see the man. Look what's in the
newspaper. Those sapsuckers in Washington are crazy as loons.
They're fixing to drag us into a land war in Asia. Old Douglas
MacArthur warned them about that, but nobody would listen to
him. First Korea and now this mess in Vietnam."

"Let me see." I took the newspaper from him and pretended
to be interested in the foreign news. He was always preaching to
people about foreign affairs. "We ought to divide the world up with
Russia," he was always saying. "Let them boss half and we'll boss
the other half. That's the way it's going to end up anyway so we
ought to go on and do it."

At nine o'clock we got into a taxi and were driven through the
streets of Houston. We went to a tall office building in the center of
town and got out and went up on an elevator to a doctor's office that
looked like a hundred I had seen before. A waiting room with
Currier and Ives prints on the wall and magazines on tables. My
father went in and talked to the doctor, then they called me in and
the three of us sat around a desk and the doctor asked me questions.
He was a short nervous man with light-colored hair and a distracted
smile.

"I'm getting a divorce anyway," I said. "My husband forced
me to make love to him. I've already had two cesareans. I can't
have any more. What would happen to my babies if I died? I hope
you're going to do this. I can't tell you what it meant to me to get
your name. I think you're a real humanitarian to do this for people.
I know people don't understand that yet. But there will be a time
when people know what a service you are doing for mankind."

"Honey," my father said. "Just answer his questions."

"When was your last period?" The doctor handed me a cal-
endar and I picked out a date and pointed to it. Then the nurse

came into the room and handed me a glass of water and two white pills. I swallowed them and looked at my daddy. He was sitting with his hands on his knees. He was with me. He was there. "It's going to be all right," he said. "Uncle James said we could trust this man."

Then the nurse took me into a room and I undressed and she put a robe on me and helped me up onto a table. She put my feet into the stirrups and tied a belt around my waist. "So you won't fall," she said. "It won't take long. It only takes a few minutes." She held my hand while the pills began to have an effect. The ceiling began to seem very far away and very pretty. The hum of a machine somewhere seemed like music. It seemed like Ravel. It was "Pavanne for a Dead Princess" but I wasn't going to die. My daddy was in the other room. He wouldn't let anything happen to me.

The doctor came into the room. He stood between my parted legs with a mask tied around his face. He spread my legs apart and put something cold inside of me and it hurt a very small bit for a second. The nurse squeezed my hand. "It's all right," she said. "You're doing fine."

"It will only take a minute," the doctor said. "Don't move if you can help it."

"You are doing a great service to mankind," I repeated. "I think you're wonderful. I think you are a wonderful man."

When I woke up my daddy was with me and he took my arm and led me out into the hallway and down the elevator and we got back into a taxi and drove through the streets of Houston. The sun was brilliant. There was the sound of a million crickets in the taxicab. A million crickets in a million sycamore trees and all of them were singing. "I don't have to have a baby. I don't have to have a baby. I don't have to die."

Daddy took me to the hotel and put me into a bed and I slept for hours. Once I woke up in the night and he was sitting on a chair beside my bed. He gave me a drink of water and another pill and I

continued to sleep until the sun was high in the sky and it was
another day. There was a tray of food on a table beside the bed and
Daddy brought it to me and fed it to me bite by bite. I got out of the
bed and went into the bathroom to urinate. There was a wad of
gauze inside me and I sort of remembered something about it.

"He said not to take that packing out of your body," Daddy
called out. It was the first time in my life he had ever referred to my
body as anything but a tool to use for athletics. He came and stood
by the bathroom door and repeated it in a gentle voice. "Sister, he
left some packing inside of you and he said to tell you not to take
it out."

"Okay." I came back out into the room and he put me back in
the bed and sat on a chair beside me while I picked at the food.

The next morning we got on an airplane and flew back home.
We flew to Nashville and got the car and drove the rest of the way.
"I want to go by the house on Finley Island on our way into town,"
Daddy said, when we were almost to Dunleith. "Uncle James drove
up from Mobile. He's going to stay out there until we're sure you're
all right. He said you might need some penicillin and he wants to
be here to give it to you if you do."

"Sure. That's fine. Let's go. He's going to stay out there?"

"Just act like everything's normal. Nobody's going to know
anything and nobody needs to. They're having a picnic out there
today for the family so we'll just slip in and tell them we had a good
time driving to the mines. Just keep your mouth shut and say we
had a nice trip."

"I'm glad he's here. I'm glad he came. I pulled that wad of
gauze out of me, Daddy. When we stopped at that filling station to
get some gas. I meant to tell you about it . . ."

"Well, tell Uncle James about it. He'll know what to do."
Daddy turned off the highway and onto the asphalt road leading to
the old summer house he had bought on the Tennessee River at a
place called Finley Island. The yard was full of cars. All my cousins
from Aberdeen were there and people from Dunleith. They were
having a party. We drove up in the yard and parked the car and got
out and started walking toward the house. My father's younger

brother James came down through the crowd and took my arm. "Let's walk down to the river, Rhoda," he said. "I haven't seen you in so long."

"I'm fine. I'm perfectly all right."

"Well, just come walk with me and tell me about it." He pulled me along a little path that led down through the woods to the river. He had his hand on my arm. I loved my Uncle James. I loved his hands, which were always unbelievably clean and white.

"Tell me about it," he said.

"There's nothing to tell. They put me up on an examining table and gave me some pills and then they did it. I had a wad of gauze inside me but it came out. I've got a Kotex on now. I'm bleeding but not too much, I think."

"How much?"

"Not too much. I've had this Kotex on for about an hour and I guess it's still okay. You want me to go look?"

"No. That's all right. You aren't hemorrhaging?"

"I don't think so. Listen, he was a real doctor, Uncle James. There was a nurse there and everything. Do you think I need some penicillin? I'll take it if you want me to. Maybe I should take some just in case."

"No, I think you're fine for now. I'm going to stay for a week. Tell me this, did the doctor do any tests to see if you were pregnant?"

"I was pregnant. I was throwing up every morning."

"But you didn't have tests made?"

"No. How could I? They might have found out and put me in jail. This way they can't prove it." I shook my head. I stopped on the path. He was making me mad now. Why couldn't we just leave it alone?

"I doubt if you were pregnant, Rhoda. You can't be sure if you didn't have a test. Do me a favor, honey." He put his hand back on my arm. "Let's tell your daddy you weren't sure. I think you imagined you were pregnant because you were so frightened of it."

"Well, it doesn't matter whether I was or not. I had to save my life. Do you think I need some penicillin? I think I ought to take some. To make sure I don't get blood poisoning or something."

"No. That's all right. It's all right, Rhoda."

"Well, I'm going to change Kotex and put on my bathing suit. I haven't had any fun for about a thousand weeks." I backed away from him. I was sick of all of this. Sick of the abortion and sick of talking about it. I went into the summer house and found my suitcase, which my father had brought up onto the porch. I went into the bathroom and took off the bloody Kotex and put a tampon inside my body instead and found a washcloth and washed all the blood off my legs. Then I put on my new bathing suit and admired myself in the mirror for a while and then I went outside to see if my mother had arrived with my babies.

Chapter
32

I healed in a hurry. I always healed in a hurry. Within a week I had completely stopped bleeding and even went out to the country club one night and started swimming laps. The water was cold and clear and I pretended I was training to swim the English Channel. One, two, three, four, five, six, seven, eight, I chanted as I swam. I saw the shores of France. I saw the cheering crowds, heard the bands, saw the banners waving.

"Rhoda." It was Charles William, standing by the ladder at the shallow end. "Come out of there. I want to see you." I heaved myself up over the side and ran to him and stood dripping water on his bare feet. "Charles William, thank God you're here. I've been trying and trying to call you but it didn't answer. How are you? What's been going on? Hand me a towel, will you?" He picked up several towels from a stack on a chair and watched as I dried myself.

"We went to Cincinnati to see a house. I heard there was a sighting. Are you leaving him again? Is this a separation or a visit? I can't wait to know." He was laughing, standing with his feet splayed out and his hands on his hips. "You haven't even seen the house we bought in Fairfields. It's the house the Morgans lived in, Dee. We went crazy in New York buying chandeliers. When can you come out? Can you come tomorrow?"

"I had an abortion. I went to Houston, Texas, and did it. It was to save my life." I sat down on a chair still holding the towels.

"Oh, Dee, I'm so sorry. Does Malcolm know?"

"Of course not. He'd kill me if he knew. So now I can't ever go back to him. Thank God. It was great, Charles William. It was the best thing I ever did in my life. I didn't care if I died as long as I didn't have to have another baby."

"The things that happen to you, Dee. My God. Are you all right?"

"I saved my life. That's all that matters to me. Don't tell anyone though. Mother doesn't know. She thinks we went to the coal mines."

"Have you told anyone else?"

"No. Why would I?"

"Because you always tell everything. I've never known you to keep a secret."

"There is a biological necessity for truth, Charles William. There is. I read that somewhere. But you're right, I can't tell this, can I? Unless I want to go to jail."

"Let's go inside and have a drink, Dee. Did you bring any clothes?"

"I have some in the locker room. I'll get dressed and meet you in the bar." I stood up beside him. Then I threw myself into his arms. He held me like a child, very very tenderly. "It was so terrible," I said finally. "So scary and terrible. I haven't been happy in so long. Haven't laughed or had fun. I want the world to change, Charles William. It has to get better for me."

"It will, Dee. You're home now. Stay here with us. We'll make it good together. You can come out to Fairfields and spend the weekend and we'll listen to music. I have all the Mahler symphonies now. They sound wonderful in those long halls. Oh, you haven't even seen the house."

"Keep on hugging me. Don't let go of me for a while." I leaned into the comfort of his chest. His big soft body was so endearing, so comforting. My friend, my true and beloved friend. "Am I bad?" I asked. "Am I terrible? Am I an evil person?"

"Of course not, Dee. You're just in the wrong place somehow.

You're not supposed to be where you are. I worry all the time about having introduced you to Malcolm. I keep thinking it's my fault."

"Where is Davie? Does he still come to see you?"

"He's here. He's in business with me. My partner. You didn't know?"

"She doesn't care?"

"She doesn't know, Dee. Or if she knows, she pretends it isn't true. I think she's happy. I take care of her. I give her everything she needs."

"I love you, Charles William. I don't care anymore what you do."

"That's what love might be. I keep dreaming it could be that."

"What?"

"Just being happy with someone as they are. Not wanting them to change for you."

"I don't think I'll ever have it."

"What?"

"Love, anything to depend on. Of course, there's Momma and Daddy and I have the boys and my brothers. That's a lot, don't you think? I mean, I'm really lucky to have them, don't you agree?"

"If that's what you want." He stood back from me, holding my hands, his feet splayed out in that ridiculous flat-footed position which made him look like a tree, a great wide-leafed oak tree, so solid and real and planted, here, in this world that he had inhabited every day of his early life and had come back to. He had been born in the Dunleith General Hospital on the first day of March, nineteen hundred and thirty-seven, and he would die there fifty-five years later almost to the day. "I'm working on a third of a heart," he told me when he called. "But don't worry, Dee. They're going to do some more tests this afternoon. I'm sure I'll get a better report tomorrow."

"Call me," I had said. "Call me the minute you find out."

"I will," he answered, but of course he never did. Davie called instead and woke me with the news. "He died trying to bum a cigarette from a nursing student," Davie said. "Isn't that divine?"

"Did she give it to him?" I asked. "Was she going to? Was she even tempted?"

* * *

"What do you mean?" I answered him now, pulling my hands away, reaching for another towel to dry my hair. "Of course it's what I want. What should I want? They're my babies. They're my family. They're all I have."

"You need someone to love. Someone to sleep with. You're a Pisces, Dee. You have to have a lover."

"Well, it won't be Malcolm Martin. I'd rather never do it again than get pregnant. That abortion was so wonderful. I'd like to have one every day. I'd get married again if I could marry Dr. Van Zandt."

"I'm sorry. I didn't mean to set you off. I know you had a bad time. Well, get dressed and meet me in the bar. Let's have a drink, for God's sake. Come on, Dee, it's over now. Let me see you smile." He tucked his chin and smiled out at me over the steel-rimmed glasses he had procured in England from the National Health Service. I started getting tickled. Also, I started thinking about gin martinis. As always, in his presence my resolve not to drink melted like snow in July.

I went down to the dressing room and put on my clothes and combed my wet chlorinated hair and went upstairs and met him in the bar and we ordered martinis on the rocks. We were sitting side by side on the bar stools way down at the end of the bar by the slot machine. "Irise hit the jackpot the first time she ever put a quarter in it," Charles William said. "She has never played it since. She wouldn't even put a quarter back in after she won. She wouldn't put in the obligatory quarter."

"My God. That's perfect. That's her perfect personality. That's exactly what she would do."

"I put it in for her. Sissy was here and May Garth. Twenty people saw it. She stuck one quarter in. The machine had only been out here about a week and she hit the jackpot. Quarters were rolling out everywhere. There was a golf tournament and the bar was packed and everyone was picking them up and handing them to her."

"How much was it?" The bartender had put the martinis down in front of us. I picked up my olive and ate it. I raised my glass. "To

us. For living to be here. Thank God you're here." Charles William
raised his glass and touched mine with it and we began to drink.

"It was two hundred and seventy-four dollars and fifty cents.
She stacked it all up on the bar and left it there for hours. We were
having drinks before dinner. She left it there until we got ready to
leave. Then she put it in a sack and took it home. I don't know what
she did with it. I never asked her."

"She's perfect. She's always what she seems to be. Always the
same. She's a perfect little doll."

"Well, not perfect, Dee. Sometimes she's disagreeable."

"When? Every time I've ever seen her she's perfect."

"She gets mad at me."

"Well, it never shows. When Malcolm gets mad at me he
makes everyone uncomfortable for miles around. Thank God I
never have to live with him again. It wasn't even his baby,
Charles William. I think it belonged to this guy who owns a
newspaper. I don't know whose it was. God, you don't know
what I've been through." I finished my drink and started in on a
second one. "Listen." I lowered my voice. "I had to fuck this
old fat doctor to get the name of the abortionist. I did it. I swear
I did." I sat back, let it sink in. "No one's killing me. That's
that. I did what I had to do."

He shook his head. He finished his first martini and drank half
his second one. It was hard to shock Charles William but I thought
maybe I had finally done it.

"Where did you fuck him?" he asked. "Where'd you go?"

"In his office on the examining table. Then we went into
another room and did it on a bed. You know what he said? He said
I had the strongest legs he'd ever seen on a girl. He said my legs
were a miracle of nature." I started laughing then. I reached out my
hands and put them on Charles William's knees and we laughed so
hard the bartender came and stood by us to get in on the fun. "Get
me some goddamn quarters," I declared. "I'm playing this goddamn slot machine. And get us some more martinis. You don't
know it, but I'm lucky to be alive."

* * *

Six martinis later we got into our cars and drove drunkenly home through the deserted streets of town. The streetlights moved the shadows of the leaves along the streets. I crouched down behind the wheel singing songs to myself. Singing *Oklahoma,* the entire score, then singing, "How High the Moon."

When I got home I went into the den and started calling people to tell them about my abortion. First I called Robert Haverty in Alexandria. "Can Hilton hear me?"

"No. She's in the other room."

"I have to talk to you. Something terrible happened. I have to tell you about it."

"What is it?"

"I got pregnant. From that night I spent with you. I aborted the baby, Robert. I had to do it. I couldn't ruin both our lives. I did it in Houston, Texas. My daddy took me."

"Oh, God. I'm sorry. Jesus. Look, I'll call you tomorrow and talk about it. I'm really sorry. In a lot of ways. Are you all right?"

"No. But I will be. I'm sorry I had to do it. So sorry to have to tell you."

"I'm sorry too. Wait a minute. Here's Hilton. It's Rhoda Martin, Hilton. She wants to talk to you. We'll come and visit you sometime, Rhoda. Or you come here. Come to see us. Is Malcolm in town? I heard he was leaving."

"He hasn't called me. He said he was going back to South Carolina. Is he there? Have you seen him?"

"No, but Hilton has. Here, I'll put her on."

"Rhoda, it's Hilton. I saw Malcolm last week at the grocery store. He's still here. Is it all over then? Are you all right?"

"I'm fine. I guess I am." I was starting to cry. "Oh, God, he was so cold. He drove me crazy. He didn't even love me."

"I'm so sorry. Is there anything we can do? Do you want to come and see us and talk to him?"

I cried while Hilton listened for a while. Then Robert got back on the phone and said he'd call me in the morning and then I hung up and fixed myself another drink and ate some potato chips. Then I

called Karla and Speed McVee. "I had an abortion," I told Karla. "It
was wonderful. I saved my life. If you ever need the name, call me
up. It's Doctor Van Zandt in Houston, Texas. He didn't kill me.
Don't tell anybody, Karla. Swear you won't tell anyone. Don't tell
Speed."

"I won't, honey. Don't worry about that. I won't tell anyone.
I can keep a secret."

"You know whose baby it was, don't you? It was Robert's."

"Oh, my God."

"You can't tell anyone. Don't tell anyone, not even Speed."

"I won't. You know I won't. I won't breathe a word."

A week later, on a Saturday night in Alexandria, very late at night
from what I could piece together afterward from the stories, Speed
ran into Malcolm in a bar and they had a few drinks together and
Speed told him that Robert Haverty and I had had an affair and that
I had aborted Robert's baby.

Then Malcolm had left the bar and gone home and gotten a
loaded Ruger he kept in a case in a locked drawer. It had hand-
carved walnut handles he had made for it the last time I had left
him. Then he called the Havertys' about three in the morning but
luckily for everyone they were in the Caribbean scuba diving so he
couldn't kill anyone that night. Then he called me.

"It's Malcolm, Rhoda."

"Jesus Christ, it's four o'clock in the morning."

"I know what you did, you bitch. I know all about it. Speed
told me."

"What do you know? You must be crazy. What are you talking
about?"

"I'm going to get those babies away from you, Rhoda. I'm
going to make so much money that your daddy can't protect you
anymore. I just want you to know that and you goddamn well better
take care of them until I get there."

"Where are you? Where are you calling from? What in the
name of God are you talking about anyway?"

"You know what I'm talking about. Speed told me everything."

"Speed McVee. He's been trying to fuck me ever since I met him. He'd say anything. I'm hanging up, Malcolm. It's clear you're drunk." I hung up the phone and went back into my bedroom and got into my bed. Then I got back up and went over to the baby bed and picked up Jimmy and carried him to the bed and cuddled up around him. I was in my own bed in the middle of my father's house. Nothing could harm me. No one could reach me or kill me or yell at me or be cold to me or impregnate me or cut me open with a knife or hurt me or take my babies away from me. No one could touch me. My father would kill Malcolm if he tried to even talk to me. I was safe. I curled my body around my sleeping child. I listened to him breathing. I smelled the lovely clean smell of his hair. I was so unhappy. I was so confused and terrified and lonely. But it was almost dawn. Already the sun was beginning to light up the skies of Dunleith, Alabama. I was home, in my father's house, in the land of my father's fathers. Nothing could harm me ever. No one could get to me or hurt me. I was safe, safe, safe, safe, safe.

"What did Malcolm want?" It was my mother, standing in the door in her soft blue nightgown. She walked toward the bed. "What was Malcolm calling you about?"

"Nothing. He was drunk. Don't worry about it. Go to sleep, Mother. You'll wake the baby."

"I'm worried about him. I want to talk to you, Rhoda. We have to talk about all this."

"Well, not now. Go back to bed. You're going to wake up Jimmy. Leave me alone, Mother. Get out of here." She stood at the foot of the bed, staring at me, trying to make me talk, but she had never had an ounce of power over me and she sure wasn't going to have any now. If it was up to her I would die having babies for her goddamn God. "Get out of here," I repeated. "Leave me alone. Let me sleep." She shook her head and moved toward the door. She left the room and I cuddled down again over Jimmy. I had been inside her body. Once I had been curled up inside her as Jimmy and Malcolm had been curled up inside of me. And something else, some terrible homunculus sent to kill me, but I had gotten rid of it. I had flown to Houston, Texas, and had it cut out of my womb. I had done it. I had saved my life and I didn't care what any of them thought or any of them did. I was going to live and be happy. I would find a way to have a happy life. Wherever there was such a thing. It was out there somewhere and I would go and find it. I rolled my head down into the fine clean ironed sheets on my little four-poster cherry bed. I moved my body around my child until we were one fine breathing thing and then I slept. In my dreams I was somewhere in New York City talking to people who thought like me and laughed like me and knew the world was funny. We raised our glasses high. It was Dorothy Parker. She was across the table from me. "I want you to meet an atheist, Rhoda," she was saying. "I heard you wanted to meet some atheists and some poets."

I woke at dawn and went downstairs and found Daddy at the dining room table with his newspaper and his poached egg. Fannin's cousin, Mayberry, was in the kitchen cooking. Daddy had searched all over Dunleith to find a breakfast cook who would come in as early as he got up and had finally found one. He and Mayberry were "what and what," as he was fond of saying. Meaning they were both highly suspicious, profoundly cynical, and almost never slept. Mayberry lived alone in a small frame house, had never married, and was probably as much Scots as my father. She was so light-skinned she thought she was above the other black people. While she cooked Daddy's poached eggs in the mornings, he called the news from the papers into the kitchen. Sometimes he got so excited he got up and went to stand beside her to read her the latest political chicanery. "Those sapsuckers are heading us into another foreign war, Mayberry. They're all fools. Nothing but fools."

"Nothing you can do about it," she would answer, steam rising from the poached egg skillet, lighting up her pale golden face, her fierce eyes never meeting his. "Nothing anybody can do about that mess."

On this morning Daddy was sitting in his chair at the table, carefully separating the white from the yellow of his eggs. He allowed himself to eat the whites, then a few nibbles of the yellow. He was less than fifty years old but he had already started his thirty-year stint of worrying continuously about his heart.

"What was Malcolm calling you about?" he asked. "You

aren't very nice to your mother, Sister. You got to be nicer to her. What did he want?"

"Nothing. He was drunk."

"I never knew him to call in the middle of the night. That's more your speed. You haven't been mouthing it around about that trip we took, have you? You wouldn't be that big a fool, would you? Even you wouldn't be crazy enough to do that, would you?" He laid the newspaper down on the table and fixed me with his eyes. Coal black eyes sunk deep in the sockets, an Irish strain. I have those eyes and so does my brother Dudley, but neither of us ever learned to use them like Daddy could.

"I haven't told a soul. Why would I?"

"Because you mouth everything around. I never knew you to keep a secret."

"I don't believe in secrets. I don't do anything I'm ashamed to tell."

"Well, you better keep quiet about this, Sister. I don't want your momma finding out about it and if that little husband of yours finds out its going to make it hard for me to get you a divorce. I had it all settled about the custody of the children and you had to go down there to Alexandria and start living with him again. Now I got to start all over."

"What could he do?"

"He could make a lot of trouble if he wanted to. So just try to settle down and don't go telling anyone else. Did you tell that sissy britches Waters boy? I heard you were out drinking with him the other night."

"No, I didn't tell Charles William. And don't talk about him like that, Daddy. He's my friend. He's the best friend I have."

"He's a queer duck, that's for sure. Well, go on and get Mayberry to cook you some breakfast. You been looking peaked lately, Sister. I want you to stop all this drinking late at night. Your momma wants you to stay home with these babies."

"I don't want any breakfast, thank you. I don't like to eat in the morning. I just came down to get some coffee." I got up to leave but he wasn't letting me go that easily. He reached out and took my arm. "You keep quiet about that trip, Sister. I mean it. You just lay

low about that for a while and I'll get Travis Jeans to try to get this
custody suit worked out. You got to help me, Sister. You got to quit
acting so crazy."

"Okay. I'm going to. I won't tell anyone. Let go of me, Daddy.
I have to go upstairs and see about the babies." I made my escape
and went into the kitchen and got some coffee and took it upstairs
and stayed up there until I heard him leave for work.

It was late that afternoon before he started in on me again. I guess
he'd been thinking about it all day, out on some road job, bossing
around the tractor drivers in the dust and heat, half his mind on his
work and the other half on me. I heard him drive up in the side
yard. Heard him whistle. Every day when he came home from work
he would get out of his car and begin to whistle a little four-note
tune he had learned from his daddy in Aberdeen. I suppose someday when that sound is lost to the world, I will think of it and weep.
One long note, then a short trill to a lower range, then a longer note,
then a short sliding stop. My brother Dudley tries to do it, but he
hasn't got the force that gave it grace. One long deep thrilling rising
note, then a short high slide, then a longer note, then a short one.

I went into the bathroom and combed my hair and put on
lipstick. Then I went into my room and took off the dress I was
wearing and put on an aqua sundress and some sandals. Then I
went out onto the porch to wait for him. It was late in the afternoon,
almost dusk. Our cousin Martha Jane was already in a porch chair
with a drink and her needlepoint. Uncle Will was coming across the
street carrying his lantern. It was a trick lantern that played "How
Dry I Am" when you turned the wick. Sometimes he brought the
lantern over. Other times he staggered across the street pretending
it was a desert. "Water, water," he would be calling. "With plenty
of whiskey in it."

I settled myself into a wicker chair and waited for Daddy to
finish changing shirts. Part of me knew better than to get around
him when he had me on his mind but the other part was drawn in
like mosquitoes to blood. I heard him pass through the dining room
and speak to my mother. I got up and stood in the doorway. "How
you doing, Sister?" he began. "What's been going on?"

"Nothing. I took the boys swimming. Little Malcolm jumped off the board."

"I got them breathing in the tub this winter," he said to our cousin Martha Jane. "You got to teach them in the tub and get them ready. You heard any more from your little husband?" he asked, returning his attention to me. "Has he called again?"

"No, I told you he didn't want anything. He was drinking."

"Well, you better remember what I told you this morning if you want us to keep these boys. I'm mighty worried about you, Sister. I've had you on my mind." He was talking to me as if his brother and his cousin weren't even there. He always talked to us that way in front of people, shaming and challenging us, putting us in our place. "What kind of a dress do you call that, Sister? Is that a divorcée dress? What do you think, Will, is this what the divorcées are wearing now? Go put a shirt on, Sister. Cover up your top."

"It's a sundress," I said. I left the porch and went into the kitchen and fixed myself a whiskey sour.

It was almost seven o'clock. Fannin was putting the fried chicken on the buffet. By dark I was drunk. By dark I was upstairs calling Charles William. "Come and get me," I said. "I can't stand it here. I have to get away. I have to go somewhere."

"Sure, Dee," he said. "Of course I will. I'll be there in half an hour." I hung up and called Speed and Karla and yelled at Speed for telling Malcolm about the abortion and then I yelled at Karla for telling Speed, then I tried to call Robert and Hilton but they didn't answer. I went downstairs and went back out onto the porch. Daddy had a full house by now. Every chair was filled with friends and cousins. He was holding forth about the labor unions and how they had blown up his tipple in London, Kentucky. "We're going to win the suit," he was saying. "I got this hotshot lawyer who's Senator Lampkin's son-in-law. It'll be a landmark case when we win it. It's slow going, though. Those damn lawyers know how to hold things up. Where you been, Sister? Come on out here. Show Miss Hannie your divorcée dress. Look here at this dress, Miss Hannie. Is this what they're wearing now?"

"I'm going out to Charles William's house for a while," I said. "He's coming to get me. I might spend the night."

"Don't go off anywhere tonight. Your mother's real upset with you, Rhoda. She wants you to stay around here from now on after Fannin leaves."

"Fannin's going to stay. She said she would. I asked her."

"Don't go off anywhere tonight. Your momma doesn't want you going off and leaving these babies late at night and I don't want you off drinking with that Waters boy."

"Well, I'm going." I left the porch and went into the kitchen. Fannin and the boys were sitting at the table drinking chocolate milk and eating pound cake and chicken and animal crackers. "I'm going out to Charles William's house," I said. "Put them to bed before you leave, will you?"

"I got a tiger," Little Malcolm said. "I'm going to eat his tail."

"I got a monkey," Jimmy added. "Fannin give it to me."

I poured some gin into a glass and gave them each a kiss. Fannin hadn't answered me. "Will you get them to bed before you leave? I don't feel like fooling with them tonight."

"You're not going off anywhere tonight and leaving us with these babies." It was my mother coming to stand in the kitchen door. "And Fannin has to get home to her family. Put that glass down, Rhoda. Stop drinking that stuff. It makes you act like a fool."

"What am I supposed to do?" I screamed. "Stay here and die of boredom? I've been taking care of them all afternoon. I took them to the pool. I played with them all day." I threw the glass down in the sink and turned and walked out onto the porch and started down the stairs. Momma was behind me and Daddy was behind her. "I'm leaving," I said. "I'm going out to Charles William's to spend the night. You're driving me crazy. I have to get out of here."

"You are not going anywhere," Momma said. "You are going to stay here with these babies. Do something with her, Dudley. Tell her she can't leave."

"I'm going out there. I'm going to see my friends. I'm not a slave to those babies." As I started down the stairs to the yard, Charles William drove up in his Buick. Daddy passed me on the stairs and beat me to the car. "She can't go off with you, son," he said. "Go on home now. Rhoda's got to stay home this evening."

"I'm going out to Fairfields," I screamed. "I'm going with Charles William." Mother tried to grab me. I pushed her out of my way. She resisted and I pushed her again and she collapsed in a heap by the live oak tree. Daddy came around behind me and grabbed my arms. Charles William got out of the car and stood by the car door. "Oh, see here," he began. "She was only coming out to visit. Are you okay, Dee?"

"Of course I'm not okay. I'm a prisoner in my own house. This goddamn place is killing me."

"Oh, Rhoda." My mother began to cry. Charles William went to her and tried to help her to her feet. "Oh, my darling," she cried. "Don't talk like that. Don't curse God."

"Go on home, son," Daddy said. "Rhoda isn't going anywhere tonight. She's going to stay here and help her mother. You come back over in the morning and bring little Irise with you. We'll be glad to see you then." He fixed Charles William with his black-eyed stare. Charles William let go of Mother and backed away. I was struggling to free myself but I could not move.

"You son-of-a-bitch," I was screaming. "You better let go of me."

"Oh, Dudley," Momma sobbed. "Oh, please, please, you two. Please stop all this."

"Can we help?" Uncle Will called from the porch. "Come on, Bro. Come sit down and let's talk this over."

"You need any help, Ariane," Cousin Martha Jane called down. "Is there anything I can do?"

"Is everything okay?" It was Irise's mother calling from across the street on her porch. "Can we help you? Is that you, Charles William?"

"I'm leaving," Fannin chimed in from the back stairs. "Someone better go in and see about those boys."

The night wore on but it did not get better. Charles William left. Mother got me back into the house. The company fixed another drink and settled down on the porch. I fell asleep sobbing with my children around me on the bed. "Nobody loves me," I was sobbing. "Oh, Malcolm, oh, Jimmy, if it wasn't for you I wouldn't have anything to live for. I might as well be dead. I'm a terrible mother. I've ruined my life. There's nothing to do. It's all over now." They patted me and moved in close. They threw their fine fat little bodies between me and the world. Think how thrilled they must have been. Their own mother to themselves for the whole night. Their wonderful mother in need of them.

Chapter
33

No matter how wrapped up we get in ourselves and our particular demons, out there in the big field something else is always happening. I had barely opened my eyes the next morning when the phone rang beside my bed. I answered it, thinking it would be Dudley calling Daddy. They always called each other at dawn to talk about their work for the day. I wanted to tell Dudley about the fight the night before and get him on my side before Mother or Daddy told him their version.

It was Klane Marengo and she sounded terrible. "I'm sorry to be calling so early," she said. "But you got to help me, Rhoda. They say I got to go to jail. You tole me the man said I wouldn't be put in jail. Now Mr. Edmund say I got to plead guilty or they might put me in the electric chair."

"What? What did he say?"

"He say I got to plead guilty. The day after tomorrow I got to go to court. I don't know what to do. I tried calling Mr. Haverty but he and Miss Haverty gone to the Caribbean to go scuba diving. Look like the whole world lined up against me now. Looks like there's nothing to do. I got Miss McVee to tell me how to call you. I just got your number this morning."

"Klane."

"Yes ma'am."

"Wait a minute. Give a phone number where I can call you back. I'll call Edmund and talk to him. I'm sure you misunderstood him."

"No, I didn't. He tole me three times. He said I got to plead guilty or they might put me in the electric chair."

"Give me a number. Do you have his home number? Give me that too." I wrote down the numbers. "You stay right there. Don't go anywhere. I'll call you right back."

I called Robert's cousin Edmund. His wife answered and then Edmund came to the phone and told me in an irritated voice that what Klane had said was true.

"But she didn't do it. You said they wouldn't put her in jail because of her children."

"The mood's not good right now, Rhoda. I'm doing what I can. We'll get it reduced to manslaughter and she'll get a light sentence and if she's good she can be paroled in a few years. It's all I can do. No one's paying me for this, if you remember. I'm doing this as a favor to Robert."

"Where is he?"

"They're making a scuba diving film. He's sunk about four hundred thousand dollars in the project. Something crazy. Well, no one can control him. He's going to lose the paper if he isn't careful."

"You can't let Klane go to jail."

"I don't want her to go to jail. She killed a woman, Rhoda. She was holding the knife. I'm doing all I can. There's only so much I can do."

"When is the trial?"

"It's a hearing. Day after tomorrow. In the morning."

"Can you put it off? Until Robert gets back or until I think of something. My daddy has lawyers. Maybe I can get one of them to help."

"I'm doing everything I can, Rhoda. Everything that can be done is being done."

I called Klane back and told her what Edmund had said. "But

don't get worried," I said. "I know lots of lawyers. I'll call some of them. Edmund isn't the only lawyer in the world."

"I won't go into a jail, Rhoda. That's it. I won't go in there."

"Where can I call you later? I have to talk to people, then I'll call you back."

"I'll be home. I was supposed to go by Miss McVee's and clean up today but I don't think I can make it. I'll be here."

"I'll call you later. Don't worry, Klane. This isn't the end of this."

"It's the end for me. If I got to go into jail. How's the baby? Is he doing okay?"

"He's fine. He's awake nearly all the time now. He's lots better. I think he's doing fine."

"You give him a kiss for me. You tell him Klane sent a kiss for his little head."

I called Edmund back but his wife said he had gone to Monroe for the day. Then I dressed and took some aspirins for my hangover and called Charles William. "Are you okay?" he asked. "I'm sorry all that happened."

"Don't worry about that. Something terrible's going on. They're putting my maid in jail. I don't know what to do. I have to talk to someone. Are you up?"

"I am now. Come on out. Can you leave? Come out here."

"I'll be there in a minute. Put some coffee on. It's Patricia's old house?"

"Yes. But don't be afraid of it. It's ours now."

"I'll be there in a minute. Oh, God, everything happens. It's because I left. If I'd stayed in Alexandria this wouldn't have happened. They wouldn't have dared do this if I was there."

"Come on out. We'll call Derry. She'll know what to do."

I hung up and stood with my hand on the receiver staring out the window. I had my hand on the telephone that had connected me with my friend. Before that I had talked to Klane. I was here in the world, connected to people, surrounded by people, people were all around me in every direction. Together we kept it whole, kept it from breaking. Nothing should break off. Klane should not go to jail. Delmonica had fallen on a knife. That was a break, a tear. But it was a web. It was flexible. If a part broke we could mend it.

I shook it off. I hated it when I began to think that way. I could barely tolerate such knowledge, such poetry, so much drama and beauty and fear.

I went into the kitchen and found Fannin feeding the boys scrambled eggs. They were in their high chairs with little pieces of scrambled eggs on their trays and arms and hands. Jimmy even had a piece in his hair. A little pat of scrambled egg right above his left ear. A golden flower in his shiny auburn hair. "You little precious," I said, and picked it off and returned it to the tray. "You angel baby, you."

"Where you going so early in the morning?" Fannin asked. She was in a bad mood today. That was clear.

"My maid from Alexandria's in trouble, Fannin. I have to talk to Charles William about it. But don't tell Momma and Daddy. Is Momma up yet?"

"She's in her bedroom. What'd she do?"

She gave me a hooded half-trusting look. Killer ants, I should have been thinking. Webs and poison, hunting groups, feeding frenzies, death by war, we come from such terrible old odds. But I didn't know enough to think such things. I just had to have an ally and the first black face I saw was going to have to do.

"She killed someone." It was the first time I had said it out loud. "I don't think she meant to though. I think it was an accident."

"I want to go," Little Malcolm started screaming.

"Me going with you too," Jimmy chimed in. They both started trying to climb out of their high chairs.

"Go on then," Fannin said. "Get out of here before you stir them up. Go on out." I fled down the back stairs and got into the car and started driving. The streets of Dunleith were fragrant and cool. It would be another hour before the heat took over and maligned the day. I drove steadily down the highway to Fairfields. I had not been on the road since the day Daddy and I had driven home from Clay Morgan's funeral. In the light of early morning the road seemed benign and healed. Cotton grew to the very edges of the road. There had been plenty of rain and the plants were tall and full, a dark rich green, with here and there the small bright flowers that precede the bolls. Everything grows and changes, I was thinking. Cotton comes up from nothing, from sun and rain and red earth, and we turn it into gold, into houses and cars and money. There is nothing to fear on this road. It was an old accident. It happened a long time ago. I'll make up for it now. I'll save Klane and that will make up for it. Nobody's putting Klane into a jail. I won't let them do it to her. I don't care what she did. She doesn't deserve to be locked up in a jail.

I turned off the highway onto the main street of the little village of Fairfields. The ladies of the town had been planting flowers along the margins of the street, poppies and chrysanthemums, iris and daisies and Scotch broom. I drove past a row of old frame houses, some very grand and some just cottages. At the very end of the street was the brick farmhouse the Morgans had bought and restored. Now Charles William and Irise were continuing the restoration. Already Charles William had built new porches along three sides. They were painted white with dark green shutters and ceilings of French blue. There was a driveway of mussel shells and a new brick sidewalk leading from the driveway to the house. The low branches of the old magnolia and elm trees were festooned with small oriental chimes and paper birds that whirled in the wind. Charles William was standing on the brick steps holding a coffee mug and waiting for me. He was wearing a pair of khaki shorts and a pale blue silk pajama top. He was barefooted. "Dee," he called out. "Come on in. Oh, divine, you're here." He cuddled me into his fine soft body. He held me for a long time. "We'll call Derry," he said. "She'll know what to do. She handles things like this all the time. This is what she does, you know." We turned and walked up onto the porch and in the front door. The front parlor had been painted a dark red. There were long red velvet drapes held back with wide velvet belts trimmed in gold braid. Golden sconces were along the walls. A huge crystal chandelier hung down from the center of what had been a farmhouse parlor. In the center of the room was the only piece of furniture, a six-foot-tall replica of the

Parthenon. "It's part of the set for a play," Charles William said.
"A production of *Medea* they did last month in Huntsville. I decorated the room to hold it. I had to have one ancient room. What do
you think?"

"My God. It's fabulous. What do you do in here?"

"Nothing. Anything you want. We could have breakfast here
if you like. Irise is making waffles. Are you hungry?" He pushed a
button on the wall. Music filled the room. "It's Mahler," he said.
"Isn't it divine?"

Irise appeared in the door. "It's the Greco-Roman wing,"
she said. "He had to have it." She smiled and took my arm and
pulled me out into the hall. "Come have breakfast. Charles William
told me about your maid, but I want to hear it all. Tell us about it."

"She may have done it. But if she did, she didn't mean to. She
has children. What will happen to them if she goes to jail?"

"Come eat," Irise said. "Then we'll call Derry. May Garth's
with her now. Did you know that? May Garth's working on voter
registration with her."

"Let's call Derry first," Charles William said. We went into the
kitchen and Charles William called the number and handed the
phone to me and I told the story to Derry. "I thought I could trust
them," I added. "Now they're going to railroad her into jail. I don't
know what to do. I don't know where to start. I don't think Edmund
will talk to me. He's mad because he isn't getting paid."

"Jim's here," Derry said. "Let me call him to the phone. He'll
know what to do. Do what he tells you to." She called him to the
phone and in a minute I heard his sweet clear voice. A voice from
another world, a scary world that enchanted me and made me feel
I wasn't good or brave or smart enough. A world that seemed to ask
things of me I could not give. The coin of the realm between Charles
William and me was imagination. In that light I thought I was
dazzling. At the sound of Derry's voice or Jim's I felt the way I did
with my daddy. Charles William was the brier patch. This man was
a river.

"What's going on?" he asked. "Tell me what happened?"

"A woman who worked for me in Alexandria may have killed
someone. I got her this lawyer and he said she wouldn't have to go

to jail and then I left and came home to Dunleith and now he wants her to plead guilty and go to jail. I promised her she wouldn't go to jail, Jim. There were four witnesses. They all say she didn't do it. They all say Delmonica fell on the knife, so why should she plead guilty? Her name's Klane and she's six feet tall. A jury might convict her of anything. She looks so fierce. I think she's a Watusi."

"Slow down. Start at the beginning. Tell me what happened." I began to tell the story as simply as I could. Irise handed me a cup of coffee. Charles William handed me the cream. They stood by listening. From the back of the house Mahler's Ninth Symphony filled the halls. Sunlight poured in through the old leaded-glass windows. Pots of red geraniums were everywhere, copper pans, blue china dishes. As I talked I began to imagine Jim Phillips and me living here. We would make love all day and do good deeds for people and then sit around listening to classical music.

"Could you meet me in Alexandria?" he asked.

"I guess so. When?"

"When is the hearing?"

"Wednesday."

"Then we need to go tomorrow. So I can talk to her before the hearing. Could you meet me there tomorrow afternoon?"

"I'll have to drive. It takes ten hours."

"I have to go to Atlanta today to finish some depositions, but I could fly there tomorrow. Where are you now? I'll call you back as soon as I make some reservations. And Rhoda."

"Yes."

"It will be good to see you again. I've been thinking about you."

"I was thinking about you too. I thought about you a lot. I'm in Fairfields, Alabama, at five-five-five-four. It's Charles William's house. I'll be right here." I hung up and turned back to my friends.

"He's going to meet me in Alexandria. He's calling me back as soon as he gets a plane. I'm going to drive down there tomorrow. I'm going to meet him there. Oh, God, he's so cute. He's the best-looking man I've ever seen."

"Let's eat breakfast," Irise said. "While you wait for him to call."

"This has got everything," Charles William added, and waved his coffee cup in the air. "You'll have to run away, Dee. They'll never let you go."

"Then I'll run away. Mother's got plenty of help. Daddy hired Fannin's cousin. They've got maids in every room." I moved to Charles William's side. I put my arm around his waist and held him close to me. Irise beamed at us and started pouring waffle batter into a waffle iron.

Jim called back while we were eating. I talked to him, then I called Klane. "We'll fix this up," I told her. "This man can do anything. The Justice Department is behind him. They can't make deals with him, Klane. He's an honest lawyer."

"Don't be bringing any Yankee lawyers down here to mix into this. You just going to make things worse for me."

"It won't make things worse. This man is brilliant, Klane. Justice doesn't stop in Alexandria, Louisiana. They send things to the Supreme Court if they do them wrong at home. Believe me, Klane. I know what I'm doing."

"You thought you knew what you was doing when you got Mr. Haverty's cousin to be my lawyer. Now look at all this mess. I can't go into a jail, Rhoda. I can't go back in there."

"You won't have to. I'll be there tomorrow afternoon. Stay where I can find you, Klane. He'll need to talk to you as soon as we get there."

"It won't do no good."

"Yes, it will. I swear it will. You have to believe it will. Will you be waiting when I get there tomorrow? Klane, answer me. Where will you be?"

"I'll be right here. Right here where you left me."

Later, after we had done the dishes and drank all the coffee and listened to the Ninth Symphony again, Charles William walked me to the car. He paused at the end of the brick sidewalk and took both my hands in his. "Be careful with Jim, Rhoda. You aren't divorced yet. Don't get in too deep."

"I want to be in deep. Besides, it's not because of him." Charles William smiled. "Well, it's not. It's because of Klane. I wouldn't go down there except for her. I have to save her. I told her I would. I promised her. You like Jim, don't you? Don't you think he's nice?"

"He's more than nice, Dee. It isn't that."

"What is it then?"

"Well, you aren't divorced. Be careful, honey. Malcolm's a killer. I roomed with him, remember?"

"What could he do to me?"

"He could take the kids. This is Alabama, honey. They don't take adultery lightly. Especially with a civil rights worker who lives in a black project in Montgomery."

"Nothing will happen. Malcolm doesn't even like the kids. All he thinks about is making money. He'll do whatever Daddy tells him to to keep from paying me child support."

"I wouldn't . . . well, never mind. Just be careful, Dee. Be careful until you get the divorce."

"I will. Well, look, I have to go. The house is beautiful, Charles William. It's perfect. So were the waffles." We hugged each other again and I got into the car and drove away. He stood at the end of the driveway waving until I was out of sight. And in the light of all that love I was emboldened. I could do anything I wanted to. I was a part of the pantheon. Child and friend of gods.

As soon as I got home I packed a suitcase and sneaked it down the back stairs and hid it in the trunk of my car. Then I took Little Malcolm and Jimmy out to the country club and spent the afternoon teaching them to swim. They were my children. Water babies from the word go. I let them stay in the water until their fingers shriveled and their lips turned blue. Then I dragged them out and dried them off and fed them bacon, lettuce, and tomato sandwiches and signed the chits with my daddy's name.

At four the next morning I left. I went into the children's room and kissed them on the heads and sneaked down the stairs and rolled my car down the hill toward Sherman Street. I had left a note in the kitchen saying I had gone out to the river house. "Dear Mother," the note said. "I am doing something I have to do. I'll call tonight. Leave me alone until then. Love, Rhoda. P.S. Don't let Jimmy alone a minute at the pool. He is jumping in the deep end every chance he gets and he can't even tread water yet."

I drove steadily down to Birmingham, then Tuscaloosa, then Meridian, Mississippi, then Jackson, then down to Natchez and across to Alexandria. I stopped several times to get gasoline. Twice I called Klane's number but the phone didn't answer. In Natchez I thought of calling Karla McVee and asking her to go find Klane and be sure she was around when I arrived, then I decided it was better to keep on driving.

I was thinking of Jim Phillips as I drove, of his kindness and his strange gentle power. The Hindus have a story of a man who is wandering in a forest all alone. He falls into a deep hole at the bottom of a tree. In the bottom of the hole is a terrible serpent. The man catches onto a root of the tree and manages to keep the serpent from reaching him. Above the hole wolves and jackals gather for a feast. Vultures circle the sky above the tree. There is a beehive on a branch above the man. A drop of honey is falling from the hive. Slowly the man undoes one hand and holds it up to catch the drop of honey. The honey falls onto his finger and he puts it in his mouth and begins to suck.

Honey of love. For the promise of one drop of this fine stuff I drove across three states as fast as I could drive.

At three I arrived in Alexandria. Jim's plane wasn't due until six. I turned off the highway and found my way to the neighborhood where Klane lived. Cars lined the street near her house. People were in her yard. I parked the car and got out and began to walk up the pathway to her house. I could hear the people talking. I could feel their eyes on me. A woman caught my eye and shook her head. A man in a white shirt got up from a bench beside the door and walked toward me. "She's gone," he said. "Klane Marengo's left us."

"What do you mean?"

"She's dead. She hung herself." He stared straight at me. Behind him other faces gathered. Children came out the door and stood beside us.

"How could she be dead. I came to help her. I talked to her just yesterday. It isn't true. I don't believe it."

"She hung herself. Hung herself right here in this house with the children playing in the yard. Yes, ma'am, she is dead." The man's expression had not changed. No one asked me in. No one wanted me there. There was not enough air to breathe. It was so hot and still. "I'm sorry," I said. "So sorry. I didn't know enough. I don't know what to do. I came to help her. That's why I'm here."

"No one can help Klane now. She's gone." This from a tall black woman I had seen before. She stepped in front of the man and took over. "You might as well go on and leave now. There's nothing here for you to do."

"I'm sorry. I'm so very sorry." I backed down the path, almost tripping over a bicycle wheel. I backed away for ten or twenty yards and then I turned and ran to my car and got into it and started driving. I started in the direction of Speed and Karla's house, then changed my mind and went into a drugstore and bought a Coke and a candy bar and began to eat it very slowly. It was the first food I had had in hours. I stood between the rows of patent medicines and magazines and ate my Hershey bar and began to weep.

Much much later I was in a hotel room with Jim Phillips. We were lying on a bed with our clothes on talking. "Don't you want to make love to me?" I asked. "I want you to. Don't you want me to undress?"

"No. I just want to talk to you. Are you all right, Rhoda? Are things all right for you?"

"No. I don't know what I'm doing half the time. Like all this mess. I wish I hadn't come down here. Why did I do this? What did I think I could do?"

"We can see about her children tomorrow and try to arrange things for them. There are things we can do."

"None of it makes any difference. It doesn't change anything."

"We can try. I have friends here who may be able to help." He patted me on the arm. He touched my hair. He kept on touching me but he wasn't trying to make love to me. What was wrong with the man? I was getting mad.

"Her sister will take care of them," I said. "But she didn't trust her sister's husband. She didn't trust him around her kids. I don't know. Sometimes I think black people are nicer to children than we are. Other times I don't."

"Some of them are better and some are worse. Try not to generalize about it, Rhoda. That's the best way to understand."

"Well, it might be the best, but it doesn't seem as true." I sat up and pulled away from him. I began to straighten up my clothes. "I thought you wanted to see me. Don't you want to make love to me?"

"Of course I do. Anybody would. But I've been going out with someone. Someone you know."

"Who? Who do I know? I don't know anyone you know but Derry. What are you talking about?"

"I'm seeing May Garth Sheffield. She's in Montgomery working with Derry. She thinks the world of you, Rhoda. She's always talking about you."

"Well, that's good. I'm glad you're seeing her. I'm glad she's got a boyfriend. She sure needed one." I got up from the bed. "What time is it, anyway? I have to call my mother and tell her where I am. God, I keep seeing Klane's body hanging from a rafter. Seeing her dead. I don't know how I got into all of this. I don't know what I'm doing here." I got up from the bed and went over to the phone and called my mother. "I came down here to try to save my maid, Klane Marengo," I said. "But she's dead. She killed herself before I got here. I'll come home in the morning, Mother. I'll come as soon as I can."

"What in the name of God? What are you talking about, Rhoda? *Where are you?*"

"She was dead, Momma. She killed herself. I'm in a hotel in Alexandria. I'll come home in the morning and I'm sorry. I'm really really sorry."

"What am I supposed to do with these children, Rhoda? They're asking for you. Little Malcolm's been looking all over the house for you. I want you to come home tonight. Go out to the airport and see if they have a plane. Just get on a plane and get yourself back home."

"I can't. I have a car. It's too late. I'll come in the morning. I'm really sorry, Mother. I'm as sorry as I can be. I'll be there as soon as I can."

"Are you drinking, Rhoda? Is that what all this is about? Little Malcolm has an ear infection. I have to take him to the doctor in the morning and I had an appointment to get a permanent but I guess I'll have to cancel that. Where are you? Where are you calling me from?" My father took the phone away from her. His voice came over the wires. "Sister, now you just settle down. Whatever's going on can be fixed. Just tell me where you are, honey. I'll come and get you tonight. You just stay put. Tell me where you are."

"I'm in a hotel in Alexandria, Louisiana, Daddy. My maid killed herself. Oh, Daddy, it was so terrible. Everything happens to me. I can't do anything right." I began to cry again, terrible tears of rage and fear and incomprehension. "Don't worry about anything, Sister," my father's voice crooned to me. "I'll be there in a few hours. Give me the number where you are. I'll be there to get you."

"Hurry up," I answered. "Hurry up, Daddy. Please come and get me. I want to go home. I want to go home and see my babies."

So my father chartered an airplane and flew down to Alexandria in the middle of the night and collected me. A man was hired to drive the car home and Jim Phillips was left to take care of Klane's children and I flew home in a twin-engine Beechcraft with my daddy.

"Don't worry about anything, Sweet Sister," he kept saying. "Your momma's got the boys and everything will be all right. That's all behind you now. They've got this new program at the stockbroker's that I want you to take. It meets on Tuesday nights and you can learn all about how to invest in the markets. Dudley and I want you in the business with us. You just stop thinking about all that mess down there in Alexandria. Just try to sleep. Everything's okay. It's going to be fine.'' He put his hand on my arm and patted me. He leaned up into the cockpit and looked at the pilot's map. He took dominion everywhere. I closed my eyes and went back to sleep.

Coda

Many years later, when we were fifty-five years old, Charles William called me on the phone to tell me he was dying. After he told me that, we decided to talk all night. We talked from four in the afternoon until seven. Then I called him back and we talked until twelve. We talked about every single thing we had ever done or could remember. He told me things I had forgotten and I told him things he had forgotten. But some things were still vivid in both our memories. My green silk dress, the Siobhan McKenna recording of the Molly Bloom soliloquy from *Ulysses,* stripping wallpaper on Dex in the June heat, and every moment of the week Klane Marengo killed herself.

"I'll never forget you pushing Ariane down in the side yard. Jesus, Dee, I thought your daddy would kill us both."

"That was the night before. Klane didn't call until the next day."

"I always think of them together. When I drove up you were tearing around in some tacky little aqua dress with your boobs hanging out and your daddy was right behind you. Then he was yelling at me to leave and Ariane was on the ground by the oak tree. I'd never seen white people act like that. It was better than a play."

"I only gave in because you were there. If I'd been alone I could have gotten away."

"Why did that bother you?"

"I was afraid he'd say something to hurt your feelings. I was afraid he'd say something about you being gay."

"Oh, Dee, upper-class southern men didn't mind gays back then. We weren't any threat to them. Didn't you know that? You were trying to protect me?"

"I think I was. I remember it that way." I started giggling. "What I can remember. I was pretty drunk."

"We were drunk a lot back then."

"We were drunk every day."

"Do you regret it?"

"Hell, no. It was how we escaped. We never would have gotten free without it. It was the gate, the open sesame. But I don't do it anymore. It's like swallowing razor blades."

"I still do it."

"I know you do." We were silent then. I wasn't going to say, You're killing yourself. "I love you, Charles William," I said instead. "I wish to hell you wouldn't die."

"Maybe I won't. It might be a mistake. I think it's a mistake."

"You could get a heart transplant. I just read this article in *The New Yorker* about the team that harvests the hearts. It's fascinating."

"I couldn't do that, Dee. I'm too fastidious to have someone else's heart. Someone I don't know."

"You're right. It could be anybody's. Jesus, think of the possibilities. Some big dumb born-again Christian from Missouri. Someone we'd hate."

"I read about this man in Minnesota who got mad because he got a black man's heart. He's suing the hospital."

"That's about par for the course. Why would anyone mind a black man's heart? Some huge sweet black heart beating out the rhythms of another continent. Nobody in the United States wants to have any fun anymore. What a bunch of pussies."

"My doctor won't believe I'm not afraid to die. He doesn't understand me, Dee, but I fascinate him, I think. He tried to talk me into a transplant. He was begging me to do it at one point."

"I'm not afraid of dying anymore. I believe in DNA, Charles William. That's the only immortality."

"I believe in art, Dee. Five hundred years is a long time. I'm tiling the entrance to Eula's old house. I wish you could see it. It's like a mosque. I'm putting mandalas everywhere."

"Don't die, Charles William. Please don't die on me."

"I'll try not to. I probably won't. I think I'll get a better report tomorrow."

But of course he didn't and his great heart heaved and stopped and now I can't call him up and read him this and see if it makes him laugh and, as the poet wrote, that makes all this difference.

"The deep blue sky was flecked with clouds of a blue deeper than the fundamental blue of intense cobalt, and others of a clearer blue. . . . In the blue depth the stars were sparkling, greenish, yellow, white, rose, brighter, flashing more like jewels . . . opals you might call them, emeralds, lapis, rubies, sapphires." Vincent Van Gogh, Arles, 1888